in the
Mists of Time

Gemma Lubbock

For the ones forever dancing x

Prologue

It began with Once Upon a Time, as all the best stories should. And a girl called Alice, who believed in magic, fairy tales and happily ever afters.

Alice lives far, far away now, but within these pages you may read her tale of true love and high adventure, a tale filled with heroic deeds, pirates, time travelling, supernatural creatures, baddies and the occasional comet in the sky, and you can carry with you the knowledge that things are not always what they seem in this world of ours.

There is magic in the world, true magic, if you dare to step just one degree away from reality and if you dare to dream, you will not find yourself disappointed.

So perhaps at the beginning of your reading of this fairy tale, suspend your disbelief and prepare to enter wonderland. For it is only by doing so, and by believing in magic yourself, that our heroine Alice can ever truly save the world.

Chapter One

A Girl Called Alice

Once Upon a Time, there was a girl called Alice. She started out just the same as you and I. She had a hint of mischief and magic about her and she lived in a place steeped in legends, in the rolling hills of the Scottish Borders, surrounded by stories of brave heroes. She loved the atmosphere in the air as she walked in the hills, sensing the echoes of footfall made long ago. But she didn't really know very much about history, she'd failed it twice at school. She couldn't remember dates and names of people who had done important things. Unless they were called William as that was her uncle's name. The school curriculum wanted her to learn about the industrial and Russian revolutions, and they certainly didn't have time to talk about local places and the heroes who had lived there with a daydreamer of a girl who didn't apply herself and could try harder.

Alice was born into a mismatched family with their own intricacies, secrets and delicacies as every family has. She grew up running around fields, chasing rainbows in the summertime, spending hours after school walking barefoot, splashing in the rivers, and looking for treasure. She had a favourite tree that she would visit, and talk to, believing it to be a knight imprisoned by a wicked spell long ago. He was always watching out for her and he was full of wisdom, as he had seen many things throughout his extended tree-life.

What marked her as different to most people, was that Alice had been struck by lightning when she was just nine years old. Alice had been playing in the field near her home when the lightning had struck her, the first flashing bolt of an unexpected storm. The raindrops had evaporated as they fell on the charred body of the little girl. Her mum had seen it happen and her father risked his own life to run out to the field to rescue her. But Alice didn't remember that bit, the last thing she remembered was the final beating thud as the electric current had coursed through her body and stopped her heart.

And then she had woken up in the hospital. A pair of brilliant green eyes peeking out from bandages, eyes that now shone with an iridescent sheen of sadness.

She had spent a long, long time in hospital, recovering. All of her hair had burned off and the doctors gave her a red bandana to wear over her bandages on her head, "You look like a pirate, Alice." they smiled at her with their words of comfort.

Her mum brought 'Peter Pan' in to read to her, as Alice had never heard the story of Captain Hook and his pirates before, hoping it would be a comfort to her little burned girl, all covered from top to toe in bandages. Then her mum brought in 'Alice in Wonderland' to read, her mum revealed how it had been her favourite story when she was a little girl, and how she had loved it so much that she had brought a magical little girl of her own into the world, and called her Alice. Tears filled her mum's eyes as she prayed that her beautiful little girl would still be there under the bandages.

Alice made a full recovery, though she always saw things a little differently than most people, perhaps as a result of being touched by something very few of us ever experience.

When she reached her twenties, her head was filling fast with what she considered to be absolute nonsense such as names and addresses of people that owed money to the company she worked for, and where all the spreadsheet documents were kept on the computer server relating to them.

And the trouble is you see, that by filling your head with nonsense, it fills all the spaces between who you are, and then it just runs out of room, as there is so much nonsense in the world and not enough room in your head for all of it at once. So to make room, you sort of lose all sight of who you are. Alice had managed to end up in a job that was slowly destroying her soul, she had forgotten completely who she was. In the words of the great Mad-Hatter, Alice had lost her Muchness. And that was very worrying indeed.

To be fair to Alice, this happens to a lot of us from time to time. There's nothing unique about losing who you are for a while. But as everyone who loses themselves knows, it is sometimes very difficult to get yourself back again. Sometimes it takes an extraordinary event like a time travelling pirate ship appearing in our garden to remind us of who we are. Don't say it won't ever happen to you, as it actually happened to our Alice, once upon a time.

Chapter Two

(Present Day)
- The Office

"I have absolutely no idea," is not the best answer in an office environment when you are supposed to be super-professional at your super-sensible job. Alice learned that when the phrase accidentally escaped her lips that morning, after the verbal backlash she received from the customer on the other end of the line. She followed it with the useful phrase "... But I can try and find out for you," and when the customer wasn't happy with that she then tried, "... Let me find out and call you back."

As was prone to happen from time to time with Alice, she had found herself stuck on the phone, as the data on the screen she had been staring at had become a strange blur of dancing numbers doing little whirly jigs with skirts on, no longer making sense to her, so she had to stall the customer and promise them a call back.

That gave her just enough time to eat a don't-panic-biscuit and try to work out what was going on with the customer's account now that they weren't shouting in her ear demanding immediate answers. If that failed, she would ask one of her colleagues what the answer was, provided they were in the office. If they weren't in the office, well, she was in big trouble. That customer would leave messages with reception asking for a call back and she'd have to stall them further until she could figure out the answer. And the phone would ring with another customer between then. So Alice would put the kettle on and eat some more biscuits. Where there's tea, there's hope.

Alice's colleague Jack had just come back from one of his cigarette breaks. He had a healthy habit and couldn't sit for longer than half an hour before taking a stroll and a puff outside. If Alice ventured outside, while she was meant to be working, especially after a call like this, she would probably run, doing a panic dance all the way to the car. That's why fresh air breaks weren't allowed for those who didn't smoke. They would escape.

There then followed an interlude of office drama. One of those moments of tension that felt as if they may well cause a world war if someone made the next wrong move. The reason for this particular upset, was the mountainous molehill of maintaining a room temperature that suited everybody. Three out of five staff had pleasantly concurred that it was cold in the room, moments after Jack had just come back from his cigarette break. So they agreed to turn the radiator up and close the office door to warm the place. The other two colleagues entered the room and wIthout prior consultation one of them opened the window. And on that airy breeze floated the daggers of treason and treachery. Time for Alice to put the kettle on again. Remember children, where there's tea, there's hope.

Alice had sat back down at her desk and Googled images of Miranda Hart quotes to update her desktop slideshow wallpaper, deciding this was acceptable as a work task as they had just had a motivational speaker trying to rally them the day before at a training day. She read the first two images and had to quell her laughter at a silly-faced Miranda mouthing the words "moist plinth" and a Miranda quote, "When I'm naked in bed and roll over, my boobs clap." Of course this resulted in her colleagues giving her quizzical looks as to just what had Alice been up to. Alice breathed deeply, moments away from office delirium, 'Must keep calm and don *a sensible* face. Not that one...thats your *funeral* face. Sensible, as in, *staring intently at a computer doing serious work* face. Not *googling comedian quotes* face', she thought. Alice hoped they weren't tracking her internet use that day.

Alice came across a quote from *The Lion King*, one with Simba as a cub looking up to the clouds "remember who you are" it read. She used to be a pirate once upon a time. But that was a lifetime ago. She shook the thought out of her head.

Alice realised she'd been staring at her screen for the last five minutes doing no work at all. She tried to look busy by printing something out, walking over to the printer looking seriously efficient and seriously focussed, only to be greeted by the helpful office printer churning out a whole load of paper into a big fan-shaped pattern all over the office floor.

She arrived back at her desk and while she sat down she accidentally muttered out loud the words "Now, what was I doing?" which, as any office worker may know, are fatal words that gave away the fact that Alice actually had no idea at all what she was supposed to be working on. She actually didn't have a clue what she was meant to be doing anymore .. well that was because she wasn't a pirate anymore. Alice grimaced and fought the thought away again, like an irritating moth it just kept fluttering out of reach only to flap right back into her thoughts again. She clicked open the customer's account who had called, and started reading their notes. The best distraction during working hours would be actual work. The first memo was one she had written to herself reminding her that this customer had a tendency to bend the truth as they had told her on three separate occasions that their gran had died, and while he may well have three dead grannies, the one he named as deceased was clearly alive and actively using social media to rant about the government. She clicked open one of his recent emails to her.

"My life has been in limbo for the last three months since my gran's death." Alice read it and thought, 'well, at least you should be a champion limbo dancer by now', but realised this wasn't quite what they meant, focus, Alice, focus. "Since my gran died last month you have made me more depressed with your threatening letters asking for money." They were lying, again and couldn't even keep their time frame right in the same email. It made Alice want to cry.

"You think you're so clever sitting there at your desk typing these harassing letters, I will take legal action against you personally for the stress you have caused me" Alice checked the account, the man now owed them three thousand pounds. She pulled up the last letter she had written to him, "Please come and see me at the office to discuss your account." Yes, that was the harassment, right there, with the word 'please', Alice groaned.

She thought back to the training yesterday, where the motivational speaker had given them a question sheet to answer.

Point One: Situation - Describe Situation or Context? *customer threatened to kill me as I asked them to pay their debt in installments to us. I was at their door and they picked up a baseball bat and told me if I ever went round again they would smash my face in.*

Point Two: Behaviour - What did the person do? What were their actions? *I felt that customer threatening to kill me was out of proportion to the request of £3.00 a week.*

Point Three: What was the result of their behaviour? *I tried to keep calm about it all but wondered why I'm doing this job.*

Point Four: Request - What do you need them to do differently? *not threaten to kill me would be a start.*

It hadn't been quite what the speaker was looking for, apparently. Alice's answers were not quite on the same level as the other staff in the room so she had kept quiet and made something similar to everyone else's answers up just in time for the speaker to come to her. Alice would have ran through that customer with a sword and set them on fire back in the day. But she had signed a contract that she would behave herself and a Pirate's word is binding. Though technically she wasn't a pirate anymore. So not only was her word not binding, she didn't have the heart to punch someone in the face ever again.

Alice waved her hands in the air to chase the memory moth away. Luckily no one in the office noticed her waving her hands in the air. She put them down and used them sensibly instead to click onto her emails. Two desks away, Stef was talking about a date she was going on that night. Alice felt a bit lonely all of a sudden.

Alice's last suitor had been in the army, and it didn't really go very well when Alice brought up her past life as a pirate. She had thought it would cover some sort of common ground with him, being in the army and all. They were having a dinner date, trying to make small-talk. The conversation ran as follows:

Alice: "So, you were in the army?"

Army-boy: "Yes". He had a very deep, well-spoken, husky masculine voice and was rather good-looking.

Alice: "For how long?"

Army-boy: "Five years."

Alice: "Did you kill people?"

Awkward pause.

Army-boy went super serious and obviously did not want to talk about it: "I was doing a job" he replied.

Alice didn't know if you were you allowed to ask people that, she had only wanted to lead onto her zombie killing story, but it wasn't going to happen. 'Don't panic', Alice thought, 'There's no tea and biscuits here to save you. Lighten the subject again'.

Alice: "Were you a stealth agent?"

Army-boy: "Er, no."

Alice: "Oh. Were you a ninja?"

Army-boy: "No, I wasn't a ninja."

Alice: "Were you a stealth ninja? Oh wow, a stealth ninja?! Really?!"

At this point a car alarm started to go off.

Army-boy: "No, I wasn't a stealth ninja." he wasn't really smiling anymore.

Alice smiled at him, trying to maintain her pleasant demeanour, inwardly cringing at how badly this was going. Then a little warning thought flitted round her head in perfect time to the car alarm outside.

Alice: "Oh...that's my car alarm. I left my parent's dog in it he must have set it off!"

Army-boy: "You brought a dog on a date?"

Alice: "Erm...sort of...yes...erm..excuse me."

Alice had left the restaurant to turn the car alarm off and didn't go back in. Her head hurt with it all. She had thought she'd done so well with the initial "be calm and don't act too keen" texting. Flirtatious not terrifying in her responses. But to no avail, he just wasn't a ninja in the army and Alice just wasn't able to tell him she used to be a pirate.

She was just an office girl, just getting by day-to-day doing mundane office work, relieved by humorous interjections and a touch of insanity. Yep, perfectly normal Alice, just doing the same as everyone else, day-in, day-out, working to pay the bills. There never was and there never had been such a thing as a pirate ship in her garden. Ever. But there it was. In trying to block it out, she had accidentally set loose hundreds of memories like moths they were fluttering all over the place and she couldn't bottle them back up, and now ...she remembered.

Alice grimaced as the memory of that first morning took over and refused to release its grasp on her, the frustrating customer not being able to compete with the adventures lurking in the cobwebs of her dusty memories.

The flashbacks and memories she strived to ignore flooded her now like waves on a sandy shore. It was too much for her to face them and for her to remember, as she had been cast away from piracy. This was the life for her now. Not great at dating, not great at her job, but getting by.

She was at the same desk where she had always been, before the pirate ship ever never appeared in her garden and she would inevitably be here forever never more.

Alice looked at her screen and typed nonsense with her hands so at least it looked like she was doing something other than daydreaming, and gave into the memories casting her back into that fateful day...

Before the beginning of great brilliance there must be chaos.

Chapter Three

(Past Memories)
The Mist Descends

I t was not long after her twenty-third birthday when the pirate ship had parked in her back garden, it was hidden in the morning mist that sometimes greeted her when she opened the kitchen blinds. The ship was quite invisible to the untrained eye. But Alice had known it was there, she could sense it like Captain Kirk spotting a Klingon ship that had gone into stealth mode.

Initially Alice had ignored it, thinking it was a figment of her imagination, like the Knight in the Tree that she used to speak to when she was a little girl. An after-effect of the lightning strike, a something that all of adulthood and growing up told her couldn't be real, a something she might have to go to the Doctor about. But she didn't like going to the Doctor, so ignoring the ship in the garden completely and utterly was the thing to do. She didn't venture outside to investigate, instead she just stopped looking out of her kitchen window, and put the television on in the living room, and had breakfast in there instead, trying to block out the mist creeping and lacing about her back windows and lurking at the back door. On the television show the presenters were interviewing people who claimed to have been abducted by aliens. Alice thought some of the people sounded really quite insane, then glanced out of the back living room window at the vast hulk of the invisible pirate ship in her garden. She knew it was there, waiting for her. She ignored it again and went to work instead.

The day dragged. Alice couldn't stop thinking about the eerie mist and the presence of the pirate ship. It had seemed so real. Julia sent Alice a text message from across the desk, "Are you okay, you look pretty tired today?"

Their office was pretty quiet. No small talk please, people are *concentrating*. To the effect that they all sent time-delayed text messages to each other so no one in the office knew they were texting each other, a completely harmless feature of the working day but one that could have dire consequences of increasing the general office paranoia to severe levels.

A mild heart-flutter flitted across Alice's chest, if only she could tell Julia about the ship in the mist. "Yes I am just feeling a little poorly. I'll work through it." Alice had replied, three minutes later. Julia's phone vibrated as soon as Alice hit send, Julia had vibrate on. They were trying to be in stealth mode here, dammit, Office Ninja Stealth Mode.

At lunch time Alice took her mind off the mist by going round the supermarket with Julia. In one of the aisles, a woman asked Alice where the hoover bags were "Sorry, I don't work here" Alice had retorted, and the woman looked her up and down with annoyance for not being able to help her. Alice found herself trying to spot them as she walked towards the check-outs.

"She must be blind as a bat, do we look like we work here, not the wonder she can't find the bloody hoover bags." Julia had remarked.

They reached the checkout queue and were appalled to find they were behind the same woman. Judging by her items on the conveyor belt the woman hadn't found her hoover bags and she gave them the dirty look directly used for useless staff who had been unable to help her. And the woman was rather taking her time, she looked at their items on the checkout belt, sandwiches and cream cakes.

"Ah, are you on your lunch break?" the woman asked them.

"Yes, but we don't get a lot of time for it" Julia snapped, not mincing her words.

"Ah, can I use your staff discount to pay for these then?" the woman asked.

"We don't work here!" Alice and Julia both said in unison, glaring at her.

That afternoon Alice outsmarted the difficult customer who had phoned that morning, getting them to cough up some money over the phone and agree to weekly payments. She felt good about herself, like she had achieved something momentous and could make her way home with a glow of a job well done. She was capable of great things in life, she could accomplish goals, she could meet targets, she was a winner.

At the garage on the way home Alice got out of her new car and couldn't open the pop-open fuel cap. She tried, and tried, pushing the little cap, checking inside the car for a lever, nothing, her new car was broken. Perhaps, she thought, someone had bumped into it and broken it, or it was a flawed model and would have to go back to the garage only that was twenty miles away and she only had five miles left in the tank. She was tempted to try to prise it open with the key but knew it would scratch her new car. She was there for a while. Mild panic was starting to set in as a male voice quietly whispered nearby "Have you tried unlocking the car, hen?"

Alice looked blankly at him. "The petrol caps don't open if the car is locked." he added sympathetically to the young woman standing stupefied in front of him.

The cashier was laughing as Alice walked in to pay for her petrol. She tried to look stunning and sophisticated when she left the shop, holding her chin up as best she could. She wasn't always a winner.

When she pulled her car into the driveway, the mist was still there, lingering around the back of her house. She could feel the heavy presence of pirate ship lurking in the garden, and could smell sea salt on the air as she stepped out of the car.

Chapter Four

(Past Memories)
- The First Brave Step

Alice could bear it no longer, she paced around her house. Either the ship was real, or it wasn't, and there was only one way she was going to find out. She had to go and face it. The mist was swirling at her back door, beckoning to her to walk into it. Alice pulled on a jumper, she shut her back door and went out into her back garden. She could sense the bulk of the ship was sitting just past that point, it sort of hovered just above her at head height, floating on a layer of mist. She could see the shadowy outline of a gang-plank which was conveniently and neatly positioned to rest upon her garden picnic table top, but it kept fading in and out of view, as if it wasn't really there when she looked directly at it.

She climbed up onto her picnic table, feeling like a mad woman. She realised, should anyone call round to visit her they would ask what she was doing standing on her picnic table, and as she found it difficult to lie, and hated being put on the spot, she wouldn't know exactly what to tell them. She struggled with the idea of simply saying "Oh I'm just seeing if I can walk the invisible plank up to the invisible pirate ship. I take it you can't see the ship? Just me then. Would you like a cup of tea? I'm sure this can wait." knowing somehow, it wouldn't quite suffice.

Thankfully no one did appear as she took her first tentative step onto the plank. Which of course was almost entirely invisible, even to her at that point, there was still just the impression that a plank was there in the mist. The toe of her canvas pump touched solid wood. She pulled her toe back in surprise and almost fell off the table. Alice's phone chose that point in time to beep a little tune. A text message, it was Stefanie.

"Hey are you going to see Dark Horse this Friday in Coopers?" Stef's text read.

"Hi Stef, right now I don't know if I'll be alive this time on Friday." Alice replied.

Alice raised her foot again and the phone beeped back.

"Lol! You crazy! Let me know! x x x"

Right, phone on silent. Foot firmly on the plank. 'Heave Ho. Don't refer to yourself as a Ho, Alice. Right, sorry.' Second foot on the plank. 'Breathe, and believe. Do not scream.'

Alice could quite clearly see the wood-grain pattern on the plank now, very worn, having been trodden by pirate boots since time asunder. Then she looked up, and the entire ship emerged from the mist and loomed into clear view. Utterly magnificent, it took Alice's breath away. It was made of a rich, dark wood and she could make out three masts adorned with crisp, clean tan coloured sails. Cannons peering out from porticos - hold on they were lined up perfectly, pointing in the direction of Alice's house - and the Jolly Roger flag billowed in the breeze. Definitely a pirate ship. No mistaking.

"Avast ye!" someone shouted from the ship, "Maiden on the plank!"

As the noise from the deck drifted down toward Alice from where she stood on the second tentative step up the plank, it became increasingly audible and sounded much like what she thought to be pirates drawing their swords and cutlasses.

"And who might ye' be?" shouted the piratey voice from the deck.

Don't panic, 'Maybe it would be a good time right now to turn around and make a cup of tea', Alice thought, 'maybe I can walk the plank later'.

"Well?" asked the voice in what was unmistakingly a hostile tone.

"Erm, it is I, Alice." Alice replied in the most confident shaking voice she could muster.

"Alice? We know of only one Alice." the voice said suspiciously, "Might ye be her?"

"Well, I'm not quite sure about that." Alice said.

"Is that so?" the voice replied.

"Are you here to shoot her house?" Alice asked.

Alice heard the stomp of boot steps coming towards the edge of the ship, then a hat appeared, a marvellous black triangular shaped hat with a huge white feather in it. Then she made out the pirate's face, terrifically handsome, slightly unshaven, blonde, wavy hair, in a long cut, possibly the same age as Alice. But as she was terrible at identifying a person's age, this could vary anywhere between twenty to thirty. Especially as at this point in time Alice really was rather terrified. She noticed he had a rather fancy white shirt on with long lace cuffs which fanned out at the bottom as he leaned both hands on the rail of the ship and peered down at her.

"You're not a pirate." says he, squinting at Alice.

"I most certainly am." returned Alice.

"You don't look like a pirate." says he.

"Well, I could beat you in an arm wrestle with one arm tied behind my back and drink you under the table good sir." Alice shouted back, trying to hide the fear she felt deep within herself.

"You couldn't drink me under the table." says he.

"I bet I could." said Alice, defiantly. 'Where did the defiance come from?' Alice thought to herself. 'Here you are standing speaking to a fully-fledged pirate with cannons on a pirate ship pointing directly at your house and you are being defiant.'

"Well, Alice." says he, "You may come on board, sample some rum, and we shall find out exactly if you are who you say you are."

'Who exactly did I say I was?' Alice thought, as she took the next few steps up the plank.

The blond pirate offered her a hand as she crossed over the wooden balustrades onto the ship. He held Alice's hand closer to his face, inspecting it as she got her balance on the deck. Alice wondered if he was about to chop her hand off.

"Why, I do believe your hand is exactly the same size as mine." he commented. He stretched out her hand and held his own hand up against it. "See?" he smiled at her.

He caught her eyes with his, which shone clear blue, like the sea after a storm, just like Westley out of 'The Princess Bride', only with a flicker of mischief dancing about them. He did not look away and Alice felt herself beginning to drown in their gaze. She blinked it away, "You have tiny hands then sir." Alice cheekily replied.

She heard a laugh from behind the blonde pirate. He spun round and scowled. "Who laughed there? Who laughed at my tiny hands?" but he was met with silence as his response.

Alice took the chance to look at her surroundings. There must have been at least twelve pirates, on a deck which was three times the size of the office room she worked in. They had more working space than her, she thought. Some of the crew were in quite bright colours, red and white stripes, others wore tanned leather and browns. Each had a gun and a sword in their hands. Pointing directly at her.

The blonde pirate was still scowling at the crew. It was getting tense. Much like Alice's office. Distraction, Alice thought, he needs a distraction to break the tension, "Are you the Captain then, good sir?" Alice asked him.

He spun back round and looked at her as if he had forgotten she had even been there, "No." he answered, annoyed, which, Alice discovered, was to be his usual tone when addressing her. "My brother is."

At that moment the pirate crew looked up, towards where the wheel of the ship was positioned up some steps on the helm. Alice turned round to see what they were looking at, and there stood a figure, illuminated by the sunlight behind him, he was almost in silhouette, and it was as if the sun rays were shining from his very body. He radiated magnificence and glory. Standing there was a person whose mere presence exuded power. There was the Captain. He started walking down the steps towards them and his face came out of the shadows. He had dark wavy hair to his brother's blonde hair, and crystal blue eyes glimmering beneath his hat, which was identical to his brother's hat save for a black feather instead of a white one. He had a dark shirt on, and wore no shoes. He was completely bare foot. Alice later learned from him that it was because it "kept him in touch with the ship." Yes this person was ethereally handsome, and he knew it. Alice was awestruck that someone could radiate such dazzling brilliance and exquisite refinery about themselves while being a real live person and without being airbrushed.

"Is that ….?" Alice tilted her head slightly to indicate to the blonde pirate.

"….my brother" he finished for her, somehow sounding a little jaded and very annoyed.

Chapter Five

(Past Memories)
The Captain's Cabin

The Captain moved to make his way down the steps, though this was more of a glide in slow motion, as these sort of beautiful people don't walk, they are so full of presence the very air seems to carry them.

"Hello darlin'." the Captain's velvety voice sent a shiver down Alice's spine.

"Good day to you Good Sir. I'm Alice." Alice nervously uttered to the Captain. She realised she'd said the word *good* in a sentence twice and perhaps, in the instance of being on board a pirate ship, that sort of mistake could prove fatal.

"Welcome to Wonderland, Alice. Welcome to the good ship Sea Rose." the Captain smiled. He had an infectious reassuring smile.

"Thank you." Alice very nearly curtseyed.

"A guest on the ship!" he exclaimed, "I'll drink to that!" he put his arm around Alice's shoulder and steered her towards what she learned to be the Captain's Cabin, underneath the helm.

"Back to work you yellow-bellied land lubbers" his brother commanded angrily to the crew, who all burst into movement about the ship, looking terribly busy all of a sudden. He followed behind Alice and the Captain into the Cabin. She was steered to a wooden chair at a table big enough to sit six people around.

"This table was my great-aunts," The Captain stroked the table top affectionately as he spoke, "It was made from one solid piece of wood. It has unfortunately split not-quite down the middle due to living on board a tired and weather-beaten pirate ship, but it is still an exquisite piece of craftsmanship." The Captain took his seat at the head of the table. "Do you mind if I smoke?"

Alice shook her head. He had already begun the process of rolling a cigarette from a tin of tobacco anyway. Alice didn't think her reply would have made any difference had she objected, he would have still lit up, and made her walk the plank for questioning him.

"Thanks Arthur." the Captain said as the blond pirate brought three glasses filled with cloudy liquid over from a side counter and placed the glasses in front of them, "Why, but you haven't been introduced, I forget myself sometimes. This is Arthur Montrose." the Captain smiled through a mouth gripping a cigarette. "Arthur Montrose, this is Alice." the blonde pirate flashed his eyes at Alice.

"And this, Alice," Arthur decided to speak, "Is Milton Montrose. My brother. My Captain."

"How do you do. Are you a Scottish pirate?" Alice asked Milton.

"Born right here in the Brave Borderland." says he, "We've come home." he smiled somewhat happily and took a draw from his cigarette.

"For a social visit?" Alice asked, attempting pleasantries.

"No. We came to find you." exhaled Milton in a puff of smoke, raising his glass and implying, with one motion of his hand, that everyone else should raise their glasses too. "And here you are. A toast to Alice. Our Alice." They clinked glasses, Alice had to stretch over the table to reach their glasses.

"Cheers." they all agreed in unison, and the two brothers downed their shots in one. Alice raised the glass, and the smell of the strength of the rum almost overpowered her senses. 'Here goes.' Alice gulped, and downed the glass. She put her empty glass down on the table.

Milton grinned at her, his eyes glistening in the light. Alice felt a smile begin at the corners of her mouth, then it emerged from hiding fully and flourished across her face.

That first night Alice didn't ask a lot of questions about why the pirates were there. Perhaps she should have, perhaps not, but she didn't, so there you go. They drank a lot of rum, they talked a lot of nonsense, and laughed almost the entire night right through till sunrise. She began to feel comfortable and safe with these two pirates, despite the knowledge that they were dangerous creatures to be around. She hardly noticed it was back to being daylight outside as they were teaching her how to play poker when the dusk turned to morning dew.

"The art of playing poker, Alice, is to don a poker face." Milton suggested.

"Po-po-po-poker face, po-po-poker face." she sang.

"What?" asked Milton.

"It's Lady Gaga." she sang lightheartedly to him.

"No it's the Queen of Spades, Alice pay attention," Arthur said.

"Who's Lady Gaga?" Milton said.

"A singer." replied Alice.

"With a stutter?" Milton asked.

"I thought it was just Alice stuttering over the words? They are so very difficult to sing." Arthur added sarcastically.

"Okay, deadpan, serious face." Alice attempted to change the subject from her singing, "I can do a serious face, watch me." she frowned at them and pulled the smile away from her mouth. "This is my super-serious face." she muttered through her clenched teeth. The brothers both burst out laughing.

"Alice, your trouble is that you are too honest. You have a lot of tics, and you are giving yourself away. People can read you like a book." Milton sighed, ducking his head slightly to look seriously concerned about this flaw in her character, "I have mastered the art of hiding my tics and to win at poker, I suggest that you do the same."

That was the pep-talk from Milton, two games into the lesson. After that, Alice won every game, much to all of their drunken confusions.

"How is this possible?" Arthur asked, annoyed, as Alice giggled uncontrollably after winning another game.

"Oh my sides hurt." she laughed, "Stop making me laugh its really, really sore!"

Arthur looked even more hurt and upset which made Alice go into another laughing fit, "Stop laughing it's not funny, you're winning every game and you're not even cheating!" pouted Arthur.

"What, were you cheating Arthur?!" Alice spluttered.

"Of course I was!" he said, annoyed, "How can you win without cheating, that's just not fair!"

"Oh. What time is it?" Alice asked them, recovering from her fit of laughter, hazily feeling an awareness creeping up on her that she had to be somewhere else when it was daylight.

"No idea" shrugged Milton.

"About six in the morning?" suggested Arthur, pointing to a round clock on the wall, "Can't seem to focus on the numbers very well for some reason."

"Oh no." Alice said.

"What? What is it?" both of them looked mildly alarmed.

"I have to go back to work." the disappointment on their faces was immediate.

"No! Stay here, with us!" Milton commanded.

"I really can't."

"As Captain of this ship I command it." Milton replied firmly, putting his fist down on the table.

"I can't, I can't call in sick."

"Why not? We have more rum. Arthur, fetch Alice another rum."

"I can't stay. I have to do things honestly. And that involves not phoning in sick. It's against my unwritten religion. If I phone in sick, karma will know I'm lying and will do something bad. Very bad."

The brothers looked at each other, "Your 'unwritten religion'?" Milton questioned, "What, have you just read the bible and other such holy books and made a religion up to suit yourself?"

"Pretty much, yeah." Alice replied.

Another look passed between the two brothers, but they said nothing, for a moment, "Alice you are being ridiculous. You are not going to go to work, you are going to call in sick. You may leave the ship but only to get your affairs in order." Milton dismissed her with a wave of his hand, "Be on your way. But be sure and return to us by nightfall. The ship sets sail tomorrow night."

"Okay, if that's an order." Alice got up, not so easily as the room was swaying a little, and hugged them both. She gave Arthur his hat back, as she had been wearing it on her head for quite some time after winning it in one of the poker games. He just scowled at her as she went to the door.

"Just one more thing." Milton said to her. She turned at the doorway. He paused, looking at her as if to build the suspense. Alice shifted the weight on her drunken feet, "You will be on the ship tomorrow night." he smiled and raised his glass to her, "What's the worst that could possibly happen?"

Alice smiled, raised her hand to her head in a salute, and left the cabin. Alice made her way down the plank, misjudged the step and fell straight off the picnic table and landed in a heap on the grass. Uninjured, she picked herself up, tottered over to her house and wavered inside. As soon as the back door was closed and she was in that familiar room, the whole episode began to feel like some sort of dream. She left a voicemail for work, donning a poorly voice she groaned that she was ill with flu, then hung up and stumbled through to her bedroom where she collapsed on the bed and fell asleep instantly.

Chapter Six

(Past Memories)
Life is But A Dream

When Alice awoke she had no idea what time of day it was as it was misty outside her window. She walked gingerly through to the kitchen and made a meal of rice, banana, peas and leftover chicken, merged together in a korma curry sauce. 'Not a bad attempt at a meal this time' Alice thought, 'and not bad for my level of culinary expertise'. The banana made it quite tasty, added to her meal as they were meant to help hangovers. And then she remembered the strange dream she'd just had about arm wrestling pirates. Her head was a bit groggy and she couldn't work out why it had seemed so real.

Alice went into the bathroom and had a shower. Standing upright took a bit of effort, she wished she had run a long hot steamy bath instead, but Alice didn't get on with baths too well. She loved the idea of having a hot deep bubbly bath, but the reality was always so very different. Any attempt to have a bath proved too stressful. When she did manage to successfully run a hot bath, it was just that: too hot. But when she put cold water in it, the water never reached "just right", and she would wind up shivering in a lukewarm bath two minutes after getting in. Baths promising dreamy relaxation and pampering didn't make Alice relax and unwind at all.

Alice stood in the shower without moving for quite some time, letting the heat from the water warm her skin. She started to sing, she loved singing in the shower. She could sing as loudly as she liked, as no one lived anywhere near her.

Alice thought she heard a little noise outside, but she put it down to the swallows who were nesting at her back door, kicking up a fuss at the nonsense song she was singing at the time.

"I put a spell on you ... cause you're mine ... I'm going out ... in a blaze of glory ... don't you forget about me ... you better stop the things you do-oooooo -oooo oooo" Alice sang, merging all the songs together.

There it was again, a quiet banging noise. Alice stopped the shower running, blinked soap out of her eyes and listened. Nothing. Silence. Onwards with the shower, she pushed the power button back on, she was just beginning to warm up.

"Oooo oooo I heard it through the grapevine." she sang. Ach that one didn't sound too great, time to shuffle the old jukebox in her memory banks,"If your memory serves you well ... we were gonna meet again anyway ..."

"Wheels on fire!" Alice heard a male voice sing quietly outside the bathroom window.

Alice paused, but didn't stop the shower. She blinked it away, as hearing voices was a sign of insanity, and started a new song, "When you're alone and life is making you lonely you can always go...."

"Downtown!" added the male voice gleefully.

"When you've got worries all the noise and the hurry seems to help I know…"

"Downtown!" the male voice sang in unison with her.

Alice went completely quiet, "Alice, what are you doing in there?" the male voice shouted.

"Having a shower." Alice replied, realising she'd just spoken to the invisible non-existent pirate. That was like acknowledging he was actually real. And he wasn't real, so Alice was in fact talking to herself.

"Hurry up will you?"

"Who is that?" Alice called. Maybe, just maybe it wasn't a pirate outside. Maybe it was a delivery man or the postie or something.

"It's Arthur! Come on, we're all waiting for you!"

'Arthur was not real, Alice, you made him up in your head. Stay in the shower and get that shampoo rinsed out of your hair.' she thought to herself, "Oh, I think I'm going to be at least half an hour." Alice spoke out loud. Trying to make the invisible pirate get bored and go away, as he wasn't real, after all.

"What? Half an hour? But you've been in there ages already."

"Well, you don't expect me to come out there naked do you? I have to get dressed as well." she shouted and heard a dirty laugh outside, "I am not coming outside naked Arthur."

"I never said anything!" he shouted innocently, "Can you just bloody hurry up woman!"

"Don't you woman me, pirate!" she shouted, stopping the shower.

"Alice will you just get a move on we have to get going!" Arthur shouted.

"I am already! This is me going getting! I'm getting out right now!" she called. It dawned on her then, the realisation that Arthur was real, the ship was real, and the excitement and anticipation hit her like the rush of hot air when she opened the oven too quickly when she was attempting to cook.

Arthur started humming 'Downtown' outside as Alice stepped out of the shower, she dried and moisturised quickly and ran through to her bedroom. Little time to plan what to wear on an invisible pirate ship that was about to set sail into the unknown. A pair of jeans, two vest tops (layers Alice, layers.) covered by a grey and white stripy jumper. And as she didn't own a pair of pirate boots, she fished into the back of her cupboard and emerged with her brown cowboy boots. She pulled out a rucksack from her hall cupboard and packed some underwear, her toothbrush, hair brush, make-up, her purse, mobile, and other such important travel items. She didn't know what else to take, she wandered round her house in a daze, she went into a drawer and pulled out her tiny pen-knife and popped it into her pocket. She packed up some food in her kitchen, including her entire chocolate supply, put it in her bag and locking the house up she stepped out into her back garden.

Arthur was sitting on the picnic table, waiting for her. He looked incredible, blond hair and blue eyes shimmering in the sunlight. He had a red jacket on today, with gold buttons and embroidery, and a pair of black cowboy boots.

"You're still here." Alice smiled at him.

"I waited for you." he said, gazing at her, he added, "I want some chocolate before everyone else steals it."

"Of course." Alice said, realising he had been watching her through the window.

Arthur stood up and held out his hand to help Alice up onto the picnic bench.

"Thank you good sir." Alice said.

He looked into her eyes and cast his eyes down to her boots, "You have cowboy boots too?" he exclaimed.

"Yes" Alice replied, "from Spain."

"Ah, mine are from Mexico. The real deal." he wiggled his black boots at her.

"Why is a pirate wearing a pair of cowboy boots?" Alice asked.

"Because it's a long story and if I told you, I'd have to kill you." he grinned.

Alice's smile vanished and worry flitted across her face, "Just kidding Alice!" Arthur laughed, "Come on we're already late."

"Yee hoo!" Alice cheered, taking her steps onto the plank, happiness beginning to find its way back to her again.

He took her hand and helped her up and over onto the ship's deck.

"Look who I found!" Arthur called cheerily as he walked towards the Captain's cabin to find his brother.

Milton came out of the cabin and strode quickly towards Alice, sweeping her off her feet and spinning her round and round. Alice was with them again, and wherever this was, be it a dream or illusion, it didn't matter, she was with them in that very moment. The rest of the world had disappeared and her heart was light again.

"Alice where have you been we've been looking everywhere for you." Milton smiled at her.

"I was in my house." Alice said.

"Oh." Milton said, "I didn't think to look there. Well you're here again. And we need to sail, the wind is wrong here now." he turned to face the deck of the ship, "Onwards ye scabbardly scumbags!" he shouted to the crew.

"I take it you are coming, Alice?" Arthur asked in her ear, "It would be a shame if you had to go home as you've only just arrived again."

"Yes I'm coming. Where are we going?" she asked.

"Onwards." he replied, as if that explained it all.

25

"To the next adventure!" added Milton.

The crew adjusted ropes and looked very busy. Milton strode up the steps to take position behind the wheel. It was then that Alice noticed that he had a dark brown leather pilot jacket on, with a sheepskin collar and cuffs. His black feather in his pirate hat wavered as he rose up the steps. He looked magnificent. She had no idea why he had a pilot coat on and realised she was staring at him with her mouth slightly open, in awe, and curiosity, at the same time she felt Arthur's gaze upon her. She turned to look at him.

"Why has he got a pilot jacket on today?" she asked Arthur.

"We're taking off." he said, annoyed, as if the answer was obvious.

"Don't you mean setting sail?" asked Alice.

"Absolutely not." Arthur said curtly, then checked himself and added, "But yes, that as well."

Milton took hold of the ship's wheel with one hand, and pulled out a compass from his jacket pocket. He looked up at the sun and squinted, then looked down at the compass, "Come on then old girl!" Alice heard him say, "Up we go!" he pulled the ship's wheel down to the left and spun it round.

The sails billowed, the ship creaked and groaned, the mist started swirling all around them. Then Alice felt a lurch, as if she was in an elevator, and she realised the ship had begun to lift into the air. She ran to the side of the ship and peered over, but could see nothing of her garden or her house, only the swirling shadows of mist.

"Wouldn't stand too close to the edge ma'am." a man from the crew said to her, "She'll pull you overboard."

"Who will?" Alice asked, stepping away from the side.

"The Sea Rose herself." he replied, "She has her ways about her." he smiled, "And she don't take too kindly to women being on board, especially those who don't respect the set-sailing."

"Do you mean the ship will push me?" Alice asked.

The pirate nodded.

"Sorry, I didn't know." Alice apologised.

"Yes, perhaps it would be best if you come into the cabin while we set sail." Arthur said, "Don't want to upset the ship, she's very particular about taking off." he smiled reassuringly, taking Alice's arm and guided her towards the cabin.

"Oh." Alice said.

"She doesn't like being watched. Maybe it's a bit like stepping out of the bath, not very dignified for an old lady, all her bits hanging out." he patted the door frame.

The cabin door suddenly swung shut abruptly and nearly hit him on the nose.

"Oi oi I was only joking!" he said to the door frame.

Alice edged through the doorway warily looking at it for any sign of a grumpy looking ship's face. It just looked like a wooden door frame.

"You can meet the crew properly later." Arthur continued, "Milton will be down soon enough once he steadies the ship."

Alice looked around the Captain's Cabin. Two chairs were visibly in use, there were drinks and ashtrays at them, two chairs were filled with what looked like clean laundry, which left her wondering who exactly did do a pirate's laundry, one chair was vacant, and one chair had a medium sized yellow soft toy sitting in it. It had very lanky felt arms, a white muzzle and a small pirate hat on its head with a skull and crossbones emblazoned on it, and it had a glass of rum in its little three fingered hand.

"That looks like Flat Eric." Alice said in wonder.

"It *is* Flat Eric!" said Arthur excitedly, "Have you met before?"

"Yes, well … he was on TV a while back, wasn't he, and I actually bought the same teddy that you've got of him … but I lost it a long time ago." she replied.

"Well, Flat Eric came on board not too long ago. Or a while ago. Well, the exact time I can't really remember." said Arthur, "But he's been part of the crew ever since."

Flat Eric then moved his head towards her and raised his glass of rum into the air as a toast.

"He's real?" Alice exclaimed.

"Of course he's real." Arthur frowned, somewhat puzzled. Arthur handed the amazed Alice a glass of rum, "A toast!" he said.

"To what?" she asked.

"To Alice!" he replied.

Milton opened the Cabin door at that moment and stepped into the room. Had the room been full of people, his entrance would have awed them into silence and the world would have slowed like in the movies. He commanded the room. As it was, there was just Arthur and Alice. Milton looked at his brother, a curious look that Alice could not decipher, then walked over to the table top where the drinks were. He poured himself a glass and raised it in the air. "To Alice." he smiled.

Chapter Seven

(Past Memories) Fledgling Pirate

Milton removed his pilot's jacket, slinging it onto the top of the clean laundry, then sat down. He looked at Alice intently through narrowed eyes. She held his look, and started drowning in his blue eyes. It was as if she was being swallowed in the depths of the ocean. It did not feel wholly comfortable, like he was scrutinising her and she didn't make the grade, "I know what is wrong with you Alice." Milton said.

".....what?" Alice asked.

"Your head. It's missing something." Milton mused.

Arthur looked at his brother from under his hat, eyes brooding.

"I know! I know what it is!" Milton leapt up from a seated position to walking that Alice had to blink to focus on him again as he strode across to the counter holding the rum bottles. He bent down, opened a cupboard underneath it and rummaged about, "Here it is!" he announced triumphantly, "You were missing your red bandana! Here it is, put it on." he held out a crisp, cotton rich-red square of cloth, "Don't tell me you don't know how to tie it." he mocked.

Alice stared at it, the familiarity of a red bandana was a strange recognition for her, a faded memory from the time she had spent in hospital as a child. She reached over the table and took it from him, "Oh I know how to tie a bandana, don't you doubt that good sir." she replied. She folded the cloth in half, into a triangle, and wrapped it round her head, almost entirely covering her hair, "Have you got a mirror?" she asked them. They looked at her as if she had asked something completely inconceivable to them.

"Absolutely not." Milton shook his head.

.

Arthur reached over and straightened the bandana for her, "Perfect Pirate Alice." he said.

Milton brought over another rum in a glass, "Let's teach her how to fight!" he suggested.

"Let's introduce her to the crew!" suggested Arthur.

"Let's get her to fight the crew!" suggested Milton.

Alice didn't much like the sound of fighting an entire pirate crew, she doubted she would make it past the first pirate, "I know!" Alice interjected enthusiastically.

"What?" they both asked in unison. As she now had their undivided attention, Alice had to come up with something more fantastic than fighting the crew with less threat to her life.

"I'll arm wrestle them!" she suggested.

"I dont think thats a good idea." Arthur said.

"You can't beat a pirate in an arm wrestle, you're a girl." Milton quipped.

"Is that a dare?" Alice asked, "Do you dare me to?"

"I'm telling you it can't be done. You girl, cannot beat a sea-seasoned pirate in an arm wrestle." he replied, gesturing with his hands to imply that Alice was a mad woman.

She surely had a better chance of surviving an arm wrestle than a full on fight against the entire crew. Alice put her elbow on the table, she raised her hand up in the air, and looked Milton straight in the eye and widened her eyes as far as they could go, conveying her *super-serious face* (which kind of hurt a little as it made her eyes dry out quite quickly after the lack of sleep the night before), and she said, "Watch me."

"You're on," Milton grinned, "Arthur, take her down." he commanded his brother, who sat down opposite Alice, blew on his hands and growled "ooh-rah" in a warming up for battle sort of way. His eyes began to sparkle and shine as a smile spread across his face. Alice raised her *super-serious* face one more bar, as far as it would go, and snarled her mouth and wrinkled her nose.

Arthur laughed, "You look so cute when you wrinkle your nose."

Alice took up his hand, "Are we gonna do this or not?"

Alice tested the pressure on Arthur's arm. He matched it. He looked into her eyes, she felt that same feeling, of him trying to reach her soul, she blinked it away and glared back. Something gave at the very back of his eyes, and his arm hit the table top. Alice had won.

"How did you do that?" Milton asked.

"She cheated." Arthur grumbled.

"I did not, I beat you fair and square." Alice replied.

"By cheating." Arthur said, annoyed.

"I didn't cheat!" Alice said.

"Best of three." Arthur declared, raising his hand.

"No." Milton said, "It's my turn now."

The brothers swapped places. Milton removed his hat and placed it on the table, sweeping his dark hair away from his face. He tidied his shirt cuffs, folding them back so that his wrists were exposed. He took a drink of rum, and when he placed the glass on the table, he took Alice's hand, examining it, "Your hand is the same size as mine." Milton said, "How very interesting,"

Alice cocked her head to one side and frowned, "Do not try to distract me sir."

He laughed, "You look rather cute when you scowl at me."

It began. Arm wrestling for her life, Alice knew, without any doubt, that if she lost this arm wrestle, she would end up thrown to the pirate crew, maybe with a sword if she was lucky. Alice looked Milton in the eyes, and felt that same power washing over her, like he was trying to drown her with the darkest depths of the ocean. Alice blinked and held his gaze. It was overpowering, suffocating, drowning. Alice blinked again, and in that quick moment that it took for her to open her eyes again, it was enough for her to break from the gaze and look at Arthur. He was watching them intently. His brother's arm gave by a fraction. Alice felt it, the muscles weaken at the same point that she had broken his soul-reaching stare. Arthur had moved, he had walked behind Alice and blew in her ear.

"Arthur that's cheating!" Alice cried out.

"What? That's not cheating. Distracting is not cheating. You happen to have very pretty ears."

Alice's arm buckled and landed on the table as she began to giggle, "That's not fair, you cheated. I go weak when I laugh. I demand a rematch."

"Alice you have to stop giving yourself away. You have just told two pirates that your weakness, your achilles heel, is laughter." Milton said, rubbing his wrist.

"Rematch." she said firmly at him.

"You would challenge the Captain of this ship to a rematch when he won fair and square?" Milton asked incredulously.

Alice felt her insides begin to churn a little which she recognised as fear. Milton had an edge to him, and she didn't know how far she could push him before she crossed that line. This was a deciding moment where Alice realised she was either going to be one of them, or be just another brief entertainment and then thrown to the crew in battles to the death. Alice knew all that just from the way the authority had appeared in Milton's last question. How very dare she? But she dared. It vexed him. And she intrigued him with her defiance.

"Very well." Milton said, "A rematch."

The air in the room grew fraught with tension. Milton rolled up his sleeves and ran his hand through his dark wavy hair, sweeping it away from his face in a focusing gesture. His arm raised to the table. Alice's hand was sweating. She wiped it on her trouser leg and took his hand in hers, her elbow on the table. His eyes were dark, the same drowning sensation began to wash over her. She felt her life starting to be overcome by the pressure of the depths of the ocean. He was using his pirate magic again. Alice wrinkled her nose at him and wiggled it.

"Alice look, a monkey." Milton said.

"That's not going to work." she growled.

"Alice you have a spider on your head." Alice's heart jumped once at Arthur's suggestion.

"No I don't." she really hoped she didn't have a spider on her head.

"Alice I want to kiss you." Arthur tried next.

"No you don't." Oh but what if he did, did he actually mean that?

"Alice your breasts are pulling faces at me from underneath your top it's very distracting."

Arthur's face appeared next to Alice's and he peered over at her chest area, "Milton I think you're right those breasts are face-pullers."

Gone. Giggled. Alice's arm was on the table.

"That's not fair either!" she exclaimed.

"He won, fair and square. Twice." said Arthur.

"Have a drink Alice." Milton laughed a reassuringly light jovial laugh. It was infectious and lost the tense atmosphere of the arm wrestle, "Arthur, have you got a light? I need a cigarette after that." he said.

Chapter Eight

(Past Memories)
And so to Sleep

They talked till the early hours, then they decided they were all really tired and wanted to go to bed. They had reached a point where any sexual desire had passed out in a drunken stupor some time ago, and sleep was the only thing left on their minds. They literally could not keep their eyes open. They carried each other through a door into a bedroom, and landed, all three of them in unison, onto a double bed. Milton put his arm around Arthur, and Arthur put his arm around Alice.

"This isn't right." sighed Milton.

"What's wrong?" mumbled Arthur, nestling his face into Alice's back.

"This!" Milton said. He sat up and grabbed his brother by the stomach lifting him into the air.

"Ow! Milton! What are you doing? Just where exactly are you throwing me?" Arthur asked.

"Look, there'll be no throwing of anyone!" Alice shouted, "I'll move!" she sat up and went to the foot of the bed, and lay flat across the bottom of the bed out of the way of both of them.

The two brothers let go of each other and lay back down. Arthur put his arm around Milton. Milton put his arm around Arthur. Alice was just beginning to feel that sleep was descending when she heard Arthur sighing, "This isn't right." he said, miserably.

"What's wrong?" asked Milton.

"I don't know Milton. You tell me." Arthur said, annoyed.

They both went silent. Thinking.

"Alice?" said Arthur.

"What?" she asked sleepily. She already had drool on her mouth and her face was sticking to the sheet of the bed because of it. Lovely.

"Can you give us a hug please?" Arthur said in a sleepy little boys voice.

Alice unstuck her face from the sheet, wiping it with the back of her hand, sat up and looked at them both. Their eyes were bloodshot, their faces unshaven and pale. Their blonde and dark hair respectively, was completely dishevelled. Two pairs of bright blue eyes shone at her in the candlelight.

Alice melted in that moment, or maybe they shot her in the heart with double-barrels of the same magic power they both possessed. No matter. In that moment she realised she loved both of them incredibly. Not in that fairy-tale falling-in-love with a handsome prince sort of way, but close to it. A love of them, who they were, as people, as pirates, as friends, and it was still a pretty deadly and dangerous feeling to descend on her. And all she wanted to do was go to sleep. Damn pirate magic.

"Fine!" Alice simmered, "If it will shut you both up so I can actually get some sleep this evening." she crawled into the Alice sized space between them, Milton put his arm around her and she put her arm around Arthur.

"Night-night." whispered Milton.

"Night-night." Alice replied.

"Night-nIght." whispered Arthur.

"Night-night." Alice said, sleepily.

Alice woke up to the alarm going off on her mobile phone which was still in the main cabin room, she'd forgotten to switch it off. They were all still arm over arm over leg. Alice took some time to take it in, a poignant memory that would last her forever. The two most handsome pirates she had ever met, one on either side of her, the sound of their breathing as they slept. As usual, with beautiful people, they managed to look incredibly dashing even when sleeping. Unlike Alice. She looked awful, she knew it, and sighed. Neither of them stirred as she got up to switch the alarm off. She crept back into the space between them and collapsed into a sleep.

When Alice woke once more she was on her own. The smell of cigarette smoke wafted through the bedroom from the main cabin room then her ears tuned to the sound of conversation and laughter. She tried to tidy up her hair as best she could and then went through.

"Good morning, dear Alice!" Milton chirped cheerily.

"Morning." yawned Alice.

Flat Eric was walking about with a chef's hat on and wearing a little white apron carrying a hand-whisk, he nodded at Alice as she caught his eye. Arthur and Milton were sitting at their respective seats at the table.

"Scrambled eggs and salmon this morning." Milton merrily announced, "Eric is a whiz in the kitchen."

"Is he the one who does the laundry as well?" Alice asked.

"I think so." Milton replied, "I don't tend to trouble myself with such trivialities."

"Oh." frowned Alice.

"So you shouldn't either!" he smiled, "Please, sit, drink some tea and eat some breakfast." he gestured that she should sit down.

Flat Eric tootled over and handed Alice a napkin, and made a place setting for her at the table. He disappeared into a room which Alice realised was a small kitchen, and came out a few moments later with a steaming plate of scrambled eggs on crust-free toast with salmon curls sprinkled over it.

"Wow, thank you." Alice said.

"Savour it." Arthur said from across the table, "It's the last of the salmon, and the last of the eggs, and the last of the toast."

"We saved them for you." Milton smiled.

Alice noticed that neither of them were eating.

"Are you not having some?" she asked, "They're delicious."

"We've had breakfast." Milton said.

"Hair of the dog." Arthur added.

Eric tapped her arm and poured her some tea from an elegant silver pot.

"Thank you." Alice said.

"And that's the last of the tea." Arthur said.

After breakfast, Alice tidied and freshened herself up as best she could. The pirates had no fresh water to spare for a wash. She thanked her earlier-self for packing wipes, which she used to scrub her face, and then brushed her hair, she styled it into a plait.

Arthur and Milton stood up as she went through to the main cabin room.

"You look lovely, Alice." Milton said.

"Mm, fresh as a daisy." Arthur agreed.

Alice couldn't tell if they were being serious or sarcastic.

"Better than you looked ten minutes ago anyway." Arthur quipped quietly.

Before Alice could react, Milton breezed brightly onto a subject change, "Come on, let us show you the Sea Rose at her most magnificent."

Chapter Nine

(Past Memories)
A Good Morning

Milton opened the door and they walked outside, into the sunlight and a brilliant, blisteringly bright blue sky. The ship really did look magnificent. She carried herself on an air of pride and triumph and she radiated a shimmery glow in the sunlight, as if the mist was emanating from her very woodwork and evaporating in the heat of the morning light. The crew were happy, smiling and chatting among themselves.

"Have a look over the edge." Milton commanded.

A rush of distrust flooded over Alice, "The crew said it wasn't safe to do that yesterday in case the ship pulled me over the edge." she said.

"Oh did they?" Milton raised his eyebrows laughing, "They love a good joke. The ship's not going to pull you over the edge. She was the one that wanted us to come and find you."

"Oh." said Alice, "But Arthur said …."

Arthur cut her off, "Come and see, Alice." he said, leaning over the edge of the ship.

Alice looked over at him, worried.

"Oh come on, what's the worst that could possibly happen?" Arthur teased, "Are you afraid of heights?"

It must have been written all over Alice's face. "Not so much a fear of heights, but more a fear of falling out of a flying ship." she tried to explain as she walked over and looked over the edge of the ship. It was a clear day, and she could see land passing by beneath them, though it was too small to make out anything more than fields, forests and the rooftops of houses. When she peered over, the wind changed, and it rushed through her hair and chilled her face. A wave of dizziness and nausea passed over her and she pulled away from the edge.

"I find a drink of rum cures a fear of heights." Arthur said.

"But I just said I'm not scared of heights."Alice replied, aware that she had turned rather green.

"Come, have a drink with me, it will cure your vertigo." he walked towards the Captain's cabin. "We shall introduce you to the crew after a drink to warm the journey."

"I might need more than one." Alice said.

"Alice what a marvellous idea! Lots of drinks!" Arthur laughed.

He walked in, went straight to the unit and popped the bottle stopper.

"What about Milton?" Alice asked, sitting at the table, putting her head in her hands to recover from her dizziness.

"Oh, don't worry, he can smell a drink at a hundred paces."

Sure enough, in walked Milton, "Call yourself a pirate Alice, you need to find your sea legs." Milton laughed.

"But we're in the air." Alice said.

"It's much of a muchness." Milton mused, pouring himself a drink.

"Who is at the helm Milton?" Arthur asked.

"Why, Alice of course." Milton replied.

They both looked at Alice.

"No I'm not?" Alice said, and feeling a twinge that she should actually know the answer already, she asked, "What's the helm?"

"That's where the wheel is, and that's where you should be as you're meant to be steering the ship. If you're not there then no one is." Milton shrugged.

They raised their eyebrows at Alice expectantly.

"Will we crash if no one is steering the ship?" Alice asked. She had no idea whether a flying pirate ship took an instant nose-dive if someone left the wheel. The brothers shrugged a non-committal response at her.

"Pretty much, yeah." Milton said.

Alice grabbed her drink and ran out of the cabin and up the steps, and clutched the ship's wheel with her free hand. Alice had no idea how to control a flying pirate ship, she held the wheel level, as it seemed the right thing to do. She took her first sip of rum, and felt its warmth fall slowly down her throat, warming her chest like it was igniting a fire deep inside her very being. Standing at the wheel of a pirate ship Alice wondered how she would explain this to anyone when she got back to work, if she even made it back alive. She could hear laughter coming from the Captain's Cabin, Arthur emerged and came up the steps to stand next to her, still laughing.

"We weren't going to crash, were we?" Alice asked him.

Arthur looked at her, his eyes with dancing with merriment, "Not at all, no." he replied, "We were pulling your weak land locked legs."

"Well, I'm over it now." Alice said.

"Told you that rum would sort you out." Arthur said jovially, "Where are we going then, Captain Alice?"

"I feel the North Wind blowing." Alice replied, feeling it was a rather good thing to come out with as she had seen it on 'Chocolat', a film about Chocolate, one of her favourite things, starring Johnny Depp.

"Then let's go south." Arthur replied.

"But I'd rather go north Arthur." Alice said.

He flashed his eyes at her and scowled, "You can't go north if the North wind is blowing in your face, the sails will want to fly south."

"But I want to go north."

"Very well. Have it your way. North it is." he spun the wheel of the pirate ship, "Heave-ho boys!" he shouted to the crew, "Alice wants to go north!"

The ship rose upwards, lurching higher into the sky. Alice clung to Arthur's arm as she steadied herself and raised her eyebrows. He looked blankly at her.

"North?" Alice asked.

"Yes. North." he replied.

"Arthur!" Alice said, relinquishing her hold on his arm and scowled a little fearfully at him, "I don't want to keep going this way north, we'll end up in space!"

"Exactly." he said triumphantly, turning and walking down the steps, "That's why I suggested we go south. Australia is lovely and warm this time of year. You girls and your nonsense." he walked away, shaking his head.

Alice was completely confused. She held the ship's wheel, feeling the smoothness of the wood and took comfort from it. The ship was still rising and Arthur had vanished in a mood. He was a strange creature, entirely miserable even when he was happy. "Can we just go steady now please boys?" Alice shouted in her loudest commanding voice to the crew. They shot vicious glances at her, muttering to themselves, Alice gathered it was to do with her indecisiveness about the direction they were sailing in. They moved around the sails, maneuvered ropes, and the ship stopped rising. Alice had a think about what had just happened. The crew had listened to her. Even though they were all annoyed at her, which was actually Arthur's fault, Alice seemed to be in charge of them while she was at the helm.

"Where to ma'am?" asked one of the crew.

"Onwards!" Alice shouted.

"Yo ho!" they all shouted back. The ship set sail again, in a safe, straight horizontal line.

Arthur came back up the steps some ten minutes later. Alice was enjoying being in the clouds that they had sailed into, feeling the moisture on her face. He held out a glass of rum.

"Thought you might need this." he grumbled.

"Thank you." Alice said.

"Milton is having a lie down." he said.

Alice didn't reply, just kept looking out at the clouds, as did Arthur. Alice was still a bit upset that he hadn't explained navigating the ship more clearly.

"We used to be like you, Alice." Arthur said quietly after a moment, Alice didn't reply, "We used to be down there. But, the world turned against us. We aren't bad people Alice. Not really. But no one sees us as nice people. Except you." he took a drink from his glass.

"I think you're a bit of a dick." Alice said, still annoyed at him. Alice shot a look at him, he looked so very sad in that moment, she didn't know what to say. He blinked the expression away.

"Indeed I am. Anyway." he cleared his throat, "Onwards!"

"To the next adventure!" Alice replied, finally smiling.

"Yes, well, for an adventure, we shall need to land." he said, his eyes beginning to light up with mischief at the thought of an adventure on the horizon, "Hmm...where shall we land?" he asked.

"Somewhere that has drink!" announced Milton, walking up the steps to the wheel.

"Have you drunk the ship dry again brother?" Arthur asked, laughing.

"Well...there is no rum left, as Alice drank it all." Milton replied, "And unfortunately this ship does not sail dry. We need to re-stock her."

Milton pulled a faded piece of parchment out from a small wooden cupboard drawer to the left of the wheel. Unfolding it carefully he spread it out on the surface of cupboard. The parchment was very worn at the edges, but the colour had held. Painted on the parchment was, from what Alice could make out, images of islands, land and seas. One part of the land had a bottle with a skull and crossbones painted over it.

"That looks as good a place as any." Milton said, pointing at it.

"Where is it?" Alice asked, not knowing of anywhere near where she lived that looked like that.

"Downwards." Arthur replied.

"Of course." Alice said, "I should have known that. Perfectly obvious to anyone."

"Downwards men!" Milton shouted to the crew.

The crew looked up at the ship platform, one scratched his head, the other raised a fist at them, and much muttering and grumbling passed between them. Alice didn't need to hear them to know what they were complaining about.

Chapter Ten

(Past Memories)
Meeting Jasper

"Why has it got a skull and crossbones on the picture of the bottle on the map?" Alice asked, "Isn't that a bad thing?"

The brothers shrugged, "Didn't make the map. Don't know." Milton said, "I acquired it in a game of poker. Magic islands. Can only reach them by map."

"I don't understand." Alice replied.

"You don't have to trouble yourself with the trivialities." Milton smiled. He looked at Alice, scrutinising her with his gaze, he cast his eyes up and down, up and down, and then looked into her eyes.

"What?" Alice asked.

"This won't do." he gestured his hands emphatically at Alice.

"What won't do?"she asked again, hoping he wasn't about to make her walk the plank for not understanding magic island landing logic.

"You will not pass for a pirate in that clothing, you look terrible. And we need you armed. We have never been to this land before, we do not know what, or who we are going to meet. You will stick out like a sore thumb and be unable to defend yourself." Milton explained.

Alice paled a little. The joy at driving a pirate ship subsided away into a quiet corner of her mind, to expose a small amount of fear sitting smoking a cigarette nervously in the background. Alice didn't smoke. It wasn't a comfortable feeling.

"Jasper!" Milton shouted, "Jasper where are you?"

"He'll be stealing something no doubt." Arthur remarked.

"How can someone steal things when he lives on the ship?" Alice asked.

"Because he is a thief." Milton replied, "Through and through. He cannot help himself."

"Jasper?" Arthur shouted over the deck.

A young boy with slicked spiky black hair and the widest eyes Alice had ever seen appeared from behind a mast at the opposite end of the ship. He had a blue top on, raggedy jeans that stopped at his calves, and bare feet. He smiled as he came closer to them, eyes widened as he gazed at Alice. He jogged lightly up the steps to the wheel. "Hello." he said, holding out his hand to Alice. He wasn't even out of breath.

Now that Jasper was up close, Alice felt tiny standing next to him, he was built like a tank. His grip almost squashed her hand. "Jasper, this is Alice." said Milton, "Can you possibly acquire her some suitable clothes to make her more pirately presentable … and a sword I think… yes, a sword as well. A sword her size."

Jasper grinned at Alice, "Are you joining the crew Alice?" he asked. He looked such a sweet innocent young boy when he smiled. Alice looked at Arthur and Milton.

"She's with us now." Milton advised Jasper, "You will protect her with your life, Jasper."

Jasper looked at Alice and smiled again, "No one will hurt her." he said confidently.

Milton looked relieved, "He's your bodyguard Alice." he said, "Don't trust him with anything other than your life. He'll steal everything else."

Jasper leaped from the wheel deck down to the main deck and disappeared from sight. He reappeared a few moments later holding some clothes, "You best go and get changed Alice." Milton suggested.

Alice made her way into the Captain's Cabin, aware of a few pairs of eyes watching her from the crew. In the bundle of clothes, Alice found a loose, dark green shirt, made of thick material, which she pulled over her vest tops, and a black pair of over-the knee shorts. There was a belt, which she tied over the shirt. When she went outside, Jasper's eyes lit up, "You make a beautiful pirate Alice." he said, "Here's your sword."

Jasper handed her an exquisite work of art, flashing silver with studded glittering gems. She wasn't sure if the clear jewels were diamonds, there was one ruby red stone set in the middle of them. It reminded Alice of the Thundercats sword, only more effeminate and delicate. It was light in weight as she tested it in her hands.

"Hopefully you won't need to use it if I'm around looking after you." Jasper said, smiling.

"It's lovely Jasper, thank you." Alice smiled.

Jasper blushed, "I 'acquired' it a while ago. I've got no use for it. Must be meant for you." he said.

Alice placed the sword in its scabbard and she found it took a bit of concentrating to fasten it to her belt safely without stabbing herself in the leg. Jasper looked really proud that she was pleased with his treasure. Milton came down the steps and looked at her. "Not bad, but there's just one thing missing." Milton pondered. He went into the cabin, and came out holding a little pot, he dipped his fingers in it and smeared two lines of black ink across either of Alice's cheeks, "Now you're one of us Alice."

"Stand and Deliver!" she cried, striking a defiant pose.

They all laughed at her.

Chapter Eleven

First Landing

"Land Ho" shouted one of the crew from the dizzying heights of the crows nest. Sure enough, the ship was lowering to a stop. Arthur peered over the side of the ship, holding onto his hat which had almost fallen off his head to disappear overboard.

"Ladders please men!" Arthur asked with a still quietness in his voice which descended over the crew. They each moved more quietly now.

"We know not what's down here Alice." Milton explained ominously, "The ship should not be able to be seen or heard except by the keen observer, but we cannot be reckless by shouting and making too much noise."

Alice nodded. Milton walked round the crew and ordered some to remain on board, and others to get ready to raid for rum. Jasper jogged up to Alice's side with a bag on his back, fashioned out of sail canvas, "Got your back" he smiled at her. He handed Alice a smaller version of his bag which she pulled over her shoulders, "For anything you might acquire." he said.

"Thank you, it's a great bag." she replied.

"I made it myself." he puffed up proudly.

Down the rope ladders they all climbed. Not the plank this time, but Alice didn't ask why. She wasn't used to climbing down unsteady rope ladders from a pirate ship. She wasn't used to having a sword attached to her hip. She wasn't used to this amount of rum in her system while trying to climb down the aforementioned pirate ladders. She wasn't used to having pirate's boots prodding her face. Nor was she used to pirates checking her out while she was trying for grim life to hang onto a ladder. 'Act like you have done this a hundred times, Alice,' she thought. 'And that you made it to the bottom safely each time and took on whatever was at the bottom of said ladders and won.'

They were on the outskirts of a cluster of houses that could pass for a small village, which was shrouded in mist. The group walked silently into the main street, where the road opened out, and Alice could see that the village was set around a large grassy green, the houses had thatched roofs and there was a church at the far end, which she could make out due to the bell tower. The whole place was silent. No one else could be seen on the streets of the village.

"Ominous." Alice whispered, "It looks just like a village I know, but much older. It looks so much like it. How strange. Only the one I know has a monument on the village green and more houses. This is really weird. I mean, it's identical, the church is in the same place, the pubs are there...."

"How brilliant," whispered Arthur, "Alice already knows where the pubs are."

Alice pointed farther down the main street, to a sign swaying eerily. It was eerie, as there was no breeze. On the sign was a crossed set of keys painted on a white background, "In thar will be the rum." Alice whispered, knowingly.

"Alice, you will need to take the lead. We have no idea if the locals will be friendly to pirates." Milton said in hushed tones.

Alice turned and looked at the six pirates clustered round her, each and every one of them giving her puppy dog eyes, "What if they don't like girls?" Alice whispered.

"Then run." Arthur whispered, "We will be right here waiting for you."

"Hiding!" Alice hissed, "Right. Fine. I'll go." Just to show them that she wasn't a coward. No one ever wanted to be the first to walk into an unknown bar, and it appeared pirates were no different to anyone else she knew.

Alice strolled as casually as she could along the street. There was a funny smell in the air, something burning, but she couldn't put her finger on it. She paused outside the entrance to the tavern, which had a step down through a low doorway and listened. She could hear murmurings inside, male voices, but no squabbling, swearing or otherwise dangerous drunken behaviour. Alice opened the door and stepped through, realising instantly that she was dressed like a pirate with war-paint on her face. It didn't matter that she was a girl, she still looked like a crazy person to people in a bar having a quiet tipple before heading home for the evening.

The barman caught her eye as she opened the door, as the bar was straight in front of her. He was drying glasses with a tea-towel. The ceiling was low, a high shelf above the bar housed ornate tankards. Six men were in the bar, that's an even fight, Alice thought, six of them versus one of her. Two men were on stools at the bar, two sitting at a table end and two standing near the fire, which was burning red hot. "Hello." Alice greeted the barman, walking up to him, clearing her throat as her voice had disappeared, "Hello sir, do you happen to sell rum?"

The barman raised an eyebrow at her, "Yes. What are you dressed as tonight then, some sort of pirate?"

"Fancy dress!" she smiled her best light-hearted-fun-filled-face at him.

"Fancy what?" he frowned, "You're wearing trousers, not a dress."

Something wasn't right, but Alice couldn't put her finger on it. "Do you mind if we all come in for a drink before the party?"

"Go ahead." the barmans lip curved into a welcoming smile.

Alice stepped outside and motioned the pirates to come inside, they strode over, "All clear." Alice said to Milton, "But something's not right."

He took her arm and linked it in his, "What is it Alice?"

"I don't know, I just have a creepy feeling creeping over me." she replied.

"Okay. Noted. Any sign of danger, run back to the ship and wait for us." Alice nodded. He dropped her arm to walk ahead and lead the crew into the bar. The pirates went into the tavern, all except for Jasper.

"I must leave you for a time, Alice." he said, "All these houses, so much to be acquired." his eyes filled with the wonder of what he could find, "I'll be back within the hour, you'll be okay with the rest of them." he smiled that same young innocent boy smile, and walked away from Alice.

She watched him go, and said nothing. Had she the power to stop him thieving, she would have asked him to stay, but this was who he was. and some quiet voice inside Alice told her it was not her place to try to quell that aching need in him for thievery.

Inside, the barman served drinks to the pirates, and they sat at a table, and tried to lighten the nervous atmosphere. Alice sat between Arthur and Milton, feeling somewhat safer sandwiched between the two of them, "What do you think Milton?" Arthur muttered quietly under his glass which covered his mouth. He took a sip from the glass.

"We come back at the dead of night. We take the rum and we set sail. This place is giving Alice the heebie jeebies."

"Ah." Arthur muttered again through his glass, "Then let's not spend any longer than we have to here."

"Aw, guys look it's just a feeling." Alice started to say, realising she was making them all feel uneasy.

"No, no, we trust your judgement Alice." Milton interrupted, "You have to trust your gut instinct. Rely on it. It knows more than you realise. More often than not, it will be right, and it is better to be wrong about being right than being wrong and being dead." Alice thought about what he had said, but got confused, so said nothing in reply.

Being pirates with a new pub to drink in, they didn't leave after one drink to return later for a looting. They sat and they drank for quite some time. They spoke to the locals who eyed them warily, even when the pirates were most jovial to them. Being slightly drunk Alice hadn't noticed that Jasper had not returned from his jaunt and she'd completely lost track of time. Then the locals left. It was only the pirates left in the bar. Even the elusive barman had disappeared. "Where is everyone?" Alice asked. The boys were still laughing and joking over their pints, but unease crept over Alice like a draught from the dying fire, sending shivers up her spine.

"Barman must be through the back?" Arthur shrugged, he got up and put another log on the fire.

After a bit of discussion about how the crackle of a log fire makes things so much more pleasant, Alice still couldn't shake the feeling that something was amiss, she got up and clambered over the bar, a tad awkwardly, and walked through to the back room to try to find the barman. No one was there. She went right round the back rooms, as silently as she could in drunken stealth mode in a pair of cowboy boots in case she got in trouble for being there. She was trying her best to take giant steps thinking that would make her quieter, and she put her arms out to the sides to make her steps a bit lighter. All the while she was listening for anything but all she could hear was the echo of her giant boot steps stomping about the place. Nothing else stirred.

Mischief took over when Alice found the liquor store room. She still had the canvas bag strapped to her back as the crew initially hadn't planned to stay long, and she had forgotten it was there over the course of the evening. So she filled it with bottles from the store room. She got four bottles of rum and some smaller bottles in it, so tightly packed they didn't even rattle or chink as she raised the bag to get it back onto her shoulders. She shook her head, took the bag off her shoulders, unbuckled her belt, took off her pirate shirt, put the bag back over her shoulders and threw the shirt back on over it. The belt and shirt secured her bag more firmly in place and hid it from view. Alice jammed small bottles of liquor into the sides of her cowboy boots, for good measure, and giggled to herself, she would never dream of doing anything like this back home.

Instead of walking back into the bar the way she had came, Alice decided to walk through one of the doors she had found, which led through what looked to be some sort of bakery, it smelled like baking dough but there was something else mixed with it that made her stomach turn. She went through another door and found herself outside at the front again. She took a breath of the cold night air which cleared the sour taste of the bakery from her lungs. Not a single light was on in any of the houses. Something was definitely, absolutely amiss in this village. Then Alice heard footsteps in the distance, pounding footsteps coming at a quick and panicked pace from one of the roads leading to the left of the green. Alice squinted, and could make out what looked to be Jasper running full pelt towards her. "Jasper?" Alice called out in the quietest loud call she could muster, unnerved by the empty villageness. The village she knew back home was so full of life and friendly people. "What's wrong?" she called.

Despite the distance, Jasper's wide white eyes caught hers in utter fear and alarm, "They're trying to *eat me*!" he shouted.

And then Alice saw them, about twenty people slumbering after Jasper, arms outstretched. They ran, but their legs didn't bend properly. "Alice, run!" Jasper shouted, "They're zombies!"

Chapter Twelve

(Past Memories)
Zombie Attack!

Alice paused for less than a second as her mind seemed to float above her body, she saw it in slow motion, taking in the scene set before her. She blinked it away and ran back into the bar. "Guys!" Alice yelled. The pirates only half heard her, "Guys!" she yelled again, this time they looked up and paused their conversations. "Zombies!" she said, unable to get a sentence of explanation out of her mouth in the sense of sheer urgency of what was waiting for them outside.

The pirates eyes were blurry but they widened in alarm as they took in Alice's genuinely terrified face and the one word she had managed to yell. They jumped to their feet and bolted for the door. The zombies were almost at their heels as they ran outside. The pirates realised they couldn't outrun them, the zombies had them surrounded.

The pirates drew their swords, standing their ground. It dawned on Alice that the stakes had changed, they were actually in real danger of losing their lives to a hoard of zombies on her first fun adventurous outing. It sobered her up pretty quickly. Death being near, this was no longer a light-hearted night out.

The pirates were outnumbered. They were barely holding their line against the first zombies to approach them. There was no way Alice could match the zombies in strength, she knew she would put all the pirates in danger if she stood with them to fight given she had only just learned how to hold her sword. She thought back to all the movies she'd seen about zombies, which weren't that many as the gore fest wasn't her favourite genre. The zombies had come out of hiding when it got dark. 'Come on….' Alice thought, 'they were afraid of the light…'

She ran back into the pub, and reached over the bar and grabbed a bottle of spirit, picked up the coal shovel and took a scoop of the burning embers from the open fire and ran back outside. She boldly stepped out in front of the line of pirates and smashed the bottle of booze over the head of the nearest zombie, then threw the contents of the coal shovel at him and ran back. In the time it took for her to sprint back behind the pirates and peer out from behind Arthur's shoulder, the zombie was engulfed in flames.

The zombie staggered backwards and fell onto a second zombie. Alice could only imagine their clothes must have been very dry, as they went up in flames quite quickly. The other zombies recoiled in horror at the light from the flames. This was enough to give the pirates the upper hand. Swords were flying, chopping limbs off bodies. The limbs disintegrated into dust in front of their eyes. It blew into Alice's eyes and stung like sand at the beach. The zombies were made of sand.

Alice ran back into the pub, grabbed more bottles from behind the bar and took another scoop from the fire. Armed and ready again she stepped outside. The closest zombie got a bottle over his head then a face full of hot ash. She ran back and forth into the bar, and out, to smash bottles over zombie heads, while the pirates plundered with their swords. Between them all, they took the twenty or so zombies out. Maybe it was forty, or a hundred, Alice hadn't been counting and it felt like a whole army had been against them. The pirates stood, breathless, looking at each other. "You saved us there, Alice." Milton panted.

"Well … " Alice broke off, trying to catch her breath, realising only then that she had burned her hand badly at some point in the process of igniting zombies, it was really starting to sting.

"There'll be more." said Jasper, "I reckon this whole place has a zombie plague."

"It wouldn't surprise me." Milton concurred.

"Nothing surprises you." Arthur commented.

"Let's get out of here, while we still can." Milton added.

Exhausted, the pirates walked and stumbled back to the ship.

Chapter Thirteen

(Past Memories)
Not so Good

Back on the ship, the crew who had remained on board gathered round them on deck, eager to see the booty from the island exploration, "Raise the ladders, take off, now, and do it post haste." Milton commanded urgently with no other explanation. They looked puzzled but ran to their posts.

Alice untied her belt and removed the bag from her back, she pulled out a bottle, opened it and passed it to Milton, "You still managed to steal drink in amongst all of that?!" he exclaimed, "Well done!"

Alice took a little bottle from her boot and walked over to Jasper, who was visibly shaking, standing leaning on the balustrade looking out into the night sky. "Are you okay Jasper?" Alice asked. He turned his face towards her. His eyes were filled with fear and sadness. Alice knew.

Without him saying anything at all, she knew. He nodded with understanding as Alice's eyes widened and he held up his arm, revealing a human bite mark near his wrist, "I cannot stay on board. I would curse you all." he murmured sadly.

"What are you going to do?" Alice asked.

"I will have to go back to the village. It is the only place for me now. I'm sorry Alice." Jasper leaned over and kissed her cheek. His lovely wide eyes were dull and filled with tears, "Don't forget about me." he said as he stepped onto the ship balustrade and jumped off the edge of the ship. disappearing into the nothingness beneath them, some trick of the ship as it had already begun its rise into the sky. Alice felt her knees buckle beneath her and she thudded to the deck of the ship, her lovely new friend Jasper was gone.

Arthur found Alice sitting in a heap a few moments later. He said nothing, just scooped her up in his arms and carried her into the captain's cabin. He placed her in the bed, put a blanket over her and lay next to her, putting an arm comfortingly around her, "Sleep." was all he said in her ear. She shut her eyes.

She didn't know what time it was when she opened her eyes. At first, she didn't know where she was. Then she registered that she was in the Captain's Cabin on the pirate ship and her hand began to sting. Her burned hand had been bandaged. It was then that she remembered the rest of the night before, and the plight of poor Jasper. Alice got up, cradling the blanket around her, and went through to the main cabin room. Milton was sitting at the table. He stood up as he saw her, he walked over, putting his arm round her and helped her to sit at the table. He took his seat at the head of the table, and looked at her, "How are you feeling?" he asked gently.

"A little shaky." she replied.

"Yes. I'm sorry you had such a terrible time on your first adventure. They're not all like that." he said.

"Jasper jumped overboard." Alice felt the melancholy ache creeping back into her body. She was glad to be seated.

"He did what?" Milton said, surprised.

"He had been bitten by a zombie, on his arm. He said he couldn't stay as he would curse us all and he jumped overboard to go back to the village."

"Oh no." Milton said, "That isn't good at all."

"Are we going to go back to get him?" Alice asked.

Milton sighed, "He's as good as dead." he replied firmly.

"But there's still a chance he's alive?" Alice said.

"No. We will not risk further lives to go back and find a dead man walking. He knew what he was doing when he jumped off the ship."

"But maybe he is okay, maybe he isn't going to turn. Maybe there's a cure down there." Alice pleaded.

"Alice, believe me, it goes against every grain in my being to leave a man behind. Its part of my code. But we can't risk it, he chose to leave, we have to respect that." Milton said somberly.

Alice sat staring at the wood grain on the table, "He made his choice." Milton said. She nodded her head sadly, "He was a valued friend, Alice, not just a run-of-the-mill member of the crew. He is a great loss to us. To me." Milton stood back up, walked over to her, knelt down next to her, and placed his hand over her unbandaged one, "I'm sorry."

Tears began to fall from Alice's face. He cupped her face with his hand, stopping each tear with his thumb, wiping them away, "Don't worry, we will always protect you." Milton said.

She looked at his face through the tears and was caught by the gaze of his blue eyes, she was drowning now in the pirate magic being cast upon her to take the pain away. Milton swept Alice up into his arms, still wrapped up like a cocoon in the blanket, lifting her off the chair and carried her back through to the bedroom. Never taking his gaze off her, he lay her down on the bed. Like someone hypnotised, Alice lay, looking into the depths of his eyes, unable to move or look away, as sleep began to fall over her once more. "Promise me, you'll stay with us, Alice." Milton whispered.

"I promise." she murmoured.

"Promise that if we do part ways, you'll always come back to us, promise that if something bad happens or if the world ends, you'll always come back for us."

"I promise." she said.

"Promise that you will always be our Pirate Alice, promise you'll never forget that."

"I promise" she whispered, falling into a deep sleep.

Chapter Fourteen

(Past Memories)
A Lesson or Two in Defence

Alice woke up in a morning light, she was lying next to Milton. His arm was round her, she was nestled against his chest with the blanket wrapped around her, but only covering the bottom-half of Milton. Alice checked, she was fully clothed, relieved there had been no dodgy pirate hypnosis, then reproached herself, 'Don't be silly', Alice thought, 'he wouldn't do that, he sent you to sleep with his strange pirate magic eyes as you were in shock about Jasper.' Milton was breathing steadily. Alice gazed at his exposed chest, covered in scars. Scars of all shapes and sizes, there was hardly an inch of skin which did not have some form of scarring on it. He had known a lot of pain in his lifetime He had one tattoo above his breastbone, roughly where his heart would be, a symbol she did not recognise. The troubles of the night before seemed an age ago, lying here next to this beautiful man. She lay still for a few moments, listening to him breathing.

There was a knock at the bedroom door, then the door opened, Alice looked up, Arthur was standing in the doorway, looking directly at her. Her heart lifted a little, but she could not read his expression, it was emotionless. "Good morning sir." Milton said cheerily, waking up at that moment, shaking his dark hair loose with his hand.

"There is some food on the table, if you are hungry." Arthur said, flatly.

"Famished." Milton said, getting up, as his brother turned and walked back into the main room.

When Alice went through, they were chatting away about the previous night, breaking bread and dipping it in steaming hot bowls of soup. Arthur looked up at Alice, catching himself as he did so, and went back to his soup, "There's a bowl there for you." he said.

"Thank you." she replied. He did not acknowledge her further.

"You need to learn how to use your sword Alice." Milton said taking a bite of bread, "I was wholly impressed by your fire throwing skills, however that will not be an option in every battle, and in almost every battle, there is the option of the sword. I will not have a member of my crew unable to defend themselves when they have a weapon which can save them strapped to their side."

Alice felt jaded, ever so slightly, that this was a criticism, somehow. She dipped her bread in her soup and took a bite. God knows what sort of soup it was it tasted of nothing and was rather lumpy, Alice couldn't help but pull a face at it.

"Tastes better with some pepper in it." Arthur said, reading her expression.

Alice took the pepper mill from the table and struggled to sprinkle pepper from the grinder into the soup, wincing as her burned hand took pressure from beneath the bandage. "How's your hand?" Arthur asked.

"Stingy." she replied, picking up the spoon with her other hand and slurping on a marginally better tasting soup, "I've had worse burns." she added.

Milton ignored the conversation and continued with his own, "You must learn to master your sword." he said, "You'll need to fight through the pain. Build a tolerance to it. If you get in a scrape in a battle, you can't go down at the first hit, you have to keep fighting. You have to step outside the pain, like it's not actually happening to you." he took some more bread from the centre of the table, "And if you do go down, you get straight back up again, and you keep fighting. Never stay down till you're dead."

Arthur looked at him and said, "Unless playing dead happens to be a wiser option." Milton looked at him, spoon in mid-air, "I'm just saying, it's a wiser choice sometimes." Arthur commented.

"Hmmm." Milton said.

"When do I start training?" Alice said, dispelling the soup stand-off.

"This afternoon." Milton said, "We can't risk landing again without you knowing how to handle your sword. You'll need to be able to protect yourself if you're with us. And if you're not with us, you're against us."

Alice looked across at him, confused at his strange accusatory tone of her being against them. He was like a different person this morning to the one who had cast her to sleep last night.

They trained Alice till she was at the point of throwing up. She didn't think it was the after effects of the anonymous soup, rather it was the most physical exercise she had done for a long time. Alice spent a fair bit of time leaning over the balustrade. She wondered where the contents of her stomach went to once it had fallen down into the nothingness of the mist that was beneath them. Did the sick just sink through the mist and land on people's heads, or did it simply vanish?

The pirates pushed her to her limits, where her arms could no longer lift the sword without shooting pains of agony. Her bandaged hand burned. She gritted her teeth and tried her best to access that part of her mind that could detach her from the pain. It wasn't easy, and she could only manage it in waves before the pain won. They moved to combative moves and steps. A crash-course in sword-fighting, it was a struggle for Alice to remember it all. The crew were going about their duties but occasionally cheered her on encouragingly if she got a move right. "You'll not be able to move in the morning." Milton said, merrily, as Alice was fighting Arthur, "All your muscles will be aching. But you will recover, and you will be stronger for it. You must practice every single day, any time you get a minute, move and practice. You have a lot of muscle to build and these moves must come to you without thinking about them."

He went over to the side to pour himself a drink then turned to face Alice, glasses filled with rum in either hand, with a rolled up cigarette in his mouth and cheeky grin on his face "En Guard!" he said. He was loving it. She knew her training would be such a great entertainment, as Alice was the most uncoordinated person she knew, Alice-clumsy-spectacular, who had to learn battle moves and sequences to make it on the pirate ship. She thought back to Jasper. She would do it for him.

Mid-afternoon, Milton ordered the crew open a cask of grog. It was then that Alice learned that there had been grog on board the whole time. Casks of the stuff. It was only the rum that was kept in the Captain's quarters and had run out. There was always alcohol on board the ship. They hadn't needed to land, they hadn't dried out after all, they had just wanted an excuse for an adventure. Jasper's sacrifice seemed belittled to her in that moment, but she tried to shake the doubt off, they all knew what they were doing after all. She tried not to add this regret to the hurt of losing Jasper. The crew were each given a tankard of grog, and the mood was pleasant that afternoon, except Alice's which was subdued and angry as she was in physical and mental pain. The crew struck up a light-hearted song. "It takes the bad spirits off the ship when they sing." Arthur said, handing Alice her grog. "It's their own way of saying goodbye to Jasper."

She took a sip of the grog and grimaced slightly. Alice wondered how Arthur knew that's what she was thinking about, but of course, they were all thinking about it, just no one was talking about it. "Tastes better after a bit of airing." Arthur said, responding to her grimaced face.

"Acquired taste." Alice replied, "like the soup maybe I should add pepper to it."

Arthur laughed at her, "God no, don't add pepper to grog. You and your nonsense."

They stayed out on deck till late that night, the crew sang songs, which eventually Alice joined in on, when she was finally officially introduced to them. They told her ghostly tales, scary tales about giant vengeful whales, sunken treasures, and about other adventures they had before she came on board. At least Alice thought they were all their own adventures, sometimes it was hard to tell. They asked her for a woman's viewpoint on how to have a successful date, and instead of shyly saying she didn't really know as she was hopeless at that sort of thing, Alice told them to brush their teeth. They all laughed and laughed together. Milton went to bed before Arthur and Alice. Milton walked over, and in front of the crew, kissed Alice's cheek. There was a hush over the crew as he did so. Alice had been recognised now, as belonging to the Captain, and was therefore to be respected as such when he wasn't there. Alice realised it was a way of protecting her.

When Alice decided to call it a night, Arthur had to steady her as she stood up, as her entire body was trembling with exhaustion and her legs were once again giving out beneath her. In the end he picked Alice up, gently kissing her forehead as he took her into his arms, and carried her into the Captain's cabin, "Thank you Arthur. Thank you for taking care of me." she somewhat slurred into his neck.

"You actually might need to brush *your* own teeth Alice, never mind the crew's." he replied, curtly.

He carried her to the Captain's bedroom, and lay her down next to a snoring Milton. He left the room, and she heard him settle into a bed which must have been in a room next door, which Alice hadn't seen before, "Good night Arthur." she called quietly.

"Good night Alice." she heard him say before she descended into a deep oblivious sleep.

In the morning they had peppery soup for breakfast, which eased the slightly hungover feeling Alice had looming over her. She felt like her entire body was broken, everywhere ached. "Grog for you. All day." Milton ordered, watching her rubbing her sore arm with her sore blistered hand, which now was only slightly less painful than her burned hand. "It's the best cure for anything."

Alice spent what she thought was about a week in a haze of sword-fighting during the day, and gathering on deck with the crew most evenings. Each night Milton would go to bed earlier than everyone else, kissing her on the cheek as he got up to leave, and Arthur would sit up with her.

The brothers sat up in the Captain's Cabin till the early hours one night, to show Alice how to take a punch. She didn't enjoy it. Being punched in the face was quite painful even after a couple of rums. But she knew why they were doing it. Not to hurt her, but to strengthen her. If the first punch to the face Alice had ever endured was on the battlefield, it would have floored her straight away. And she'd be dead. So she took the punches they threw straight at her face. And she learned how to make a fist and punched them right back. The first few times they laughed at her, "You hit like a girl." they had said. It had been enough. Then the brothers began to bruise too. Alice was changing, she was getting stronger.

It was a crash course in being a pirate. By the end of that training time, Alice's muscles had toned, her skin had tanned and she wore permanent black stripes across her face. Her mark. She was one of them now. The ship had meandered lazily this whole time. Sometimes surrounded by mist, sometimes not. Alice couldn't be sure if it was ocean or sky they were sailing across.

Chapter Fifteen

(Past Memories)
This is Our Time

It was on the morning of the seventh day of training that Alice had remembered her life back home. Somebody said something that threw her old life back into existence. They asked if anyone had a something to write with and Alice remembered a tub of pens on her desk at work. She sat on the helm steps leading up to the ship's wheel, and bowed her head. "What's wrong Pirate Alice?" Arthur said, coming over.

"I'm going to have to go back to work." Alice muttered, without raising her head.

"Ah." he placed his hand on her shoulder, patting it twice, and not removing it, "But you see Alice, on board this ship, time doesn't really behave itself as it should. Sometimes days repeat themselves, sometimes time goes backwards. Sometimes it just jumps merrily about the ship and no one can quite remember what it was they were doing five minutes ago or what they were supposed to do next."

"What do you mean?" Alice asked him.

"That down here? On this ship? This is our time. Don't worry about everywhere else. If you need to return home, you will do so at precisely the time you are supposed to. In time for tea, no doubt." he sat on the step next to her.

"What if I don't want to go home for tea?" Alice said quietly, "What if I want to stay here, with you?"

Arthur gazed out across the ocean, which was where the ship was sailing at that moment. Alice followed suit and gazed out across the waves. Sailing a vast lilac and blue ocean that stretched as far as the eye could see, it was beautiful. Arthur said nothing for some time, and when he did reply, he changed the subject, "Let's have a party tonight! To celebrate!"

"What are we celebrating?" Alice asked him.

He paused to think again for a brief moment, perhaps still waiting for a wave of inspired genius to pass under the ship and whisper reasons for celebration into his pricked piratey ears, "That life is good. Right now! That's enough for me. Who knows, I might even dance with you!" Alice looked at him but he couldn't read her expression, "Dear me Alice, don't take away the only excuse there is to have a party from me!"

"I didn't do that, I just looked at you?" Alice replied.

He frowned, "Do you have a pretty party dress?"

"No." she smiled and her eyes lit up at the thought of dancing, "But I shall pretend I do."

As the sun began to set over the ocean it cast its golden glow over the crew, as the light changed to the evening sky there appeared on deck an accordion, a fiddle and a tambourine. This was a different night from the other nights when they sat around singing songs to still the evening sunsets. Alice was asked to sing the first song, so she sang "Sunny Afternoon" by The Kinks and taught the crew how to sing it too. The crew then sang different songs, songs that filled the deck with energy, songs that made their feet lift up and dance without even thinking about it. Alice danced with each and every member of the crew in turn, despite her aches and pains, and she felt relief from the pressure that she hadn't even noticed she had been building up during her training week.

It was years ago now, those dances on the ship deck, but a few lines of the feet-tapping songs stuck in Alice's memories that were lively and defiant:

"Dare you dance in the mist

 to the old pirate jig

yo ho yo ho

listen at the echoes

 of the ocean in the sky

yo ho yo ho

know that on this day of days

the pirate ship does fly"

"We had bets that you wouldn't make it past the first day's training." shouted Tri-Cap Tam above the din, he was Alice's dance partner at the time, "We're glad you made it, you're fun. Most of the other girls were made to walk the plank within the first hour of being on board." he smiled and spun Alice round, "Yes, Milton can drive us all pretty hard. Girls included. But you came through. We're glad out of all of them, it was you."

Alice was going to ask him questions, but she was whisked away by another pirate. Alice hadn't realised that the constant scrutiny from Milton the last week had been in any way threatening. She thought it had been concern when he pointed out her mistakes and said she still wasn't good enough, throwing his fists on the wooden beams in temper. Alice had thought it was concern that she was putting herself in danger unless she improved. No, in actual fact, he was measuring her, weighing her up. And if she didn't make the grade, he would get rid of her.

Milton sat with Alice for a while, during the short time he came out that night with the crew. "You are doing well." he said.

"I will be better tomorrow. I will be as good as you tomorrow!" she had replied, a bit drunk, a bit overly positive, trying to get thoughts of lots of girls walking the plank out of her mind, and failing to do so.

"No Alice, I want you to be better than the best. That is why I am teaching you. I want you to go out into the world better than I ever can be. My Alice, I am so glad to have found you at last. To know you, is an honour." he had a sad expression on his face. Looking back, Alice would swear he knew things that no one else did, that he could see things she would never begin to be able to see, he was so worldly wise. She had looked at him, wondering what to say in reply. Then he smiled, kissed her cheek, announced his goodnight to the crew, and went to his cabin.

Chapter Sixteen

(Past Memories)
Too Much First Thing
in the Morning

The training on the ship deck was over. Alice woke up that morning relieved that she wouldn't be faced with another day's training. Milton was sitting on the soft seats underneath the large window of the cabin room, smoking a cigarette and holding a cup of steaming coffee in his hand, "Good morning." he greeted her, "How are you feeling?"

"Okay, thanks." said Alice.

"There's coffee in the pot and soup on the hob. Arthur and Eric are out on deck, fishing."

"Okay."Alice wandered into the tiny kitchenette to pour herself a coffee. It was thick, black and disgusting. She didn't dare look at the soup, she thought she'd be getting that for lunch too. Her stomach was adapting to the meals of the pirates and becoming less hungry at breakfast time.

"The coffee tastes better with some sugar." Milton called through.

"Thanks." Alice called back.

The sugar bowl contained brown sugar which was stuck together, and a spoon that had been used a hundred times to stir the tar-like coffee. Alice poured two spoonfuls into her cup and stirred it. Complying with pirate hygiene, she put the wet spoon back in the sugar dish. "How are you feeling really though?" Milton asked her as she came back through with her coffee.

She thought about it, the depth of his question, a being put on the spot about her feelings sort of question that required more than a generic reply, "I'm okay thanks, I'm still a bit hurt about Jasper but feel stronger in myself now."

"That's good." Milton replied, looking out of the window and taking a draw on his cigarette. "Can I ask you some hypothetical questions Alice?" he asked her.

Alice blew on her coffee. "Are they going to be really difficult?"

"That depends on you." he smiled, flicking the ash off his cigarette and shifting his position on the seat, "As Captain of this ship, I have to make many difficult decisions and live with the consequences. I carry pride at the decisions I know to be right and could see their effects straight away. For a time I carry guilt at decisions I have made that have had serious consequences, but what I do not do though, is burden myself with extra worries. I see each worry as a weight upon my ship, and with too many worries on board, the ship would sink. I have to let them go, or they would destroy me."

"You're talking about Jasper aren't you?" Alice asked.

"Partly, yes. You might think me heartless for not going back for him, but that is the decision I made as the Captain. It is my burden and do you know what I did with that burden?" Alice shook her head, "I let it go." he replied, "It was Jasper's decision to leave, he had already been bitten, and I carry no guilt for that."

"But if we hadn't gone down there ..." Alice started.

"But we were going to go down there regardless." Milton reminded her, "You cannot stay on this ship endlessly and never seek out the next adventure. Some of them will carry a price. But to stay on board for all of eternity, well, you will never have lived. You may as well have stayed in your little office and not come on board at all." he sipped some coffee and continued, "Now, was Jasper not tasked with staying by your side and protecting you?"

"Yes." she replied.

"And did he not break a direct order from his Captain to go and thieve the place?"

"I could have stopped him." Alice said, the guilt welling up at this point. Milton noted her change in tone.

"No, Alice, it was not your place to stop him. It was his place to stay and follow a direct order. Had he survived the zombie attack and come back on board, I would have had him thrown off the ship anyway for disobeying my command and putting your life in danger." he looked directly into her eyes as he said this.

Alice felt the weight of his sentence sink in. Milton had just taken the guilt away that she had carried all week, "Okay, Alice, let's give you something else to think about. Would you mind topping up my coffee first though?" he held out his cup.

"Will you have me beheaded if I don't top it up?" Alice asked him, half smiling.

"Of course." Milton offered a half smile in return, a smile which terrified Alice in a way, as she couldn't tell if he was being serious or running with her joke.

Alice went through to the kitchen, topped up the coffees and returned. She sat on the seats next to him and waited. Milton blew on his coffee cup, took a tentative sip and began, "In a made up scenario, you have two crew members on board, Murray Makepeace and Henry Hungermonger who are cause for concern. Henry Hungermonger had eight wives, each of which he had killed because they couldn't give him children in the times that he was on dry land. He also had many mistresses at different ports."

"What an asshole." Alice muttered.

"Murray Makepeace was sent on board your ship as a scout by an enemy, and betrayed your entire crew to them, but he is an excellent seaman. You need twelve men to run your ship and can only get one to walk the plank. Which one of the two would you keep?" he finished, sipping on his coffee.

Alice looked out of the window and bit her lip. She was the best part of indecisive the entire time, this morning was no different. Who was to walk the plank first? Murray Makepeace or Henry Hungermonger? She didn't like the sound of either of them, "Can't they both walk the plank?" Alice asked Milton.

He shook his head, "You decide, fair and simple. Which one will you keep and which one will you kill?"

"And why am I having to kill one of them?"

"Because I'm telling you to." Milton said as if that was explanation enough, then added, "Okay for the purposes of this example, let's pretend you only have enough food left on board for twelve men as rats ate part of your food rations."

Alice tried very hard to think like a pirate instead of like herself, "Murray Makepeace to walk the plank." she finally said.

Milton leaned forward, "Right answer, but why?" he replied.

"Because Murray broke his oath of loyalty and betrayed his kinsmen. Henry could have been the best battle planner in history, his crime was a personal one. So in a battle situation, I would have to keep Henry and kill Murray."

"Clever girl!" Milton laughed.

"But I'd cut Henry's balls off." Alice added, "And hang them round his own neck so that every woman knew he was a cheating liar."

Milton laughed and laughed, "The balls maketh the man! You'd lose your war planner by doing that! But very well. Here is another for you: You are a passenger on a ship heading for your holidays. There are well to do people, poor people, crew and slaves on board. There is a storm, the ship wrecks and maroons you on a small island. Some people die, sad, I know." Milton said without any emotion or empathy in his voice or expression at all. "Your survivors include the Captain of the ship, some crew, some slaves, some well-to-do and some poor people. No one knows what to do. There is one gun between you all. You are going to starve unless you get organised. You need shelter. You need to hunt for food. You have women who are going into hysterics." Milton paused, taking a sip of his coffee, "What should happen? Should there be a leader of the group? How would you lead such a diverse group? It is nearly nightfall. The Captain of the ship says that he should lead as he led the passenger ship. What do you do?" Milton leaned back, rolled a cigarette slowly and methodically, and watched Alice.

Alice thought about it, "I'm really not sure," she said, "the Captain could split us into groups and we could have hunters and shelter makers."

Milton shook his head, "Alice, at least try to think outside the box." he insisted.

"Well, you could leave them all to it and go off on your own." she suggested.

"And when the rescue party arrives unannounced and you're off having a shit in the woods you get left behind. No, you're stronger as a group." he replied.

There was a long pause. Alice really tried, but didn't know what Milton was expecting from her. "I'm sorry this one is over my head. Can you teach me." she asked, "What would you do?"

Milton smiled, "What would I do? Well …" he took a draw on his cigarette and exhaled. "I'd march right up to that Captain and I'd chop his fingers off, and I'd tell everyone that they could expect the same if they went against me. I'd take that gun and I'd point it in the hysterical women's faces and I'd tell them that they'd be getting a mouthful of gunpowder if I heard so much as a peep out of them and they were to strip their pretty dresses to make rags to start the camp fires, and also for my own amusement." he stared into space at the thought of the women stipping their dresses.

Alice waved a hand in front of his face and he returned to the room, "Oh yes, then I'd use the gunpowder to start the fire, on the beach to signal for help. And I'd hang any trouble makers."

"Oh." Alice said.

"You cannot presume just because someone is called Captain that he is the right person to lead a group on a deserted island situation. That Captain was captain of a passenger ship, not a survival expedition. A passenger ship, might I point out, that marooned while under his command. That should tell you straight off that he is a bad leader."

"Oh." Alice said, "I never thought of it like that."

"You must question everything, Alice." Milton insisted, "If I can teach you anything, learn that. Everything they have ever tried to teach you just might be a little wrong and needs undone. That is what it means to think like a pirate. There are rules for pirates, and there are rules for other people. Never forget which side you are on. Never be scared to question something."

"I won't." Alice said.

"Good." he smiled, "Any further questions?"

"Just one." Alice said, "The village we went to on that map, it was so familiar to me, it was like a village I knew back home, only the houses were thatched instead of tiled. It looked the same but older."

Milton stubbed out his cigarette and exhaled a big cloud of misty grey smoke into the air. "That's because you're on a time travelling pirate ship." he smiled, "Did you not know?"

"Time travelling?" she asked, her eyes filling with wonder, "How does that work?"

"Alice I don't have all the answers, and even when I do, I am not about to ruin a good story with the truth. Why trouble yourself with the trivialities of it all? I am Captain of a Time Travelling Pirate Ship. It works, it travels through time. I like to think of it as magic rather than dissecting it with science. Would you prefer I gave you a mathematical equation to explain the same thing to you?"

"No, but if you're time travellers, aren't you affecting history each time you land?"

This made Milton smile a self-knowing smile, "History books are often written years after the events, sometimes by those who write their own families into important events so they look important in the right social circles. No one actually really knows what happened, it's all just intellectual sounding guesswork. Sometimes all they have are names and dates on a gravestone and they make the rest up. "

"But if it is written down in the history books, isn't is a fixed point in time that has already happened?" Alice asked.

"They've already written their history books, they can't re-write their records of events. But yes, we can re-write history." was Milton's explanation, which didn't make sense to Alice at all.

Milton laughed and continued, "Did you ever read the term 'ritual sacrifice' before? Its when the experts don't have an explanation for what's right in front of their noses. I'll bet Arthur and I are on some of the stone carvings and egyptian hieroglyphs in the most important museums in the world. We'll be standing there drinking a toast with the Pharoah Kings, showing off our swords or the latest booty, we'd be buckled over laughing at the pharoahs bad jokes, and the experts will tell you we were being beheaded as some sort of religious sacrifice."

"You've been to Egypt?" Alice asked.

Milton nodded, "That's a story for another day though. If you succeed in changing history by being there Alice, they'll never know it happened that way, will they?"

"But wouldn't they then have written something else in their books, as you've changed the world as we know it?" Alice asked, her head beginning to hurt.

"But they have already written the books, Alice, so history won't change according to the books that have already been written."

"I don't understand." Alice said.

"Sometimes, you don't have to understand, Alice. Just accept it is what it is, relax and enjoy it. Worrying about the ins and outs of time travel will just confuse you and you will spend so much time worrying about it you won't end up on any adventures at all."

Arthur and Eric came back into the Cabin, "Did you catch anything?" Alice asked, eagerly breaking out of the headache inducing conversation about time travel she had found herself in.

Eric held up a bundle of small fish, "Eric caught some mackerel. I didn't catch a thing." Arthur said.

"And Alice is going to catch some Paper Tigers."announced Milton, standing up and stretching, "She needs a lesson on unnecessary worrying." he added, walking out of the door.

"Paper Tigers?" Alice said to Arthur.

"Oh you're going to love this adventure!" Arthur smiled wickedly.

Chapter Seventeen

(Past Memories)
Chasing Paper Tigers

Alice and Arthur sat at the table in the Captain's Cabin while Eric busied himself in the kitchen with the mackerel. Alice felt the ship changing speed and beginning to draw to a stop, "You'll need your sword for this one Alice." Arthur said.

She took her coffee cup through to the kitchen and went through to the bedroom to buckle her sword to her side, "I'm ready." she said, going back through.

"Great." Arthur said, "I'll take you to Eyeball Paul, he's the expert on Paper Tigers."

"Are you not coming with me?" Alice asked.

"No, been there, done that." Arthur said nonplussed, "I'm going to do some more fishing while you're away."

Arthur took Alice outside and along the deck, to Eyeball Paul, who was a short man with unkempt grey hair, a grey top and a black bandana on his head. he had only one leg; where his other leg might once have been was a wooden stump. He grinned as Alice approached and Alice finally recognised him as the pirate who had told her the Sea Rose would drag her overboard if she stepped too close to the edge, despite the fact she had danced with him on deck on previous nights. "What can I do for you?" Eyeball Paul asked Arthur and Alice.

"You're to take Alice to battle the Paper Tigers." Arthur said in a friendly tone.

"Is that so?" questioned Eyeball Paul, his eyes lit up mischievously, he raised his wooden leg and tapped it with his hand.

"Did the Paper Tigers do that to your leg?" asked Alice straight away.

"Aye, that they did. Tis a hard lesson to learn, battling the Paper Tigers." Eye-Ball Paul purred pirate-like at her. Arthur couldn't hold a laugh in, Alice looked at him suspiciously. "We'll be taking Vincent with us as well, to watch our backs." said Eyeball Paul to Arthur.

"Very well. Just don't be out till after dark if you're taking him with you." said Arthur, and he turned to Alice, who was standing a bit wide eyed and worried, "Alice, you have nothing to worry about. You've done your training now, the rest of your time here is to be enjoyed for the adventures they are." and with that he wandered away.

"Righto." Alice said.

"Stay here Miss Alice. I'll go and fetch Vincent from his cell." Eyeball Paul said.

Alice did some stretching while she waited for Eyeball Paul, then he emerged from below deck with a huge man Alice hadn't met before. The man had slicked back dark hair and a pale complexion, he wore a navy shirt and tattered jeans and had icy green eyes, "This is Vincent." Eyeball Paul said.

"Ah, how pleased I am to finally meet your acquaintance." Vincent said in a thick accent.

"We've not met. How do you do." said Alice holding out her hand.

"I have a tendency to stay below deck." Vincent explained, "But I make an exception on this occasion."

Eyeball Paul and Vincent lowered the rope ladders which disappeared into the thick mist which was hovering just below view of the deck, "After you Vincent." motioned Eyeball Paul.

"With pleasure." smiled Vincent, Alice saw that he had incredibly glossy teeth.

"After you, Alice." said Eyeball Paul.

"Okie dokie." said Alice, clambering down the ladder.

They made their way through the mist and emerged into a green landscape, lush woodland surrounded them, giant ferns grew all around them, "We need to walk to the next clearing." whispered Eyeball Paul, "Draw your swords, you never know where these Tigers be at."

Alice pulled out her sword, Vincent pulled out two slightly curved swords and held them in both hands, while Eyeball Paul pulled a small knife from a sash belt that he had slung round his chest, she hadn't noticed it before as it was hidden under his outer shirt. "What are you going to do with that?" Alice asked quietly, "It's a teeny tiny knife."

"Throw it." Eyeball Paul said, "I can teach you how to use them if you like?"

Alice nodded, "Yes please, the more weapons I know how to use, the better."

"Very well, a lesson on fighting Paper Tigers, with knives, for Miss Alice today."

They walked through the undergrowth, Eyeball Paul led the way. Alice had to raise her feet above her knees to step up and over the thick green weeds beneath them. Then they were in a small clearing about the size of the ship's deck. Something flashed, a movement, that shot towards Eyeball Paul, it flew through the air and started to grow in size, emitting the beginnings of a roar as it did so, then quick as a flash, Eyeball Paul had thrown his knife through the air and the thing disintegrated into dust. "What on earth was that?" Alice asked.

"Ach, that would be a Paper Tiger." Vincent advised, "They're harmless really, they roar and they snap at you, but if you pour water over them they go all soggy and that's the end of them."

"And if you set fire to them, well, that's more fun again. Whoosh! They go up in a big ball of flame!" Eyeball Paul laughed.

"Don't smell too good afterwards though." Vincent said.

"Aren't they alive? Thats cruel to kill them just like that." Alice said to them.

"They aren't really alive. They have no souls." Eyeball Paul replied, "They are like bits of paper, fluttering in the wind, which is why we call them Paper Tigers."

"But they look alive! They have faces and they move and they roar, they must have life in them to move about." Alice was confused.

"Not really. They are just illusions. Try your best not to worry about them." said Eyeball Paul.

"The more you worry, the bigger and more ferocious they become." Vincent said calmly.

"Oh right." replied Alice, "But they already look pretty big and fearsome from here."

Another one chose that moment to leap out at them, claws outstretched, mouth agape, teeth baring down on them. Alice screamed. Vincent carved it into shreds with his two drawn swords. It fell in little tiny paper shreds that fell like confetti all around them, "They really do look like they're made from paper." Alice said.

"Yes." agreed Vincent, "We think they are like the leaves of autumn trees, fragile little things really. Perhaps they are some left over illusion from a long-forgotten magician's parlour tricks."

"But it was trying to kill us?" Alice asked.

"No, it wasn't. It is paper Alice, paper cannot kill you." Vincent said.

"Well, what would happen if it actually landed on us?" Alice asked.

Vincent smiled wickedly, "Good question. Eyeball Paul, stand still for a moment, will you?"

Eyeball Paul grinned, "A challenge of death is on the cards!" he said.

"No! It really isn't!" Alice gasped, "You can't!"

"This is going to be fun!" laughed Eyeball Paul. He took a couple of paces away from them and stood still. Sure enough after a moment there was a rustling in the trees. Out leaped another paper-like creature, the colour of browns and oranges like the autumn leaves. Eyeball Paul stood staring at it, arms outstretched, "Come on then!" he challenged the creature.

The tiger was flying through the air, paws and claws outstretched. It reached Eyeball Paul, hit him and broke in front of him, crumpling into little shreds of paper. "Fear nothing, Alice." Eyeball Paul said, triumphantly.

"It collapsed as you weren't scared of it?" Alice asked.

"Yep." Eyeball Paul said.

"But I'm terrified of them. What would they do to someone like me?" Alice said.

"There's only one way to find out. Alice versus the Paper Tigers!" Eyeball Paul grinned.

"No!" Alice said.

"It's okay, Alice, we won't let anything happen to you." Vincent said.

"Not much, anyway." Eyeball Paul laughed.

Alice swallowed a lump in her throat, her hands were beginning to shake with adrenaline, this wasn't good, "Never enter the clearing with fear in your heart, Alice, they will sniff it out and it will draw more of them to you." Vincent said, noticing her sword trembling.

Alice stepped out into the clearing, Vincent stepped behind her so that he and Eyeball Paul were only a few steps away from her. She raised her sword in her hands and heard the rustle in the undergrowth. It was coming for her. The tiger pounced out from the bushes, in mid air, claws outstretched. This one was jet-black. It got bigger and bigger as it flew towards Alice till it was the size of a grizzly bear. Alice screamed and dropped her sword. Vincent stepped forward with an instant movement and ran his sword through the tiger, it snapped once at him and was gone, "Well, ain't ever seen a black one like that before." Eyeball Paul said, scratching his head.

"He was the most vicious I've seen." agreed Vincent, "Not the best one to start with, Alice. Sorry."

Alice picked up her sword and tried to calm her breathing, "You ready for another?" asked Eyeball Paul.

Alice nodded. Another rustle, and Alice was ready for it this time. A white tiger this time, it flew through the air and stretched its claws out, bearing its ferocious teeth at Alice. She was terrified, it got bigger and bigger, she swung her sword, and it was gone. Her sword impacted nothing and she spun round with the force of it not making an impact. When she looked about her, fronds of white paper were fluttering through the air like snowflakes.

"And a white tiger too. Alice you're drawing all the rare ones today." remarked Eyeball Paul. "Right, now, we need you to learn how to still your mind, so that when they start to come towards you, they don't grow any bigger. I like to visualise Florence's breasts back in the Courtroom Tavern, there's nothing distracts me better than than the sight of her heaving cleavage."

Vincent laughed, "Our Alice may need to think of something other than breasts. Alice, you need to still your mind, breathe slowly and try to step away from the situation in your mind, fear is based in your mind and overcoming it means the difference between winning, and losing."

"Like shadows in the dark in your house." Alice said, "There's nothing there to be scared of."

Vincent laughed, "I myself would make another comparison, but yes, something like that."

"Okay." Alice took deep breaths, "I'm ready."

They battled a few more tigers and Alice began to get quite brave to the point that she started enjoying herself. Now that she was over her first nerves, her training kicked in and her sword hit each target, "You Cardboard Cut-Outs!" she yelled as she smashed her sword through another one.

"Okay Alice," said Paul, "now, let me teach you how to throw the knives. Vincent, keep an eye on the bush in case any leap out at us while I show Alice how to aim with them."

"Okay" nodded Vincent, "I will keep a look out." he brandished his swords in anticipation.

Eyeball Paul handed Alice a knife and adjusted her grip on it till he was happy with the way she held it, "With these, you gotta learn how they feel in your hand, that's your body learning their weight, and how to throw them without you even knowing." Eyeball Paul said, "You aim with your eyes, and you throw with your eyes. Your body does the working out in between. Before you throw, if you have time, exhale, and on the breath in, pick up another knife."

Alice nodded and aimed, her hand behind her head, "No, like this." Eyeball Paul adjusted her arm.

They were there for another hour or so, Eyeball Paul making sure Alice was fully confident with knife-throwing as well as losing her fear of a fight. Then they went back to the ship, where a lunch of soup and mackerel awaited Alice on the Captain's table, and she could trade stories with the brothers and Eric about their encounters with the Paper Tigers.

Chapter Eighteen

(Past Memories) Ship Ahoy!

Alice went out onto the deck after lunch with Arthur, at that point they were sailing on the ocean waves. Arthur walked over to the Carpenter who was pouring seawater from a bucket over the base of the main mast, "Can't stay on land and sky all the time." the Carpenter said, "Have to keep her moist."

Alice looked intently at him once he had said that, but he was deadly serious, Alice looked at Arthur questioningly, "Yes, he does has a bit of a strange relationship with the ship." Arthur agreed, "But it does neither of them any harm."

Suddenly, there was a yell from Eyeball Paul in the Crow's Nest, "Ship Ahoy!" he shouted. "North by Northwest!"

"What direction does that mean?" Alice asked.

"If you're not sure, just look to where he's pointing to lass." the Carpenter said to her, wiping his hands on a dirty rag.

Alice looked up, sure enough, Eyeball Paul's arm was extended out, pointing in the direction that she had just been advised was North by North-West. "Why, tis the Royal Fortune herself lads!" Eyeball Paul shouted down to them, "Roberts' flag's a flying!"

"... Pirate ... Roberts?" Alice asked Arthur, "As in, the 'Dread Pirate Roberts'?"

"Yes, do you know him already? Pirate Hussey." Arthur said.

"No. But I have heard of him. I thought he was a made up character in a movie though."

"He is as real as you or I. He is a most fantastic pirate. You will be honoured to be able to say you have had the honour of meeting him. But I am loathe to introduce you to him as he will undoubtedly try to steal you away from us."

"He won't succeed." said Alice.

"Well he usually manages to steal crew from us every time we happen to bump into him." Arthur replied.

Alice smarted a little at being called a crew member, she didn't really know why, "Well, if I'm just a general run of the mill crew member, maybe it would do me the world of good getting experience on board another pirate ship." she huffed.

"Oh, Alice, stop being such a girl and over-thinking things." Arthur sighed.

"What?" Alice asked.

"It was two separate sentences, he'll steal you, he steals crew, not the same things." Arthur said, exasperated with her, "Go with him if you like." he continued, "It would give me a rest from having to tell you we don't want you to go!" Arthur walked away, as usual, very annoyed with Alice.

Alice had managed to wind him up so much that there could have been steam coming from his ears. Of course, because he had walked off, it was then that Alice had a chance to process what he said, realising that he hadn't meant any of it at all in the way she'd heard it, and she needed to apologise to him, but he had walked off. She growled at him instead. The Carpenter who was still within earshot, laughed, "There be a tempest brewing in him, lass, you'd be best to leave him to cool off."

"He's infuriating." Alice glowered.

The Carpenter laughed again, "Ye be perfectly matched then."

Alice, again, took a moment too long to process this, and just when she had opened her mouth to reply, the Carpenter said, "Well, must be getting on, this ship doesn't mend herself. Well, not without a little assistance from the gentle touch of my hands." and with that, he walked off.

Alice was left staring out to sea, looking out across to the ship that was navigating in their general direction. Being infuriating was an entirely new concept to her. She'd never noticed that she could infuriate someone before, she'd always considered that she was rather nice to everyone she met. "I'm not infuriating." she said to no-one, "I'm not." Alice determined that she would try very hard to be less infuriating in future, if only she could figure out what it was about herself that made people infuriated. Perplexing herself, she decided to practice sword moves instead, accidentally imagining that it was Arthur she was lunging at with her sword. That infuriating …. pirate.

The other ship drew closer. It was magnificent, a good deal larger than the Sea Rose. A man stood proudly at the prow, donned in a deep red jacket, with white lace cuffs, and a gold chain about his neck which was finished with a heavy-looking cross-shaped pendant. He was leaning on a shimmering sword, and he was topped with a magnificent large hat with a maroon coloured feather waving in the wind. He stepped gracefully over onto the Sea Rose, noticing Alice almost immediately in amongst the entirely male crew who were gathered on deck to greet him, "My my, what an exquisite gem!" he said, taking Alice's hand and kissing it intently, gazing into her eyes with his. "Milton, my dear fellow! Who the devilling deuce is this dish?" Roberts turned to seek Milton.

"She is Alice." Milton said in a most dignified fashion, stepping forward. Even he seemed to be putting on airs and graces in his introduction to Roberts' boarding, if that was even possible.

"*Thee* Alice?" Roberts flashed a look at Milton.

"*Our* Alice." Arthur muttered, ruefully.

Roberts laughed, "I see. I fear by the end of my visit I will have persuaded her to come aboard the Royal Fortune, for she would be a most attractive addition to the vessel! Which one of you has laid claim to her that I may fight him manfully in a duel to win her hand?"

There was an uncomfortable silence amongst everyone. Or at least, Alice felt there was. She didn't belong to any of them. Yet, she belonged with them. Whose duty was it to answer Roberts, and how? If she wasn't claimed, why, Roberts could just whisk her away there and then! Her eyes widened a little, fear beginning to rise, "She is mine." Milton replied, with a grave finality.

"Ah, Milton." Roberts smiled, "It would be such fun to be beaten by you once more in a duel, but I fear I am rather fond of my locks, you see they have only just taken on their lustre again since the last time you chopped them off. Very well, I shall have to kidnap her instead! Ha-ha!" he laughed, a viciously infectious laugh, full of mischief and without a care in the world.

"Come my friend." Milton gestured, "Tell me your latest exploits and adventures. We'll talk of good women later, I'm sure you have a good deal to share."

"A good deal more than I care to remember, and a few more I'd rather forget!" Roberts laughed in reply.

"I meant adventures! Not women!" Milton laughed, "I have heard enough tales of your exploits with women if I were to write book about them the sheer weight of the volumes would sink my ship!"

"Ah your ship!" sighed Roberts wistfully, "How I wish she were mine to command."

"We all have different paths and different curses." agreed Milton.

"Hmm." said Roberts, "But, perhaps this is the wrong impression for my new belle, Alice. Destiny winds a twisted path." Roberts said insightfully, "I can see that you are just beginning to fulfil your own."

Roberts gazed at her, and continued, "But, I have had a long journey with naught but my crew and their familiar stories for entertainment these past long few weeks. Time for such talk can be much later in the evening."

"Yes, best served with a drink of rum in our bellies!" Milton laughed.

"Don't look so serious, Alice." Roberts said, "If the world were meant to be taken seriously there would never be any point in anything now would there. That's why God invented sack races."

"Sack racing?" Alice asked.

"Indeed, if you want me to race you in the sack we shall save that for later on Alice." Roberts replied cheekily, "But first, some food, please, before any strenuous activity. What's on your menu?"

Alice could feel herself blushing at his innuendo and tried to control her breathing to take it away, luckily no one noticed, "We have soup of a non-descriptive flavour. Goes well with a generous dose of pepper." she heard Milton say.

"Peppery soup, excellent. I shall have some peppery soup." Roberts smiled, he took off his magnificent hat and ran his hand through his glossy dark hair, bringing it back to life after it being flattened by the voluminous weight of the hat. Another one, Alice sighed, another incredibly attractive man that just exuded handsomeness. It was easy to see how he could have women falling at his feet.

Milton said, "To the cabin." he gestured for them all to make their way to the Captain's Cabin. "Chef! Some soup for our distinguished guest!" Milton called before entering the cabin through the doorway.

Alice looked around, Eric was nowhere in sight, but she knew somehow he would hear the order of food being called and the order of soup would appear, for the exact number of people. Arthur cleared his throat behind her, "Could you get us all a drink please, Alice?"

She realised she'd been staring at Roberts, and feeling a bit flustered, she went quickly into the Captain's Cabin and straight to the drinks cabinet to prepare the drinks. Arthur came over to stand near her, "Well, he's certainly a bit of a dish, isn't he?" Alice said quietly to Arthur as she poured rum into four glasses.

Arthur wore a scowl as his facial expression, "If you say so. Can I have my drink please." he took the drink from her hand without another word. Alice realised he was still in a mood with her from earlier, so sat down between Roberts and Milton in order that she could hear their stories. Arthur wouldn't even look at her to crack a smile at jokes they would normally both have found fantastically funny.

Alice couldn't believe the real life Dread Pirate Roberts was sitting in front of her. The first and original Dread Pirate Roberts, she learned. Over the course of the evening she even managed to give him the idea for a marvellous retirement, "I do believe I am beginning to tire of pirating." Roberts had sighed wistfully.

"Well, you could always retire." Alice said.

Roberts looked at her, ponderously, "Yes, I could retire, settle down, take a wife, raise some children …" he raised his eyebrows at her, "Are you volunteering to help?"

Alice laughed, "No, not like that. I mean you could land your ship one day, change your entire crew over except for one trusted person who is going to be the next Dread Pirate Roberts. When you hire a new crew, you could pretend to be first mate and call your chosen successor by the name of Roberts. The new crew will be none the wiser and you could get off at the next Port and retire, but your name will continue to plunder and trouble the seven seas and you could keep the profits."

"That is a genius idea, however did you think of it?" Roberts asked.

"I read it in a book once." Alice smiled.

Chapter Nineteen

(Present Day)
Remember the Sirens

Alice's phone rang on her desk and pulled her out of her memories. She felt like she was waking from a dream, and realised she hadn't done any work for about half an hour. The phone call lasted about fifteen minutes, mostly consisting of the person on the other end of the phone complaining about things that were nothing to do with Alice. She ended the call feeling drained and started typing up the notes. She looked away and then went back to the screen. She realised she'd written " sirens" instead of what she'd meant to write. There was no escaping her memories ...

The Sea Rose sailed away from the Royal Fortune and Milton pulled out his parchment map once more. He ordered the crew to sail to the next island, which was marked by a symbol Alice didn't recognise. On arrival the whole crew except Eric got into rowboats and rowed towards the island. Alice could make out a sandy beach surrounded by smooth rocks on either side, which was where they were aiming for as they rowed. There were figures on the rocks, with long hair, "We're in luck boys, there's a group of women waiting for us to land." Eyeball Paul shouted to the other boats.

The women sat on the rocks on the water's edge, their toes caressing the water. There were four of them, "I don't like them." Alice said.

"Well, you wouldn't, would you Alice, you're a girl." Arthur snapped at her.

"It's not that. There's something about them I don't like." she replied.

"Like what?"

"I don't know, I just have a bad feeling about them."

"Well, if it's just because they're prettier than you then …"

"It's not that. And they aren't prettier than … oh forget it." Alice sulked in the rowing boat. As they rowed closer she glowered at the four luscious ladies. One of them smiled at her and Alice hated them even more. They were sirens, Alice was sure of it, she'd seen an eighties movie once with stop-still animation monsters and thought she remembered them from there, they were definitely bad guys. "I don't think we should go over to them." Alice said as the crew pulled the boats up onto the beach.

"Oh Alice don't get jealous! We're allowed to speak to other women besides you! Look at them, they're gorgeous." Arthur said.

The four women were exquisitely beautiful, and enchanting. Their long thick hair was precariously positioned to maximise their allure. They hadn't been singing as the pirates approached but as they came within earshot one of them struck up a haunting melody, which the other three then sung along with. Alice looked at the crew, who were open mouthed, staring at the four girls. "Really, keep it in your pants boys." Alice mumbled loudly enough for the pirates to hear.

"Good afternoon ladies." Milton said delectably, taking off his hat and bowing.

The ladies smiled at him and giggled shyly. One of them spoke, the one with the darkest hair, that looked like she'd just stepped out of a salon, it was so healthy and glossy. Alice hadn't seen a bottle of shampoo in weeks, she reached for her own hair subconsciously. "Good day to you, sir." the lady murmoured murmourously with her voluptuously velvety voice, "And good day to your merry band of men as well."

Alice looked at the women and they looked at her, cat-like, they flashed their eyes at her, 'Yeah yeah ignore saying hello to the only woman in the group, just give me your unbelievably attractive dirty looks why don't you'. Alice thought.

"What brings you to our island boys?" the blondest blonde one said. Her hair was light, soft and golden, she had a glowing sultry tan about her perfect complexion.

'And she can take a running jump off a short plank as well', thought Alice, 'bloody perfect people, gah.'

"We are looking for a place to camp." Milton said, "Do you ladies happen to know of anywhere a band of weary pirates can lay their heads for the night?" His eyes were dancing with mischief.

"Disgusting." muttered Alice.

"Go back to the boat if you're that bothered." Arthur turned and said to her, "It's not like you're going to be any fun the mood you're in."

Alice withdrew to the back of the group, hurt and rejected. But what was her place with the pirates anyway, she was merely a distraction, a brief entertainment in their lives and something more interesting had just come along. Milton had already reminded her that her time with them was short term, a holiday, a temporary amusement.

Alice wasn't missed when she turned and walked back to the rowing boat and made her way back to the ship alone. Her arms burned with the effort of rowing the boat on her own and she struggled to tie it up, then fought with the rope ladder to clamber back up onto the deck. From where she stood catching her breath and rubbing the life back into her arms, she could see the light of a camp fire start up, and hear the crew's raised voices and laughter matched with the high pitched jingle jangling melodic laughter of the decidedly evil siren women. She trudged up to the ship's wheel and ran her fingers lightly over it, "I'd quite like to go home now." she sighed miserably.

She felt a tap on her right leg, a little tug on her crop trousers. She looked down, it was Eric. His little fuzzy head with wondering eyes looked up at her questioningly, "The crew have gone to the shore to party with women more beautiful than I will ever be. They told me they didn't want me around Eric, and I'd like to go home."

Eric shook his head and frowned.

"I was just trying to say I didn't really like the look of the incredibly beautiful women as I'd seen this movie once with Sirens in it and I was worried that's what they were. But they all said I was jealous. I mean, okay, maybe I am jealous a little bit Eric, but it wasn't meant to come across like that I just feel so left out now."

Eric climbed up to the bannister railings so that he was at eye level with Alice, he reached out his tiny paw hands and gave her a little Eric sized hug. He pulled away, still resting his paws on her shoulders, and looked her in the eyes, concern on his face. He jumped down and walked away. Alice sighed again, alone again, or, Eric returned with two tankards filled with rum, he offered one to Alice. He had sprinkled spices into it and it smelled wonderfully comforting.

"Thank you." she sniffled. Eric looked across the distances to the campfire light. They could both hear the crew's party on the shoreline, "What sort of women lounge around on the beach singing to men apart from sirens anyway and lure them away to dinner?" Alice said, the rum warming her chest.

Eric slammed his tankard down and his eyes widened. He ran into the cabin. Alice could hear him rummaging about, knocking things over. He came back out and motioned Alice to follow him back into the main cabin room. He had lain out a book on the Captain's table. He pointed his three-fingered hand at the page he'd opened. There were illustrations, in ink and watercolours of lustrous women in posturing pouts and poses. "Oh my god, that's them!" Alice said, "That's exactly them!" She peered more closely at the book, "Not just similar looking luscious ladies, but the exact same ones! I saw these women on that island earlier!"

Eric pointed at the page, imploring her to read the text, Alice read out loud, "I write this as a warning to any sailors who stray too near Honeydew Island - do not set foot on the land!

Sailing close by an island, one of the mainsail winches seized fast. we had no option but to drop anchor and try to work her loose. Taking the opportunity, a scouting party went ashore to find fresh water. They did not return. I took a further four men in a boat to try to rescue them, but it was too late. When we landed there were women sleeping, around them were scattered the clothing of my men, and then we realised that the bones about them were human remains. There was nothing left of my six crewmen. We were back in our boat, rowing for our lives when one of the women awoke and they came after us. I will never forget their faces as long as I live. Their chins were caked with the dried blood of my men, their bellies distended from gorging all night on the flesh of my crew. I have drawn their likeness lest you should ever have the misfortune to sail here. Death awaits all men on this island." Alice sunk into a chair, "What are we going to do?" she asked Eric.

Eric took another drink from his tankard, a thoughtful sip, the sort of sip that formulated plans of action. Alice did the same, only hers was a large gulp, and it burned her throat on the way down. Eric pointed at the clock hanging on the wall.

"You're right, I don't think we have much time." Alice said.

Eric frowned. Alice frowned. Eric got up and went over to a drawer. He pulled out a black bandana and the charcoal paint. He walked over, climbed onto the table and tied the black bandana round Alice's head. He painted her two black stripes onto her face. "I agree. Stealth mode. Ninja style." Alice agreed, "Eric, Death awaits all men on this island. But me and you? You and me? We are not men." she downed the rest of her rum, and stood up, "Let's get the bitches."

Chapter Twenty

(Past Memories) Stealth Ninjas

Alice ran out of the cabin and down into the depths of the ship to the weaponry room. She tucked six small daggers into her boots, and pulled on a leather belt diagonally across her which had more attached to it. She looked around for more Alice-sized help, and found another small sword, not in any way as exquisite as her own, which she tucked into the back of her shirt over her shoulder. She ran back upstairs and out onto the deck. Eric was wearing a black bandana too with war paint on his face and his dagger sized sword belted up at his side. He threw a salute at her and jumped over the deck, climbing down the ladder onto the rowing boat.

Urgency was in the air, as the party on the shore had gone completely silent. Alice climbed down into the rowing boat in stealth mode and picked up the oars, her arms protesting at having to row again. She rowed with all her strength, helped by the waves rolling towards the shore, but she guided the boat away from the main shoreline and landed it slightly further up, so that they would not be seen, heard, or scented by the sirens.

Alice stepped as quietly as possible out of the boat and stooped as low as she could in the shallow water to secure the boat, and then they both ran across the sand, quietly. She knew that with the light of the fire, normal human eyes wouldn't see much else beyond the glow of the firelight, but she didn't know about the sight of sirens. She motioned Eric to stop and signalled for him to move away from her so that they would have two angles of attack. Eric signalled that he was going to climb up into the trees, Alice nodded, Eric left her. She was on her own now, no one to tell her what to do to make this attack actually work. One little Alice with aching arms against a dozen supernatural beings.

'What you need here, is True Grit, Alice.' she thought to herself. She crept forward in the sand, hiding behind some large rocks where she was able to peer out at the scene in front of her. Taking it in took mere moments. There were the twelve women, naked, busying themselves with the crew. Alice's gut sunk into the depths of the sand around her. She could see crewmen that were tied up and bound, they were semi-conscious, their eyes half-open with strange smiles upon their faces, under some sort of drugged bewitchment. The Carpenter was dangling upside down by his feet above the cauldron, on a raised stick frame. His throat had been cut and the blood was dripping from the wound into the cauldron pot. Alice felt herself retching and fought it back, any sound or movement would give her away. Two sirens were crouched over another body, the body was twitching as the women were in some sort of feeding frenzy, sucking the life force from the man beneath them. The noise came across to Alice now, the sickening sound of suckling sirens. Alice looked for Arthur and Milton, they were slumped next to each other, being ignored by the sirens for the time being.

The two sirens near her were done, they stood up and hauled the unconscious body of the man to his feet, they dragged him over to the contraption hanging over the cauldron, tied a rope round his ankles and hauled him upside down. He still had the dazed stupor look on his face, smiling, when they slit his throat, holding out their hands to catch the blood pouring from him. Drinking from it, and laughing.

Alice took all this in while she had pulled a dagger from her sash and weighed it carefully in her hand, one miss, and her position would be revealed too soon. She aimed for a siren who was draining the life out of a still body who she recognised as Tri-Cat Tam, and threw the dagger. The knife hit the siren in the back of the neck and she collapsed silently on top of her dying prey. 'One down….' Alice thought. She saw another chance, another siren, away from the main group with her back turned to her. Alice reached for another dagger, aimed, and threw. It flew silently through the air and again hit its mark in the back of the woman's neck through billowing locks of flowing hair. The siren went down without a noise.

Alice could hear the sirens chanting and groaning with pleasure as they smeared blood over each others bodies. Alice forced down the bile in her throat again. Four of the women were approaching Milton and Arthur. Alice didn't know what to do. This was the move that was going to draw hell down upon her. The women had crouched down over Milton and Arthur. Alice grabbed a dagger out of her boot. She tested the weight in her hand, kissed the dagger, aimed and threw. The dagger sunk into the naked breast of a blonde haired woman. As the siren screamed in pain, Alice could see sharp pointed fangs in her mouth glinting in the firelight. Quick as a flash, Alice took another dagger which flew through the air and into the stomach of a dark-haired olive-skinned siren. Screams lifted into the air, screams of anger, screams of pain, reaching Alice's ears and burning them like poison in the air. Alice held fast.

The sirens dropped all the men and gathered around their injured sister, warily looking around them, hands outstretched like claws, waiting to attack. Alice saw another siren at the back go down, hit by something - it must have been Eric!

"Stop this!" one of the sirens cried into the night, "Stop this!" she called again, "Stop killing my sisters!" The siren had dark hair and wore a thin crown around her forehead.

Alice's face contorted into a snarl, "A life for a life!" she shouted at them, not caring that her position would be given away. She stood up, drawing her sword at her side and the one from over her shoulder and walked out into the clearing, swirling the two swords in her hands with confidence, like Vincent had shown her when they battled the paper tigers.

"You!" the siren who had already spoken said.

"I am going to kill each and every one of you." Alice snarled, "These are my men. This is my crew. You will pay with your lives for what you have done to them! Those of you left alive are going to die slow and painful deaths."

The sirens hissed at her, but the crowned siren glared at them, "Be silent!" she commanded.

"Lusicosa she has killed our sisters!" one of the other sirens hissed.

The Queen, Luciosa, turned and glared at her, "Look at her! Can you not see she is like us?" Luciosa turned to Alice, "I did not see it before when you first landed, but I do now, you are one of us. One of the magical creatures. Tell me your name that I know who you are."

"I am nothing like you!" Alice replied, "I am Alice."

89

Luciosa's eyes widened, "Thee Alice?" a silence descended on the sirens and they all took a wary step back away from Alice, "We will let them go." Luciosa said quietly.

Alice had no idea how she had them all in fear and awe of her. She raised her swords above her head ready to strike.

"Stop!" Luciosa pleaded, "We will let them go!" she looked into Alice's eyes, pleading for the life of herself and her sisters, "You have my word, we will let them all go. Sisters, undo their bonds." Luciosa commanded, never taking her eyes from Alice, who still had her swords held above her, ready to launch at them.

The sirens ran over to the pirates and loosened the ropes round their wrists and ankles, the men swaggered to their feet and the sirens pushed them all towards Alice, "They will follow you." Luciosa said.

"Give me one reason why I shouldn't kill each and every one of you right now. You will do this again and again to other men who stray into your path." Alice challenged her.

"It is our nature, Alice, we are predatory creatures." Luciosa offered as an explanation.

"You revel in death." Alice replied.

"We have our rituals." Luciosa said, "They are part of what we are, part of the old magic. That is what you are tied to as well, the old magic. It dances all over your soul in a way I have never seen before in anyone. I swear this to you now, Alice, on the oath of the immortals, that we will repay our debt to you for sparing us today, if you let us live, we are indebted to you."

"If we ever cross paths again, I will take your lives." Alice vowed.

"We will meet again." Luciosa said to her with absolute certainty, "I can see how much hatred is in your heart for us, but we will promise not to shed any more blood between us and you."

Alice scowled at Luciosa and narrowed her eyes, she lowered her swords to her sides. She did this because her arms were aching and screaming with the effort of holding the swords above her head, and she didn't want Luciosa to see they were beginning to tremble with the strain. She looked at Luciosa, Alice felt the adrenaline beginning to lessen in her veins, she didn't know if it was some magic which the siren standing in front of her was trying to do, or if Alice was genuinely reaching the end of her pluck for this particular adventure. She even pitied the creature in front of her, pleading for its life with fear in its eyes. Something gave inside her and she relented, "Very well." Alice nodded at Luciosa, "Until we meet again."

Luciosa sighed with relief and nodded, "Thank you." Luciosa whispered, "Thank you."

Alice took a back step, and another, then turned and walked slowly away from the sirens. She had learned from a movie long ago that you must never run from anything immortal. Sure enough, the men followed her, swaying and staggering, still in their drunken daze. Eric came running to her from his hiding position, he indicated that he had her back while she escorted the men across the beach. She nodded, deciding to say nothing until they were off the island, lest the sirens realise it had only been little Alice and Eric against all of them.

Chapter Twenty-One

(Past Memories)
Fall-Outs

Alice ordered the men into the boats to row back to the ship and they obliged. She decided to abandon the boat that she and Eric had landed further up the island as she wanted to get away from it as quickly as possible. Once in the boats, off the island, the strange spell that was upon the men began to wear off. Alice was in the boat with Milton and Arthur and Eric, her final fierce guarding of her friends to ensure she had done her best to get them safely off the island. She had been staring back at the island and the dull camp-fire light for quite some time when Arthur spoke, "What in God's name just happened?" he asked, "Where are all the beautiful women? Why are we heading away from them back to the ship? ... Anyone?"

Milton stared grimly at Alice, she felt his stare and looked back at him, "Should I have left you all to die there?" she said angrily at them, "It is as much as you can do to even look at me nicely."

Milton's expression changed to hurt, "Alice, we would all be dead if it wasn't for you. Words cannot begin to express the risks you just took to save us."

"A simple thank you would be a start." Alice growled.

Milton leaned over and hugged her, "Thank you, dear Alice."

Alice burst into tears, "They were so scary!" she cried.

Arthur rolled his eyes, "Alice you have just taken on the deadliest women in the world and beat them, and now you're crying about it? That isn't brave of you at all. Call yourself a pirate, all you did was stop us from getting laid!"

Milton turned quickly towards Arthur and struck him on the face. It was the first time that Alice had ever seen Milton so angry at his brother. Blood trickled slowly down Arthur's nose. He leaned forward and pinched it, trying to stem the flow, and he went quiet. Milton pulled Alice towards him and let her cry into his shoulder, "It was a very brave thing to do, Alice." Milton calmly soothed, "I know no other girl who would have risked her life just to save a group of foolhardy worthless pirates who should have known better in the first place."

"I was so scared!" Alice whimpered.

"I know." he said, holding her while she cried.

Alice woke up in the Captain's bed. Arthur was sitting on the side of the bed, watching her, waiting for her to wake up, his face was bruised from where his brother had struck him, "I'm sorry Alice." he apologised, "Thank you for saving me, thank you for saving us."

Alice looked at him, though no words needed to be spoken between the two of them.

"Would you like a drink of rum?" Arthur asked, nervously.

She nodded, Arthur went out of the room. She heard voices murmouring in the main room, Milton's "and be nice to her!" command clearly audible. Arthur came back through with a tankard of rum and a plate of broken biscuits, "I have brought you some biscuits as well." he proffered the plate proudly, placing them on the wooden table next to the bed and stood looking at the table for a moment.

Alice waited. Arthur inhaled as if to speak, then changed his mind, he looked at her, his gaze catching hers, "I'll be next door. If you need anything." he added awkwardly.

As he walked out the door, Alice said, "Thank you for the broken biscuits." his footstep faltered, his head lifted a little, then he walked through the doorway.

A few moments later, Eric tootled into the room to see her. He put his little hand on hers and looked at her, "We did okay, huh?" Alice asked him. Eric nodded, "We couldn't have saved the other men, could we?" Alice asked him.

Eric shook his head. He climbed up onto the bed and sat next to her, he took a broken biscuit from the plate, Alice did the same. She took a drink of rum then offered the tankard to Eric, who took a drink as well. Watching Eric take the tankard, she noticed a ship's wheel was etched into the side of the silver metal.

"That was the bravest thing I've ever done in my whole life." Alice whispered, "And the most terrifying."

Eric leaned on her arm and passed her the rum. She took a sip then passed it to him, "Eric, they'd all be dead if it wasn't for you and me." Eric had a sip of rum and passed it back to her. "Those sirens were mean, Eric, they were wicked creatures." Another drink each. And a pause for contemplation. And another drink. Then, "Those stupid boys!" Alice shouted, "Stupid, stupid boys!"

Eric made a fist and jeered with her.

"Bloody sirens! Bloody boys!" Alice swore loudly.

Arthur and Milton heard the volume and the cursing growing louder from where they were sitting at the large table in the Captain's Cabin. Milton was writing additional notes in the book Eric had found, next to the images of the sirens, with a white feather quill pen, much like the feather usually found in his brother's hat.

"Looks like Alice is feeling better." Milton said.

"Shame the same can't be said for my head. God knows what those women did to us." Arthur replied.

"They preparing to kill you, Arthur." Milton said, without looking up from his notes.

"Well, whose bright idea was it to go to the island anyway?" Arthur replied.

"Yours, I believe." Milton looked up to glower at his brother.

"It was not mine, I agreed with Alice that it was a bad idea." Arthur argued.

"It *was* your idea, Arthur." Milton glared.

Arthur glared back. Sparks flew between them, then both of them were on their feet. A couple of punches were swung, noses were bleeding again, heads locked together, when suddenly a sword appeared between them, precariously and delicately touching the tips of their noses. A trickle of blood began to slide down the blade. The brothers drew their eyes further down the blade to find Alice glaring back at them.

"You both decided it was a good idea." Alice growled, "You're both a pair of idiots, and you are quite possibly both the worst pirates I have ever met. And if you keep fighting about it, I will cut your tongues clean off and feed them to the fishes!" Alice was holding the tankard of rum in her other hand, glaring at them both in turn fiercely with the fire at the depths of her eyes, and she realised she was swaying ever so slightly.

Arthur took the tankard from her hand and took a drink. She turned, her face furious with anger at him. He raised his eyebrow at her and smiled cheekily beneath the rum, his bruised face was covered with blood, he was not a pretty sight, "That's … my …. rum." she growled at him.

"What are you going to do about it?" Arthur asked her.

Alice took the tankard from his hand, raised it up and poured the contents over his head, "Help yourself." she said.

Arthur's face glowered with rage, which then moved into incredulous shock, "You deserved that!" Milton laughed, his big hearty cheering laugh.

Arthur wiped the rum out of his hair, dripping rum drops everywhere, still very annoyed. Alice burst into peals of laughter. At the sound of her laughing, Arthur looked at her, smiled, and started laughing too, the tension in the air was finally broken. Eric produced a towel which he handed to Arthur, who began wiping his face. Milton went over to the counter and poured everyone a fair measure of rum.

"Do you think that parchment map of yours is actually perhaps all the places to be avoided when you're sailing the seven seas Milton?" Alice asked.

"You might have a point." Milton laughed.

"Definitely the worst pirates I have ever met." Alice said again.

"We're the only pirates you have ever met, Alice." Arthur countered.

"I've met the Dread Pirate Roberts too." Alice turned to glare at him again.

"Oh yes, about that …" Arthur started but Alice walked over and grabbed a tankard.

"Do you want this over your head again?" she said to him.

He laughed, "No, absolutely not. You win. Being the worst pirates is far better than being the best anyway."

Out on deck the crew were subdued after the loss of their crewmates. Rum was poured and passed around and it demanded that their spirits were lifted. It was the only remedy to the traumatic events of the night. The ship's sails billowed as she strove to sail her crew far away from the sinister island. And by the end of the night, Alice had recounted her tale of saving the pirates from the sirens, only by then it was becoming a polished tale of brave adventure. A tale that at the time was truly terrifying to live through, Alice realised that sometimes the best stories only come with laughter long after the wounds had been cleaned and healed.

The night was drawing to a close. Alice was listening to Milton and Vincent talking to each other, and could hear the ocean waves lapping against the ship, it was so still and quiet Alice could hear the ship's wood work creaking and the sail's swaying motions with the gentle breeze. "How many people attended that funeral Vincent?" Milton was saying.

"Wheech wan?" Vincent asked in his thick accent.

"The one in Glasgow. You know, Gizella's. There were hundreds turned out for it, hundreds. Gathered round the graveside. You couldn't see it for people! You must remember Gizella's funeral."

"Yes, but they were all men." Vincent said.

"Yes, I suppose it was all men, mostly." Milton agreed.

"Huh?" Alice said.

"Gizella was a prostitute." Vincent said to her as an explanation.

"Well it was the biggest turn out to a funeral I've ever been to. She was quite a popular lady." Milton said, "Were you there Vincent?"

"No sir. I was in the cells. I was in prison at the time of Gizella's funeral."

"What for?" asked Alice.

"You know, I am not quite sure. I must have done something illegal though." Vincent said, "I have been in prison many times." he added.

"Oh." said Alice.

"Oh thats right, we busted you out after the funeral!" Milton laughed, then, changing to a fierce face, he asked, "Do you know what they did to Vincent, Alice?"

"No." she answered.

"Vincent here is a Romanian Prince. He inherited vast lands off his aunt, with a mansion, filled with worldly goods, and lands as far as the eye could see. The mansion ended up being taken over by pimps and their prostitutes. He tried standing up to them. They jammed his head in a door, splitting his skull open, crushing it like a watermelon. We had to take him to a witch doctor to set him right, who fixed him up, but he still has his off moments now, bit of dodgy re-wiring." Milton explained.

"That's absolutely awful." said Alice.

"Yeah, one day we'll go back and get those bastards." grimaced Milton.

"Not yet!" pleaded Vincent, "Not yet, Captain."

"No, not this day." agreed Milton, thinking, "Let's go to the beach tomorrow instead. I fancy a day off from all this pirating."

Alice looked at him warily.

"It's okay, I know one that's perfectly safe." Milton replied.

Chapter Twenty-Two

(Past Memories)
A Day at the Beach

The next day they parked the ship, as it were, or anchored it, if you prefer, so that it hovered directly over the beach of a little bay which was completely deserted. It had beautiful white glistening sand and a tranquil turquoise blue sea. The sand met rocks on either side and behind them, which rolled into steep dunes.

"Its beautiful!" Alice exclaimed from the deck of the ship. She clapped her hands, excited at the thought of having a beach day, throwing off her boots on deck, in anticipation of feeling the sand between her toes.

"It is your holiday after all, Alice." Milton smiled.

Alice paused as Milton referred to her as being on holiday with them, a reminder that Alice's time on the ship was limited and it was in his mind that he intended her to go back home.

The sun was shining and there was only the gentlest of warm breezes, perfect for breaking the full heat of the day. The pirates took their boots off too, they all rolled up their trouser legs though Alice was the first off the ship, she was bouncing about on deck waiting for the plank to get lowered much to the pirate crew's amusement. They didn't know what to make of their Alice who had turned into a bouncing ball of excitement so each one side-stepped to let her onto the beach first, she ran off the end of the plank and ran straight down the beach to the water, splashing into it, the water was warm and refreshing.

Alice skipped about a little, wandering along the edge of the water where the waves broke the sand, little shells adorned the beach. She looked back at the boys, some of them had already started to set up a cricket-type pitch. She saw that Milton had walked over to sit at the warm rocks and was smoking a cigarette, some way from the rest of the crew, he exhaled a puff of smoke, smiled and waved at her as her eyes found him, hhe smiled and waved back. He threw away his cigarette, and proceeded to take off his top and trousers. Sporting a pair of long-johns, with his chest bare, he climbed the rocks, jumped and was in the sea, swimming slowly and leisurely about the water.

Alice cast her eyes back to the beach, pocketing some little shells like she used to do as a small child. She walked further up the beach, sitting down on the sand she pulled out all of the shells from her pockets and made them into a pattern, which began to take the shape of a ship's wheel, or compass. Arthur was playing in the game of cricket, while flagons of grog were on the go to quench the thirst of the competitive pirates. Alice smiled, lying back she rested her head gently on the sand and looked at the clear blue sky, happy and content. Someone came up to her and sat down by her side. She glanced sideways, squinting at the silhouette in the sunshine, "Hello Arthur." she acknowledged.

"I gave up. They were all cheating." he replied.

"Which means you were the one that was cheating." she sighed. Alice got up and wandered about, leaving Arthur sitting drinking a tankard of grog by himself. She wandered across to the rocks at the edge of the beach, gazing at rock pools, and the little crabs skirting about in their miniature worlds of deep maroon coloured anemones and seaweeds.

Arthur was watching her, "What are you doing, Alice?" he asked, "Don't wander too far."

Alice groaned, as if she was five years old and needed telling to be careful on the beach. But she said nothing, just waved at him, mostly a wave expressing him to shut up and go away, to leave her in peace and tranquility however brief it may be. She climbed higher up. Instead of leaving her be, he stood up and came over to her, "Seriously, don't wander too far." he called.

"Why Arthur?" she replied, annoyed, "Why can't I wander too far?"

"Because I worry about you." he said.

"Arthur, I'm perfectly fine. It's not like there's going to be a sea monster leap out of the ocean and eat me up. I'm fine."

Arthur cleared his throat to get her attention, raising his hand he pointed out to sea. Sure enough, there was a giant green head with dangling tentacles, apparently the head of a sea monster, staring right at them.

"That one's okay, he's like a giant seal." Arthur smugly explained, "But there's others too in this part of the ocean, more dangerous than him. The beach and cove are perfectly safe though." He tried very hard not to laugh at her. Very hard indeed. Alice was staring open mouthed at the sea monster. She stared and stared, she allowed Arthur to take her hand and guide her, still staring, back down from the rock pools and back down onto the beach.

"Come and swim in the sea with me, Alice." Milton called, sensing an intervention was required, "It's lovely and warm."

Alice looked at Arthur, "I promise it's safe." he said laughing She took a mouthful of his beer, took off her outer shirt, and waded into the sea.

Captain Milton met her as the increasing depth of the water meant her footing was just becoming unsteady and helped her to get her balance floating in the water, "It's lovely." she spluttered, spitting out a mouthful of seawater.

"Tilt your head back." Milton suggested laughing at her poor attempt at swimming in the sea. "Your body has a constant, small amount of oxygen in the blood at all times. If you tilt your head back, and relax, you will float."

Alice didn't believe him, but leaned back in the water, sure enough, she felt her body begin to ease to a low level near her chin, and she found herself successfully floating in the water. She looked at the sky and languished on top of the gentle waves, she could hear the cheers of the pirates on the beach playing their game. She could hear the gentle lapping of the sea against the rocks nearby, and the stronger waves of the ocean crashing against the other side of the rocks. Remembering the sea monsters, Alice swam back to the shore and walked back to Arthur, who tried hard not to watch soaking-wet-Alice with dripping clothes walking towards him, but failed.

"Wet t-shirt Alice." he leched unapologetically, "I can see your bra. And your boobs." he handed her dry over-shirt to her and she wiped her face with it, then pulled it over her wet shirt.

In a magical feat known only to those girls who have spent their time in school changing-rooms in P.E lessons feeling body-shy know, Alice was able to pull off her wet underneath t-shirt from inside the outer-shirt without exposing any of her body parts.

Arthur smiled at her, "I am so glad you are with us."

"Yes, but you are nothing but a womanising pirate, so of course you'd say that right now when I'm nearly naked." Alice replied, throwing her wet t-shirt in his face.

"We are who we are, aren't we." was Arthur's muffled reply.

"Yes, I know exactly what you are."

Arthur sighed, pulling the t-shirt off his face, "Let's not fight, Alice, I can't bear it. Please, just sit with me a while."

"Okay." Alice sat down next to him, resting her head on his shoulder. She could smell his hair, feel the softness on his neck, she was sad for a moment. For some reason, she was struck that she desperately wanted to wrap her arms round him and give him a hug. But she didn't, he was a womanising pirate and it did her no favours to allow herself a strong attachment towards him. But neither of them moved.

Milton made his way out of the water, his body glistening with the dripping ocean water. He looked at them in an odd way, then smiled and waved, Alice smiled and waved back.

"Oi! Will you two get off yer arses we have a game to play here and we're a pirate short Arthur!" Eyeball Paul shouted from where he stood in the game.

Arthur kissed the top of Alice's head lightly, which she took as his way of asking her to move off his shoulder, then got up and made his way back to the crew and their game. Milton walked past her smiling, saying "time for my snooze" as he went.

Perfect bliss, everyone was happy. Alice stayed where she was, watching the waves roll in, and watching them go out. If time could stop, just for a moment, and rest there in a forever picture of right now … she smiled.

But nothing lasted forever. It was now just a memory.

Chapter Twenty-Three

(Present Day)
The Wonderment of
Menthol Vapours

Memories are often evoked by certain smells. Memories that tell us we didn't dream it all. Alice longed to forget the smell of Pirate Pumps, oh how they ponged. Those wafty gusts of stinking stale gases. Men, stuck in enclosed spaces, drinking grog and farting the unburst bubbles out of the other end. It was vile. One of the smells that lingered for life, once they were whiffed, they were never forgotten. And once remembered, the smell stuck, no matter how much perfume was sprayed over the memories, the pirate poo particles lingered in her nostrils for days. Why she'd remembered the stench, Alice had no idea. She cursed herself for remembering it. She tried very hard to distract her mind before those little electrons jumped along the circuits to the smell activator cells. But it was too late. The stink was upon her. Turning green, she rummaged in her bag under her desk and came out with a tub of Vicks Vapour Rub. She smeared the clear gel under her nose, the menthol vapours reaching up her nostrils and burning her sinuses. Finally, she had discovered something that overpowered the residual smell memory of pirate pumps.

"Have you got a cold, Alice?" Kayla asked her.

"Erm ..." Alice stalled, "Well, I think I might have a bit of a sniffle." Alice continued, sniffing, "So I'm just trying to chase it away before it turns into anything nasty."

"Ah, okay." Kayla said.

Alice knew Kayla thought Alice was acting strangely, even just by that response, Alice knew. Alice looked at her computer screen. Then Kayla was standing next to her, Alice jumped, "I have a lemsip drink, max strength here, might help you. I'll make it for you, I'm going through to the kitchen anyway." Kayla said.

"Oh thank you, that's so kind of you." Alice smiled, inwardly cringing. She hated lemsips, and was now going to have to sit and drink one because Kayla thought she had a cold, as Alice had thought that saying she had a cold was easier than explaining she had a rotten smell memory stuck up her nose. Now if Alice tried to explain anything, Kayla would think she was mad, and Kayla already thought Alice was strange. Oh why hadn't she just gone and told Kayla the truth.

Kayla came back through with the lemsip, "That should chase it." she said to Alice.

"Thank you." Alice said, "I hope it does." Alice would make sure the lemsip would chase the non-existent cold away and would never mention it again. Alice took a sip of the lemsip and grimaced, it tasted like Pirate Pumps.

It hurt again. Alice pulled out of her memories, she stood up from her desk for a break, and went downstairs to the vending machine for a bar of chocolate, Arthur's favourite, on her way back to the office. She re-did her makeup in the toilet before entering the office with a brave face, no one could tell she had been crying again. She wondered if she should go to the doctors, but what could they do for her sadness and melancholy? Tell her to cheer up, that it was all made up stories in her head? Put her in the insane asylum? Or give her anti-depressants, and she wasn't keen on that idea. What if the pirates ever did come back for her, but the chemicals in the medication stopped her from believing they were even there and it stopped her from seeing them again? She didn't know what else to do to distract herself and try to cheer herself up all over again, so she decided to make some adventures of her own that weekend.

The next day, Alice packed a picnic lunch in her rucksack, pulled on and tied up her walking boots, wishing that there was an easier way of fastening walking boots than by never-ending boot laces, took herself in her car and drove to the bottom of the waterfall known as the Grey Mare's Tail. Alice had to drive past Tibbie-Shiels Inn, which rested on the shores of St Mary's Loch and subconsciously her eyes cast over the Inn for any signs of land-bound pirates in the pub. There was just the usual array of well-loved motorbikes belonging to passionate bikers who had stopped off for scampi and chips. She drove on, parking in the National Trust car park and got the guilt, so fished in her glovebox for some coins for the parking meter, knowing that there wouldn't be a car park attendant for miles around, but if she didn't pay, then someone would know and she'd come back to a ticket on her car, or maybe one in the post days or weeks later, and she could do without that stress and worry.

The waterfall began its roar in front of her, the noise travelling to her ears as she stepped onto the greenery away from the car park. It was beautiful already, surrounded by steep rolling border hills on either side of the small road. Sheep grazed nearby her, she looked again. They weren't all sheep. Some of them were goats with lovely silken looking coats. She thought they might be cashmere goats, but couldn't be sure. She edged warily away from them. She knew that there was a loch at the top of the climb, and that was where she was aiming for, not for a day being head butted by goats down a mountainside. She just had to make a start. She crossed a stream and came across a man-made cairn stone-circle, she read the information panels there, then started up the small steps on the lowest part of the hillside. She stopped to catch her breath quite a few times. Each time she looked down, the car was smaller and smaller beneath her. Sometimes, the edge of the path had a sheer drop to the left, where the waterfall was, and the effect was mesmerizing, drawing her to lean and look further over the edge. Once or twice she had to lean over towards the right, to the safety of the hillside and clutch at the grass to re-ground herself before walking again.

Alice reached what she had taken to be the top of the waterfall, from her original view from the car park. But instead of a loch, the view ahead of her turned into even more rolling hills, and even more babbling waterfall cascading down the hillside. She wasn't at the top at all. Eventually, the path became less steep, and started to even out. Alice walked passed overgrown rocky ruins, barely perceptible in the moss and bracken. She wondered how people could have lived all the way up here, but when she looked around her, it was like another land, another world entirely, there were fields and plains, rivers and hillsides all around her, maybe they never needed to venture to the bottom of the hill at all.

The stream and path curved round to the right and Alice meandered along with it, rounding an uphill corner, she came upon the loch. Surrounded by yet more, even higher rolling hills, the loch was eerie. There was a slight mist in the air above the water, so faint it was almost imperceptible. There was a small island with a very small tree, a weather-battered, weary looking tree, growing on it, and at once, Alice knew this to be a magical place she could feel it in the air. She walked round, following the path to the right, which became a much thinner trail. Her boots were enveloped by boggy marsh in places. She reached a spot where she felt like stopping, and stood, gazing over the water. She pulled her rucksack off, sat down, and ate her sandwiches. She remembered that she'd read somewhere that people in the olden days used to throw food and offerings into the water lochs to appease the Gods that lived there. She threw all of her crusts into the water where they sunk into the dark depths below.

"If you can hear me, hello, my name is Alice. I'm a bit lost at the moment." she said somberly, "You probably don't know me if you just lived up here as this is my first visit, and you probably get bothered by tourists all the time coming up here, but I'm really not trying to bother you. I'm just feeling very lost. And very alone. All by myself, in fact." she paused, biting her lip as a tear fell down her face.

As if in answer, a random wave broke the surface of the loch and rippled towards her. It broke before it reached the shore, "Oh. Hello." she said, smiling at the water, there was no further movement.

"I miss all my pirate friends." she continued, "I wish that I could see them again. But I know I can't." she sighed, "Anyway, thanks for listening. I bet everyone comes up here and tells you their problems. Sorry for troubling you."

Alice looked across the water again. It was another world, this water, a place that the modern world hadn't been able to touch. Magic seemed to dance about the surface like electricity in the air, invisible, but still there nonetheless. Alice silently ate her banana, her healthy option, took a drink of water then bit into her chocolate brownie. The banana would counteract the calories in the brownie. She threw her last morsel of brownie into the water, "Thanks again." she said, packing her bag and beginning to make her way back down.

She felt mildly better on the top half of the walk, feeling like she had just accomplished something. Then her legs just about gave way as she reached a point where the hill turned into a sheer drop on her right hand side. Her eyes made the whole world go a little bit dizzy and she reached to her left to grasp the hillside. She looked at the side of the hillside and found herself looking straight into the face of a goat. Her step faltered and she got a terrifying leap from her heart into her mouth in that split second that her foot tried to find a grip in the loose gravel again. It was so quick, but enough to get her heart racing at a ridiculous speed thinking she was going to fall off the edge of the cliffside.

Now she just felt like a fool and an idiot, a complete idiot, risking her life to go to a loch at the top of a mountainside to make a wish to a god that didn't even exist except in folk tales, and nearly get head-butted off the hillside by a goat. No Alice, she told herself, this was not the best idea you've ever had. You have had a lot of bad ideas in your lifetime and this is up there with the best of them. Then she was at the bottom of the hill and sitting in her car, untying her soaking wet boots. Her legs were trembling uncontrollably with exhaustion and adrenaline. But she had done it. She had made herself have an adventure. Rain started pouring down onto her car, torrential rain so heavy it was bouncing back up off the car bonnet. She was grateful that she hadn't been caught in it, and put the radio on to wait out the storm. She shut her eyes for a moment, and remembered back to a time there was a heavy storm this one time on the Sea Rose.

Chapter Twenty-Four

(Past Memories)
A Storm Awakens

A storm had broken out, the mist had darkened all around the ship, it was black as night. "I have a bad feeling about this." Alice said with a sense of foreboding.

"Given that this is a storm, Alice, you might just be stating the obvious." Milton said, looking across the deck at the crew who were steadying the sails and bracing the ship.

"No, it's more than worrying about lightning hitting the ship, or me again, it's something more."

"Like lightning hitting the ship isn't bad enough?" Arthur asked her.

"How many times has the mist from the ship turned into a storm, Milton?" Alice asked. Milton turned his head to look at her, realisation dawning on his face.

"Never, actually." he acknowledged, "I have never known it to be so. We have dealt with storms on the seas before, but never in the mist itself."

The cloudy mist echoed and rumbled with the noise of thunder, "Tis the Devil's magic." said Eyeball Paul ominously, who was within earshot, "It's not safe Captain. This weather is unnatural, it's building into a tempest. If you cast your gaze portside, you will see the eye of the storm is gathering."

"Which way is portside?" Alice asked.

Eyeball Paul growled at her and pointed, she looked and saw the clouds were swallowing the remaining light from the sky, lightning flickered beneath it.

"We must land." the Captain grimaced, "We must be brave, men, we do not know where we are landing."

"As usual." muttered Arthur, "It's not like we ever actually really know where we are landing."

"This is serious." chided Milton, "There is some sort of dark magic at work here."

The crew lowered the ship, they set her down and she settled on a shallow river, which Alice could make out from the side of the ship, a normal ship would never have been able to settle in such shallow water. Milton, Arthur, and Alice, disembarked, Milton ordered the crew to stay on board though the crew wanted to leave with them, their hands itching at the swords by their sides. The three of them made their way down the gangplank and found themselves in a glade in a woodland. They looked back at the ship, it was in a safe position, resting peacefully in the water, with a dark sky looming ominously above them, "Let's see where we are then." said Milton.

They walked out of the glade and happened upon a path in the woods, which was wide enough to be a trail road. They hadn't walked very far along the path when along came a man leading a donkey, he appeared to be a trader of some sort. His shoulders were set low, slumped as if carrying a heavy burden, his eyes were shadowy, and his donkey looked just as weary ,the man leaned heavily on his staff.

"Hail stranger." called Milton, "Might I enquire as to where we can seek shelter from the storm?"

The stranger gave Milton a funny look, "That sir, is no storm that will ever break. It is conjured from the Hermitage Castle of the Lord De Soulis. Want that I could never walk within its walls again, but I am obligated to trade with him."

"A conjured storm?" Milton questioned.

"Aye. He is a wicked man. Ye would be best never to go there."

Alice looked out from the edge of the woods and saw that the eye of the storm hovered and spun directly above a terrifying and dark hulk of a castle squatly silhouetted against the skyline.

"And where might ye be from?" The peddler asked them, "Ye be strangers to this land, if ye have never heard of the name of De Soulis and the fearsome reputation that goes afore him."

"We are pirates." said Milton, "Pirates of the finest calibre."

"Is that so?" pondered the peddler, "And where might your ship be, sir? This land is fifty miles to the nearest ocean, ye have travelled very far on foot."

"We have it harboured." answered Milton, trying to be vague.

"Is that so." said the peddler again, with a strange glint in his eye.

"I think that we would be best to turn around and return to where we came from, now that we know this storm can be avoided. Many thanks, and good day to you sir." said Milton.

"Good day to you." said the peddler.

Milton waited for the peddler to start walking away before turning back to the direction of the ship. He led them silently back to the glade at the riverbank. Just before boarding, Arthur said, "Do you think there was something odd about him?"

"Like what?" Milton asked.

"I don't know. I just got the sense that there was a touch of magic about him."

"Alice's paranoia is rubbing off on you, Arthur." Milton said.

Alice looked at Milton, he had a distant look in his eye, and she thought it contained a fleeting glimpse of doubt and uneasiness, "Sorry guys, I shouldn't have said that I had a bad feeling." Alice said.

"Not to worry. Ever onwards!" Milton smiled at her, but it didn't quite reach his eyes, nor chase away the worried look that was haunting him.

As they boarded the ship none of the trio noticed the peddler, watching them from the edge of the glade. The peddler shook his cloak and hit the base of his staff upon the ground, his shoulders straightened and his stood upright, his face changed into that of a man in his forties with dark hair and glistening green eyes. His donkey transformed into a big black horse which stomped its hooves and snorted away its disguise with smoke coming from its nose. He was known in these parts as Lord De Soulis, and all who knew him, feared him. He gazed at the magnificence of the pirate ship, which, with his being steeped in the knowledge of old magic, he could see as clear as day.

"At last I have found it." De Soulis cackled with glee, "The ship that can control time! And before the year is up, it will be mine!" he spun his cloak, jumped up on his horse and galloped off into the woods to return to his torturous tower.

Chapter Twenty-Five

(Past Memories)
Being Locked in a Tower
Isn't Much Fun

The Sea Rose next landed on the outskirts of a small village that Eyeball Paul knew, where the crew were welcomed at the tavern and drinks were placed on the tables as soon as they walked through the door. Alice learned it was the year 1649 by asking a man near the door who gave her a puzzled expression but answered her nonetheless. She had walked out of the bar for some air and to have a look at the village, she noticed that there was a group of girls standing on the village green so she walked towards them but was grabbed instead by the man she had just spoken to and found her arms being bound in a rope.

"What are you doing?" Alice cried out.

"Don't you say another word, witch." he snarled in her ear.

"Witch? I'm not a … " she received a slap across her face.

"I said be silent!"

Alice heard a commotion, other men were tying the hands of the girls she had seen just a short distance away from her. She was dragged over to them and tied up with them, their legs were bound together only allowing for shuffling movement, and they were marched along the road and up a hill towards a large castle. The other girls were barefooted, dressed in rags and tatters, their hair was loosely tied up or braided, their faces covered in a layer of dirt and grime.

Alice had three girls in front of her and one behind her, she shuffled along with them pleasantly enough, convinced that at any moment they would stop and the guards would set her free, for one of three reasons she could think of right at that moment:

That they would ask her name and when she said "Alice" and they said the usual "Thee Alice?" she would lie and say why yes, she was Thee Alice and they would let her go.

That she plainly looked nothing like a witch. She didn't have a pointy hat or a broomstick for a start.

That the pirates would come and rescue her. It would help if they actually knew where she was being taken, but still, they would come, they were, after all, only in the pub down the road.

The girls were shuffled across a drawbridge. Alice saw a coat of arms above the gateway, but she wouldn't know one coat of arms from another to know who's family this castle belonged to. She noticed some colourful flowers nearby as she walked over the drawbridge, but that too, didn't help give away their location. Alice expected to be dragged down into the dungeon, but heard a gruff-looking guard shout over their heads, "It's full, the damn prisons full, whatcha doing bringing them here for? You'll have to lock them in the tower. Thank gawd Her Ladyship isn't here or she'd hang me for this. Still, better than being burned at the stake isn't it ladies?! On you go, get these witches outta my sight."

Alice scowled at him. If she was able to set curses on people, she would definitely set one on him, he was vile. He had a chain of keys on his hip and a whip in his hand. He had a scar running down across one eye, and a huge fat distending stomach that protruded out of his clothes. She took him to be the prison warden. He coughed as Alice walked past him, "What sort of queer witch is this?" he said to anyone listening. He must have been in the habit of talking out loud when he was around his prisoners to put the fear in them, "Not a local lass. I'll bet you're the one leading our girls astray with your crazy witchy ways."

The girl behind Alice, who she learned to be called Marissa, chose this moment to accidentally tread on Alice's heel. Alice tripped and stumbled, falling towards the guardsman in a very undignified way, unable to steady herself with her hands tied behind her back. He side stepped back, aghast, "You're trying to hex me!" he said, as he kicked her back into the line.

Then she was through an entranceway, heading up a small starting set of steps which then led to a larger spiral staircase, Alice copied the other girls and held her tied hands gently on the centre of the spiral staircase for balance and to help guide her up the dimly lit stairwell, they passed two floors and then they were ushered into a door on the third level. They were locked away in the room, hands still bound, legs still attached to each other in the chain, the guard kicked at a pot on the floor and grunted.

"What's he saying?" Alice asked Marissa.

"Thats our piss-pot." Marissa replied.

"But its tiny." Alice said, "How is that one pot for everyone to pee in?"

"You strange you are, we always has to share it." said Marissa, "You throws the dumps out of the window if you have to."

It had been the thought that it was all a big mistake that had kept Alice calm about the whole thing. Or some sort of suspended disbelief, a misplaced reality, she wasn't really locked in a tower in another time and place but she was actually back at work in the office, texting Stef from across the room about the latest gossip. But no, she actually was stuck in a tower and going to be burned at the stake tomorrow, and in the meantime, she had to watch five other girls pooping into a pot.

"Speaking of which, I gotta go, girls." the girl at the front of the chain said, shuffling across to the pot and hitching up her rags. Alice gagged, this was worse than the pirate ship.

Alice tried to take her mind off where she was, "Marissa...where are we?" she asked.

"You's in the tower of the Dirle Town Castle, Miss...."

"Alice, I'm Alice." she replied.

"Excuse me." someone said from over Alice's shoulder. Alice turned and was greeted by the sight of a steaming pisspot wafting its contents in her face directly at eye and nose level, "I need to chuck this out of the window." It was the girl from the front of the chain, she smiled cheerily at Alice, "Been holding that in a while!"

Alice didn't know what to say, she was trying not to inhale as she side-stepped out of the way. The other girls had to hop and shuffle about too so that the lead girl could reach the window, "I hope you don't mind me saying, but you do seem surprisingly chirpy for someone about to be burned at the stake." Alice said to the girl.

"That's as I know we're not going to be." said the girl.

"Oh?" asked Alice.

"It's like the guard said, you're a real witch, and you're going to save us." The girl threw the contents of the pot out of the window, all the while smiling at Alice.

Alice felt the polite smile on her own face freezing, "But I'm not a witch." Alice replied.

"It's okay, you're among friends here. You don't have to deny it with us." The girl smiled, shaking the drips off the pot and pulling it back inside the window, "I'm Agnes. This is Edith, and Mina, and Isabella."

"How do you do." said Alice.

"Cor, I ain't half pleased to meet you, a real witch." Edith said shaking Alice's hand.

"You're here to save us!" said Isabella.

"Agnes would know a real witch when she saw one." said Marissa behind Alice, "She made it rain once. And she made Jake Evelynn come out in a rash, so if she says you're going to save us, then she must be right."

Alice didn't know what to say, so said nothing, just kept smiling uncomfortably. The sun was getting lower in the sky and she was out of options, the tower was well secured, locked, and too high to climb out of. Agnes hobbled across to a shelf that had some flint and candles on it, she lit one and placed it in the alcove above the shelf, i cast an eerie orange glow about the room, "I'm not a witch, Marisa." Alice whispered over her shoulder to Marissa.

"But you're our only hope." Marissa said in reply.

"Don't say that, we can't be done for." Alice said, turning to face her.

"Well, the men will come at first light, they drown you to see if you float, and then they burn you at the stake." Marissa replied.

"I don't like the sound of any of that. Why were you all arrested? Isn't there some sort of trial first?"

"Well, we were getting our water from the well and this chap on a white horse came trotting into the village. He was dressed in a deep maroon cloak, he was an older man, but still very handsome so he was, he said he was looking for someone, but Morag, well, she got jealous of us talking to him so she told the Magistrate that we was witches and here we are." Marissa said.

"What, they just took the woman's word for it?" Alice asked.

"Yes." Marissa replied, "She's a merchant's daughter and has a lot more say in the village than us, we're just peasants' daughters."

"Thats insane." Alice said.

"It happens everywhere, someone shouts 'witch' and that's the end of someone who's done nothing wrong except annoy a rich fella's daughter."

"Or wife!" Isabella called, "Do you remember poor Fiona over from West Farm, the laird took a shine to her and he imposed his rights and took her, he got her knocked up so he did, and his wife had her half drowned then burned at the stake, the wife stood and watched the burning. They say you could hear a baby screaming in the fire."

"It should have been him what was burned alive." Edith growled.

"Then there was Maggie Shaftoe and Tess Hardie from The Grange, they were out picking berries and had a flagon of whisky with them, next thing you know, they're up on them stakes for being caught trying to raise the devil with their dancing and their singing. They was only drunk and having a laugh." Isabella said.

"Bloody hell." Alice said. However the mention of singing had given her an idea. "Girls, do you like singing?" she asked them, "If I teach you a song, will you sing it with me?" They murmoured an agreement of sorts, "Okay, Agnes can you pass me a candle please?" Alice asked.

Agnes lit another candle from the one burning in the alcove and passed it along the line of girls to Alice, who placed it on the window ledge. It flickered a little in the breeze.

"Marissa, I need you to stand next to the candle, stop it from going out, but hover your hand over it if you can so that its like a signal light, like this." Alice waved her hand on out outside of the window, in front of the candle flame, "If everyone else can gather round the window with me."

The girls shuffled closer to the window. Alice cleared her throat, "It's a song called Downtown by Petula Clark. I realise you won't know what that is, it goes like this, 'When you're alone and life is making you lonely you can always go, Downtown.'"

Alice's voice wavered a little as she sung. She looked at them expectantly, "Okay, now you try."

"Wont we get in trouble for singing?" asked Isabella.

"Who knows, but we're going to keep singing until someone stops us, okay?" Alice rallied.

The girls successfully sang 'Downtown' for ten minutes until the guard came into the room, "You girls better button it, or you'll be feeling my whip across your backs."

"Not if we curse you first." Alice snarled at him.

He moved as if to strike her, Alice raised her hands, "I call upon the Watchman's Curse," she began to say, it had the desired effect, he moved back.

"You stop that!" he said to her fearfully, "take that curse offa me right now!"

Alice laughed, "Or what you going to do, kill us?" she raised her bound hands in the air for dramatic effect as if she were conjuring a spell onto him.

His eyes widened, "Just keep the noise down." he said, going out.

The girls whooped at Alice, "Little bit scared of witches round here then." Alice said.

"What's the Watchman's Curse?" Edith asked, shyly.

"I dunno, I just made it up." Alice answered.

"Cor, making her own spells up, what a witch!" Agnes replied.

"Right ladies, I need you to sing that song again." Alice said, changing the topic from her witchiness.

They started singing again, and sang for another five minutes or so before Marissa stopped them and said, "Alice, somethings just went past this window, a shadow or something, I don't know what it was."

"A shadow?" Alice started to say, however there was a thud from above them, at that moment and a rope ladder suddenly appeared dangling down outside the window. Marissa moved the candle out of the way, and a pair of black boots, then legs and a shirt and then the full figure of a man appeared and jumped lightly into the room.

"Alice! We have found you!" he said happily in a thick accent.

It was Vincent. Alice hobbled over to him and hugged him as best she could. Vincent leaned out of the window and tugged twice on the rope ladder. Another pair of boots came down, and Arthur was the one who came through the window.

"Alice!" he exclaimed, "There you are!"

The girls stances changed immediately with the appearance of two men that knew Alice in their tower prison, hair was quickly tidied and flicked flirtatiously over shoulders and eyelashes were batted beautifully, "We've been looking everywhere for you." exclaimed Arthur, "Then I heard our song."

"Our song?" Alice asked.

"Yes the one we sang together in the shower." Arthur replied.

The girls turned suspiciously to Alice, "I was in the shower, he was standing outside." Alice explained.

"Then we saw the candle in the window signalling to us, and we knew where to find you." Vincent cleared his throat, Arthur glanced guiltily at him, "Okay, Vincent had a lot to do with it as well. He has good eyesight in the dark." Arthur added. Vincent coughed again, "and he heard the singing first."

"And you are not alone, Alice." Vincent smiled, "You have many attractive ladies with you."

The girls all blushed, but no one except Vincent could see this in the dim candlelight.

"Yes, we're all just hanging around here waiting to get burned at the stake first thing tomorrow morning." Alice said nonchalantly.

"How have you managed to get yourself into so much bother, we only went for a drink." Arthur asked.

"Well, can we maybe do the angry-at-Alice bit later and do more of the escaping part just now please?" Alice asked Arthur.

"The ladies will be coming with us, no?" asked Vincent.

"Don't see why not. We could drop them off at the next place we go to." Arthur shrugged.

Arthur and Vincent cut the ropes between the girls ankles, and one by one they ungracefully clambered out onto the window ledge and were hauled up the rope ladder, to find themselves on board a mist covered pirate ship parked on top of the castle tower. The ship set sail post haste to get away from the village.

Chapter Twenty-Six

(Past Memories)
Setting Down in Whitby Town

M ilton came out of the Captain's Cabin, saw the girls coming on board and went back in and closed the door behind him. Alice gingerly opened the door and peered round. Milton was sitting in his chair at the table, head in his hands. He looked up at the door, then his eyes focussed on her face, "You're found." he said.

"Yes. Thank you for coming to find me." she said.

"Wasn't my idea." he said, "I would have left you given half the chance."

Alice couldn't tell if he was being serious, "I would have been burned at the stake if you had." she replied.

"And you've brought women with you I see. Who are they?" he asked.

"Wenches from the village!" Arthur said excitedly, coming through the door behind Alice, "I've claimed the girl in the green dress." he added.

"You've claimed none of them. Leave them to the crew." Milton said firmly.

"But … "

"I said leave them be." Milton's face was dark and brooding, "You got us into a lot of trouble the last time you got involved with women."

"They were sirens." Arthur said defensively.

"You lose your head when you chase the women, no foresight at all with you, just led by your lust."

Alice felt extremely uncomfortable.

"Yes, okay Milton." Arthur said, backing down.

"Alice, leave us." Milton said, "Go get yourself some food and have fun with the others on deck."

Alice squeezed passed Arthur in the doorway and went back outside. She was greeted by a hug from Eyeball Paul, "Good to see you Alice!"

"Thank you." she replied.

"Take no notice of him in there." Eyeball Paul said indicating the Captain, "He's been worried sick about where you were, he's been shouting his mouth off and even threatened to give us all thirty lashes if we didn't find you before nightfall. Then night fell and he locked himself in his cabin. Once the Captain stopped stomping about the deck making all that racket shouting at us all, Vincent said he heard you singing and sang it to us, and Arthur recognised the song."

They could hear Milton shouting at Arthur from inside the cabin, "Arthur's used to it Alice, water off a duck's back. Come on get in with the party." Eyeball Paul said as he took her arm and dragged her into the crowd of crew and girls. There was inevitably a bit of a party on board that night, with the sudden influx of single ladies who were more than willing to thank the crew in their own particular ways for saving them. Marissa and Vincent were dancing together, her green dress splaying out in a fan, as Vincent span her round, Vincent's eyes were filled with delight.

"Looks like he's in love." Eyeball Paul chortled, "Does a pirate no good to fall in love. Their heart belongs to the sea and she can be a jealous woman, she'll take him away from his land locked lover and he'll be torn in two forever more."

"Is this like the time you told me the ship was going to cast me overboard in a jealous rage?" Alice asked him.

"Erm …" replied Eyeball Paul, "So they say." Marissa and Vincent were kissing now. "Urgh, leave them to it. Young-uns." Eyeball Paul grimaced.

Later on, Alice sat on the helm step leading up to the ship's wheel, sipping a rum, taking in the scene on the ship, and also to steady herself after a lot of dancing. There were women wandering about, Alice wasn't used to it. Marissa and Vincent were canoodling, holding hands and giggling, their heads bowed close together.

Arthur came out of the cabin, a little paler than when he had gone in. He found Alice drinking her rum, "Eventful night." he said, "May I?" he gestured to sit next to her.

Alice scooted across the step a little to make room for him and offered him a drink of her tankard. He accepted it gratefully, "We are going to land at a little coastal town that Vincent knows, to drop the ladies off first thing tomorrow morning." he said matter of factually. "Maybe you could come to bed with me tonight, you don't class as a wench, Milton wouldn't mind."

Alice looked at Arthur, he had a soft look on his face that she'd never seen before, "Or not." he added, "As I'm a womanising pirate."

Alice nodded, "Got it in one."

Arthur looked away from her across to the women, "Can't blame me for trying, you are rather attractive, Alice."

"It wouldn't matter who was in your bed, you just want to get laid." Alice said, the rum talking for her.

"But you know I'll always be yours, Alice." he murmoured quietly.

"And what good is that coming from a womanising pirate who runs off with sirens?" she laughed.

"I would never let anything hurt you."

"Except yourself." she pointed out, "You would unintentionally break my heart, just by being who you are. Anyway, Arthur, I am not going to sleep with you tonight just because Milton says you aren't allowed a wench and I'm the next best thing. I'm not a wench, I don't put out at your command, you can say all the sweet nothings you like to me."

Arthur frowned, "I didn't know I was."

"Well it's not going to work." Alice got up, somewhat unsteadily, and walked down the steps, leaving Arthur sitting alone.

The next morning the ship landed in ocean waves near a coastal town, which Alice recognised instantly as Whitby, as there was an ominous looking abbey silhouetted on the top of the craggy clifftops. The Sea Rose sailed merrily into the harbour and was docked mist free next to ones that looked very similar to her, so Alice knew they were not in Alice's own time period and she couldn't go out and relish a packet of fish and chips and an ice cream. Just the thought of greasy salt and vinegar splashed chips made her mouth water. The crew lowered the gangplank and the girls and crew disembarked. On the road, Agnes caught up with Alice,

"Plenty of work in this town for us girls!" Agnes giggled, "Alice, we don't know how to thank you enough for saving us."

The pirates escorted the girls as far as the nearest tavern and there they said their farewells. "Ah my sweet Marisa." Alice was within earshot of Vincent, "I cannot bear to leave you."

"My Vincent." Marissa purred.

"Wait for me, my darling, I will return from the sea a rich man for you."

"I will, my love." she said in a sultry voice.

"And promise me, you will not venture out after dark in this town, it is not safe for you and I am not here to protect you." Vincent said.

"For you, my darling, anything." Marissa replied.

Alice had to walk away. "Honestly." Eyeball Paul said to her as she walked past him, "He falls in love with every woman he meets, that one. He'll have forgotten her in a fortnight."

Arthur was just in front of her, she caught up with him. He looked terrible, he was grey-faced with shadows under his eyes. "Are you okay?" she asked him.

"It is no concern of yours." he answered.

"I'm only asking, Arthur." she said.

"Well you needn't trouble yourself over a womanising pirate."

Alice looked at him but he wouldn't look at her.

"Do you mind, I want to be on my own." he said curtly to her, walking into the next tavern.

Alice turned back to Eyeball Paul who looked at her and raised his hands up in a "I dunno" expression. They took a walk up a brightly lit alleyway, Alice savouring the sunshine on her face, and the bustle of the people passing by them. They went into a tavern, where they asked for spiced rum. The barman scratched his head and said to them, "We don't do none of that spiced rum here."

"Oh." they said, having a think about what else to drink.

"But we do do our own version of a rum recipe." the barman suggested helpfully.

"So you do have spiced rum?" Eyeball Paul asked.

"No. But we have our own spiced rum." the barman replied.

"Yes, that's what we're asking for." Eyeball Paul said.

"Local recipe." Barman.

"Yes. Thank You." Eyeball Paul.

"Spiced rum." Barman.

"Yes. Please." Eyeball Paul.

Vincent walked into the bar just as Eyeball Paul was about to pass out with exasperation at trying to order a drink, "Barman, three rums, if you please." he requested straight away.

Eyeball Paul and Alice watched incredulously as the barman smiled at Vincent and said, "Right away sir." to him.

"How did you do that?" Alice asked, "We've been trying to get served for ages."

"I speak the local dialect." Vincent winked.

Alice and Eyeball Paul looked at each other, confused.

Chapter Twenty-Seven

(Past Memories)
Night Begins to Fall

Alice, Vincent and Eyeball Paul had a jolly hour or so drinking in the taverns along the shoreline street, they'd lost track of time of course. They bumped into Arthur in one of them, where he was swaying unsteadily at the bar counter.

"This is my Alice!" Arthur slurred to the man next to him, "But she won't have me as I'm a good for nothing womanising pirate."

"Aren't we all, lad." the man nodded in agreement and understanding.

"Alice." Arthur hiccuped in a high pitched voice, "What are you drinking? Lemme bayou a drink."

"Spiced rum please Arthur." Alice sat at the stool next to Arthur.

"Ah we don't do none of that spiced rum here." said the barman.

"Yes, so we've learned, don't tell me you have your own local recipe?" Alice asked.

Arthur leaned his head on Alice's shoulder, for it had become very heavy all of a sudden. The barman placed her drink down and tended to Vincent and Eyeball Paul. Alice ignored the Arthur on her shoulder and took a drink from her tankard, which tasted exactly the same as the rum from the last few taverns and their local recipes.

"The people here are really friendly." Vincent said within earshot, "My Marissa will be very happy here."

"Much like Vanessa from the Algarve." Eyeball Paul laughed, "And Carlotta from Venezuela."

"What can I say, my heart, it loves all the women." Vincent smiled.

Arthur's head rose back up from Alice's shoulder. He put his arm round her and squeezed her breast, "No." she said firmly, pulling his hand away. He clasped her hand instead and refused to let it go. She gave up and let him hold it, rather her hand than her breast.

A man entered the bar and brought a gust of cold air with him. He stood on the other side of Arthur and ordered a drink. Alice felt Vincent and Eyeball Paul bristle behind her, "Sandy Jake! Watch him Alice." Eyeball Paul whispered into her ear, "Milton had him thrown off the ship a year ago."

Sandy Jake greeted Arthur like an old friend, holding him in an overly familiar embrace. Arthur's hand left its steely grip on Alice's and was gripped by Sandy Jake's handshake. The man acknowledged Eyeball Paul and Vincent, and looked at Alice, "She yours Arthur?" Sandy Jake asked.

Arthur turned his bleary eyes towards Alice, "No, no she is not mine." he bitterly moaned.

Alice couldn't hear the rest of the conversation as their heads were turned away from her. She talked with Eyeball Paul and Vincent, who advised her it was time to go back to the ship.

"I'm staying here." Arthur slurred.

"But we must go back to the ship before nightfall." Vincent said gently.

"I'm staying here with my friend Sandy Jake." Arthur said firmly.

"Arthur, come with us, please." Alice said.

"Leave me be, wench!" Arthur said, "Go on, leave."

Sandy Jake laughed.

"Not without you." Alice said. She tried to take his hand again but he pulled it away. Eyeball Paul took her arm, "Come on Alice, you will have to leave him."

"Yes, Alice, go on. Leave." Arthur said again, bitterly.

"Okay Arthur." she gave in, admitting defeat.

"I'll look after him." Sandy Jake smiled and looked at Alice. He had gold glinting teeth.

Alice went outside where Eyeball Paul and Vincent linked arms with her.

"He knows his way back." Vincent said.

"Milton won't sail without him." Eyeball Paul said.

"I should go back and get him." said Alice.

"It is pointless, you won't move him when he is like that." Vincent replied.

Back at the ship, Milton was out on deck, pacing, he stopped when he saw Alice, "That is everyone except my brother, where is my brother, Alice?" he asked her.

"He is in a tavern, he wouldn't come back with us." Alice explained, "He met someone called Sandy Jake and refused to leave."

Milton grimaced, "You shouldn't have left him alone with Sandy Jake!"

"Well I didn't have much choice, he wasn't for moving." Alice said defensively.

"We must be out of the dock before nightfall, he knows that, I made myself quite clear to him!" Milton said, pacing further.

"I can go back and try and get him." Alice suggested, feeling guilty.

"No. You'll take me and show me where he is." Milton said, "Vincent, guard the ship let no one else board the vessel, there is trouble here if Sandy Jake is in town, it follows him like the scent of blood to a hound. If we do not return within the hour, then raise the ship."

"Without you on board, Captain?" Vincent asked.

"Without me on board. I will not put my entire crew in danger of when the night falls down in Whitby town."

"Very well Captain."

Chapter Twenty-Eight

(Past Memories)
The Captain Steps Forth

Milton even troubled himself to pull on a pair of boots to walk into Whitby town. He had his hand on his sword the whole way. "Why is everything so urgent tonight, Milton?" Alice asked trying to keep up with him.

"The air is bad here and the ship is unsettled." Milton replied.

"Isn't there trouble everywhere we go?" Alice asked.

"Yes, but that's not the point. The ship must be away from here by nightfall and on her way." he offered no other explanation.

They rounded the corner and reached the tavern that Alice had last seen Arthur in with Sandy Jake.

"On her way where?" Alice asked as they reached the doorway, finally realising that Milton had a destination in mind when he spoke.

Milton didn't answer, he pushed the door open, but the two stools where Arthur and Sandy Jake had been were empty. "Where is that damned fool." Milton muttered, stepping out of the bar again, "Dammit." he bit his lip, thinking.

Alice looked around the street, alleyways, bars and taverns met her gaze from all directions, Arthur could be anywhere.

"We must find him." Milton said, "You take that side of the street and I'll take this one."

Alice crossed over the road, dipping into each bar entrance on her side to check for Arthur, while Milton did the same. They reached the end of the street to no avail, and proceeded up an alleyway, Alice stayed on her side of the street, then there was some steps, leading down into darkness, on her side. She heard a strange strangled noise, almost Arthur-esque, but it was cut short, she stopped walking. Milton stepped out of a bar on his side and noticed her stopping, so he crossed over.

"What is it?" he asked.

"Not sure." she said quietly, pointing down the steps, "I thought I heard something down there."

Milton drew his sword, it glinted, a long thin blade covered in some sort of oriental writing down one side, Alice recognised it as a samurai sword. Alice drew her sword as well, they went as quietly and stealthily as they could down the steps. Arthur was lying in a crumpled heap at the bottom of the steps, with Sandy-Jake crouched over him. Alice's eyes adjusted to the darkness and saw that Sandy-Jake was licking Arthur's ear where dark liquid was coming out, which Alice realised was blood.

In two strides Milton had stepped forth and thrown Sandy Jake through the air before Alice had really fully taken in what was happening.

"I thought I warned you once before." Milton snarled at Sandy Jake.

Sandy Jake landed on his feet and crouching, hissing at Milton. He was cornered, the alleyway was closed off, Milton was blocking the exit and Alice blocked the steps up to the street. Milton stepped towards Sandy Jake who leaped up and clung to the side of the building. It was then Alice saw his gold teeth were missing, and in their place was a glistening set of fangs, glistening in the eerie Whitby lamp light.

"He's a vampire!" Alice called in alarm as Sandy Jake leaped through the air.

"No, you don't get away this time!" Milton shouted.

Milton jumped up into the air and took a step in the mid-air, gaining extra height with this ninja move, he swung his sword up into the air above his head and brought it down, hitting Sandy Jake's leg and took his foot clean off at the ankle. Sandy Jake fell to the ground clutching the bottom of his leg at the same time that Milton landed nimbly on the ground. Milton swung his sword again and struck Sandy Jake's head clean off. Sandy Jake's body disintegrated into dust.

Milton put his sword away and ran to his brother, "Help me carry him." he panted at Alice.

Alice ran over and together they lifted and carried Arthur's lifeless body back to the ship.

Vincent was watching for them and as they came into view he ordered the ship cast off. They were barely on board when the ship sailed away from the dock. They laid Arthur on the Captain's bed, where Vincent crouched over his body.

"Well?" Milton asked him.

Vincent looked up, "He is only slightly poisoned. I can cure this."

Alice looked at Vincent suspiciously as he crouched over Arthur's face, she couldn't see what he was doing, "Vampires?" she asked, "In Whitby?"

"I thought everyone knew about Whitby's vampire population." Milton said looking at her, irritated.

"What about the girls we just dropped off here, won't they get eaten?" she asked.

"They'll be fine, they know not to go out after dark." Vincent said, his voice slightly muffled.

"And what are you, some sort of stealth ninja?" Alice asked Milton, "You literally stepped in thin air back there."

"It's all in the reflexes." he replied.

Vincent moved away from Arthur, who groaned.

"Where am I?" Arthur asked.

"You're on the Sea Rose, you're safe." said Vincent.

"Someone pushed me down the stairs." Arthur mumbled.

"Nothing broken, no bones, it was well that he was drunk when he fell. Drunks fall a lot better." Vincent said to Milton.

"Thank you my friend." Milton said, placing his hand on Vincent's shoulder.

"Where's Alice, is she gone?" Arthur asked.

"No she's here." said Milton.

Alice walked over to the bed and took Arthur's hand, and squeezed it.

"Hello Alice." Arthur mumbled.

"Hello Arthur." Alice replied.

"I never admit to these things normally, but I think perhaps I should have come back to the ship with you." he sighed wearily.

"He needs to rest." Vincent said.

"Very well, let us leave him for now." Milton said.

Alice went outside onto the deck to get some air, Whitby was sailing out of view, and then it vanished into a haze of misty fog.

"We are leaving this town, and my Marissa." Vincent sighed, "Come, Alice, drink with us, we could all do with one after that."

Chapter Twenty-Nine

(Past Memories)
May I Have This Dance

The crew decided to play music to chase away the the evening's events, as they so frequently did, changing the sombre moods to laughter again. For them it was saying goodbye to the girls, for Alice, it was to chase away the visions of Sandy Jake crouching over Arthur's body. The music struck up, the dancing began, and Alice felt her mood changing to happiness again.

The hours stretched on, Alice was content but weary, the smile never leaving her face the whole night. When the night quietened down, Alice stood at the side of the ship, taking in the starry night about them. Arthur came over to her as the songs changed to a more quiet melody, "May I have the last dance?" he asked, bending over, one hand behind his back and the other outstretched to take hers.

Alice looked at him, still smiling, happy that he was there. He was expecting her to refuse him in a ridiculous way, she could tell by the expression on his face, but instead of arguing, she simply took his hand in hers and allowed him to lead her to the deck come dance floor. Arthur placed his hand around Alice's waist and lifted the other hand in hers slightly in the air, and they danced. The stars were glistening all around them, and they were reflected in the ocean waves. Alice leaned in closer to Arthur, and could feel his steady breathing. Time slowed down, it was as if it were just Arthur and Alice, dancing arm in arm, on a pedestal with the rest of the world far beneath them. It felt right, and safe there in his arms, moving slowly to the soft, gentle music. "You look beautiful tonight." Arthur whispered in her ear.

"I'm happy." she replied.

"As am I." Arthur murmoured.

Alice looked up into his eyes, and could see the stars reflected back in them. He brushed some hair behind her ear and he smiled at her, then his eyes grew sad. The song ended and he let her go, "Thank you for the dance." he said.

It was quiet now, all around, "I'd like to go to bed now, I think." Alice replied.

"A perfect ending for you, my dear Alice." Arthur said, quietly.

"Thank you Arthur. I'm so glad you are okay now." she said.

He smiled, somewhat painfully, "And so to bed you must go. Good night, Adieu, Fare Thee Well." he gestured that Alice would walk in front of him through the Cabin door.

Alice kissed Milton on the cheek as she walked past him where he was sitting at the table smoking a cigarette, and curled up on the bed where Arthur had been recovering only a short time before.

Though she fell asleep quickly, time behaved in an unusual way that night, she couldn't tell how long she had been asleep for, she didn't know what time it was when she awoke, though it was still late in the night, she could tell that much. She didn't wake up properly, she didn't know if she had even woke up at all, or just dreamed the snippets and scenes she remembered hearing that night.

Alice heard Milton and Arthur's voices in the main room, laughing together, arm wrestling in light-hearted spirits, and the familiar smell of rolled up cigarettes drifting into the half open doorway. Then the world went dark again. She regained bleary consciousness once more, tuning in to the sound of Milton and Arthur saying "Ow" at intervals, and laughing, and talking the rest of the time about punches. Alice knew that they would be sitting cross-legged facing each other and seeing who could hit the other the hardest.

The next time she came round, their voices were sterner, fading in and out of her half-asleep hearing range. Milton saying, "Do not cross the dangerous ground You can go no further with this."

Arthur responded angrily, but Alice could not hear it "......"

Milton: "I am your Captain! And you follow me, do you not?"

Arthur: "I would cut off my own arm for you, brother, you know that."

Milton: "Then you would be wise to say no more of this. She is our Alice, and she is *the* Alice, but ……. Alice ……. the answer is No, do I make myself clear?"

Arthur: "Yes, brother … my Captain."

Milton: "We will speak no more of this."

The next time Alice woke up, her eyes opened enough that she could make out the silhouetted outline of Flat Eric standing in the open doorway, staring at her. He raised his little three-fingered hand and pointed at her, there were footsteps that walked over to the door, and the door was pulled closed.

Alice's brain would think nothing of it that night, it refused to be pulled fully into the world of awake-ness to make sense of it, and in the morning light, she would dismiss what she had heard as not being real, and that she had conjured it from her own imaginings. She had no chance to ask them about it as things took a grim turn that morning, and it was a memory which only came back to her now, sitting on the park bench at lunchtime, with the night's strange conversations echoed in her memories. But it was so long ago now, that she would fill in the gaps that she had heard with her own sentences, it was too broken a memory to keep replaying and she could not hope to ever understand it.

For it was the next morning that Milton told Alice it was time for her to return home. She was devastated. The morning began with a breakfast of strong coffee in the main room of the Captain's Cabin, Arthur must have been sleeping in his room, while Milton was standing with his hands clasped round his lower back, staring out of the large cabin window into the sea and sunrise when he asked Alice to tell him about her dreams, in what she thought was just a general conversation of curiosity.

"Tell me about your dreams, do you have any?" Milton asked her.

"Not really." Alice replied, "Other than the obvious, like wanting to win the lottery." she laughed, but Milton didn't break a smile.

"What about a family, would you like a family one day?" he didn't turn to face her.

She realised he would be able to see her in the reflection if he chose to gaze that way, as she could see the glimmer or glower of his eyes in the window reflection.

"I've never really thought about it. I've never really thought about settling down at all."

"Don't you think it's time you did?" Milton asked abruptly.

Alice found her mouth hanging a little open, no idea where this conversation had come from or where it was going. She hated being put on the spot about life-invasive questions that demanded somewhat prophetic answers that lasted for five minutes and sounded super-intelligent. She needed time to think about things, to take it in and come up with a feasible argument, but he didn't give her time to reply, "It's too late for us here. We are what we are. We are unable to change our course and will be Pirates till the day we die. It's not too late for you."

"What do you mean, 'too late'? You sound like you are unhappy? I don't think it's ever too late for people to change if that's what they ..."

"That's because you are young, and very, very naive." Milton chastised her, "I don't mean to sound patronising, but you are very naive. You have no life experience at all."

"Well you do sound patronising." Alice said defensively, "I might well be naive, but I'm not stupid, I'm allowed to think the way I do. I'm allowed to believe people can change whenever they set their mind to it. They just have to want to change."

"Well, perhaps for some people it's too late." Milton replied.

"Too late for what? God you can sound so depressing sometimes. What's wrong? You won't feel any better by tearing me to bits. I'll cry, as I'm a girl, that's what we do, and then you'll feel bad as I'm crying and there was no need for you to be so mean to me in the first place."

He laughed. She heard it, a very small, faint but audible laugh, "Ah, Alice, you always make me laugh. I'll miss that."

Alice thought she'd heard correctly, and an unease rose in her throat, "You're just too nice." Milton continued, "Call yourself a pirate."

"Well, what else do I call myself while I'm on board a pirate ship?"

"A stowaway." Milton replied, "A wannabe pirate."

"I am not a wannabe!" Alice's face flushed.

Milton laughed again, "You can't even do an angry face, Alice."

"I've killed zombies and sirens." Alice said.

"You got seasick on the rowing boat." Milton countered.

"I was sick before we went on it!" Alice felt tears burning at the back of her eyes, now was not the time for tears, Pirate Alice. She didn't know what she had done wrong to aggrieve him so badly this morning.

"Just what exactly does it take to prove myself to you? What have I done wrong?" she asked.

"You have done nothing wrong, Alice. It is simply time for you to return home." Milton said plainly.

There were the words, she didn't know that they had been coming this morning, and they hit her square in her stomach.

"I feel responsible for you, all the time." he continued, "Every time I wake up I worry about you. Where you are, what you're doing, whether we're going to end up in an adventure that gets you killed."

Ah those words. The other girls had been made to walk the plank within the first hour of coming on board, Alice got her heart ripped out later, after she thought she had toughened up and was able to take care of herself. After she thought she was part of the crew and that she belonged there, after she thought she knew who she was, and loved herself when she was with them. That was the very point that Milton decided he had had enough of her being on board the ship. "We are on route to your house this morning" Milton said, with no emotion in his voice.

A tear slipped down her face, she hoped he hadn't seen it. Alice refused to cry in front of him, "I will pack my things together and be ready to leave." she said holding back her tears with everything she had. Milton said no more to her.

She packed her canvas sail bag, the gift from Jasper, and Milton did not look up when she stood with it in the main room, "Goodbye then." she said, but he did not reply.

Alice left the cabin with her packed bag and went up onto the deck and looked around her. That was the last time she would see the sky from on board the ship, she knew it, she could feel it in her being. Though she hadn't known she was going to be asked to leave before she went into the cabin, she knew now that she wasn't going to be returning to the ship ever again. She breathed it in, the smell of the wood, the comforting smell of the sea air, her lip quivered, the tears that fell down her face burned her skin, as if they were tiny rivulets of red hot molten pain. The rest of the tears she swallowed, refusing to let them fall as it hurt too much to cry. Instead, the tears found their way to her heart, burning it through and through until that too hurt too much. Her heart did the only thing it could to ensure its own survival before it broke completely, and it hardened the molten tears and turned them into a thick core of ice.

Alice felt the ship lowering to a stop, it had arrived at her house, "Thank you." she whispered with a wavering voice to the ship.

She walked bravely across to the balustrade, with her chin up and her head held high, where the plank waited. The crew had gathered there to say their goodbyes, shaking her hand and hugging her farewell. Lastly were Vincent and Eyeball Paul, they had tears in their eyes as they hugged her. She raised her hand in a farewell salute to the ship, the crew raised their hands to their heads and saluted their goodbye to her. Alice's hand held for a moment then began to shake. She turned away and used it to grasp the side of the ship, then climbed onto the plank, and walked down steadily into the mist, and then she was back in her garden, standing on the picnic bench. She refused to look back at the ship, she walked steadfast, across her garden to the back door, where the grey swirling mist ended. She pulled out the house keys from their hiding hole, unlocked the door, and walked in, shutting the door behind her.

Alice sighed, her shoulders dropped, her head lowered, her eyes filled with sadness. She wandered through to her bathroom, threw off her pirate clothes, leaving them discarded in a heap and she stepped into the shower, turning the water up as hot as she could bear it, letting the water wash over her and wash her adventures away. "When you're alone and life is making you lonely, you can always go, Downtown." she sung quietly and sadly to herself.

Chapter Thirty

(Present Day)
Where There's Tea, There's Hope

Alice looked across the desk at the computer screen and sighed, she got up and walked through to the kitchen to make a cup of tea. As she waited for the kettle to boil, she leaned over and lowered her head into her hands on the counter worktop. She wished her memories would leave her, if she had no memories then she would be quite content to live in her little nine to five, she was sure of it. She hit her head off her arms, trying to jostle her memories out of her head, but it wasn't working. And just as she was doing that, the kitchen door opened, Alice stood bolt upright, reaching instantly for the tea cannister, trying to look like she had been preparing tea the whole time and not just insanely hitting her head off the countertop, it was Stef.

"Oh hey! There you are!" Stef said cheerily.

"Oh, hey. Just makinging a cuppa, do you want one?" Alice tried to sound cheery too.

"What's wrong?" Stef asked. Stef always knew. Always. Where no one else noticed, Stef spotted the slightest facial change that gave a Sad Alice moment away.

"Just missing someone." Alice said.

"Is it a guy?" Stef asked, Alice nodded, it was a whole lot easier to just agree.

"Ah." Stef said, knowingly, "How about we go for a glass of wine after work, take your mind off it?"

Alice nodded and smiled, "That sounds like a great idea."

"I have stuff to tell you!" Stef said smiling.

"Oooo! Gossip!" Alice exclaimed, slightly distracted from her melancholy.

"Mm-hmm!"

"Its definitely a date then!" Alice's smile remained on her face, "Thank you Stef."

That evening the two girls turned into four girls as Kayla and Julia caught wind of the hint of wine alluring the air and decided to join them. They walked along to the bar closest to their office, ordered four rosè spritzers and set to the gossip, where Alice giggled and laughed at the stories that unfolded. After half an hour and their withdrawing home for the evening becoming all too imminent, they all agreed that it was too much fun gossiping and they would all stay for a few more drinks and get taxi's home later.

Alice got home at midnight and spent an hour dancing round her living room singing her head off to old familiar songs, rounding off the night with the Bugsy Malone soundtrack, "We coulda been anything that we wanted to be." she sang as loudly as she could, doing all the moves as if she was in a crowd of pirates, correction people, not pirates, Alice.

She went to sleep in a good mood, happy and content. She took the good moments when they came and hugged them to her like comforting blankets. She woke up, however, with a hangover complete with nausea and the shakes, after forgetting to end her evening with her staple hangover survival cup of tea and a cheese toastie.

"Not the best idea to drink on a school night." she grumbled barely audibly into the toilet bowl.,"I'm blaming the wine. What did you go and drink wine for, Alice?" But the flashbacks of girly giggles argued back, "I have an hour to get myself ship-shape." Alice groaned on the bathroom floor.

She crawled through to the kitchen, hauling herself up by her cooker handle and leaned on the counter to put some eggs on. The smell of cooking eggs sent her straight back through to the bathroom. She tried again, this time succeeding to swallow a mouthful of egg roll and a mouthful of tea before throwing up again. She tried a banana instead. It stayed down. Then the shower, and while she wasn't wholly fit and able, she was ready for a slow day at the office.

When she arrived the other three girls looked to be in the same condition as her, coping, but hoping for a world disaster to close the office and send them all home for the day. "The boss has called an emergency meeting this afternoon Alice." Stef mumbled to her, "Hows your head?"

"Awful." Alice replied.

"Same." Stef replied.

"Boss....meeting...?" Alice asked blearily.

"I know. It had to be today, huh." Stef replied.

Alice brewed a strong coffee in the kitchen and splashed her puffy eyes with water. None of the girls would survive an emergency meeting at this rate.

Chapter Thirty-One

(Present Day)
It was all just a Dream

At lunchtime, Alice sat on a park bench, and she started to cry, she blamed the tears on the wine toxins leaking out via her eyes, as she never cried normally. She had her doubts that any of her pirate adventures were ever real at all. She used to carry the red bandana that Milton had first given her in her handbag, the only last remaining hope that they had not forgotten about her, convinced that one day they would return for her and she'd pull it out of her bag and wave at them from a distance, and they'd laugh at her, and all would be well again. But as each day passed, the bandana wasn't enough to stop the doubts that now resided in her mind that she had simply dreamed a crazy series of dreams and the red square of cotton cloth got put in the back of a cupboard. After all, there had been no pirate ship in her life for many years now. They had forgotten all about her. Those memories that meant so much to her, those precious times that she so often found herself lingering over, were more precious than pirate gold. She clung to them for dear life, terrified they would disappear, sinking like a heavy laden sea chest into the sands of time. These memories she cherished, they were everything to her, but they had cast her away, and she had been forgotten.

The days had passed in a dull ache. Weeks had merged into nothingness. The corners of her mouth no longer rose up to the smile that had been lost the day they made her leave. There was no match for the bullets that had been sunk deep into her heart that first night on the pirate ship when Milton and Arthur looked at her with their deep drowning sea eyes in the candlelight. The ice that had formed a shell around her heart and would not allow it to heal was formed from their mist filled ocean magic.

Here she sat again on the bench, day after dreary dreadful day, lamenting her heartache at losing the adventures and the greatest people she had ever met. Who didn't even exist, "Time out is what you need Alice." she said out loud to herself, "You need a distraction. Some holiday time. Stop crying and have yourself a merry little adventure, stupid girl."

An adventure at least for two weeks as she could get holiday leave from work. Maybe she could book a flight to Las Vegas. It would be a whole heap of fun there. Maybe she could win a fortune on a roulette wheel and never have to come back to work. Only she didn't have enough money for a ticket to Vegas. Let alone a full holiday. Unless she won money when she got there. Then she'd never come back. She'd become a gambling addict and spend all her winnings, and trawl the streets scrabbling in trash cans for food, and end up living in a flood tunnel underneath the big city, spending the change she found in slot machines to still try and get that one big win, no stop there, overthinking it Alice.

Alice handed in her annual leave sheet to her manager and asked for two weeks off work, which was signed off without any question, her boss being preoccupied with organising the agenda for the emergency meeting later that afternoon. Alice then successfully managed to jam the photocopier so that an engineer had to be called to come and repair it.

"That could have set the whole office on fire if it had been left any longer." he said to Alice, as she was trying to explain to him how she had managed to jam it so badly.

Then the fire alarm had went off, and they all had to evacuate the building. There was a bit of chaos as they didn't really know how to evacuate properly. "Who went to the front of the building and who went to the back, does anyone know?" asked the person taking the register.

"Has anyone seen Monica? If she is still in there I am not going back into save her."

"Didn't the repair man say Alice had set the photocopier on fire this morning?"

"Did he not bother to put the fire out while he was fixing it?"

No one was talking to Alice as they went back into the office, for she was to blame for having to stand outside in the cold and rain for twenty minutes as she had set the office on fire apparently, according to everyone except Alice.

Despondent. That's the word used to describe quite how Alice was feeling late on that Wednesday afternoon. A week to go and no plans for her holidays. And it was raining. Stupid girl, believing in invisible pirate ships. Look where that got you, she thought, the whole office hates you as you are hungover and clumsy and stupid for ever believing in pirates in the mist.

"Picked a good time for your holidays." said someone, she didn't know who, they all sounded the same, all of them with the same tone of annoyance at her for setting the office on fire and disrupting their day, "Meant to be thunder and lightening storms the whole time you're off." they added, somehow gleefully as if this was Alice's karma for setting the office on fire.

"Thanks." Alice said, "I'll be sure to wear a raincoat, lightening never strikes the same place twice." The person looked at Alice oddly and walked away.

Maybe a few days of house rest would be just what the doctor ordered, Alice was losing her grasp on reality, it was hanging by its fingernails, dangling over a deep dark precipice of a crevice, or maybe hanging off the edge of a plank on an invisible pirate ship. Did she just dream the whole thing? She knew she did, for years she had known really, that it was a result of too many late nights and alcohol induced vivid dreams, she needed time off, and a good sleep.

Chapter Thirty-Two

(Present Day)
A Strange Meeting

T he team were pulled into the main board room at three o'clock, the meeting timed to run until the end of the day. They each made a cup of coffee, the last chance for a drink to get them through the final two hours of the day, and took their respective seats. Their manager walked in, carrying some paperwork, with a worried look on her face, "What's it going to be, another budget cut?" Kayla asked.

"Maybe a pay rise," Julia murmoured sarcastically, "That'll be right."

"Right girls! ... And Jack," their manager said, "I have some news. I need you all to be prepared and remain calm, with no interruptions until I have finished, okay?"

"Well this sounds serious." Kayla muttered.

"I've never heard this starting speech before." Julia said.

"Girls, please." their boss said, "I can't actually believe I'm saying this. It's like something out of a science fiction film." she stifled a giggle.

"Are we going to need a drink after this?" Stef asked humourously.

"I need one now!" their manager laughed, but they realised it was laughter filled with the nervousness of utter dismal despair.

She fished around in her pocket for her reading glasses, put them on, and picked up the first sheet of paper, "What I am about to tell you is being announced only to the Government, and you are bound by your contractual obligations not to divulge what I am going to tell you. To anyone. Discussing it outside this room is not permitted. If you want to talk about it during work time, you must come back into this room to do so. Right … " she took a breath and read a pre-typed script from the sheet, "Nasa have advised the President of the United States that there is a rogue comet heading towards Earth. They are going to look into this further but the British Government has advised us to set up contingency plans in case its path is on a direct collision course as suspected."

"Whaaaat?" Julia said.

"I know, it doesn't really affect our level, but given that we are government employees in debt management, they have allowed us in on the knowledge." their manager said.

"I don't understand." said Stef fuzzily.

"People will change their spending habits, so we have to be prepared." their manager explained.

"Oh." Stef said.

"But the public don't know about this, right?" Alice asked.

"No Alice, not yet. They are going to have to investigate further so they can say with a hundred percent certainty that this comet is going to hit us directly and they've not made a mistake in their calculations. But it is a distinct possibility and we have to be prepared."

"How big is the comet?" Alice asked.

"I don't know, Alice." her manager replied.

"When is it scheduled to hit?" Alice asked, the caffeine clearly having kicked into her system.

"I don't know, Alice." her manager said, a little defensively.

"Do you know when they'll be able to announce that they know if it will actually be a direct impact?" Alice asked.

"No I don't. Alice will you please stop asking unnecessary questions and try to focus on the task in hand. It is not for us to worry about whether this comet is going to hit or not. We are tasked to set up a contingency plan so that we can cope with the volume of work that may result once this is announced to the public."

Alice looked at her manager, somewhat incredulously. Her manager continued, "That is what we have been asked to do, by Friday. So I need us all to put our heads together and draft a plan of action in this meeting today. So, does anyone have any suggestions as to the measures we can put in place should people stop paying their debts to us?"

"Hire a temp to help work with the increased admin and phone calls?" Julia piped up.

"Oh yes, I'll write that down. Well done Julia." their manager said.

"We could all agree to work a little overtime." Morag said.

Alice looked at them all and suddenly felt like she was watching them from outside a bubble, "We could maybe do with getting a little more information about this, don't you think?" asked Alice, "Like, when this comet is going to hit us? I'm not signing up to loads of overtime when there's no real reason for it."

"Alice, that's not really very constructive. There is no comet on a collision course."

"But you just told us there was."

"No, I didn't." her manager's face turned taut, Alice felt the girls sitting near her tense up.

"If you had listened, Alice, I said Nasa are not announcing this as it might be absolutely nothing to worry about, but our chief executive has asked us to prepare a contingency plan to keep us in line with the other government agencies."

"But ... they have announced it? To us. Doesn't that mean that there is something serious about it all?"

"Yes, the deadline of this Friday! That's the serious part! Think of it more like a 'what-if' scenario, if that helps you, okay? We aren't in any danger, they would tell us if we were." Alice felt like her boss was patronising her now.

Alice refrained from talking any further, just nodding her head, she was just upsetting the room and she had already done enough damage just hours ago by (not) setting the office on fire. She looked out of the window, out at the cloudy grey sky, but what if there was a comet, and it actually was on a collision course?

Nothing changed when they left the board room at twenty minutes past finishing time. Nothing at all, except that the team ensured the emergency contingency plan was submitted on time. No one spoke again of the comet as there was no further news or office meetings about it, it wasn't released into public knowledge, nothing on the television or internet, the whole thing could have been a fake scenario made up by the chief executive to test their reactions, no doubt Alice had failed.

Chapter Thirty-Three

(Present Day)
It's all a Conspiracy

On her second last day of work before her two weeks annual leave,, Alice looked out of the window, it was finally a clear day with no clouds in the sky, and there she spotted a distant light high above them. At first she thought it was a bird, then a plane, glinting in the sun. But she was convinced she could make out a round shape with a pointed end, like a comet and a tail.

"Stef, can you look out this window and tell me if you can see something in the sky?" Alice asked.

"Any excuse to down tools for a bit." Stef said, scooting her chair across to Alice's desk, "Where am I looking toots?" Stef asked.

"Up at about twelve o'clock in the sky, above the house with painted windows."

"Uh-huh."

"There's a little glowing thing, can you see it?"

" ... Nope, don't see it."

Alice sighed.

"Oh ... hold on." Stef added, "Yep, see it now. Looks like an aeroplane."

"Mm-hmm." said Alice, "Only, it's not moving very fast like an aeroplane, is it?"

"What ... do you think it's the c ... the thing we're not allowed to talk about?"

"Mm-hmm." said Alice.

"No way!" Stef squealed, "Is it online?" Stef added, "Have you checked?"

Alice shook her head and grabbed her keyboard, she quickly rattled words into the screen. Nothing. Nothing on Nasa's site, nothing on Google, nothing on other search engines, nothing on the conspiracy sites, which she thought would have something if a comet was visible to the naked eye. Then, she found something on Youtube: 'What Nasa isn't telling you about Comet N18-XRU' She clicked play and a man's voice, dead-pain in tone, came over the speaker. Alice quickly clicked the mouse and pressed buttons to adjust the volume so the whole office didn't walk over and call them out for not doing real work.

"Nasa scientists…" (The man began in his deadpan tone) "…have known about the approach of Comet N18-XRU since May of this year. Government officials were advised to draw up contingency plans for mass-world devastation this week. But they have blocked all attempts to broadcast this knowledge on the world wide web and the international press. Any attempts to publicise this comet has led to mysterious disappearances. No one is allowed to know we are all doomed to die."

"That was us, we're the government officials!" Stef whispered.

The man continued, "Nasa have discovered this comet is on a direct, I repeat, direct collision course with earth, and they don't want you to know! It is estimated to be six miles wide. The dust from the comet will block out the sunlight for months, or even years creating freezing temperatures. The oceans will flood the continents. Effectively guys, this comet is going to wipe out all life as we know it. At its current speed, it is estimated to hit Deep Impact: Earth on September nineteenth of this year. Be warned people, this is the killer comet they are not going to tell you about as there is nothing they can do to stop it. Nasa is relying on the fact so few of us look to the stars these days and won't notice the comet, to stop world wide riots for as long as possible. But it is there, in the sky, if you look hard enough even with a pair of binoculars. This is Grey-Watcher, until next time, if there is one, over and out."

Alice saved his link to her favourites and closed the screen.

"He's scaremongering." Stef said, "He's found a memo in a wheelie bin about the emergency contingency plans, and he's scaremongering."

"Pretty convincing though, huh!" Alice said, realising it was better if she agreed with Stef.

"These people need to get a job, nothing better to do with their time than make stuff up out of nothing." Stef added, scooting back to her desk.

When Alice got home that evening she went up into her attic and rummaged around until she found her pair of bird-watching binoculars. She triumphantly went back down to the ground floor and pulled on a thick jumper, then walked in her socks outside into her back garden, clambered up onto her trampoline and lay flat on her back on it and aimed her binoculars at the dark night sky. They didn't show anything, Alice aimed them at the kitchen light, still nothing but black nothingness. She jumped back down and jogged over to the kitchen light to look at what could be wrong with the binoculars, of course she'd forgotten to take the lens caps off.

Back onto the trampoline, pointing the uncovered lenses up at the sky, everything was blurry and out of focus. "Dammit." Alice said. She pointed them at her kitchen window, twisting the dials until objects became clearer, then directed them at the night sky again. This time she dropped the binoculars straight onto her face.

"Dammit, Alice you clumsy clutz! How can you make something easy so bloody difficult for yourself?" she scolded herself, rubbing her nose. She raised the binoculars again, and stuck her tongue out, seriously concentrating now. Then, there it was! She tried to hold the binoculars steady while she pulled her face out from under them to gaze at the sky. She was focussing on the right object, the thing that she had spotted earlier that day at work, that was not normal behaviour for a plane or star, to still be in the sky at night as well as during the day. Her eyes were back in the lenses, she twisted the dials as gently as she could until the blurred edges became sharp, then blurred edges again. She moved them back. Sharp and clear again, focussed on a bright orange object, rounded at one end with a distinct blue tail radiating from the back of it.

"Bloody. Hell." Alice said, "This things real!"

She realised she was all alone in her garden, she had no one else to tell about it, no one would believe her. Alice lay on the trampoline for a little while longer, gazing through the binoculars at the object in the sky, then she went back inside her house in her soggy socks, grabbed a half finished bottle of wine from the fridge, grabbed a glass and curled up on her sofa with her laptop, punching Youtube into the search screen and finding the next installment of the Grey Watcher's videos, the familiar deadpan voice spoke loudly into her living room.

"Hello, this is Grey Watcher. This might be my last broadcast, I think they have found me ...." Alice watched the three minute video with awe. She clicked to watch it again, but the video wouldn't play a second time, instead being replaced with an error message that the video had been removed for copyright infringement. Alice moved her search on to how to survive the end of the world scenarios.

The next day, on her lunch break, Alice was to be found in the supermarket. The first thing that went in her trolley were six bottles of spiced rum conveniently on offer, she hadn't had rum for a very long time. Then, she filled the trolley with tins with extra-long expiration dates on them, super-cheap, store branded ones, six tubes of store-brand toothpaste, a new tin opener, chocolate, dried foodstuffs, and lots of store-brand sanitary pads. It was a start anyway. Cheap as she was trying to be for beginning to stock her survival cupboard, the total bill came to over a hundred pounds, "That'll fairly keep your cupboards stocked!" the check-out girl said, passing pleasantries.

"Yes, I just thought I'd better just in case I get snowed in for winter." Alice said, smiling at the check-out girl.

Stef bumped into her in the car park, "Hey Alice!" she said cheerily, then her gaze fell on Alice's bags of shopping, big open bags, giving away their contents of white labelled tins, "Whats with all the tins?" Stef asked, "Oh my god, wait, you're stocking up for the end of the world, aren't you?!" she started laughing.

Alice gulped.

"Oh you crack me up Alice. You know that's not going to happen!"

Alice shrugged guiltily, "Well there's no harm in being a little prepared."

"I'd sooner have cupboards full of wine and just get drunk if we're all going to die!" Stef laughed.

"I'm not planning on dying." smiled Alice, with a little touch of pirate mischief dancing round her face for only the briefest of moments.

"You're crazy!" Stef laughed and started to help Alice load the heavy bags into her car boot.

"I know." Alice replied, "Completely off my head. I drive myself crazy with my craziness."

"Well you're in good company, we're all mad here!" Stef laughed, "Do you know, I'm sure that's a quote from Alice in Wonderland, have you read it?"

"My mum named me after the book. She read me the story when I was in hospital after I was struck by lightning when I was nine years old."

Stef laughed again, "Oh Alice, you and your jokes. I'm away into the shop to get my lunch, see you back at the office, crazy girl!"

"Strange things are afoot at the Circle K!" Alice replied, locking her car and taking her trolley to the full trolley park.

That afternoon Alice tidied her in-tray and put her out-of-office on her emails all set for her two weeks annual leave, which were co-inciding just nicely with the end of the world which nobody knew about. She looked round at her colleagues as if it was the last time she was going to see them all, but kept quiet about her worries and said her cheerful cheerios to them on the way out of the office at the end of the day.

Chapter Thirty-Four

(Present Day)
Coffee on a Summer's Eve

O nce Alice got home she unpacked her car, putting the tins into plastic boxes she stashed them stealthily in her cupboard, as if she were storing some dubious secret, and made herself a cup of coffee. She looked at the steaming cup, then at the six bottles of rum on the counter waiting for a home, she hadn't had rum in her cupboards for quite some time. She opened one of the bottles and poured a splash of rum into the hot coffee, then she took herself out into her back garden. The summer was just beginning to draw to a close and a slight coolness was floating in the air. Alice sat on her back step and placed her mouth over her coffee cup, even the steam vapours offered the scent of spiced rum to comfort her senses. She took her first sip.

Alice did a double take as she thought she saw a misty blurry space appear in her garden, like a little cloud was floating there, but it was almost invisible. Alice rubbed her eyes at her tear ducts, thinking it was just her eyeliner drying her eyes out. No, the cloud was still there. Alice felt her heart beat a little faster as it dawned on her that maybe, just maybe, the pirates hadn't forgotten about her. It had been six years since she had seen them last, dropping her off in time for tea, saying goodbye, telling her they couldn't take her with them. That for her own good, they were leaving her behind to settle down, to raise a family, not to run around looking after pirates and having fantastic but somewhat dangerous adventures.

Alice's heart stopped beating faster, 'Good girl Alice', she thought, 'Well trained now aren't we. Had six years to have your heart's hopes raised and shattered again, we won't allow that to happen today.' But that little cloud was still there. Alice walked closer to the little misty cloud in her barefeet, feeling the cool grass beneath her toes, which was wet as she tiptoed closer to the cloud. The cloud was real then, as far as Alice could tell. God she hadn't even had a full shot of rum and she was hallucinating. Alice went back into the house and shut the back door. She took a drink from her coffee cup, the rum warmed her throat. She looked out and watched the cloud from her back window, it had become denser now, more of a dark grey cloud and far more visible.

She took another sip of her coffee and steadied herself for whatever was coming, she had been waiting a very long time. The cloud slowly darkened, the shadows floating about formed distinct silhouette shapes which then focused into solid matter, becoming a little rowing boat with a solitary figure, sitting with their head in their hands, underneath a flamboyant pirate hat with a white feather in it.

Without flinching, Alice stepped outside again and walked over to the boat with her cup of coffee still in her hand, and looked at the figure sitting there. She waited, sipping quietly on her coffee, her hands were steady. They knew she was there, and they knew she was waiting for them to look up. He raised his head, "Hello Arthur." Alice said warily. After all this time, she didn't know yet quite how she felt for seeing him, she noticed that that he was unshaven, his eyes bloodshot, and his cheeks flushed, he was in a bad way, Alice kept her breathing steady.

"Thank God you're here." he said, relieved. Alice said nothing in return, she just looked at him, "Milton is gone, Alice." he began to sob, putting his head back into his hands, big choking noises coming out of him. Alice put her empty coffee cup onto the grass and stepped into the boat to sit next to Arthur.

"Where's he gone?" she asked softly.

"He's....dead." came the reply.

The news hit Alice like a train crashing into her chest, the world closed in around her, the dark cloud closed out any light and all she could do was hold Arthur while he cried. They sat there for about ten minutes, in that little rowing boat, not saying a word to each other. "Do you want to tell me what happened?" Alice eventually asked him.

"They killed him. I wasn't there. I wasn't there to save him. I wasn't there!" Arthur cried.

"Who killed him?" Alice asked. It made no sense, to her, Milton had seemed completely undefeatable.

"A man in a maroon cloak, by the name of De Soulis, and his hateful army." came the reply. Arthur wept, "The ship is gone, so is the crew, some of them are dead and the others had scattered with the wind before I even got back there. They left, running to all four corners of the earth for all I know. No ship, no crew, no Captain, no brother. It's all pointless. Just this boat, it's all I have left of the ship, and just rowing, rowing and rowing. I didn't care if I lived or died. I wanted to drown in the water but I was too coward to do it. I rowed and rowed. And I just wanted to see a friend. I missed you, right then, and hoped, somehow that you would find me. And you have."

"You were in my garden." Alice pointed out.

"No, I was lost at sea." Arthur sniffed.

"Well you're in my garden now." she softened her tone, "You're safe. Do you want to come in and have some rumfee?"

"Rumfee?" he said.

"It's my new drink. Coffee mixed with rum. Why I never tried it six years ago on the Sea Rose I'll never know." she replied, keeping her tone light to stop her mind from reeling with it all.

"Six years ago?" he looked puzzled.

"Yes, that was when you left me here." she replied.

"Alice, we dropped you off in your garden a little over a week ago." Arthur said, "Milton knew De Soulis was after us and wanted to keep you safe."

Alice couldn't believe it, six years for her had been just a week to them, "It's been six years since I last saw you. I was twenty-three when I met you and I'm twenty-nine now." Six years of thinking they had forgotten her, and they had actually done it to keep her safe from harm.

Arthur's face dropped even further, "I think I'd like to try that drink now."

"Yes I think I need another one." Alice replied, holding her hand out to help Arthur stand up and get out of the boat. He pulled the boat to the edge of the garden so that it was touching the walls of her house and tied the rope round a plant pot to make sure the boat wouldn't drift away at high tide.

Alice guided Arthur to sit at a stool at her kitchen breakfast bar while she filled the kettle. She looked at him, a completely dishevelled version of himself, wide-eyed and utterly lost. She went through a hundred thoughts and a range of emotions in the time it took for that kettle to boil, a hundred questions that she wanted to ask, but knew she couldn't bombard him with them. She practised her breathing, taking slow breaths in and out to steady herself, the pirates hadn't abandoned her to forget her, they were trying to protect her, and now they were gone.

Arthur sat with his head in his hands, holding his hair in knots, his hat on the countertop, "I wasn't there Alice." he sighed, "I wasn't there for him."

"Where were you?" she asked gently.

"I was with a wench in the village near to the castle, you remember it, the castle with the storm swirling around it." he told her, "We had wound up there again as another storm appeared in the mist and made us land the ship, but I know now it was the same storm." Arthur creased his face with pain, then continued, "The wench got me drunk so badly, I think she drugged me I've never lost my senses like that before, I was out cold, I don't know how long I was out for but when I came round I was in a ditch and I couldn't find my way back to the ship. I knew that we had docked in a river, I wandered the wrong way and double-backed on myself going further upstream, and when I found my way back, De Soulis and his army had already arrived. Bodies of the crew were lying on the ground as I crept closer and then, they started ripping the ship apart, pulling planks off her, tearing her to bits. I saw De Soulis's men carry Milton's lifeless body into the castle nearby and one of them laughed and said he was dead. There was blood all down his face." He broke off, wiped his face with his hand then continued. "The rowboat was sitting in the river, stuck on some branches so I got in it and rowed away, the misty cloud came down and the river turned into the ocean and I just kept rowing."

"Thats awful, Arthur I'm so sorry. There's nothing I can say or do that will take your pain away." Alice said.

"I know." he said, holding back another racking sob.

The kettle clicked as it boiled just as Alice's doorbell rang, "Strange, I'm not expecting anyone." she said, heading out the kitchen to the front door.

Chapter Thirty-Five

(Present Day)
Pirates in the House

Alice turned the door lock, and when the door opened, Flat Eric was standing there looking blankly up at her, carrying a little rucksack in his three-fingered hands. "Oh." Alice said, "Hello Eric. Haven't seen you for a while."

Eric said nothing, he simply sauntered into her house, down her hall and into her kitchen. "Eric!" exclaimed Arthur, "Where the devil have you been?"

"He must have heard the kettle boiling, from where ever he was." Alice muttered, amazed.

Eric shrugged, and sat on the stool next to Arthur, his face barely came to counter level, he looked at Arthur and put his three-fingered hand onto Arthur's arm. Alice stood in the doorway, astounded, "I thought we lost you in Lewes." Arthur said.

Eric raised his hands in the air with exasperation.

"Did you lose Eric?" Alice asked Arthur.

"Yes, at the last stop before the last one, that's a long story too." Arthur said.

"Well, Eric, would you like a Rumfee as well, seeing as you're here?" Alice asked.

Eric frowned.

"Its coffee with rum, Eric, she's claiming to have invented this new drink, as if we never thought of doing that on the ship." Arthur said to Eric.

Alice scowled fractionally, and pulled three cups from the cupboard and made three coffees topped up with spiced rum. She opened the kitchen door and said, "Shall we take these through to the living room?" promptly carrying the three drinks through and walking away from the two pirates in her kitchen.

She put the cups on a small dark coffee table, while the two pirates wandered through in their own time. She lit the wood-burning stove and sat on the fireplace step, while the pirates sat on the sofa, Arthur looked out of the window, "Nice view of the hills, Alice." he said.

"Yes, isn't it? I love my little house. That's Minto Hill and that one further away has the ruins of Fatlips Castle at the very top." she said, "you can see Ruberslaw hill out the back too."

The two pirates were making polite pleasantries while recently interred into Alice's home, they took equally polite sips of their coffee cups, "Not bad at all." praised Arthur, "This is something I could get used to drinking."

Flat Eric nodded and raised an eyebrow at the drink.

"You made a terrible job of lighting that fire, Alice." Arthur said, stretching his legs out.

Alice silently fumed, Arthur had taken a mere five minutes after a disastrous announcement and six year absence to return to his usual irritating self. She opened up the stove doors and threw more firelighters into the fire.

"It'll be fine in a minute it just needs cleaning out, it's a bit choked." she said.

"Or you just don't know how to light fires properly." Arthur replied smugly.

"I'm going to go out and get some more sticks and logs." Alice said, standing up and picking up the log basket, "Don't trouble yourselves to help me." she added, "Just make yourselves at home."

Arthur raised his coffee cup at her, "Thanks, we will."

Alice walked out her back door across to her shed to fill the basket. She had to chop some more kindling sticks with her axe as she'd used all her others up, and as she picked up the axe she realised her hands were shaking with nerves. When she returned to the house, she almost dropped the log basket at the back door at the sight of her house interior, within a mere fraction of the afternoon of Arthur and Eric's arrival and within only fifteen minutes of her absence, the house had been pirate-ified. There was water all over the kitchen floor, dishes everywhere, cupboard doors were swinging open. She carried the log basket through to the living room in total awe of the destructive power of domesticated pirates. The carpet in there was covered in crumbs and plates, and fire ash added to the colourful new blends in her carpet near the stove, there were broken ornaments and all of her shoes were scattered about the floor.

"Why are my shoes all scattered about the floor?" she asked Arthur.

"I don't know, I didn't put them there." Arthur replied.

"How have you managed to get my house in such a state?" she asked.

"I don't know it wasn't me." he replied.

"Well you're the only pirates in here!" she said angrily, "And what is that smell? Urgh!"

"It must have been Eric." Arthur said.

"You've been here for less than an hour and my house is completely trashed! Who's going to tidy it all up?" Arthur looked at her fearfully, Eric shook his head, his mouth bulging with something in his mouth, he chewed and swallowed it, gulping it down in guilt. "Neither of you are volunteering for that then. Now may not be the best time to tell you the world is going to end as there's a comet in the sky hell bent on destroying us." Alice glared at them.

"Well you won't have to tidy your house then." Arthur replied.

Alice growled and opened the stove doors, stabbing at the ash with a metal poker, "Alice you're not doing that properly it will never burn." Arthur stood up and bent over the fire taking the poker out of her hands, "I'll show you how to light a fire." he said, "We even cleaned it out for you." he gestured at the ash strewn all over the hearth and her carpet.

Alice gave up, she picked up her coffee and took Arthur's vacant place on the sofa. Alice sipped at her coffee, and realised that the scene that had just played out in her house had been a complete distraction for them all, and at the moment there was a silence which was beginning to allow it all come flooding in again. The television remote was sitting on the arm of the sofa so she flicked the screen on, the voices of a boy band came out of the box.

"Who on earth is that?" Arthur asked as he played about with the stove.

"One Direction." Alice replied.

"Hmm. I'm not sure if I like them or not. Catchy though." he said, humming along to the song as he lit the fire with a match. Of course it flared up instantly and burned successfully after that point.

Eric tapped her shoulder and indicated to his empty coffee cup.

"What, would you like another one?" Alice asked.

Eric nodded.

"He'd get it himself, but he can't reach your countertops, you made them too tall for him." Arthur said, staring transfixed at the boy band dancing on the screen.

Alice grabbed the two empty cups and carried them and her half full cup through to the kitchen, muttering to herself that it wasn't her who had designed the kitchen. She put the kettle on and took a sip of her own drink. Standing in the kitchen and being out of the living room, she briefly felt that familiar feeling like it was turning back into a dream she'd just had, that Eric and Arthur weren't in her living room driving her insane already, but then the sound of Arthur's voice carried through, he was telling Eric what had happened to his brother, the ship and the crew.

Alice had the drinks ready, but she left the two pirates a little while longer before going through to the living room. Fresh tears had been shed by the boys, "They're singing a really sad song Alice, can you stop it somehow please?" Arthur sniffled.

She put a coffee cup down next to him, "You just need to change the channel, Arthur."

"Change the what?" he asked.

Alice realised he didn't know how to work her television, so picked up the remote, popped it up to the next channel to get rid of the sad song instantly, and was about to pull up the programme schedule menu when she realised she was watching a news broadcast actually talking about the comet. They watched the screen, with mouths open. "You just mentioned that didn't you." said Arthur, "I wasn't listening to you properly."

"Yes." Alice replied, in shock.

It had been released to the public. All attempts to thwart the course of the comet had failed and it was on a collision course with their precious planet Earth. The programme had even shown images of the comet and its icy tail, heading straight for them, with a direct impact hit estimated for two weeks time. They were all doomed to die. The three friends sat in silence, watching video clips of experts talking about the comet, others advising what to do to prepare for the end of days, "What are we going to do now?" Alice asked.

"With two weeks left to live and with you two my only friends left in life?" Arthur started to say, but went quiet, no mad or crazy ideas jumping to mind. Eventually he added, "I think we should get in my boat and row away. See where the sea takes us. Maybe it will transport us far away from this time where the world is going to end."

"Its an idea." agreed Alice, "But what about all the people here? Millions of them, Arthur, including my friends and family."

"We don't have a bigger boat to take them all in." Arthur said.

"Then we need the ship." Alice said, "I don't want everyone to die. If we find the ship then at the very least we could try to get some people on board and save them."

"The ship's gone Alice." Arthur said.

"You said they were dismantling it? Not burning it?" she asked.

"Yes. They were pulling it apart piece by piece." Arthur confirmed.

"In which case could we get it back?" Alice asked.

Arthur frowned, "And do what, rebuild it ourselves? They were carrying it in bits into the castle. Alice, you're not going to be able to rebuild the ship. We haven't even got a crew to help us, never mind the army you would need to invade the castle. And ultimately, the ship doesn't work without her Captain." he was forlorn and dejected,

"Oh." Alice was stumped, "Then what else are we going to do in the two weeks we have left alive? Just sit here and get drunk together?"

"Well, my first idea was to row away and see where we end up but even that seems like a lot of effort for nothing. What else could you and I get up to with our last two weeks on earth together?" smirked Arthur, the faintest hint of a forgotten smile dancing on his lips.

"Not that." said Alice, scowling at him.

Maybe it was the rum, but she felt a new emotion stirring inside her, a feeling that she had never felt before in her life. It tasted like blood in her mouth. It was revenge. "My idea might not be the best one." said Alice, "But seeing as we are doomed to die, why don't we go out all guns blazing, the way the best heroes are supposed to? Let's put a new crew or army together, let's go on a last adventure, and mostly, let's claim vengeance on the man you call De Soulis. I don't want to sit here and watch the world end all around us, I want to do something with the last days of my life."

Arthur sighed, "My idea was a whole lot easier and a lot less like hard work."

"I think that's the reason you came back to me right now Arthur, you say you left me a week ago, but for me it's been six years and you've appeared just as I hear my world is about to end."

"Do you still believe in fate, Alice? You and your silly unwritten religion. LIke any of this is meant to be. Like De Soulis was meant to take Milton away from me."

"I don't have all the answers, Arthur, I'm sorry. I just like to find a reason in things. That maybe you and I and Eric are meant to do something now. Or maybe I don't just want to sit around here feeling helpless for the next two weeks. You've been wronged, and De Soulis is still out there."

"Not in this time period he's not." Arthur replied.

"A mere triviality, on the scale of things." Alice's voice echoed the words spoken to her all those years ago.

"If we go back in time, then we can stay there, the world won't be ending then." Arthur replied.

"I want to try to find a way to save my family and friends." Alice implored him.

"You're crazy." he shook his head.

"All the best people are." Alice replied.

"You are sentencing us all to death with your crazy notions about getting the broken ship back and killing De Soulis."

"I am going to die with this comet coming anyway." Alice sadly said.

"No you aren't because I'm here to save you." Arthur replied.

"What about everyone else?" Alice asked.

"Alice, the boat won't carry any more people." he said, "If you told even one person about it, more would come, and there just isn't room." Alice stared at the fire, burning brightly now in the stove. "Alice, you have two weeks left to live in this time period. I have a boat which can get the three of us away from here. Sail away with me, let me take you away from this doomed time and we will be safe together. I can't say I will be the best company, but at least you will be alive."

"Alive for one last adventure." Alice said faintly.

"It won't be your last adventure if you come with me away from here." he said.

"What if I'm meant to die in two weeks time, the same as everyone else? What if my death is a fixed point in time and I can't avoid it no matter which time period I go to?" she asked him.

"You're overthinking it Alice. As usual, you over think things and worry too much about things that haven't happened yet." he replied, "Have another rum."

"Yes, I think that's the best idea." Alice said, getting up and going into the kitchen for another drink. "Time travelling is really confusing, especially when it's the end of the world."

"While you're there get us one too." Arthur called.

Alice walked back through and grabbed the two mugs from Eric and Arthur. When she went back through to the living room, Arthur and Eric were both lying on the living room floor, amongst the scattered disarray of shoes and mess, arm wrestling. She sat on the sofa and watched the news channel flashing up more and more stories from around the world of the chaos that was beginning to unleash as the human race began to panic. Arthur sat up, and then got down on one knee in front of her. He took her hands in his.

"Arthur what are you doing?" Alice asked.

"I'm asking for your forgiveness." he said.

"For what?" she asked.

"For whatever I've ever never done to make you cross with me, except for your shoes being in here, as that really wasn't me." Alice felt a tiny crack run across her ice covered heart.

"Sail away with me, my Alice, and let's see where we end up." Arthur said.

"Yes, I think I shall." she said.

Arthur kissed her hand, his eyes shining with tears. Alice looked into them, and realised she didn't have that strange sensation of drowning in them like she used to on the ship. His magic pirate powers were broken, "Let's get going then." he replied, "no time like the present judging by that news you're watching, you'll have rioters at your door in no time."

"I need to phone my family and speak to them." Alice stood up.

"Probably best not to." Arthur replied, "I think we should just strike while the iron's hot and try to row out of here right now. Phone calls are going to upset you and may take a while, what are you going to say to them, they'll want to see you these last two weeks how will you explain you've gone?"

Alice nodded reluctantly, "Then let me pack some supplies."

"As long as you remember to bring the rum. Food is overrated." Arthur said.

"You should try my cooking sometime." she laughed.

Alice got up, went into her bedroom and opened her cupboard door. She reached into the very back of the cupboard, at the bottom and pulled out a familiar bag made out of sail canvas that she hadn't touched for six years. She untied it and reached inside, pulling out a washed clean set of pirate clothing wrapped around a cutlass sword, the gifts from Jasper. The sword glistened as she pulled it out of its scabbard, glowing back to life as it warmed in her hands, the touch of the metal upon her skin bringing back memories of the battles they had seen together. She got changed into the clothes, and packed her rucksack and the canvas bag with items she thought she might need, and then placed them and the plastic boxes filled with tins in the kitchen by the back door. "I'm ready." she said walking into the living room.

Arthur and Flat Eric looked at her, Eric had Arthur in a headlock, "Let's go then." Arthur said standing up, dusting himself off and leaving the room with Eric still hanging off his shoulders.

Alice switched the television off and looked around at the room, saying a silent goodbye to the comforting space that had been her home for many years now, then went outside. Arthur and Eric had moved the rowing boat to the grass in the middle of her garden and were loading the boxes onto it. "Oh almost forgot the rum." Alice said, going back into her kitchen. She packed a bottle in each of her two bags then put three into a bag on their own, and left the half full one out for the journey. She went outside and locked her back door, and took her place in the little boat.

Chapter Thirty-Six

(Present Day)
Row, Row, Row Your Boat

They sat still in the little row boat. Nothing happened. They sat longer and nothing happened.

"Maybe the magic's gone?" Alice suggested.

"Nonsense." Arthur said, "You always talk nonsense, Alice."

Alice noted that Arthur sounded a little like his old self when he was annoyed at her, "So what, we just have to wait then?" she replied impatiently.

"Well, I just sat in the boat, rowed and thought of you." Arthur leaned over and took the open bottle of rum from her hands and took a drink from it.

"So, do you think we should row now then?" Alice asked.

Arthur gulped, sighed with satisfaction and looked at her as if she was mad, "I have my hands full just now, you'll have to do it."

"Hands full?" Alice raised her eyebrows.

"Yes, I'm terribly busy too."

"Busy? Doing what?" she asked incredulously.

"Holding an extremely heavy bottle of rum while supervising you. I am the Captain of this ship don't you know."

"It's a rowboat not a ship." Alice corrected him.

"Well every boat needs a Captain, and I are it, little lady." Arthur said, smiling. He had such deep shadows under his eyes when he smiled it was as if the moon had cast a beam onto a dark winter's night, lighting up the dark shadows where once there had been the sun.

"So you want me to row?" Alice asked. Arthur just gestured flamboyantly with his hands. "And how am I supposed to row on grass?" Alice leaned over the edge of the boat.

"Careful now, or you'll fall out and drown." Arthur warned her, adding, "then who's going to row me about?"

"Why, Eric can of course." Alice was exasperated, as she couldn't possibly drown in a garden of grass.

"He can't, he only has tiny arms and tiny feet."

"Smaller than your hands." Alice said.

"Leave my tiny hands out of this. You always comment on my tiny hands." Arthur whined.

Alice growled then picked up the oars and made rowing motions on the grass. Nothing magical happened. "Put some effort into it Alice. Come on!" Arthur ordered.

"I'm trying!" Alice said, "Its not working."

"Hmm." Arthur said.

Flat Eric tugged on Arthur's arm, he leaned down and Eric whispered something in his ear, "You know, I think you might be right Eric." Arthur whispered loudly back.

"What was that?" Alice asked.

"What was what?" Arthur looked around him, "I was just thinking though," he continued, "Maybe we can't get back the same way that I came in this time. Maybe too much time has passed here."

Alice looked out across the lawn as if she were waiting for it to transform into an ocean before her very eyes. It didn't do that. "You may be onto something there." she agreed.

Flat Eric rolled his eyes and folded his arms.

"This is merely a problem that needs to be overcome by the Captain of the ship." Arthur said, "For the magic to work, this boat must be in motion. It must be set sailing. Do you happen to have a river nearby to your house?"

"Yes, the Teviot, it's across the road and at the bottom of a field." Alice pointed at the direction of the river, but realised she was pointing at her house as the river was on the other side of it.

"Then that is where we must go." Arthur said.

"We can't carry the boat all the way down to the river, it's too heavy." Alice said.

"No, I agree, we're not going to. You are. I'm going to carry the important stuff, like the rum." Arthur replied.

"That's not going to work, you'll have drunk the lot before we've even got down to the river. And no!" she added quickly, realising what he'd ordered her to do, "I'm not carrying the boat on my own!"

"Eric will help you." Arthur suggested.

Eric shook his head.

Arthur looked around, and smiled gleefully, "Then we shall borrow that horse in the field who can tow it for us!" he exclaimed triumphantly, pointing to a black and white gypsy cob in the field next to Alice's house.

"Well, where did he come from?" Alice said, "I've never seen him before."

Arthur jumped out of the boat, "Do you have a rope Alice?" he asked.

"Yes, in the shed, but what are you …?"

"Don't worry about it, I've got it all figured out." Arthur interrupted. He went rummaging in her shed and came out with her rope. He climbed the fence from her garden into the field, muttering to her, "I used to know a horse whisperer, who showed me a few tricks of the trade, don't you know."

He somehow managed to successfully approach the gypsy cob without spooking it away, the horse seemed quite bemused by the pirate heading it's way. It allowed Arthur to halter it with the rope and they walked meekly round the field, through the gate and into Alice's garden. "He says he will happily tow the boat for us down to the river." Arthur said, patting the pony's neck.

"You can talk to it?" Alice asked.

"Well, not as such, no. But that's what he said." Arthur replied.

He fashioned a harness out of the rope and secured it to the boat. He unloaded some of the supplies and placed them on the lawn to lighten the weight for the pony. The pony began to walk quite merrily. Alice found herself holding open the gate to allow the pirate with the pony towing the rowing boat out of her garden. Eric waved at her from the boat. She tried to lift the back of the boat to stop it scraping badly along the ground.

They held up the traffic on the main road as they crossed it, Alice offering apologetic expressions as the pirate in front of her ordered the angry and panicked traffic to a standstill so the stolen pony towing the rowboat with a three fingered yellow monkey sitting inside it drinking rum could safely cross the road. And then, they were across the field and at the river. It was situated down a banking and could not be seen from the roadside. The boat was carefully lowered into place on the water. Arthur turned to the river bank, looking for something.

"Where are the supplies?" he asked.

"In the garden where you left them." Alice replied.

"Well, why aren't they here?"

"Because you left them in the garden!" Alice spluttered.

"What sort of First Mate are you? The crew carry the supplies and the Captain steers the ship." Arthur said.

"Well, we'll have to go back and get them." Alice said.

"Yes, you will." Arthur replied, settling himself into the boat with his half drunk bottle of rum. "The Captain must stay with the ship, and make sure no one steals it. Eric will help you." Eric looked at her and took her hand, guiding her away from Arthur before she could utter expletives at him.

"Right, fine. We'll go back to the house." Alice muttered to Eric, "But if Arthur dares go off without me after all this, I'll hunt him down and chop his head off." Eric squeezed her hand and patted it reassuringly.

Once back at the house she realised she'd been set a difficult task, as carrying the supplies included the heavy boxes filled with tins of food. So she loaded it all into her trusty wheelbarrow, helped Eric clamber to the top of the pile in the barrow, and began the march back to the boat. It was a struggle, she nearly toppled the wheelbarrow a couple of times, but Eric leaned over to help counter the balance, and held onto loose objects. Sweating and breathing heavily, the stolen pony on the riverbank came into view after what felt like an eternity. Then the boat. But, and for this Alice had to stop and focus her eyes again, there were two figures sitting in the little rowing boat ahead of her.

Chapter Thirty-Seven

(Present Day)
The Gypsy King

Arthur was sitting next to a red-haired fellow, who was wearing a white singlet and raggedy khaki shorts.

"Alice!" Arthur said, smiling, "This is the King of the Gypsies!"

"Hello, nice to meet you." Alice said breathlessly, looking at them both sitting so pleasantly in the little boat together.

"And it is most lovely to meet you, my dear!" The King of the Gypsies said to Alice.

Alice looked at Arthur, hurt, "I didn't know you were planning on leaving me behind. Again."

"Aren't you coming with us?" The King of the Gypsies asked.

"There isn't any room for me in the boat." Alice said sadly, thinking of the people she was leaving in this time period.

"Urgh, she does this all the time." Arthur muttered to the Gypsy King.

The King of the Gypsies smiled at her, "In that case, we're gonna need a bigger boat!" he laughed, "Until then, we'll just have to all cosy up together."

He had a merry laugh, light and easy, as if he had never known a single hardship in the world. Yet, something in his eyes told Alice he had known many hardships indeed. Alice couldn't help but smile as the Gypsy King kept laughing.

"Come on, come on board Alice!" he sang in his lilting voice, "And what a merry crew we will make! All aboard!" the pony stepped towards the boat, "Not you, Norris!" the Gypsy King said, "You stay there and help us along the verge, sir, if you please. Back, back! Thank you!"

The pony Norris snorted and stepped backwards. Alice unloaded her wheelbarrow, passing the Gypsy King the supplies, who packed them carefully away under the benches of the boat. She helped Eric step up onto the boat, then the Gypsy King took her hand and helped her on board. "Your hand is very pretty, Alice, it should be adorned with jewels. Here, have one of mine." he took off a small gold signet ring which was on his pinky finger, "This one should fit you."

"Thank you, but I can't accept that." Alice stammered.

"It's a gift and you don't have a choice!" he laughed, "Dear Alice, don't you know who I am? I am the King of the Gypsies, even an esteemed someone such as yourself cannot refuse a gift from the Gypsy King!"

Alice looked at the ring, it was a solid piece of gold, with the detail being the shape of a heart. "Thank you." she said, placing it on the middle finger of her right hand.

"If you ever find yourself in bother with the gypsies, you show that ring to them. And tell them you have the blessing of the Rom Baro to go where you please and no harm will come to you by them."

"What are you two whispering about?" Arthur piped up behind them.

"I was saying that you and I go back a long way, my friend, but it takes an act of bravery for you to try to steal my horse!" the Gypsy King laughed.

"To be fair, I didn't think he was your horse." Arthur said.

"Who else has a horse like mine, that can understand perfect English?" the Gypsy King asked.

"Really? He can understand everything you say?" Alice asked.

"Yes, he understands everything perfectly well, don't you Norris?" the King directed his question to the cob, who, in perfect timing, snorted in response, "If you insist on stealing the Gypsy King's horse, the Gypsy King is sure to follow suit."

"Does that mean we have stolen you, as well as your horse?" Alice asked.

The Gypsy King broke into a laugh, "I suppose it does!" he laughed jovially, "I suppose it does. Get your prisoner a drink Captain! And let's get this ship on the road, or river rather!"

"Where are we going?" Alice asked.

"Downstream!" Arthur said.

"You shall tell me your tale along the way Arthur, and what brings you to my part of the world." the Gypsy King said.

Arthur pushed the boat away from the riverbank edge. Alice noticed that the boat was attached to the rope, which was attached to Norris. Norris began a slow meander alongside the boat. The river seemed a lot calmer than when she remembered it from her walks. Arthur and the Gypsy King spoke together, Alice leaned back and trailed her hand in the cold water, listening to the murmur of their voices, the steady pace of the pony, and the air around them, which seemed so still, yet carried the song of the river. A slight breeze whispered through the branches and birds occasionally chirruped around her. It was mesmerising. She hadn't been on a boat since her pirate days. The outside world and its worries floated away and she began to lose track of time and dozed off.

She opened her eyes to see Arthur sitting watching her, "Hello sleepyhead." he smiled.

"Hello." she replied, wiping her face, which was slightly sticky with drool, a typical thing have would have to happen when in the presence of the Gypsy King. Alice looked around at their surroundings. The river had widened slightly, the trees looked older. "I've never seen this part of the river before." she said wearily, "How long have I been asleep for?"

"It's amazing what you can miss when you're not looking." Arthur said.

"Well, I would think I would miss things if I wasn't looking for them." Alice said, still half asleep, "But if I was looking, I would know this part of the river, and I don't know it."

"Well, you don't know everything, do you?" Arthur replied.

"I never said I did know everything." Alice bit her lip, the equivalent of biting her tongue. For some reason she felt like bursting into tears. It had been a long day already, "What time is it?" she asked.

"Time for you to have a drink." the Gypsy King smiled softly at her.

"Shouldn't it be getting dark soon?" she asked.

The Gypsy King shrugged his shoulders, "It would be nice if time slowed down sometimes, wouldn't it, rather than rushing the day away for night to come in its place?"

"Have you slowed time down? Can you do that?" Alice asked him.

The Gypsy King burst out laughing, "No, no, nothing as spectacular as that. But I do have my ways about me." he said mysteriously, "Your husband here has filled me in on what's been going on with you both."

"He's not my husband." Alice said.

The Gypsy King laughed again, "Och you have much to learn. And not much time to do it."

"What do you mean?" Alice asked.

The Gypsy King leaned forward, "Time waits for no man, but its terrified of women." he laughed again, "Och what a merry little outing this is." he smiled leaning back again.

Alice looked across at Arthur, who was rolling himself a cigarette. He looked up and raised his eyebrows at her, licking the cigarette paper, "The Gypsy King isn't coming with us, he is just guiding us to the rest of the river." Arthur spoke through the paper licking process.

"Nay, my path isn't to go on your adventure, I have my kindred folk to look after during this time. I was making my way back to the camp from my own travels and stopped for a midday nap and when I awoke Norris was gone. I followed my sixth sense and the trail of hoof prints leading to a boat down at the river and here they were, Norris and Arthur waiting for me, and then you appeared."

"Are your folk in the same time period as me?" asked Alice.

"Yes they are. And my place is with them as we spend our last days together." the Gypsy King said.

"I wish there was a way to stop it." Alice said.

The Gypsy King replied, "My magic is not great enough to stop a comet in its path of destruction. Nor are all of my people's magic combined together. This I know. We are not the ones that can stop it."

"Isn't there anyone who can? There must be something someone can do." said Alice.

"It would take the bravery of great heroes able to conduct great magical feats to save us and I don't know that we have any of those lingering around. I know of only one legend from the old tales who would have been able to do such a thing with any chance of success." the Gypsy King said, "But their story became mere whispers long ago, and now they are only wisps on the wind exiled on the forgotten moorlands. No gypsy speaks their tale anymore, they are long forgotten, but I remember who they are. The Gypsy King remembers them."

"Are they a real person?" Alice asked.

"As real as you are sitting in the boat with me." the Gypsy King smiled.

"What time period were they from, could we find them and bring them here?" she asked, hope stirring in her.

"They are dancing in the mists of time, Alice, as all the legends and heroes tend to do." he said, "And they vanished a long time ago, probably never to return. I would imagine if you choose to seek them, by the time they are found again, it will be too late."

Alice reached out her hand, "Can you pass me the rum please."

The Gypsy King cast off his seriousness and smiled again, "With pleasure, dear Alice, sit back and let the river take you where it flows. But och, this is my stop. Norris! Halt sir, if you please!"

The pony on the bank snorted and stopped walking. Arthur and the Gypsy King pulled the boat towards the edge of the riverbank and the Gypsy King got out.

"It was a pleasure to meet you, Alice. Arthur, go well." he smiled at them.

Arthur shook the Gypsy King's hand and held it clasped with his for a moment, "Thank you, and farewell old friend." he said.

"Yes, farewell," the Gypsy King glanced at Alice, "I'm glad you found her again." he whispered quietly to Arthur.

"As am I." Arthur said.

"You take care of her, Arthur, she's precious cargo."

"I know. I will." Arthur replied.

The Gypsy King jumped up onto Norris' back and with one final wave to them, rode away up the banking and out of view.

Chapter Thirty-Eight

(Present-Day)
Pirate at the End of the Peninsula

"Well, where to now?" asked Alice as Arthur stepped back into the boat.

"I think it's time I visited another old friend." Arthur said, taking the rum bottle from her grasp, "He lives down the river somewhere this way."

"Why do I get the feeling that he lives miles away from here, but this river is going to magically transport us there?" Alice asked.

"As you would be right." Arthur said.

"Oh." replied Alice.

"I had a long chat with my old friend the Gypsy King while you were sleeping, and it made me think of Mad Minn."

"Mad Minn?" Alice asked.

"Yes, Mad Minn. He eats too much Mackerel, all the oils saturate his head, but he's perfectly nice."

"Seems like a good a plan as any." Alice shrugged.

"Then let's go then!" Arthur smiled, "Eric, ready the boat to sail! Onwards crew mates, ever onwards!"

The little boat even seemed to pick up its pace in the water with the announcement that they had somewhere to go. The river turned a corner and became narrower, and over their heads was a great twisted and knotted canopy of alder tree branches from trees on either side that had met in an archway above their heads, like old friends holding each other upright over the water. The river then got thinner and thinner, till it was nothing but a stream, and then it dried up all together. Alice looked overboard, expecting to see a dried up riverbed, but all she saw were fern leaves, which the boat was now resting on, "Is that the end of the river?" Alice asked.

"Oh this looks familiar." Arthur said ignoring her question, "Come on people, disembark, Eric help me secure the boat I don't trust Alice's knot tying skills, don't want it to float away at high tide."

Alice stood up, stretched and stepped out onto the soft bed of ferns then helped Eric climb out of the boat. They were in completely different woodland to the alder woodland that the boat had floated past only a short time ago. This one was tall thin Scots pine, sparsely laid out, with lots of pale green vegetation and fern leaves everywhere. She even spotted a couple of Monkey Puzzle trees hidden amongst the pine woods.

"Right then crew, follow me!" Arthur commanded to Alice and Flat Eric.

"What about the supplies?" Alice asked.

"They'll be fine here, the boats invisible to the unknowing eye, remember?" Arthur said, walking away from them down the hill.

Alice reached into the boat and pulled out her sword, attaching it to her hip and pulled her rucksack onto her back. Eric looked at the tangled pathway of ferns and high grasses and looked at Alice.

"Do you want a piggy back?" she asked.

He nodded and held up his hands for her to lift him up.

"Do you know this Minn man, Eric?" Alice asked him as she lifted him up to sit across the rucksack and started walking to catch up with Arthur. Alice could feel Eric shaking his fuzzy little head, "Hold up Arthur!" she called, quickening her pace down the banking to try to catch up with him.

Arthur, Alice and Flat Eric reached a dirt track of a road some way down the banking, which they began to follow, snaking its way steeply down hill. Alice could hear water lapping upon a shore, she peered out to her right and saw waves of a vast expanse of water, she felt Eric turn his head to look too.

"Wonder where we are." Alice said to Eric on her shoulder, "Are you sure you know the way, Arthur? Have you been to his house before?"

"No, never." replied Arthur, "He moved here some time after we parted company."

"Then how do you know he lives down here?" she asked.

"This house belonged to his father. I knew this Pirate's father as well as him." Arthur said, as if that would help, "He was a remarkable man. And if he was going to have a house, it would be at the very point where the land meets the sea and you can go no further. Of course, the house is hidden from ordinary folks, it's not on any map so we just have to go with my gut instinct, which of course is always right."

Arthur was right of course, despite Alice's protestations that the road was about to run out and vanish into the water. Sure enough, the track curved round its final bend to reveal its secret hidden cottage. The dirt track led down to the front door, but the track also ran parallel to the water's edge which had come into clear view out of the trees. The water lapped at the edges of an old stone wall which supported the track, and it was beginning to crumble and some bricks had fallen into the water. The cottage was very small, Alice guessed it might have two tiny rooms in it and probably no upstairs. It was built onto a craggy rock side, and half of it seemed to float as the waves lapped against its walls. It had a magnificent view of the vast water, at the other side of which Alice could see a fantastic castle, also built onto its own craggy outcrop. She could make out tourist coaches parked outside it, so wondered if she was still in her own time period. She looked up at the sky, and sure enough, spotted that menacing light of the comet above them. Then she wondered why tourists were still visiting and going about their holidays when the world was about to end.

Arthur knocked at the door and the three of them waited with pleasant smiles on their faces in anticipation. There was no answer. Arthur waited a bit longer, so as not to seem impatient, then knocked again. Mad Minn wasn't in. Arthur tried the front door, it was locked, "He's not here." Arthur sighed, resignedly.

"And we don't give up." Alice reminded him. Alice looked around the front door for any sign that the pirate was just away for a while rather than having the house locked up and perhaps gone away for a long time. There was a bottle of white wine chilling in the long grass to the right of the porch.

"I don't think he's gone for long, he's got wine chilling." Alice said, but Arthur didn't hear her, he had disappeared up to the left of the house.

Alice noticed the track did actually continue that way but it was grassed over and overgrown, and there was a small cabin a little further up past the cottage. Alice heard rummaging in the cabin, Eric pointed towards it so she walked to it. Arthur came out of the open door, brandishing a magnificently clean hat, a sailor's white cap on his head.

"What do you think?" Arthur asked with the slightest hint of a smile at the edges of his mouth.

"Not sure." Alice replied, "I thought you were a pirate, not a sailor. Have you turned good all of a sudden sir?"

"Never!" he exclaimed, going back into the shed. A moment later he came back out, wearing a pristine black bowling hat, "How about this one?"

"Now you are trying to tell me you have become a sophisticated gentleman?"

He thought about it, "Never!" he exclaimed, and went back into the shed. A moment later he came back out, donned in a deerstalker, he placed his head in his hand and changed his face to a quizzical expression, "How 'bout this?" he mused.

"Sherlock Holmes?!" Alice laughed, "A Pirate Detective?"

Arthur wandered about the small space around the cottage for a while, in the detective hat, looking for clues as to the whereabouts of his pirate friend, "Well," Arthur said after a while, "I think it's clear he's not here."

"Well you've cracked the case there Arthur Holmes." Alice replied.

"And look!" he cried out, "I have found a bottle of wine cooling in the long grass by the porch!"

"Well done, magnificent detective skills …" Alice exclaimed.

"What?" he said, "Why are you looking at me like that?"

"I'm not looking at you like anything sir." Alice said, smiling, then changing the subject, "Are you going to drink the chaps wine?"

"No, I shall leave it here. Then he will know we've been." he said.

"But it was here when we go here." Alice said, puzzled.

"Well, yes. And he will know we've been and had the good manners not to drink it. He obviously left it for us knowing we were paying him an unexpected visit." Arthur's face was completely serious.

"Or, I could just leave him a note." Alice suggested, "Pop it through his letterbox." Arthur frowned at that suggestion, "As well as leaving the wine." Alice added, "Then he will double-ley know we've been and have had the good manners to wait upon his return to drink his wine."

"Magnificent." he agreed, "Unless it is better manners to drink the wine?"

Alice looked at the wine cooling in the grass then looked at Arthur.

"Okay I'll leave it." he said, walking back into the shed.

Alice rummaged in her bag and found a slip of receipt and a pen, she left a note for the pirate on the back of the receipt saying that they'd been. She didn't know what sort of pirate he was, whether he was like Arthur, not quite of this world, with a whole ream of unknown magical abilities to his disposal, or like herself, with a full fleet of technology to his disposal, so she added her mobile number at the bottom of the note and hoped for the best. Arthur came out of the shed in his pirate hat.

"Right let's go." he declared.

"Where to?" Alice asked.

"Onwards." he announced, marching back down the track, past the cottage and up the road where they had came from.

Alice followed him back up the track, when she stopped to look behind her it was as if there wasn't a road at all, the heavy vegetation had closed up all around it obscuring it from view.

"That figures." Alice said out loud.

"What?" asked Arthur.

"Pirates and their disguises. You have the mist, this pirate has shrubbery at his disposal to hide his tracks."

"And his monkey puzzle trees." Arthur said, pinching Alice's arm.

"Ow, what was that for?"

"I just saw a monkey puzzle tree."

"And why does that involve pinching me?"

"It's what you do when you see one. How do you not know that already, Little Miss I Know Everything?"

"You just made that up that is not a magical rule sir."

Arthur burst out laughing, "Don't talk nonsense."

Alice looked at him.

"Let's go to the pub." Arthur said.

"Is there one round here? How do you know if you've never been here before. Hold that, stupid question, you'll sniff it out with your pirate instincts."

"Exactly. You really don't need to ask as many questions as you do, do you." he said, marching along the track.

Chapter Thirty-Nine

(Present Day)
To the Pub

The dirt track met a tiny single track tarmac road, "Left." Arthur said.

Two hundred yards later there was another junction, "Next left again." said Arthur.

"Well, we have found our way away from there, but I'm not sure we'll ever find our way back again if he does contact us." Alice said.

"Nonsense." said Arthur, "Pirates never get lost. They always know exactly where they are at all times. Built in nautical navigation."

"Yes, yes, it's all very well that you know exactly where you are, and he knows exactly where he is, but *we* may not find *him*."

"Well, he will have to find us then." Arthur replied, "If he knows where he is, then he will have no problem knowing our whereabouts will he?"

Alice was beginning to tire now, Eric patted her shoulder reassuringly, "Can we just stop and wait for him somewhere then?" Alice asked, resignedly.

"That's exactly what we're doing Alice, once we reach the pub we'll wait for him there." Arthur said. They walked in silence for a bit.

"Wait a minute. You've gone quiet." Arthur turned to look at her.

Alice stared straight ahead, not responding lest she be drawn into another ridiculous magical discussion that was actually just 'head for the pub the pirate will be there if he's not at his house.'

"Did we, did we? Did we just have our first argument?" he asked.

"What do you mean our first argument, we argue all the time?"

"Our first argument as a couple." he said.

Alice refused to look at him, she took a deep breath, "We are not a couple." she sighed.

"That's exactly how couples argue." he muttered.

"What?!" Alice asked.

"On a scale of one to ten, where one equals a complete stranger, and ten equals a couple, where would you rate that argument?" he asked.

"We weren't arguing!" Alice shouted.

"Yes we were."

"No, we weren't!"

"Yes we were."

"No, we weren't!!"

"Yes we were. Oh look here's the pub."

Alice was ready to strangle Arthur, luckily he had already stepped into the safety of the doorway where there would be witnesses. He knew Alice was ready to cause him physical harm and was avoiding being in close proximity to her. He waited for her and held the door open for her as they walked in.

"Ladies first." he smiled sweetly at Alice.

She glared back at him, the most murderous glare she could muster.

The young woman behind the bar gave the happy couple strange glances as they entered the room, "Fancy Dress?" she asked in a thick accent which reminded Alice of Vincent.

"No, just two pints please." Arthur replied.

The barmaid looked blankly at him, then shrugged her shoulders. Alice liked her. Something about her demeanour was slightly familiar, though they had never met before. They were the same height, the girl had short glossy raven black hair, one side came down to shape her face, the other side was shaved and had a bright pink stripe running through it. She had her nose pierced and the gemstone glinted in the bar lighting as she turned away from them slightly stroppily, it was amazing how quickly Arthur could annoy other people. Alice smiled apologetically at her as the woman presented the two pints, Alice paid her, seeing as Arthur only carried a bag of gold coins with him, which, for some reason weren't acceptable currency in this establishment.

"Its legal tender." he had tried to explain to the girl.

"You cannot buy a beer here with it." she said in her accented velvety voice.

'Maybe she's a vampire.' Alice thought.

"And you look like the devil's come stain on a nun's dirty knickers." Awful Arthur replied bitterly.

Alice was aghast, but the girl didn't change her facial expression. Alice realised later that she perhaps didn't understand his insult, as she was from Romania and it was lost in translation, thankfully. Arthur was sent outside for a cigarette by Alice, much to his confusion, as to further vex the bar girls frustrations with him, there was a law in this time period which meant he wasn't allowed to smoke inside the pub.

Alice seized the opportunity to talk to the girl behind the bar, trying to smoothe over the creased frown on her face from the ream of Arthur insults. She discovered the girl was a retired trapeze artist from the circus who had decided to move into a Scottish croft and live off the land. Arthur came back in, with a man on his arm, grinning from ear to ear, "I found him!" Arthur announced to Alice and Eric.

Chapter Forty

(Present Day)
A Pirate Walks into a Bar

Alice took the man in, from top to tail, he was tall, with a dark mop of hair, carrying an air of superiority about him, he was wearing a rainbow striped-shirt, only a pirate could pull off a shirt like that, he had a happy face, as if he found his entire life an amusement.

"Aren't you barred?" Alice's new trapeze lady friend growled warningly at the rainbow-shirted pirate.

"Davina, my sweet, sweet barmaid! How are you?" the pirate ignored Alice and Arthur, to move straight into sweet talking the annoyed barmaid. Alice looked at Arthur, he shrugged at her and sat down.

They waited, supping their pints quietly, watching the rainbow-pirate talking to the barmaid, then watched the barmaid's face change, becoming as bright and cheery as the rainbow-pirates, and then he eventually came back to them with a pint in his hand. 'That was his pirate super-power in action', Alice thought to herself, 'Right there'.

"So, you've found me at last!" he said to Arthur, "What a surprise, here I am driving down the road on my way home from a mind-blowing two day party at a castle and there's my old friend Arthur having a cigarette outside my local. I applied the brakes on my car then realised I don't have any brakes, as I lost them in a poker game, so it took me a while to turn round and drive back to the pub."

He turned to Alice and smiled, his eyes twinkled and she felt myself warming to him and smiling right back, "My name is Mad Mackerel Minn." he held out his hand.

"Pleased to meet you Mad Mackerel Minn, I'm Alice." Alice shook his hand.

"Ooo, Alice." he laughed wickedly, "My friends call me Minn. And seeing as you are with old Arthur boy here, any wife of his is a friend of mine."

"I'm not his … " Alice started to correct him, but already his attention had passed to Flat Eric sitting next to Alice, who shook his hand and then picked up his half pint glass carefully in his three-fingered hands to have a much needed drink.

Minn turned back to Arthur and they started talking about Milton, Alice felt Arthur tense up beside her, so she put her hand over his under the table. He took it and held it tightly, Alice watched his face, putting on a brave smile, keeping it together as they talked about what had happened. Minn lost his smile, but the kindness never left his face, he had heard about the loss of his comrade, apparently they had been crewmates in their younger days, the three of them held captive and tortured together, and then made great escapes together, Milton was an older brother to him. Minn leaned over the top of the table, Alice panic grabbed the three pint glasses out of the way just split seconds before they tipped over, and Minn put his arm round Arthur, slightly squashing him.

"I love you, man." Minn said, "If there's anything I can do, just name it."

"Join us in our boat." Arthur said, wiping tears from his eyes, "We can get away from the comet. Alice has a plan that involves getting revenge on the guy that did this to Milton, the crew and the ship."

Minn looked at them, taking in each of their faces, "You're serious?" he asked. Arthur nodded. "Wow Man." Minn said, "This is going to need *a lot* more alcohol. Let's get a carry out and talk back at my place."

Alice grimaced at the bar bill which she was having to cover, damn pirates. Luckily Minn had a car as she didn't fancy walking all the way back to the hidden cottage.

"You'll need to squidge up in the back there, I only have one back seat as I lost the other one in a game of poker." Minn said as they loaded the boxes of booze into the car boot, "My house is pretty hidden, even if I was to show you the way, you'd never find it yourselves." Minn continued.

"We found it earlier today." Alice commented lightly.

"You did? Oh. I'll need to tighten the foliage." Minn said, "Keep the riff-raff out. Can't have damn tourists crawling about the place."

"Are you calling us riff-raff, Minn?" Alice asked him, confused.

He laughed his hearty, cheering laugh that touched her frown and tried its best to turn it upside down, "No, no, not at all. You're pirates, like me."

"Don't listen to her, she's full of nonsense." Arthur said.

"Now now." Minn said, "That's no way to talk about your wife."

Alice opened her mouth to protest but Minn had already jumped into his car.

"I am not your wife." Alice said quietly to Arthur, as she stepped into the back of the car, "Why does everyone keep saying I am?" she added, fastening her seatbelt grumpily. Arthur looked at her and smiled.

"I love you too honey." he said, "Eric will need to sit on your lap, keep him safe."

Alice bit her tongue and concentrated on helping Eric into the back of the car, Arthur was driving her insane, and she was glad of having another human for company.

Chapter Forty-One

(Present Day)
Here's to Friends

When they reached the hidden house at the end of the peninsula again, Alice let Minn and Arthur carry the carry-out into the house and announced she was going to go for a little walk as she needed to get some air and stretch her legs. The men shrugged their shoulders at her, their priorities were over the cans of beer in their arms now.

Alice was unfortunately bursting for a poo. It's not often written about in the history books, but she had been on the road for many hours and did not want to enter Minn's house for the first thing she needed to do was to stink the place out with a long held-in poo. Girls don't poop, you see. She liked to keep that illusion going as long as possible, as do so many people in the story books when writing about women. Women are an enigma, they didn't fart, they certainly didn't poop, they didn't get hairy whiskers on their chins and legs that they had to wax off, it was all part of their feminine mysticism. Alice wasn't sure what happened to women when they broke that unwritten code of sharing the knowledge that they too could brew the worst smelling poops in the world, but she certainly didn't want to be one to do that. But sometimes, when nature calls, it ignores all the rules, Alice had to poop right then.

She took herself up a dirt track, further away into the woodlands and the ferns. She found a nice spot overlooking a tiny inlet, a boat was docked in the water and she hoped there was no one settling in for the night there, choosing to look out their round windows at that moment only to see a girl pulling her pants down to relieve herself. It was quite a good view, across the water. The air was still, the water making lovely lapping noises upon the shore. She felt a bite on her bum and knew a midge or two had managed to find her private nakedness within seconds of her pulling her pants down.

And the relief afterwards was immense. Probably half of the frustration and anger she had thrown at Arthur had been because she had held in a poop for hours on the rowing boat. She pulled up her pants, scratching the midges away, hoping no ticks had crawled into her trousers ready to latch onto her inner crevices later. She walked back down the dirt track and heard Arthur's voice calling her name.

"Where have you been I've been worried sick about you." he shouted angrily.

"I've been for a walk, that's all. I told you where I was going." Alice said.

"No you didn't. You said you were getting a bit of air and when I came out for a cigarette you were gone! I've been shouting and shouting for you." he said. He looked genuinely concerned.

"I'm sorry. I didn't think I'd been gone for long."

"Don't go off like that again." he said, "Please."

"I wont." Alice said reassuringly, and secretly wondered how she could ever take a private poop again if she wasn't allowed to wander off into the woods herself anymore, "I'm going to go in for a drink. Midges are getting me."

"Okay, I'll be in once I've finished my cigarette." Arthur said.

Alice walked into Minn's house for the first time. The porch had a red naval jacket hanging up on old cast iron hooks, and old empty green bottles stacked in a layer of dust. She walked through to the hall and looked to the right, the room she could see there had no flooring, so she couldn't go in there. The room to the left was lit by candlelight, she wandered slowly through, Minn was crouching over a portable gas heater, trying to light it, Alice noted the big cast iron stove behind him and to the right of that was a very thin and very steep wooden staircase.

"Hello." Alice said. Minn glanced up, "Might I get a rum please?" Alice asked.

"Yes, it's in the kitchen."

"Where's that please?"

"Just behind you."

Alice turned in the candlelight to see a sink just behind her, in an alcove in the wall. The house was tiny. Pans filled the sink, covered in mouldy food and fat globules, she saw the carry-out bags placed upon a little table and was glad to have accidentally acquired her pint glass out of the pub. She opened the rum bottle and poured some in.

"Can't light the stove." Minn said, "Chimney's blocked."

"Ah." Alice said, taking a sip of the rum. It beautifully burned her throat, she felt like she had been waiting for that first burn for hours and hours, it glowed with satisfaction in her tummy.

"Not got running water either, so if you need to use the loo, you need to just go outside." Minn added, "It's all a bit of a work in progress at the minute."

Alice looked around at the room, paint peeling off the walls, the smell of years of dust in the air, "Its nice." she said, politely.

"It's a bit of a burden." Minn said, "I can't fix a house."

Alice looked at him, "And I can't fix a broken pirate ship or save the world either, but sometimes we are given things that we do not ask for in life." she didn't know where that comment had come from.

Minn finally paid Alice some proper attention, he looked at her, taking her in and tried to assess her with his gaze, "Do you play guitar?" he asked.

Alice shook her head.

"Alice is a great singer." Arthur said, coming into the room at that moment.

"No I'm not." Alice said.

"Minn plays guitar." Arthur told her. Minn stood up and picked up a guitar, he began to play, and finally Alice felt the troubles of the day begin to slip away.

The hours passed and the candles had burned almost to their wicks when the four decided it was time to sleep. Minn said he had beds upstairs, so they made their way up there. Alice had to use her hands and go up the stairs almost like a step ladder, the steps were so steep. There were two half height doors on either side of the staircase, as the roofline was slanted steeply, there wasn't room to stand upright.

"I'm afraid that room is unusable so we'll all have to share this one for the night." Minn said, walking into the room on the left. It had two single mattresses on the floor, "If we push these together there'll be room for us all."

Minn and Arthur moved the mattresses and lay down with a gap between them. Alice sighed and took her place between them, trying her best not to lie on the gap between the two mattresses, and Eric clamboured next to her. Minn pulled some blankets over them all. Alice was asleep within seconds, though she woke up some time during the night as she was getting kicked by Arthur, who was having a bad dream and was lashing out. Minn was snoring on the other side of her. She got a kick in her stomach but caught Arthur's fist as it came towards her face just in time.

"Arthur! she whispered, trying to wake him up out of the nightmare. He didn't hear her, stuck in the dream he was still kicking at her legs. "Arthur!" no response.

She needed to go for a wee anyway, so she got up, shuffled past the sleeping boys and clambered awkwardly down the stairs. The morning outside was still enveloped sleepily in those beautiful secretive moments before dawn, mist was swirling all around her, she found a comfort in its presence, as if it was naturally part of being with the pirates. She wandered up the grassy track, listening to the first of the birds beginning to serenade her with their singing.

On the way back down Alice found a pair of binoculars lying on the ground in the woodlands, she picked them up and took them back to the house with her, climbing back up the steep staircase. Arthur was sleeping soundly, she lay back down between them all, though it took her a good hour or so to get back to sleep as a thousand thoughts span dizzyingly round her head like a thousand marbles pinging around all at once on a pinball machine.

Alice woke up to the smell of bacon sizzling from downstairs and Arthur's arm around her waist, Minn was still fast asleep on the other side of her, she peeled Arthur's arm off her and went back downstairs where Eric waved a fish slice as a good morning at her, "Morning Eric, breakfast smells good." she smiled.

He deftly flicked some bacon into a roll and handed it to her without a plate, "Thanks." she said, "No Ketchup?"

Eric shook his head and waved his hand around the space he had to work in, as all professional passionate chefs would do when asked if they have ketchup in a kitchen with no working sink, no cupboards and no fridge.

"Point taken." Alice said, and with her mouth full of roll she added, "Still tastes great though. Missed your cooking." Eric smiled at her, "Eric, I've lived on my own for six years and still haven't gotten any better at cooking. I even tried going to evening classes." He raised his eyebrows, "Yes, okay I went to the taster session as they were offering free tasters then I forgot to sign up for it, but I tried. I'm never going to be a chef, Eric."

Eric shook his head and waggled the fish slice at her.

"I know, never say never, but I don't think God gave me cooking genes" she replied, taking another bite of her roll, "Just a pair of good old denim ones."

Eric smiled a big smile at her comment and handed her a hot mug of coffee to go with her roll.

"You're amazing, thank you." Alice managed to mumble through her mouthful of roll.

Arthur came down the stairs, followed by Minn, "That smells amazing, where did you find the bacon, I don't have any here, I just go out and catch fresh mackerel when I want to eat." Minn asked.

Alice looked at her bun like it was about to sprout legs and run away. Eric gestured to a bag on the floor, which Alice recognised as being from her house, Eric must have packed his own supplies from her cupboards, including the buns. Eric flicked some more bacon onto a bun and passed it to Minn.

"Great, thanks man." Minn said, "So Arthur, when do we set sail on this boat of yours to avenge the death of your brother?"

"Oh, have we decided we're doing that?" Arthur asked, clearing his throat.

"I think it's a great idea, let's go out with a bang!" Minn said, taking the biggest bite of bun Alice had ever seen a man take.

"The world isn't going to end in that time period." Arthur started to explain.

"We all have to die at some point." Minn said, "And I think I'd like to go out fighting."

"I have tried to explain this to Alice, if you come with me on the boat, back in time, then you won't die. The comet will hit here and not there and you won't die."

"Yes, but we would die if we were here, so I'd like to go and get this man, De Soulis, while I have a breath left in my body." Minn chewed his food looking expectantly at Arthur.

Eric handed Arthur a coffee, "Yes, thanks Eric, I think I need that." Arthur said, "These two are loco."

"Are we taking my car or the row boat?" Minn asked.

"Well we kind of need to go back in time and only the rowboat can really do that." Arthur said.

"Could the boat take the car back in time if we tied the boat onto the car roof? It's a bit comfier in the car." Alice asked.

"What are you going to do with a car in the thirteen hundreds, Alice?" Arthur scowled.

Alice chewed thoughtfully on her roll, "I dunno, but theoretically if we could take a car back in time, we could just take a tank instead and just blow De Soulis up."

"What a great idea! But where are you going to acquire a tank from?" Minn asked.

"It's no good anyway, a tank would sink the boat." Arthur said.

"Bad idea then." Alice said.

"How do we know the boat can take us back to De Soulis' time period?" Minn asked.

"Because it brought me here to Alice, and you just have to trust me and not ask complicated questions." Arthur offered as an explanation.

"Questions like Alice here asking if we can take a tank back in time?" Minn replied.

"Well no, but, oh, let's get going then, no time like right now." Arthur took a deep breath, "There's no point standing round here asking whether we can or can't take a tank in a row boat, we simply haven't got a tank, it wouldn't fit in the boat anyway, and I'm beginning to get uneasy thinking that a comet is edging closer to us the whole time, and I'm not willing to waste any more of my precious time in this time period trying to find a tank that none of us can even drive."

"Agreed." said Minn, "Though how hard can it actually be to drive a tank?"

"We're not getting a tank!" Arthur groaned.

Chapter Forty-Two

(Present Day)
Boat on the Water

Arthur, Alice and Eric waited outside while Minn packed up some belongings, pulled on the long red admirals coat in the hallway and locked up his house. "Two seconds, guys." he said, jogging up to the cabin and going in, he came out wearing a small black triangular hat and brandishing a sword. "This sword was my dad's." he said, "I never thought I'd get the chance to use it."

"Impressive." Arthur said.

Alice helped Eric onto her back and they walked up the track and into the woodlands, to the spot where the boat was tied, Arthur and Alice stopped walking, and Minn stopped behind them.

"Why've we stopped guys?" Minn asked, pulling a small package wrapped in tin foil out of his pocket.

"To get into the boat." Arthur explained.

"Great, where's the boat?" Minn asked, unwrapping the tin foil to reveal flakes of fish. "It's Mackerel. Want some?" he offered the package to Alice, she shook her head.

"Where's the boat man?" Minn asked Arthur.

"Right in front of you." Arthur replied.

"Will it work here or will we need to set it on water again?" Alice asked.

"I think it will need to go on the water." Arthur replied, "Minn, help me lift the boat and carry it down to your jetty?"

"What boat, Arthur there isn't a boat here." Minn replied.

"Okay, Minn, you're going to have to trust me. I need you to hold your hands out, like this, while I pass you part of the boat, and you will have to help me carry an invisible boat down to the jetty, okay?"

Minn laughed and put his tin foil wrapped mackerel back in his pocket, "Okay man." he said, holding out his hands in front of him.

"Okay, are you ready? I'm going to lift it and put it into your hands." Arthur said.

"Yeah man." Minn said.

Arthur lifted the boat, clearly visible to Alice and placed the front of it into Minn's hands, which dropped instantly with the weight of the boat, "Woah, what the?" Minn said, "It's actually invisible?"

"Hopefully just for a short while to you." Arthur said, "Once it's on the water and you're sitting in it, I think you should be able to see it."

They once again walked down to the hidden cottage, where at the jetty Arthur and Minn waded ankle deep into the water and Minn laughed as he set the invisible rowboat down into the water, "In you get Alice, ladies first, into the invisible boat." he laughed. Alice held onto Arthur's arm and stepped into the boat, sitting down, which to Minn looked like she was sitting in thin air.

"Right Minn, you next and I'll push off." said Arthur. Minn raised his leg in the air to step into the invisible boat, "A little to the left Minn." Arthur said. Minn moved his leg which was suspended in the air to the left, hopping a little in the water as he did so.

"There." Arthur said.

Minn lowered his foot and hit solid surface, "Wow." he said, trying to figure out how to get the rest of him into the invisible boat.

"Can you see it yet?" Alice asked.

"Not at all." laughed Minn, "It's insane."

"How strange." muttered Arthur as he pushed off from the jetty.

"I can see the fish from here swimming beneath us!" Minn laughed, "Imagine how many fish I could catch if I had a boat like this, they'd never see me coming!"

"Alice have we got any rum left on board this vessel?" Arthur asked, settling into his seat in front of Minn.

"Yes, a quarter of a bottle left." she didn't tell him about the other ones she had stashed away.

"If you please." he gestured for it, she passed him the bottle and he held it up in the air.

"To the good ship Revenge and all who sail on her." he said, taking a gulp, passing the bottle to Minn.

"To the unknown!" Minn said, taking a gulp and passing it to Eric, who held it up in the air, then gestured emphatically, took a gulp and handed it to Alice who said,

"To friendship!"

"That's lame." Arthur said.

"Yes, that's lame Alice." Minn laughed.

"Screw you both then." Alice retorted, taking a second drink from the rum bottle.

The ship floated on the water, Alice looked across at the tourists wandering around the castle on the other side of the sea-loch, she could see the flashes from their cameras going off.

"Man I can't get used to this I still can't see the boat guys." Minn said a few moments later, "Do you think the tourists can see us floating above the water with no boat?"

"They can't see us, we are invisible to them." Arthur said confidently.

"Just why are the tourists still going about the castle and not flying home to their loved ones?" Alice asked.

"Maybe they just want to finish their holiday to Scotland before they die." Minn suggested, laughing a little too wickedly, "They have a little under two weeks, they have time to fly home yet, maybe it's a once in a lifetime thing for them, coming here."

"Well it is now, literally." Arthur said, "Once in a lifetime. Speaking of which, why are we still here and not travelling through the mist back in time, hmm?" he directed the question at Alice.

"You say this like it's my fault." Alice said.

"Well, you're not rowing, are you?" he replied.

Alice growled and picked up the oars, heaving them into the loch water and beginning to row. As she did so, the mist instantly swirled up from the oar paddles, as if it had just been waiting that whole time for her to begin to row, it snaked and spiralled up the oar shafts and drifted round the boat.

"That's more like it." Arthur said.

"Oh! I can see the boat now!" exclaimed Minn, "Bye-bye little fishies."

Alice rowed and rowed, feeling a tingling of magic in the air all around her. She felt the pressure on the water against the oars change, and then the worst thing that could have happened, happened. There was a tug on one of the oars from the water as she was trying to lift it out of the water, something pulled on the oar again, and the oar fell out of her grasp.

"The oar!" Alice exclaimed, standing up and trying to reach for the oar in the misty murky water.

"Alice, be careful!" Arthur said, standing up and leaning to try to reach for her, to catch her as he could almost pre-empt what was happening in front of his eyes.

But he was too late, Alice was reaching backwards and then she was falling out of the boat and down into the water. She screamed briefly, there was a splash as she landed in the water, her hands reaching up to them from the water, and then, Alice was gone.

Chapter Forty-Three

(Back in Time)
Of Monks and Men

Alice fell through the water, holding her breath with her eyes closed, it was cold, so cold, and she was falling deeper and deeper into the depths of a deep, dense dark ocean. Then she felt air upon her skin. but it was still dark. She opened her eyes, moving her hands around her to get her bearings, her hands lifted out of a shallow water, she felt pebbles beneath her body, and she realised she was now lying in a stream. She struggled to raise herself up from the water.

"Where on earth have you just appeared from? The depths of hell no less! Sire we have a witch, a witch here I tell you!" she heard a voice over by her left hand side shouting in panic.

Alice came to her senses quickly enough to know she had to start running lest she was captured and locked in a tower or worse, with no pirate ship to come and rescue her this time. She struggled to her feet, which were heavy in her wet shoes, and ran, splashing out of the stream and up a steep banking. There were voices coming after her, trying to hunt her down, she could hear them, at least four men. She ran and ran across a field and towards a cluster of lights she could see in a dusky haze, sprinting as fast as her legs could carry her.

As she ran closer to the building she realised there was a large tall wall all around it. The voices chasing her were growing closer now, threatening to kill her once they caught her, to string her up on the nearest tree and spill her guts out. She ran along the wall, hoping against hope that she would find the entranceway. A pair of large doors loomed up towards her. There was a giant door knocker on the doorway, ornate brass, the shape of a human face with the knocker in its mouth. Alice grabbed the big door knocker and hit it against the door three times, "Help me, please, let me in!" she cried out.

There was a stir in the air around the door and it swung open. No one was on the other side to greet Alice as she dived through the giant door, so she shut it quickly behind her. She saw a large block of wood, which was the bolt lock and lifted the wood onto big holding hooks over the door she had just closed, she leaned against the door, heaving for breath, at least for the time being she was safe.

Alice turned around to take in her surroundings and found herself in the grounds of an abbey which was a small distance away from her and the entrance gate. Directly in front of her was a small grassy moated bridge, which she crossed to reach the main buildings of the abbey. It was eerily quiet, she turned her head but could not hear her pursuers outside the door, none the less, she quickened her pace, briskly walking around to the right, through an archway and up some steps. Through a closed door she could make out the sound of monks in prayer, a melody in their voices as they chanted their latin words, she kept walking, wary of meeting anyone now in this strange place. Alice wandered through a garden, a square shaped lawn with square segments filled with herbs she could not identify. She caught her breath back and inhaled the scents, some she knew, like juniper and lavender others were unfamiliar.

Alice walked through the garden and out an archway which she realised was an enclosed graveyard within the tall wall. She chose a well hidden spot and sat down to rest her aching legs behind a large gravestone with an ornate carving of a robed lady watching over her. Her feet were aching and her muscles burned. Her eyes were heavy, she was weary and desperate for sleep. She closed her eyes only for a moment, just to rest them, and drifted into unconsciousness.

When she awoke it was completely dark, and she had been covered with a thick rough woollen blanket. There were lights on in the abbey, and although the archway door back from the graveyard through to the abbey was now closed, she could see that it had been left slightly ajar as light shone through it. She stood up, sore and and aching, rolling the blanket up and limped over to the door, she must have pulled something on that sprint out of the stream.

She pulled it open and closed it fully behind her as quietly as she could. There was a single candle burning in an alcove near the door, which revealed the beginning of a set of stairs which she hadn't seen on her way through earlier, and there was darkness everywhere else in the abbey. Whoever had put the blanket over her had left the candle for her as well. She went gingerly up the stairs, feeling every knee bend with weary muscles. The top hallway opened onto a corridor with doorways, the third doorway along had its door open, and it led to a chamber filled with long tables and benches. The tables were all clear except for one place setting, where there was a plate of bread, cheeses and a bowl of soup. Alice sat down and tested the soup, which now only contained a hint of warmth. She tore the bread, placing slices of cheese on top of it with her fingers and hungrily eating the lot, her starving senses overwhelmed with the taste of the simple fresh meal. She finished and yawned, rubbing her neck which was still aching from falling asleep against the hard slab of stone outside.

Alice left the room and wandered further along the corridor. A candle lit the way to one more set of stairs and another corridor, with the fourth door being an open door of a small chamber containing a small single bed with another rough blanket on it. She shut the door and collapsed on the bed. It was only marginally softer than the stone slab she had fallen asleep on outside. She took her rolled up blanket and tried to use that as a pillow, but it made her face itch. She got up and rolled it out flat beneath her for an extra layer of padding, using just the one blanket for covering, but that was no better and the longer she lay there the colder she became. She gave up, got under the two blankets, wrapping them tightly round her body and used her arm for a pillow. Exhausted she finally fell asleep.

Alice awoke with a start, her eyes adjusting to the candle light. She didn't know what time it was, she could hear the noise of people shuffling along the corridor outside the chamber doorway, footsteps with a steady pace. Not a panicked pace, so she didn't have to jump into fight mode. It was still pitch black of the middle of the night outside. She lay her head back down to sleep, taking a while to get even remotely comfortable again, wrapping herself up like a cocoon in the two blankets to try and regain the warm she had lost by waking up. Then the chanting started up, and the sound of praying.

"For heaven's sake, it's the middle of the flaming night." Alice muttered ever so quietly to herself, "What are they doing praying at this time?" she closed her eyes again.

Then it was daybreak, the sun came beating into her window, hitting her face, the heat waking her up. She rose, and splashed her face in the basin of water which was on a wooden stool by the narrow bed. Down the stairs she went into the dining room, hearing voices there, echoing up the staircase.

Two men were sitting at one table, and five monks were silently eating on the other. She noticed place settings had been laid out next to the two men and not the monks, so she obliged and took her place next to the men.

"And who might ye be?" The man who spoke to her was a middle-aged man.

Alice noticed he had dark hair, he was unshaven with a dark complexion.

"I am Alice." she replied.

"*Thee* Alice?" he asked.

"No, just an Alice of no consequence." she said slightly miserably.

"Ah." The man said, "We are all waiting and wondering about *thee* Alice. Shame you are not her, I would have liked to have said to my wife when I return home that I had met the Actual Alice."

"Oh are you married?" Alice asked politely to make conversation.

"No, but I will find myself a wife at some point, and have lots of children, once it is safe for me to leave this place." he said, squinting his eyes at her, "Might ye be taken?"

"Yes, yes I am." she lied, politely and quickly.

"Ah. So you are not the Alice of the legends?"

"No, I'm not, sorry."

"Shame, I would have liked to have had her as my wife." he smiled, "A fierce spirit such as hers, I'd be the one to tame her! Hah hah."

The other man spoke to her, "My name is John, John Balliol, and this is my companion of many a year, Malcolm Wallace, though he is currently claiming sanctuary within these walls for crimes against the state, much like yourself. Please, do have some breakfast."

"Thank you sir, I shall eat, for I am quite hungry." Alice said.

"Have you travelled very far?" John asked.

"You might say that." Alice said, trying to saw a dainty lump of ham off a large chunk of meat on her plate. She gave up, picked up the large chunk and attacked it with her hands and teeth. The ham was an amazing flavour, rich, strong and meaty, she had never tasted ham like it, those monks knew how to cook.

"You like it?" John asked, just as Alice had taken a mouthful of food.

She smiled apologetically and gestured at her mouthful of food, Malcolm laughed into his drinking chalice, John smiled politely and continued to talk, to allow her a chance to eat.

"The pigs are hand reared in the orchard, feasting on the apples that fall from the trees, as well as the food scraps. They are then spit roasted, along with the apples. It really is rather good don't you think?" She nodded in acknowledgement, her mouth still full of food.

A beautiful lady entered the dining room, a heavenly sort of human who floated on the air rather than walked anywhere, this lady had the ability of her every movement being perceived in slow motion. Her skin was flawless, ivory light radiance, contrasting with her dark hair, which was tied back and knotted in a celtic plait. Her gown was a rich and vibrant red, with golden flowers and intricate details, though it didn't pouffe out like Alice expected a lady's dress of an unknown historical era to do, it was neat, lightweight and hugged her figure. Alice could make out beautiful red shoes peeping from the slightly raised hemline.

"Ah, Dervorgilla, my sweet angel!" John rose to his feet and kissed the Lady Dervorgilla on both cheeks, took her hands in his and gazed adoringly into her face.

"My beloved husband." Dervorgilla replied. Her voice was like new born kittens caressing the air with the sweet sound of their first plaintive mews. Alice chewed as quickly as she could.

"This is Alice, my sweet." John said as an introduction, "She arrived last night."

Dervorgilla took in the ragged clothes, the crumpled, unkempt hair and the look of startled rabbit, complete with stuffed cheeks, on Alice's face, and the layer of ground in dirt covering her skin. Alice smiled, trying her best to look pleasant and cheerful with a mouth full of ham. She wiped her hand on her filthy top, realising it was still slightly damp, and held out her hand, "Nice to meet you m'lady." She realised she was offering a mud-splattered hand to the beautiful immaculate lady and regretted it instantly.

Dervorgilla took Alice's mud-covered meat-greasy hand without hesitation and held it, Dervorgilla's hand was soft, gentle and warm. "It is an honour to meet a hero as brave as yourself, Alice." Dervorgilla said, smiling an elegant smile full of grace and beauty.

"She says she's not *thee* Alice, my love." John said.

"You don't think you're thee Alice?" Dervorgilla asked her, the smile playing at the edges of her mouth, like newborn kittens with their first ball of wool.

By now, Alice's mouth was finally void of food, "No, sorry. I've been asked that many times, and I'm definitely not. No legend with me, I'm just plain old Alice." she smiled, the sound of her own voice jarred coarsely on her ears, not kitten-like at all, more like a hacking old scabby hyena hiding at the back of a zoo pen.

"Well it is still a pleasure to meet you even when you're not quite sure of who you are just now." Dervorgilla purred, still smiling with some sort of knowledgeable wisdom about herself.

"Ladies, if you will excuse us?" John said, "Malcolm and myself have business matters to discuss that are most pressing."

"Do consider my marriage proposal over breakfast." Malcolm said cheerily to Alice.

The two men rose from the table and walked away. Dervorgilla sat at the table and prepared herself some breakfast. The girls made small talk over breakfast, growing quite close quite quickly. Alice liked Dervorgilla, there was something familiar, and warming about her., Alice discovered that Dervorgilla was the same age as her, and that John was considerably older.

"I was thirteen when we were married. He is my husband, and I love him." Dervorgilla revealed.

Alice stopped in her tracks, the words sinking in, as usual with Alice, words spoken to her took a few moments to decipher, even when spoken in plain English. "Thirteen? But you were just a child."

Dervorgilla smiled, "Yes, I was very young. I was lucky that my husband was a good man, and respected me. We did not consummate the marriage until I was fifteen years of age. A lot of the women I know are not so lucky."

Alice put her slice of pie down, feeling a wave of nausea passing over her.

"It is the way of things here, Alice. Perhaps it will change one day, but our families need to trade us off as we come with lands and titles, to the most advantageous political adversary."

"You poor things." Alice said.

"It is not so bad." Dervorgilla smiled, "My husband is kind to me. I am loved, and I am not just a token wife, so I have a fulfilling life with him. Is it so very different for you?"

"Well, I have worked since I was fifteen, my last job was in this thing called an office, which was a bit dull and a bit depressing. I had to ask people for money that they owed the company. Then, one day, a pirate ship appeared in my garden and I went on adventures with them! Sword fighting, and everything, it was fantastic! But they sent me back home and life became even more dull and boring. Then Arthur reappeared."

"Who's Arthur?" Dervorgilla asked.

"He is a pirate." Alice preened proudly, "Of the finest calibre."

"I see."

"He was a shadow of who I knew as he'd just lost his brother, the time traveling pirate ship and the whole crew to a really nasty man, only now, I've lost him again and I've ended up stranded here with no real way of finding them again."

"It is interesting that you think of yourself as stranded, perhaps you have been sent here to learn something." Dervorgilla suggested.

"I wonder who designed life to be like school." Alice replied, "We are never done with learning. Can't life just be fun and light-hearted instead of all these lessons?"

"To help you grow to who you need to become Alice, your life will be full of lessons." Dervorgilla smiled, "For example, I see that you have a sword affixed to your hip, so you have learned how to use a sword, which means now you can defend yourself. And if you didn't know that, then someone would kill you, perhaps before you can fulfill some purpose."

"A purpose?"

"Yes. I believe in you, Alice. God has sent you here, to us, for a purpose and you are on this path for a reason. I am extremely privileged to have met you."

"I think you're getting me confused with the other Alice again." Alice said.

"Only time will tell me that." Dervorgilla said mysteriously, "If we knew everything about ourselves and what we were going to do, before we have done them, then wouldn't it spoil all of the adventures along the way?

You may as well have stayed in your office and not done anything at all. But then, if you had, none of it would happen. What you have called lessons, you are also able to refer to as adventures."

"You've lost me." Alice said.

"My apologies. Let us take a walk in the grounds and I will try and help you find yourself again." Dervorgilla suggested, rising from the table. Alice rose with her and they made their way outside to the herb garden, "Do you mind if I remove my shoes?" Dervorgilla asked, "I find it so very refreshing to feel the grass beneath my toes."

"I think I'll take mine off too. Alice smiled, remembering Milton's aversion to shoes, the times when he would strut about the Sea Rose in bare feet, and she wondered if all the best people preferred to have no shoes on.

Chapter Forty-Four

(Back in Time)
Sack Races and Such

Alice listened to the birds and the air of calmness about them, she felt the cool grass between her toes and relished it, then all of a sudden, she missed Arthur, lost somewhere on the sea in the rowboat. "Are you in love, Alice?" Dervorgilla asked, noticing the change in Alice's expression.

Alice paused, "What is love?" she diverted the question away from herself, "I look at you, and it is obvious that you love your John. Yet you didn't choose to marry him. I used to think love was about finding a man, falling head over heels as soon as we made eye contact, and just knowing he was the one for you, but you are the most in love couple I have ever seen."

"I am very blessed." Dervorgilla replied, "I believe God brought John and I together so that we could do great things."

"You have very strong beliefs." Alice said, "You are so sure of what you say. I have trouble even making the simplest decisions, I'm so indecisive, yet you have this inner knowing about everything."

"I feel it in my heart. When it is right, it feels right, and I am happier for it. You must have more faith in yourself, be strong and stick to those feelings. Follow them down whatever path they lead. You will be helped and guided along the way."

"But not everyone seems guided."

"Do not worry about them. You are not in control of their destiny, you must follow your own path."

Alice thought for a moment, "Are you able to walk away from it? Turn your back and do something else instead?"

"Well, Alice, you can stop trying to control everything, you can let go of it, or you can be dragged. I'd sooner follow my path than be dragged backwards along it and find myself getting lost along the way as a result. Why keep battling with yourself? You are who you are. You will not be lost when you are fulfilling your soul's' purpose. And you know when you have it right, as you will shine for it. It will radiate out of you and inspire others to do the same. I would say follow your heart, it knows what is best for you."

"Thank you." Alice said, "I don't come from this time period, I guess I am feeling completely lost."

"I know." Dervorgilla said, laughing a little, "I gathered that when you told me about the time travelling pirate ship and 'this thing called an office'."

"Well, where I'm from, there's a comet appeared in the sky, and it's on a direct collision course for earth and it is going to wipe everyone out. I got on the rowing boat with Arthur, and I left."

"You mean that comet up there?" Dervorgilla asked, pointing at the sky. Alice looked up and gasped, her eyes focussing on the bright light in the sky above them.

"How can it be here as well?" she asked incredulously.

"I do not know." Dervorgilla said, "The monks spotted it and said it shouldn't be there."

"Oh my God, sorry Dervorgilla, I didn't mean to say that, I mean, oh my gosh, I can't believe it's here as well, how is that even possible?" Alice sunk to her knees in the lush grass, "If it's here too, is it everywhere? In every time period?"

"It could be." Dervorgilla said thoughtfully, "This time travelling ship that you mention, was it destroyed?"

"No, Arthur said the man had his army dismantle it and they were taking it into his castle."

"Then from that, I would understand that this man has perhaps harnessed the magic of the ship and perhaps he has something to do with a comet that can transcend time." Dervorgilla said, bending down to Alice, and reaching for her hand. Alice looked into her new friends eyes.

"We're all doomed." Alice murmoured.

"No, Alice, we are not." Dervorgilla smiled with that same knowing look about her, "I prayed to my God last night when the monks told us about that comet in the sky, I prayed for him to send a sign that he would save us. And you appeared that very night, knocking on our very door. You are going to save us Alice."

"Erm, no, definitely not me." Alice replied.

"Follow your path Alice." Dervorgilla said, helping Alice back to her feet, "And if it's really not for you, if it makes you that unhappy? I'm sure the world would let you go, back to your boring job, and it would try to find another way to save itself. But it will try its best to convince you as it thinks you're the one to save us all. Or would you rather be standing with the rest of us waiting to die when the comet comes, wondering, 'but what if I'd tried'?"

"But I'm lost, so lost." Alice said, sadly.

"I think, perhaps, you are exactly where you need to be." Dervorgilla replied, "Come, back inside, you need a bath and a change of clothes."

Dervorgilla was fascinating, she spoke without pre-judgement, she just followed her own heart and answered Alice with what she felt needed to be said. Alice looked at her as they walked back inside the abbey buildings, this lady, the same age as her, who was so sure of herself, carrying an air of knowledge and certainty about her, and she admired her for it.

"I would love to be as strong as you." Alice said to her.

Dervorgilla laughed, "I am so glad to have met you Alice, you make me laugh. You, as strong as me! Why, it is the opposite way round! I wish I were as strong as Alice!"

Alice was still feeling quite lost and uncertain, so said nothing.

"We shall give you some new clothes, ones that are more in keeping with ladies in this area, to help you on your way. You shall have one of my gowns! I know they shall fit you as you are so similar to me!" Dervorgilla took Alice's hand.

Alice had felt like a big cumbersome heifer around Dervorgilla, so didn't know how she was able to be the same size as her. Dervorgilla led Alice up the stairs to her own bed chamber, where a serving maid waiting outside opened the door for them.

"Please wait outside Marabella." Dervorgilla asked.

The maid curtseyed and the two friends stepped inside the room. Dervorgilla walked over to a trunk, which she opened and rummaged about in, pulling out a light green gown and held it out for Alice.

"Thats too much, really, I can't." Alice said, aware that each individual stitch on Dervorgilla exquisite gown had been hand sewn, and there was a great many stitches, probably sewn in candlelight by pixies, and spun with the silken threads from silk worms who lived in only one place in the deepest darkest reaches of underground caverns in the outer hemisphere, accessible only by dragons.

"It is nothing. It will help you on your way. You shall have a dress and you will say 'thank you Dervorgilla'." Dervorgilla ordered.

"Thank you Dervorgilla." Alice repeated.

Dervorgilla smiled, " I believe I have been given my privileged position so that I can help make people's lives a little easier. That is why I am building my abbeys, to make sure my people get an education, and food in the winter. My monks will look after them."

"*Your* Abbeys?" Alice asked.

"Yes. My John prefers to talk of politics with his colleagues and friends, so this gives me something to do while he is busy. He understands this is my purpose and supports me in this. We will raise our family together in a few years time, and neither of us will have much time to do the things we enjoy, like we can now. Though hopefully we will strike the right balance and raise our children well so that they too can care for their people."

"You are so kind." Alice said.

"Well, I have had a lot of thinking time. I don't work, so I have done a lot of studying, and this is the most comforting role for me."

"You still have fun though, right? I mean, your life isn't entirely serious all the time, is it?" Alice asked.

Dervorgilla thought and said, "I am calm, yes, and happy, but you have certainly lifted my heart by coming here."

"Sack races!" Alice said, "Let's do sack races this afternoon. Us, John, Malcolm and all the Monks."

"What are 'sack races'?"

"We step inside sacks, or maybe those wooly blankets will do, and jump to the finish line to see who wins."

"Won't people fall over?"

"Yes, that's part of the fun."

"The monks will not do it, they have strict times for their prayers and rituals."

"Didn't you say they were *your* monks?" Alice smiled at Dervorgilla mischievously, and a light flickered across the Lady's face, like a kitten discovering its first Christmas tree.

So, that afternoon, Lord John Balliol, Lady Dervorgilla of Galloway, Malcolm Wallace and the Cistercian Monks of the as yet un-named abbey spent the afternoon running about in hessian sacks. Dervorgilla and Alice had tied their dresses up for the occasion and though the Monks had originally agreed to play only if they held onto a vow of silence, Alice's antics in trying to teach them how to race in sacks broke them into peals of laughter which repeatedly burst out of them for the rest of the afternoon.

They laughed and laughed, playing more games that Alice could remember from her childhood, hopscotch, the three-legged race, dooking for apples and more. They broke for a late supper in the dining hall, freshly baked doughy bread, cheeses, and meats. It was delicious.

"This has been such fun!" Dervorgilla said.

Alice's heart lifted and she took it as a sign that she had done the right thing, Dervorgilla had grown up too quickly.

John smiled, "You are an entertainment, Alice, thank you for returning the smile to my Dervorgilla's beautiful face."

"Ah Alice, how I wish you would marry me. We would make a beautiful son together, and he would be called William, for it is a most noble name." Malcolm sighed wistfully at her.

Alice's thought process was clearly visible at that moment, working its way from both of her ears, round her already troubled little mind, and at the exact moment her thoughts made contact and the electric currents connected, Alice dropped her drink all over the floor, "William? You would call your son William?" she questioned Malcolm.

"Yes. William Wallace." Malcolm squinted at her, "It is a good name, is it not. If you are not happy with it we can choose another, as my wife I would allow you that much."

Alice paled.

"What is it Alice?" Dervorgilla asked her.

"Wow." Alice said looking at her plate shaking her head with amazement, "Wow. You're William Wallace's father?"

"Well, he hasn't been born yet." Malcolm replied quizzically bemused.

"I know him. I mean, I know of him. William Wallace saves Scotland, he's one of the greatest heroes to have ever lived." Alice muttered into her chin, realising she was going to sound completely mad to the people around her.

John and Malcolm looked at each other. Dervorgilla said nothing, keeping her secret knowledge of Alice's time travelling capabilities to herself.

"His reputation precedes him, Malcolm!" John laughed. "Have you heard of our children too, Alice?"

"No, sorry, I don't know this part of history very well. I don't recognise the name Balliol, I'm sorry. But you are such nice people, I'm sure only good things will happen to you."

"Well, Alice, my children will be in line to the throne." John said, "The blood of the Kings of Scotland courses through my Sweetheart's veins."

"Wow. Well, I didn't know that." Alice said, "Sorry your highness." she turned seriously to Dervorgilla, "I probably wouldn't have suggested sack races if I'd known you were the Queen."

All three of her companions burst out laughing, "I'm not the Queen, Alice!" Dervorgilla said, "I am in line to the throne, that is all."

"Well, I think you'd be tremendously good at being the Queen." Alice replied.

"My ladies, if you please." said Malcolm, "Alice, can you tell me why you said that my son saves Scotland?"

Alice looked at him and did her best to answer honestly, after all it was her unwritten religion to tell the truth when asked a direct question and she was sitting in a really rather religious place, "Because I'm from the future. I don't know how I ended up here, in this time. We used to sail on a time-travelling pirate ship, but the boys lost that and we've not been able to navigate quite so well since. I'm trying to find my pirate friends again but I don't know if they are even in this timeline."

Malcolm blinked at her, then burst out laughing, "You are quite honestly the most funny little lady I have ever met! Why you must marry me, for I would laugh every single day!"

"They would hang her for being a witch." laughed John, "With her predictions about your son and her notions of time travelling!"

"I'm definitely not a witch." said Alice, "I met a lot of them locked in a tower, once and the pirate ship landed on the roof and rescued us."

"Landed … on a tower roof?!" John laughed.

"Well, yes." Alice said, knowing full well what was coming … and yep, there it was, peals of raucous laughter.

"You are crazy!" John laughed, slamming his chalice on the table and rubbing the tears from his eyes with his hand.

"Yes, I've been told that a few times before." agreed Alice.

"A time travelling pirate ship. Have you ever heard such stories? Next you'll be telling us you have slain a dragon!" John laughed.

"Can you get those round here?" Alice asked.

They burst out into yet more laughter, "Dragons aren't real Alice!" Malcolm laughed.

Alice sat back smiling, and let them laugh while she took a drink of the weak plum wine from her chalice, she'd seen a sea monster once, so she knew dragons were real, just because they'd never seen one. Dervorgilla joined in the laughter, catching Alice's gaze across the table with that same knowing look in her eye.

Alice drank some more wine, feeling a slight madness of sorts was beginning to descend upon her, with the freshly born butterfly thoughts flitting and flapping about her mind that perhaps Dervorgilla was right, and she was going to have to try to save them all. Every single one of them, from every single time in the entire history of the world. No pressure at all. But she definitely wasn't going to marry Malcolm Wallace, she was drawing the line right there.

Chapter Forty-Five

(Present Day)
A Brief Interlude

———— ⚬⚬⚬ ————

"Did you feel that?"
"Feel what?"
"Something just brushed past me."
The two tourists stood and looked at each other, cameras poised.
"This place must be haunted."
"Yes, I think so too."
"It was on my list of places to see before … you know … the world ends."
"I know honey. Maybe the ghosts are saying goodbye."

———— ⚬⚬⚬ ————

Chapter Forty-Six

(Back in Time)
Onwards

Alice woke up the next day feeling fully refreshed and full of purpose, she was convinced there was something magical in the monks plum wine. Then she remembered where she was, and that the world was going to end, and she groaned. She pulled herself off her small thin bed, dressed into Dervorgilla's lovely gown, ran her fingers through her unkempt hair which she plaited as best she could, and went down for breakfast.

She was alone in the dining hall, the monks were already up and out doing their chores. They had left her a place setting and delicious fresh bread and even warm plum wine to start her day with. Dervorgilla entered the room, she was dressed in an outdoor cloak.

"And it is today that you leave us Alice." Dervorgilla said as if continuing a conversation they were in the middle of having. "You must find a way back to your friends and save the world, and there is no time like the present to make steps towards doing that."

"I have no idea how to reach them." Alice said.

Dervorgilla swooshed her cloak about and paced the floor, in most graceful slow motion, "I would suggest that you finish your breakfast and set out with a mind to finding them today, and perhaps you shall do just that. But you will not find them by staying here."

"That's true." Alice said, finishing her warm plum wine.

"Can you ride, Alice?" Dervorgilla asked.

"Yes, I've ridden most of my life, on and off."

"We will give you a horse. It will give you God's speed to help you on your way." Dervorgilla said.

"That is too much." Alice protested.

"It is not to me, Alice. It is the least I can do. I can see something in you, that you perhaps cannot see yourself. You have a spirit so strong, and you are capable of doing great things, I would like to be able to help you on your way and you must catch up with yourself post haste. Come with me, I will help you choose your horse, come come."

Alice obediently followed Dervorgilla out of the abbey grounds and along to a field, where several small horses were grazing. They had pretty shaped heads and thin legs with beautiful feathers covering their hooves, they reminded Alice of unicorns, they were so elegant and graceful in their movements. Dervorgilla entered the field and walked among the ponies.

"Our horses are perfectly designed to travel the rough terrain over long distances. They are sure footed little things, they can find their way even in the darkness. This one is mine, she is as fast as the wind when she needs to be." Dervorgilla said, stroking the face of a cream coloured one.

Alice looked at the ponies. Three of them moved away from each other, revealing one which had been hidden from sight until now. He was a grubby brown colour with a star on his forehead, though his lower legs, mane and tail were black. He stepped forward with curiosity and Alice walked towards him. The pony snorted at her and chewed its lower lip.

"Ah, I see, he has chosen you. Very well. You shall have Casper." Dervorgilla smiled. She raised her hand into the air and a foot servant appeared out of nowhere, carrying a bridle, "Saddle him up please Frederick, and make sure Alice has a plentiful supply from the kitchen to help her on her way." Dervorgilla bade him.

"Yes M'lady." Frederick replied, placing the bridle over Caspers nose and leading him towards the gate.

"Dervorgilla I can't take the pony, how will I ever get him back to you." Alice said, biting her lip.

"Alice, you are being gifted the pony to help save the world. I do not expect him to return, but I do expect you to succeed. What you are actually worried about is the road ahead of you. Do not worry about it.

Know and trust that you will be protected as much as possible along the way."

"Thank you." Alice said, "For everything you have done for me."

Dervorgilla smiled and began walking out of the field, "Dear Alice." was all she said.

The little horse Casper was waiting by the gate of the abbey for Alice, with Frederick. Casper was loaded with two bulging saddlebags, and Alice could even see her sword neatly tied onto the saddle, "Hello Casper." Alice said to him, "Will you take me to my friends?" The little horse bowed its head a little and nuzzled her arm.

Frederick helped Alice get up into the saddle, "I packed all your things ma'am." he said.

"Thank you." Alice said.

"Godspeed." Dervorgilla said, "Farewell, my friend Alice. And may we meet again some day."

"Good bye Dervorgilla." Alice said with a tear in her eye.

Alice squeezed her heels into Casper's sides and they were off. The little horse set a good speed and they made steady progress up a dirt track road away from the abbey. Alice looked once back over her shoulder and waved, though she didn't know if anyone would see her.

"Right, where is it we're actually going then Casper, do you know?" Alice muttered to the pony, he moved his ears to the side a little, listening to her, "When I last saw my friends, they were rowing a boat in the year twenty-twelve. This is craziness."

The little pony kept walking it's brisk little walk. Alice shut her eyes, but felt like she was losing her balance so opened them quickly again, she listened to the sound of Casper's hooves clip-clopping along the track and the noise of a gentle breeze in the old trees around them, "My friends were rowing away from twenty-twelve, and towards De Soulis, but I don't know what year he is in."

Chapter Forty-Seven

(Back in Time)
Pesky Marauders

Alice could hear another noise now, the sound of water babbling along its course. She guided Casper along the track until they reached a turn-off, a smaller more winding path leading downwards. The water was louder now, and then round one more corner, she could see a large river, this wasn't the stream that she had found herself lying in on arriving in the realm of the abbey, this was a larger more powerful river. It was running very low and shallow, Alice realised they could walk across it and had just guided Casper to the river's shingle stone edge when a voice called out, "Halt, who goes there?"

She turned and saw three vagabonds standing facing her, with staffs in their hands, their arms folded and cross expressions on their faces.

"I am Alice." she said, hoping it would have the desired effect.

"Never heard of you." grunted the first gruffian. "But I tell you what, you can give us your horse there and we will forget we ever saw you. Could do with a horse like that us gypsies don't have one so pretty."

Alice realised her sword had been too neatly packed to be pulled out at short notice. Dervorgilla last words echoed round her head, "Know and trust that you will be protected as much as possible."

"You can't have him, he's on a mission from God." Alice replied curtly to the man.

"Ah you are one of the loons from that Abbey." the man said.

"You bet I am." scowled Alice, fire flashed in her eyes as she leaned towards the man's face, "And you're trying to rob the only person that can stop the comet in the sky. You really want to be responsible for the end of the world? I warn you now, I've not had a fair matched fight in a long time. Three against one, I'll take you all out with one hand tied behind my back. Go ahead, make my day. "

The man raised his eyebrows, not expecting fighting talk from a lady dressed so finely, "Very well, a duel it is then." he raising his fists.

"God dammit I am trying to save the world here do not get in my way! How can you still just sit by this river and rob passers by when the world is ending, do you not have family to hug on your last days? Do you not have better things to do with your time than fight with people trying to save the world?" Alice said jumping down to the ground from Casper.

The man laughed, an irksome idiotic laugh that meant he hadn't understood what Alice had said. Alice tried one last tactic.

"While we're at the introductions, before I kill you, I'd like to know your names so I can tell them to your King when I see him."

"How do you know our King? He's not been seen round these parts for years." the man drawled, stepping towards her.

"I really don't have time for this." Alice sighed.

Alice clenched her hand into a fist and punched the man square in the face as hard as she could. She kept her fist taught and raised it to his eye level, "That ring that's just punched you and left its mark right there on your grubby fat face says I'm on pretty good terms with the Rom Baro, wouldn't you say?"

The other two men squinted at the ring mark on their companions forehead and their face changed expression completely to one of fear, "I'm sorry M'Lady, I'm sorry, I had no idea you was our friend." one of them said.

Alice scowled at them, inwardly cheering with relief that the Rom Baro ring had worked its magic, "Go home to your family. The world is coming to an end." she said, getting back onto Casper.

"What do you mean by that, are you some sort of witch?" one of the men asked.

"A witch of the very worst kind." Alice confirmed, "I'm trying to save the world with my magical powers."

"Is our world ending?" he asked.

"Haven't you looked at the sky?" Alice asked.

The man shook his head. All three of them looked up at the sky, Alice pointed to where the comet was visible overhead.

"Oh my life, the sky is falling down." the first man said.

"We must tell the King!" the second one said.

Alice sighed, "I'll leave you to it then." she said.

She tapped her heels against Casper's sides and they waded into the river. Halfway across the river it grew deeper, Casper stayed sure footed but Alice's gown trailed into the water. The little pony stepped up the banking on the other side, and they broke into a canter to get far away from the men.

The sun was beating down and it warmed Alice's skin, she could feel her dress beginning to dry, they rode along the pathways for miles. They rode past two clusters of houses that Alice took for villages, trotting quickly past the entranceways lest someone else accost them. They meandered along the pathway, Alice choosing random paths at junctions, still not entirely sure where they were going, but trusting that they would get there somehow.

They stopped when Alice's stomach told her it was time to eat, Casper grazed at the grass but all the while watched Alice She ate a delicious meal of fresh bread and meat from the abbey. Then they were off again, clip-clopping along the paths and dirt-tracks. They followed another river, keeping it to their right, Alice feeling that at least she was heading in one direction. The path brought them over a little bridge and past a toll house, Alice looked but there was no one around so they continued down a track which she realised then crossed the river. Casper snorted once at having to cross another river. Alice stopped for a moment to think about it. She had no idea where they were going. Then she noticed a mist creeping down the flow of the river, getting closer and closer until it was almost upon them. The mist lapped at the water's edge, Alice tapped her heels on Casper's sides to encourage him to walk through it.

"Here we go." Alice said, "Let's see where we end up this time, Casper."

Casper's ears moved towards her, Alice could barely make out the edge of the other side of the river, as the mist was swirling all around them. Casper waded through the water then stepped up the banking on the other side of the river never losing a step.

"You'll have to guide us, Casper." Alice said, unable to see anything at all.

Casper pricked his ears forward at her command and stepped forwards. Alice held her hands underneath his mane, warming them up. The air was different, Alice knew without any doubt that the mist was the same magical mist that used to surround the ship. They walked onwards.

Chapter Forty-Eight

(Lost in Time)
Forever Fatlips!

W hen they reached the other side of the water, the mist cleared. Alice looked behind them, the mist was mysteriously gone, not a single sign of it having been there remained.

"Now how does that work without the ship?" Alice muttered, "If Milton was here, he would say not to trouble myself with such a triviality, Casper. You didn't meet Milton, he was a brilliant pirate."

The little horse lifted his head into the air as if nodding in response. Something akin to butterflies stirred in Alice's stomach when she looked ahead of them and caught sight of a magnificent tower standing atop of a craggy hillside farther along the pathway they were on.

"I know that place!" Alice proclaimed with wonderment to Casper, "That's Fatlips Castle! I can see it from the windows of my house, in the future, it looks a little different, but I'd know that hill and castle anywhere. My God, that must have been the Spittal-on-Rule Toll across the Teviot as well, I've come home."

Alice sat for a moment in the saddle, she'd just ridden through the place she'd grown up at, only in another time in history. She shook her head, not understanding any of it. Casper decided to keep walking.

"To Fatlips it is then." Alice said.

They rode up the craggy hill, up a meandering path which passed a locked up small tower house along the way, "That's Barnhill's Tower." Alice acknowledged.

215

She was feeling a hundred times better now that she knew where she was, even if it was in a different time period. The path grew steeper towards the top of the hill, her little pony puffed a little, even his sure footed stamina was wearing out a little now. Alice dismounted, her legs were aching and she was glad to be able to stretch them. They were almost at the top of the hillside, where the spectacular little castle came into view after some particularly steep steps.

The lower part of the castle was hidden from view by a mist. As if it was waiting for her, the mist disappeared almost as soon as she saw it, revealing a fully in tact tower. Fatlips didn't look quite the same as she knew it in her time, but it still imbued its powerful presence on the landscape, a single-room structure of four storeys high, made of light grey stone.

"Hello old friend." Alice said loudly, smiling at the castle.

"Hello down there!" the castle shouted back.

Alice stopped mid step. Castle's definitely didn't talk.

"Alice, is that you?" And how did Fatlips know her name, they hadn't even met yet?

Then a figure was running down the hillside towards her, she tensed up ready for a fight, then to her complete joy and amazement she realised it was Arthur. She dropped Casper's reins and ran towards him, he lifted her up and span her round, hugging her tightly in his arms.

"We thought we'd lost you!" he said burying his face into her neck, breathing her in, "I am so glad to see you."

"So you're here then." exhaled Alice, slightly squashed. Arthur put her down.

"Fancy seeing you here." Arthur smiled, "Knew you'd find us."

"Yes there doesn't seem to be any escaping you. What made you come here?" Alice asked.

"Well, we sat in that boat and rowed and thought, what would Alice do. We saw the castle through the mist and thought, Alice would definitely go there. We camped out and just waited. It's been about a week now. We didn't really know what else to do."

"I think that's the very best thing you can do when you're not sure of what to do. Though saying that, I met a lovely Lady who ordered me to take steps forward when ever I wasn't sure what I should be doing." Alice said, walking back to Casper and picking up his reins.

"Well, we'd never find each other if both of us sat down and waited. I agree that you walking and finding me is better than me walking and not finding you, as I have a tendency to bump into things and hurt myself along the way." Arthur smiled.

"You're driving me crazy already." Alice said.

"Come and have a drink and tell us where you've been. Minn has a fire going."

"Where's the boat?" Alice asked as they made their way up the final section of path to the castle.

"Hidden away in the trees." Arthur said, "It's safe, though we found your secret stash of rum, it might be mostly gone now.."

"Oh Arthur."

They were up at the castle now, Alice walked up and touched the walls of the castle, a familiar anchor in a time she didn't know, the brickwork was warm and grainy to her touch. Minn appeared from round the corner of the castle.

"Alice! Thank God we've found you!" he ran up and hugged her.

Arthur took Casper's reins and led him away to unsaddle him.

"Come and sit by the fire and tell us what's been happening." Minn said, gesturing to the campfire just outside the castle doorway, "Eric made soup."

"Soup, great. Pirate soup." Alice said, missing her Abbey food immediately, "I have some bread in my saddle bags." she said turning, but Arthur was already coming over carrying them with him, and her sword. Eric opened the bags and pulled out the bread, sniffing it suspiciously.

Chapter Forty-Nine

(Forever Fatlips)
Alice Waves her Magic Wand

The friends sat round the campfire, and ate the soup, Alice recounted her adventures with the Monks and Dervorgilla. As dusk was beginning to fall around them, they heard footsteps coming up the hillside and a cheerful whistling could be heard echoing off the castle walls.

"Who could this be?" Arthur asked.

"We're not expecting anyone else." Minn said.

They looked up expectantly, waiting to see who was coming. The whistling stopped as the figure walked round the final corner and came into view, "Well hello there!" came the happy cheery voice of the Gypsy King.

"Hello Sir!" called Arthur, "Fancy seeing you here!"

"Hello." greeted Alice, "I thought you were going to be with your people for the end of the world?"

"Are you not my people?" asked the Gypsy King incredulously, "I thought that's who I told you I was coming to see."

"But you left us in twenty fifteen to go and see your people?" Alice said.

"And I came to meet you here." he laughed, "Oh Alice you are a funny girl so you are. Can I have some bread I'm starving and is that soup on the go? It makes you quite hungry this time travelling business."

Alice sat back down on her log by the campfire, her head spinning. But she was glad to see him, the happy cheery Gypsy King whose laughter bounced off the walls of the tower like the flickering camp fire light.

"Isn't it good to be around friends." the Gypsy King smiled, "Tell me Alice, have you been dancing yet?"

"Dancing?" Alice asked.

"Dancing in the mists of time." he laughed, "Och you, I can see it in your eyes someone has reminded you who you are. There is a fire lit up in their depths that wasn't there the last time we spoke."

"Isn't that just the campfire light." Alice said, staring at the flames.

"You and I both know that's not what it is." he said, putting his hand on hers. He lifted it up to gaze at his ring, "Ah yes, and this has saved your life already."

"How do you know about that?" Alice said.

"Och, I have my ways about me." he smiled, "The Gypsy ways." he winked.

"Right, who wants beer. I'd say it's beer o'clock about now wouldn't you?" Arthur said.

"Och funnily enough I've brought some with me." the Gypsy King laughed. He whistled shrilly and there was a whinny from further down the hill, "Give him a minute." the Gypsy King said, holding up his hand as if to press pause on their conversation, "It's a steep hill." Moments later Norris came plodding into view, puffing and snorting steam out of his nose, he had two large beer kegs strapped to either side of his body.

"You never fail to amaze me." Arthur said, slapping the Gypsy King's back.

"Well, what can I say, it's the end of the world." the Gypsy King rolled his eyes and smiled back, "Let's celebrate."

A few hours later, Alice was leaning on the Gypsy King's shoulder, "But they all want me to save the world." she slurred drunkenly, "An' howmay supposed to do that? I'm just me."

"Because that's who you are. You're Thee Alice." The Gypsy King said.

"What am I supposed to do, magic up an army with my magic wand?" she said, supping more beer.

The Gypsy King gazed into the embers of the fire, "Well, it's worth a try. Maybe it's time to muster up the great heroes who will fight with you, call them to arms."

Drunken realisation dawned on Alice's face, "It's time to set the Beacon's Alight." she said, "Set Fire to the Night!"

She jumped up and ran down the hill into the darkness, surprisingly nimble for being completely drunk.

"Where's she off to now?" Arthur said getting to his feet protectively.

"Och, she'll be back in a minute." the Gypsy King laughed, "Alice is about to do some magic."

Alice came back with branches and sticks in her arms, "I'm gonna build a great big fire over there. An' am gonna magic some heroes." she panted.

"Do you need a hand?" Arthur asked.

"Yes please." she said, her little legs scurrying her up the very last part of the hilltop from the castle, where the craggy ground finally broke free of its grassy covering. She threw the sticks onto the ground there.

"Put the sticks right here thanks." she said, scurrying off down the hill again.

The boys groaned and got to their feet.

"She always makes us do something. We can't just have one night of sitting doing nothing when she's around." Arthur grumbled.

"She's trying to save the world Arthur." Minn pointed out.

"With sticks? Is she going to build a nest for the comet to land in? There's a comet in the sky and she's building a nest of twigs. Surely we have a better plan than this." Arthur said.

The Gypsy King burst out laughing, "Arthur be nice to your wife and do as you're told."

Arthur grumbled and picked up a branch. The pile of sticks became a huge pile, taller than Alice in height. She stood with her hands on her hips, happy at the pile they had all made.

"Can I go and sit down now?" Arthur grumbled.

"Mm." Alice said, "I'm not really sure what to do now." she turned to the Gypsy King for help. He shrugged his shoulders, "It's just a plain old bonfire at the minute though, how is it going to become a magic one to call the heroes?" she asked.

"I think you need to say something when you light the fire." the Gypsy King suggested, "It helps direct the Flames on the Wind."

"Like a spell?" Alice said.

The Gypsy King nodded.

"I can't do spells." Alice said.

"Call yourself a witch." the Gypsy King said, raising an eyebrow.

"But I'm not a witch."

"That's exactly what a witch would say. They never admit to being witches in case they get drowned then burned at the stake. Wise move Alice. So, just say one of your witchy spells when you light the fire."

"I don't do spells. Seriously, I'm not a witch." Alice said.

The Gypsy King grinned and winked at her, "Well wave your magic wand then. I don't know what witches do. They're so secretive all the time."

"My magic wand?" Alice frowned, "Oh, I know." she ran back down the hill to the castle, picked up her sword and ran back to them, "This is as close to a wand as I can get." she smiled.

"Right, well, now you need to light the fire and cast your spell." the Gypsy King said.

Alice sighed, ran back down the hill and grabbed a burning stick from the embers of their smaller camp fire. She ran back up to them.

"RIght boys, link hands." she ordered.

"What? We're not holding hands." Arthur said.

"It's what witches do in the movies, they stand round their fire and they link hands." Alice explained.

The boys reluctantly linked hands, Minn, Arthur, Eric, and the Gypsy King. Alice crouched over the dry bonfire and held the alight branch over the dried leaves. It set on fire immediately, roaring to life. She took a step back and held her sword up to the sky, catching sight of the comet's glow as she did so.

"I call to the power of Ruberslaw in the East, I call to the power of the, erm, Cheviots, they're sort of in the West. I call to the power of the Dunion in the South and I call to the power of the Eildon Hills in the North. Hear the names of the heroes, and find them. Wherever they may be, please, let them hear my plea, and bring them to me."

She paused to catch her breath and tried to think of heroes she could conjure, but of course, she had put herself on the spot, and her mind went blank. She thought of her Uncle William, who smiled and waved at her in her mind.

"Hear me!" Alice called out, "Sir William O'Rule, hear me now! William Armstrong, hear me now! And Sir William Wallace, hear me now!" she looked across the valley into the night sky, "We need your help. We need you to come to our castle and help our fight! ... Please, erm ... come here tonight and ... aid our plight!" She raised the sword higher into the night sky, the gemstone glinting in the burning beacon light. She looked around and there, in the distance on Bedrule Hill, a beacon lit up and answered her flame.

"Its working!" she cried.

They could make out another fire that lit up further up the valley as well. The message was moving out, "You're calling in the big guns there! William Wallace. Wow. Wonder if he'll show up seeing as he probably died over a hundred years ago." Arthur said sarcastically.

"I've never done this before, I couldn't think of anyone else." Alice replied quietly.

"Except people called William it seems." Arthur replied, "What about the Dread Pirate Roberts, Long John Silver, or oo, how about people we actually know, or just people who are alive in this time period, that could actually maybe come and actually help us?"

"I'm sorry, do you want to give it a go?"

"William Wallace, William O'Rule, William Armstrong, they're not even from the same time as each other! How do you expect them to get here?"

"By magic." Alice said, sadly, her eyes pooling with hurt.

Minn walked up to them and put his hand on their shoulders, "Guys, please. The war is out there, not between the two of you."

"I am sick of him, Minn! I really am!" Alice cried and ran down the hill and around the corner of the castle.

"Leave her, Arthur." Minn said, "You will only make it worse."

"She's acting like a child. Running away." Arthur said.

"You were wrong to do that Arthur." Minn turned to Arthur, angrily, "All she wanted was for you to believe in her so she could believe in herself."

Arthur looked to where Alice had run to, noticing her pony was missing now as well.

"She's gone Minn!"

"And with good reason, why should she stay?"

Arthur stormed down from the craggy crest of the hill and into the castle, grabbing a tankard and filling it with ale on his way in.

Chapter Fifty

(Forever Fatlips)
Calling all the Heroes

Minn sat at the camp fire, thoughtfully, waiting. He didn't know he was waiting, but that was actually what he was doing. The Gypsy King and Flat Eric joined him, all sitting in pondering silence, waiting. About an hour or so later, a solitary figure rode up to the tower on horseback, with a banner flying proudly into the sky, galloping to a halt at the two men and the three fingered monkey sitting by the dying embers of a fire.

"Men of Scotland!" the man shouted, commanding everyone's attention immediately.

Minn looked up, knowing then this was the very moment he had been waiting for. The man had long wild hair, his face was painted blue and he had a crazy look in his eyes, "Warriors among you know my name! I am William Wallace! Who has summoned me here?"

"What the … ?" Minn said, jumping to his feet, "William Wallace?!"

Arthur came out of the doorway, "Whats all this noise? What's going on out here?" he asked grumpily.

William Wallace had dismounted at that point, he walked past Minn, and brandishing the biggest sword Minn had seen in his life, placed its point upon Arthur's throat, "I want to speak to the person in charge." William Wallace snarled at Arthur.

Despite acknowledging the fact that his entire life that had been steeped in magic, Arthur chose that moment to pass out in incredulous disbelief, though mostly this was with the admittance that Alice had been right, and that she was gone just when they needed her the most, and that, maybe, was all his fault.

Minn and Wallace sat at the table in the main hall of the tower which was lit by candle light and by the glow of a fire in the large fireplace, their heads bowed to discuss battle tactics, while Wallace ate some of the Monks bread with Eric's soup. Arthur was perched in a window alcove, drinking away forlornly to himself, "De Soulis has a magic army, an impenetrable fortress and he himself is said to be unable to be killed by sword or bow." Minn described the situation to Wallace.

"So we have to defeat an army and break his magic spells before we can even get to him?" Wallace asked.

"Yes." Minn gulped.

"We think the remains of the pirate ship are powering the magic behind the comet. So by our reckoning, if Arthur can get close enough to the ship, he may be able to counteract it. Somehow."

They looked across at Arthur, who at that moment had ale slipping down his chin. His slumped body betrayed that he wouldn't even be able to stand up if he tried.

"Looks like we're going to have to work that part out later." Wallace commented, "Meanwhile, we're going to need someone that knows the layout of the land from here to the De Soulis castle."

They were suddenly distracted by footsteps coming up the spiral staircase, and the entrance was darkened by a big burly bearded man framed in it, "But my, that fellows in a fine state." The burly man said, looking at Arthur slumped in the alcove.

"He's lost his Alice." Minn replied, "*Again.*"

"*His* Alice? Not the same Alice as *thee* Alice?"

"Yes, that one." Minn confirmed.

"Oh dear. Losing *thee* Alice is very bad indeed." the man agreed.

"Yes it is." Minn said, "And it's pretty much all his fault." Arthur groaned in his alcove.

"How did he manage to lose her?" the burly man asked.

"He told her she couldn't do magic. It upset her a bit."

"But *thee* Alice can do the greatest magic in the world, how can he not know that if his Alice is thee Alice, it's as clear as the silly little nose on his face. It's in all the legends and stories told about her."

"He didn't believe in her, so she went away and we don't know where she's gone." Minn replied.

"He is meant to be leading our men into battle, into a war. They may lose their lives, but they will not follow a drunkard like him." Wallace said.

"Ah, well, you see, our leader was sort of actually Alice." Minn said, apologetically, "It was Alice who summoned you all here to hopefully help us, and our Arthur over here has turned into a bit of a wreck without her."

"Then you need a new leader. And urgently."

"Would you, erm, would you oblige?" Minn asked William Wallace.

"Would you mind?" Wallace asked, puffing up his chest a little as if he was born to lead all matters of importance.

"Not at all" Minn replied.

"Well, I am becoming rather skilled in this field … " Wallace smiled.

"Yes, we have heard of you." Minn said.

"Alice," Wallace added, checking himself with a remembered memory, "My father said he met a mysterious beautiful lady called Alice once, when he was a guest in the House of Balliol. He told me that if I should ever meet her, that I was to help her as we were indebted to her. Now I know what my role is in her destiny. To lead her forces when she cannot. It would be an honour, and a privilege."

The big burly giant of a man walked across to Arthur and sat at the stone seat opposite Arthur. He almost filled the space and dwarfed Arthur, "Pull yourself together man! You need a drink in you lad, here, drink this."

"I think he's already had too much." Minn stood up from the table, to prevent the man feeding Arthur any more liquor.

"Ah lad, he's never had a drink like this. Home brewed right here to our sacred recipe. The waters of the Rule will revive him! It'll put hairs on his scrawny little chest and make him as strong as a Bull!"

"Who are you?" Arthur slurred.

"I am William O' Rule." the man said proudly, popping open the cork of a goatskin pouch, taking a swig of the strong smelling contents.

Arthur groaned, "She got you here as well then."

"Of course she did. I answered the beacon, you never ignore the firelight when a call goes up, you and your men must answer." William O'Rule handed Arthur the goatskin, and he took a swig, "Give it time to kick in lad." O'Rule leaned over and patted Arthur's shoulder, which almost knocked Arthur off the seat, then got up and walked over to the table.

"Sorry I don't know who you are, but Alice seemed to think you were tremendously important in some way." Minn said, shaking O'Rule's hand.

"Well, I'm honoured." O'Rule said.

"I'm Wallace, William Wallace." William Wallace said, standing up and shaking the burly man's hand.

"Pleased to meet you son, I'm William O'Rule." O'Rule said.

"My men have mustered from all over my land to answer the beacon's call. We have been summoned to fight, and we will follow you, Wallace, as some half wit has managed to lose Alice and now we can't follow her. That I could meet her in my lifetime, would have been a true honour." O'Rule continued.

"Yes it takes a real idiot to lose thee Alice." Minn agreed.

"I can hear you!" Arthur slurred, raising his voice, "I can hear you all! She is my Alice, she belongs to me! She is my wife!"

"How can you say that when you don't believe in her?" Minn snapped back.

"I'll fight each man to the death for her! She is mine!"

"That's all very well Arthur." said Wallace, "But you appear to have misplaced her in your carelessness, and we could really have done with her being here about now."

"I will find her." Arthur replied.

"Then you will need to get your act together." Wallace said calmly.

Arthur glared at him, stood up and promptly fell face first onto the floor.

"Ah yes, the Rulewater Reviver goes for the spirit first, then the body." O'Rule laughed heartily, walking over and picking Arthur up with one hand, placing him back onto the alcove seat again, "Couple more mouthfuls of this and he'll be good as new." he popped the cork open and poured some more of the liquid down Arthur's throat.

Another set of footsteps came up the spiral staircase. The men waited in anticipation to see who was going to walk through the door, although Minn had an inkling that he already knew. A man entered the room, with a pirouette, a pivot and a point of his toe, sporting a green beret with a feather in it, and swishing a swaying cape, he was the complete opposite of William O'Rule, smaller framed and light on his feet, sporting a well trimmed goatee beard and moustache. "William Armstrong at your service." the man said to them bowing and swaying his hand in a spiralling movement, "Also known in these parts as Kinmont Willie, Border Reiver, thief and notorious outlaw. I have heard the beacon's call, and I have come with my men."

"Greetings, what year is this sir?" Minn asked him.

"Fifteen hundred and eighty three." Kinmont Willie replied with a flashing smile.

"Nay, tis Twelve Ninety Eight sir," William Wallace said.

"You mean Thirteen Fifteen." said William O'Rule.

"Gentlemen, I don't think we are in any of those times at all." Minn said, "Alice has summoned you, not just across the lands, but across time as well."

"Bad boys, bad boys whatcha gonna do, whatcha gonna do when they come for you?" Arthur sung in his alcove. He stared out of the window, he could feel it in his heart that something was very wrong with his Alice, wherever she was, "My Alice needs me. She has got herself an army." he said, standing up, straight and tall on his feet, "And I am ready for a fight."

The men looked at him incredulously, and smiles flickered across the great warriors faces. "Then let's go to war!" William Wallace roared with a rallying cry.

Chapter Fifty-One

(Forever Fatlips) But Where is Alice?

Alice had ridden her pony and was making her way steadily across the Teviot valley, the landscape familiar to her now she had her bearings and Casper was confidently finding his way in the darkness. She wasn't sure where she was going, her head was imploding with all the pressure, and the thoughts that they were all only days away from dying from a burning comet in the sky and she couldn't figure out how to save them, she was an idiot and a failure and there was nothing she could do. She was just trying to find somewhere to step outside herself for a while, but she couldn't run fast enough to outrun herself.

She didn't hear the horses behind her until it was too late to do much about it. She turned and found herself surrounded by six men on horseback. She spurred Casper on, he was quick but their large horses were faster on the level ground they were on. She tried to unbuckle her sword, but couldn't manage before one of the men caught up with her, she punched him in the jaw, and he fell back. Then there was a man on either side of her, and then the world went dark as she was hit on the back of her head and her limp body fell to the ground.

Chapter Fifty-Two

(Forever Fatlips)
Alice's Army

Arthur and his new army of some two hundred men left Fatlips Castle the next morning and marched across the miles of moorland towards Hermitage Castle. The three Williams had brought their best fighting men with them, who were all spoiling for a fight. The men sang along the way, one struck up a set of bagpipes and they chanted war songs in time with their steady march. The songs of the bagpipes were rallying battle songs, which drew local lads out of their homes, out of their fields, and onto their horses to join in the march to Hermitage. The army grew in size and bravery as it marched closer to their destination.

Between them William O'Rule and Kinmont Willie navigated every pathway and road, and kept the entire force well hidden. They made camp for the evening in a hidden wooded hill glen that Kinmont Willie knew of, with an air of agitated anticipation stirring among the men. They were to rest there for the night and attack at the first hint of the rise of the morning sun, De Soulis's army commanding too much power in the moonlight on their own soil.

Arthur and the three Williams snuck into the woodlands close to the castle while their army was settling down for the evening. They made slow movements, keeping their heads steady, moving only their eyes to communicate with each other. Kinmont Willie motioned them to stop.

They had a good view of the castle from where they stood in the woodlands. It was hideous, dark and imposing, oozing an air of hostility all around it. The castle was built of grey stone, a vast structure looming over the landscape. It had a gigantic archway dominating the main wall, reaching almost to the top of the structure where there was a small square window on either side at the top. It looked like the entrance to the mouth of hell, a dark and ominous gateway.

An eerie red glow surrounded the castle, casting a halo of fire against the night sky. There was a wooden platform walkway around the top of the castle, which they saw was guarded with corner look-out posts. At least twenty men stood along the look out posts. Arthur clenched his fists by his sides, that walkway wasn't there when De Soulis attacked them and took his brother from him, that walkway was what was left of the Sea Rose. They had seen enough, they turned and went back to their camp.

Once back at the camp they went into a main tent where Minn, Eric and the Gypsy King were waiting, and sat together, finally speaking, "That walkway is the old ship, or what's left of her." Arthur said, with certainty.

"He's cast some strange spell around that castle, a protection spell. Did you see the glow of magic in the air? There'll be no getting past it even if we defeat the entire army." William O'Rule said.

"What we need is a magician." William Wallace said.

"And just where are we going to find one of those at this late hour? And one that would go up against De Soulis himself?" Kinmont Willie asked.

At that moment, there was a murmour of disturbance among the army. Trying their best to be quiet, but the men were not happy at something happening further away, where Arthur and the Williams couldn't see. A scout ran up to them, "A stranger walks among us sirs." he panted, "Says he must speak to our leader. Says he knows Alice."

Arthur stepped forward towards the scout, "Bring him to us." William Wallace commanded.

The scout nodded and ran back to the men, and emerged a few moments later with a man in a deep maroon red cloak, a long hood covering his face, "Greetings." the stranger said, unfurling his hood. He was handsome man, perhaps in his late forties, "I've been waiting for you." he said calmly. His voice was serene, carrying wisdom in the air around him.

"State your name and business here." William O'Rule said gruffly.

"I am Michael Scott." the stranger smiled, "I am a magician. I am here to help you."

"Well that is unbelievably convenient." Kinmont Willie smiled, "A magician turning up just when we need one."

"You said you know my Alice?" Arthur asked him.

"She has been captured by De Soulis' men. They have her locked in the castle. I have been watching De Soulis since he conjured the comet, trying to learn how to stop him, but it is too much for my powers alone. I saw his men bring Alice into the castle, leading her pony with her. I knew who she was when I saw her, but I don't think De Soulis knows her."

"You seem to know a lot old man." William Wallace said, walking over to Michael and scrutinising him. The man tried not to flinch at this intimidation tactic.

"De Soulis was my apprentice. He was like a son to me. I cannot believe he has stooped to such wickedness. He threw me out of his castle when I visited him, I was hoping to reason with him, but his mind is too far gone. I know I was lucky to leave with my life, though it would be difficult for him to kill me, I know now that he would feel no guilt in doing so."

"And what do you want by coming here, to us?" Wallace asked.

"I wish to help you. I think together, we can stop him." Michael said, clasping his hands together as if in prayer.

"And how can we trust you?" Wallace said.

"I am the only magician you have." Michael said.

"If you betray us … " Wallace warned.

"I will not betray you. I wish to live. This is the only chance we have to stop the comet in the sky."

"What do you mean?" Wallace asked.

"Do you not know?" Michael paled, "It was De Soulis who conjured the comet. He used the magic from the ship to warp time so that the comet is going to destroy every time that ever existed in some crazy plan of world domination."

"How is that even possible?" Kinmont Willie exclaimed.

"Don't even try to think about it." Minn muttered, "It just messes with your head."

"So killing De Soulis should stop the comet?" Wallace asked.

"Theoretically, yes." Michael said, "But he cannot be killed by any sword or mortal weapon."

"Can you kill him with a magic spell then?" Arthur asked.

"No. But I have a rope made of sand that can bind him." Michael said.

"Rope made of sand … of course." William O"Rule said, perplexed at how that would help them.

"Okay then." Wallace said, "We will attack the castle just before dawn. We need to take them by surprise, any ideas how to get in there to wrap your enchanted rope round De Soulis?"

"I think I might be able to bring the mist in again from this distance, for some ground cover, if the ship doesn't object." the Wizard Michael said, "He may have harnessed her magic, but the ship should answer when we call, as some of her crew are with us. If I knew where the wheel was, I could do so much more. That's her heart, you see."

"We'll cut some of the branches of the trees to disguise ourselves in the woods." Wallace said, "The mist will give us cover and we can move at least some distance with the tree branches as cover."

"Good plan." William O'Rule nodded.

The men talked a while longer then retired to rest, they had a long day ahead of them.

Chapter Fifty-Three

(Forever Fatlips)
Battle at the End of Time

The next day found the Wizard Michael Scott sitting cross-legged on the ground in the woods near the castle. His head was bowed and he placed his hands in the moss at his sides, palms down. He picked up his staff and placed it in front of him into the ground, resting his head and hands against it. His lips moved and he tilted his head to one side as if he was listening or looking for something, even though his eyes were closed. The army stood in utter silence behind him, waiting. The army was on edge, day would be breaking soon and they would be spotted.

William Wallace had ordered them to chop tree branches down and hold them above their heads, a camouflage to hopefully hold off the inevitable point at which a glint of a sword or a flash of armour in the dawning sunlight would give them away.

"Lady of the water." Michael said quietly, "Sea Rose. I ask that you shroud us in your protective veil once more. Allow us safe passage to pass our enemies undetected. Lady of the water, recognise the members of your crew here today and help to keep them safe." Michael frowned, "She is weary." he said out loud to those near him, "She says this is not what she was made for. She misses the ocean."

Michael twisted his head again, "She is showing me something." Michael peered at something, though his eyes remained closed, "Alice is inside the castle … in the darkness … it's so hard to see … ah, she is locked in a chest that came from the ship. The Sea Rose is upset, Alice is part of her crew and the Sea Rose is trying to protect Alice by veiling who she really is to the eyes of De Soulis. He cannot capture the heart of the ship completely, she is still of the ocean. We can stop his spell yet!" Michael opened his eyes.

Arthur was sitting staring into space, chewing his lip, his hands clenched fiercely, fingertips biting into the palms of his hands, "He has my Alice locked in a chest?"

"If he knew who he had, she would be dead already." Michael said.

"I'm going to destroy him." Arthur said, flashing his eyes directly at the Wizard Michael.

"I know." Michael said calmly.

Something began to happen around them, from under their feet, from the mossy ground beneath them, a thick mist began to rise.

"By god, it's worked!" Minn whispered incredulously.

Arthur and Minn recognised the smell of sea salt in the air. The mist swirled around their legs and rose, covering their waists, then their bodies, and kept rising to the tips of the branches that they held above their heads.

"Right men." William O'Rule said quietly but officiously, "We will fight, on this day, for freedom! Let our hearts be fearless, our swords be sharp. Let fear fill the eyes of the enemy before us and let them fall like droplets of rain upon our fiery swords! On this day, we shall not fail! For Freedom!"

The army grimaced and nodded their heads, they could not cheer lest they gave themselves away, but silently each man kissed their hands, made a fist and placed their hands upon their breastplates then placed their hands to their sides.

William Wallace looked at him and raised an eyebrow, "Stirring words, sir."

"You can use them sometime." O'Rule smiled.

"For Freedom." Wallace tested the words.

"For Freedom." O'Rule agreed, "Ready men!" he called quietly.

The men shook their legs awake.

"Onwards!" Wallace raised his sword in a forward motion the air as a signal to move.

The army walked out of the woods, but the mist moved with them, covering their bodies. Arthur, Michael and the three Williams led the way, each footstep taking the mist forward with them. Arthur had a set look on his face, gritted teeth, with murder swirling in his stormy eyes. A storm of a thousand raging seas was stirring inside him now, waiting to be unleashed on the one who had stolen his Alice away.

Chapter Fifty-Four

(End of Time)
The Darkness of Hermitage Castle

De Soulis rose from his slumber and while walking to get his robes, glanced out of the window to look at what the day was going to bring. Something was amiss, but he couldn't put his mind to it, having just woken up. There was a low lying mist about the woodlands, hopefully promising a good day once it had cleared. A day of damp air and midges, he decided on wearing an airy long-sleeved garment.

There was a knock at his door. He yawned, walking over to it running his hands through his dark hair, and pulled the door open expecting his maid with fresh water for his wash-basin. Instead he was met with the ashen faced gaze of his commander.

"Spit it out, what's the problem Brutus?" De Soulis snapped.

"The trees sir, they have come alive and are heading towards the castle. The woods are coming for us!" Brutus announced.

De Soulis had never known Brutus show fear before. He had known him for a long time and he had been by his side through many of his evils and had delighted in them as well. For Brutus to show any sign of fear was most unusual. De Soulis grabbed his cane, donned his sweeping deep maroon cloak and marched up the stairs to the ramparts to see for himself. He gazed out at the ground beneath his impenetrable tower. He saw for himself that the woods were indeed moving, a mist swirled about the treetops which were marching toward the castle.

"What sorcery is this?" De Soulis cried. He raised his cane into the air, the gemstone at its point glowed a sea-green eerie light into the air about it. He closed his eyes, searching.

"I can see no-one." he said to Brutus, "Only my own magic. Which they will not get passed. But Brutus, take your men and chop the trees from their rooted legs which carry them."

"Yes sir." Brutus said.

"You are protected, Brutus." De Soulis reminded him, sensing the unease still around him, "Trees will not beat me!" he smiled, "The laws of nature must not approve of my being here. Perhaps they think I have outstayed my welcome. They will all burn for their treachery against me. Go man, and destroy all of them."

De Soulis watched his army march out from the castle gate towards the woods, then turned and strode down the stairs and entered a chamber. The Lady Marion was standing by the window, gazing out, also watching the army make their way to the woodlands beyond. She had long sleek mousy hair and wore a white gown, she turned as the door opened.

"My sweet lady." De Soulis said as he entered the room.

She looked fearfully at him, "I had hoped it was my Walter come for me."

De Soulis paused, and sighed, "But who is this Walter you speak of m'lady? You are my love."

He walked to a table and poured two goblets of red liquid from a decanter. He hovered his hand above her goblet and muttered something under his breath.

"Here, my sweet lady, drink with me, It will soothe your anxieties." he held out the goblet, and Lady Marion took this from him, hesitantly.

De Soulis raised his goblet to his mouth, smiling as reassuringly as he could, and she did the same with a confused look on her face, sipping it slowly. He stood next to her at the window, breathing her in, her feminine fragrance, the smell of her hair, the scent of her warm skin, so alluring in his ominous castle with its lingering stench of fear, blood and all the desires of death. He placed his hand gently on her lower back and felt her entire spine go rigid with fear straight away.

"I am not here to harm you, my love." he pleaded, "Please, drink with me. All I want is for you to be happy."

De Soulis looked out of the window and sighed sadly, which had the desired effect and Lady Marion felt guilty enough for his sadness to drink the contents of the goblet. He smiled to himself. He leaned over and whispered into her ear, spellbinding unrecognisable words, her eyelids drooped a little as he lightly brushed her ear with his mouth. He turned and gently stroked her face with his hand affectionately until the fear fell from her eyes and a glazed veil went over them.

"Be it that I could have had you any other way, my love." he said, "But you are mine by right and I will claim you as my own. It is in the heat of battle that the greatest warriors are forged. When life is so close to death it can hear it whispering in the darkness next to it. When the two worlds are drawn close together, that is when a true magician is made."

De Soulis guided Lady Marion to the four poster bed, where she lay down and he shut the curtains around them.

A while later, De Soulis rose from the bed, wholly satisfied, and confident in the knowledge that he had seeded a son with his claimed bride. He picked up his staff, threw his cloak around his shoulders, left the room and locked the door behind him. He could still taste her on his lips, she was the ultimate purity he had ever taken. He went upstairs onto the battlements, the smell of blood was in the air. The taste of her mingled with the blood in the air and excited him. His army could not be seen beneath the mist but he could hear a battle being carried out. He frowned, something was very much amiss.

That stupid girl he had locked in a chest in the cellars had told him that the mist would come and claim him. He swore and made his way downstairs, across the courtyard and down into the darkness of his dungeons. Once down there he pounded his fist on the sea chest and unlocked it. Alice was curled up in a ball inside, but still she looked at him defiantly when the lid opened, "Who are you to know of this?" he demanded, "Who are you?"

She said nothing. He grabbed her and hauled her out of the chest so that she stood, her feet still in it, and struck her across the face. She had been hit a few times already since her capture, her lip burst open from an earlier wound, blood beginning to brim and make its way down her face.

"Answer me you insolent bitch!" he struck her again across her eye.

Alice spat the words along with the blood out of her mouth, "I am Alice."

De Soulis lessened his grip on her collar, "Thee Alice?"

She licked the blood from her mouth, "There's only one like me you asshole."

"I have had you in my possession this whole time?" he laughed, "But you're the only one that can stop me! And you're mine! Hah hah!" he clasped her shoulders, "I should have claimed you! Had but I known! I have thee Alice!" he hauled her out of the chest and slammed the lid shut, "Rather that I claim you now, what a fine demon you will breed!" he snarled, punching Alice in the stomach and ribs several times, then he forced her stomach-first over the chest she had been locked in.

She was too weak to fight against him, her limbs were seized up from being locked and huddled up in the chest and each movement pained her. He crouched over her and licked the blood off her face, his panting increased in her ear, and he laughed, fiddling about between her legs, lifting her gown, groping her, grunting. Alice tried to scream, she was coughing and choking back her own blood. Her arms were pinned underneath the weight of his vast body, and her legs were too weak to kick out. She shut her eyes tightly, trying to block it all out.

Then suddenly his heaving body was off her. Alice was too scared to move, she had no idea what was happening, there was a glowing light, shouting, clattering and noise all around her. She heard what she thought to be Minn's voice, "I have his staff. Quick Michael, bind him!"

And then a set of arms were round her, she flinched, "Alice, Alice my love, I'm here." Arthur's voice in her ear, just where De Soulis had been moments before, "Oh my God she's covered in blood." Arthur's voice, panic ridden. She was lifted into the air into someone's arms, a cloak was flung about her, she was aware that she was being hurriedly carried up the stairs and out into the blinding light of the day.

Chapter Fifty-Five

(End of Time)
Thee Alice

Alice was lain down on the trunk of a tree, Arthur's face met her eyes when she dared open them against the harsh hurtful light of day. "Oh my Alice, what has he done to you?" Arthur said. Alice looked at him, through one swollen eye and one eye smiting from the brightness of the sunlight, and she whimpered weakly.

"He will die a thousand deaths for this." Arthur snarled, rising to his feet. He ran over to Michael who was standing looking worriedly at her nearby, "You will tell me how to destroy this sick evil man or I will take your head from you right now, I swear to God I will run through you! You didn't protect her from him! You, with all your powers you could have stopped this!"

Michael lowered his head, defeated and crushed. He shook his head, "That, I could not."

Alice cried, she was hurt and broken, she pulled the cloak further over her, trying to make the world disappear. Arthur stepped forwards to her, placing his hand on her shoulder. Alice screamed and tried to pull away from him, Arthur stepped back and ran his hands through his hair, clasping it as if to tear it from his head. Minn grabbed onto him to steady him, "Tell me how to kill him." Arthur said, turning on Michael again.

"I will tend to Alice and try to heal her as best I can." Michael said, "And I will tell you how to defeat De Soulis."

He motioned for Arthur and Minn to enter the tent, out of Alice's ear shot. Arthur and Minn left a few moments later, with steely looks upon their faces, Arthur was clutching De Soulis' staff. Arthur looked at Alice, crumpled under the cloak that hid her from the world, then turned and walked away.

Michael came out of the tent and brought out a medicine satchel with him. He walked over to Alice. "Alice, I cannot undo all that has been done to you. And I could never have stopped it from happening." he said, crouching down slowly next to her and opening his bag, "Your destiny is beyond my control. But I can help you now."

He pulled out a vial with green liquid in from the bag and transferred drops into another vial with clear liquid in, "You are going to have to find an even greater strength within you my girl, this war is not quite over and the next part is something only you are capable of doing. It is your destiny, and you are bound to it. But I suspect you already know something of that already, don't you?"

Alice opened her good eye, sobbed and nodded, "Open your mouth, Alice." he asked gently, "This is to help with the pain."

Alice opened her mouth, flinching with the pain that caused fresh blood to roll down her face. Michael wet a rag with the clear liquid and softly wiped the blood from her face. "Killing De Soulis isn't going to undo all of his spells." Michael said, "I know now that it won't stop the comet in the sky." Alice's good eye widened, "I know a little of the spell he weaved now that I have been inside the castle. The spell is heavily imbued with his magic and with the ship's magic, but it is also bound with the earth itself. It will take a sacrifice of innocence to stop it."

"It's me, isn't it." Alice whispered hoarsely, her shoulders slumping forward, "That's why everyone knows who I am."

Michael looked very sad and nodded mournfully, "I may be able to harness the magic of the ship by fashioning arrows from the wood, that when attached to my magic rope, it may send you where nothing else can, and no one else can go except you."

"Firing an arrow into the heart of the comet you mean?" Alice tried to comprehend the magic Michael was envisioning. Tears stung Alice's eyes.

"It is okay to cry. The bravest heroes are allowed to cry." Michael said.

Alice sniffed "I don't feel very brave right now."

Michael breathed in deeply, "It is an unknown. What you are expected to do goes beyond the realm of most human understanding ... " Michael paused and tended to her wounds. " ... But you know, don't you, that no one else can do this?"

Alice nodded, her pained expression hurt Michael's heart. He thought some more, striving for the right words to say to this broken young girl before him, to give her the strength that no one should ever have to find.

"Heroes are not wise before the adventure. They are made that way through the hell fire they walk through. It is after a heroic deed is done that they are identified and recognised as heroes. Your soul has been touched by time travel, and you are ever so slightly magic yourself. A natural ability that you have never truly realised." He paused, cleaning his cloth in a dish of water, "All of your experiences up to this point have been preparing you for this, Alice, all the people you have encountered, all the conversations, all the pain, all of the training, all of the learning, it's all led you to being who you are right now. It is a rare thing to find someone who is already recognised as a hero before the deed has been done. I like to think that means the entire world knows you will succeed."

"It's not written in any history book." she whispered, "Maybe because it happened after they were already written."

"You are a wise soul." Michael said. He worked at another medicine concoction for a few moments, in respectful silence.

"No pressure or anything." Alice said, "There's just me that can do this."

"Just Thee Alice." Michael said.

"It would be. Tell me how to do it." she whispered.

"Alice on the next full moon night, and that is tonight, you must stand on the tallest hill in the land, brave bold Ruberslaw, and cast a magic arrow into the sky, and command it to take you to the comet."

Alice sat silently for a moment, "Promise me, Michael, that you will help my friends. Help Arthur if I don't come back."

"I will make no promises that rest upon you not coming back." Michael said, "What I will promise to you here and now, is that I will do everything within my power to aid your success. It is written in my destiny to help you. It is a cross I have borne for many years. De Soulis has taken many lives and caused so much suffering, and those deaths are on my hands as well, as I taught him how to use magic ... If I had taught him differently ... "

"It wasn't for you to know." Alice said.

"Thank you for your comforting words, Alice. But this debt knocks at my door and calls me by name, and I must answer before my own magic turns against me. It breaks my heart that I am going to be part of my son's downfall. We wizards have very deep souls and this is something that hurts me very much." Michael said sadly. "It is like sitting in the eye of a dark storm right now, all around us is spinning, and once the wind is gone and the dust settles, what it looks like outside the cloud is anyone's guess. De Soulis has darkened the skies of the heavens and even the angels cannot see the outcome. It entirely depends on you, now. You are our last hope."

"Right." Alice said, tilting her head so that her chin sank a little.

"Alice, while there is still light radiating from your heart I will not give up hope. Hold onto that light tightly, for it may be all you will have to guide you safely home again."

"What do you mean?" Alice asked.

"Do you still not know?" Michael asked, "What you hold in your heart, what everyone can see plainly except you, is love. Pure Love, True Love. The strongest magic of them all. The man that holds that place in your heart is the luckiest man alive, he is what drives you and the rest of us ride on your coat tails."

Alice grimaced, "I do not love any man."

"When all of the light from our world is gone, there is only going to be one grain of light left in you and you must be able to recognise it and call it by name … or you may never come back. You will be given to the darkness."

Alice looked away, "I shut my heart away long ago, never to let it hurt again. It is turned to ice."

"And a comet is made of fire. It will melt your icy heart and it will consume you and turn you to ash. But I know it is your destiny to live, happily ever after, as all the Princesses do in all the fairy tales."

"I'm not a Princess." Alice said, miserably.

"Oh yes you are." Michael said strongly, "You're the only one in this fairy tale."

Alice wiped the tears gently from her aching face and laughed bitterly.

"I know." Michael said, soothing, "I know lass. A life lived in hope Alice, that's all that I ask you to hold onto when you go. When all else is lost, we must live in hope."

Alice nodded, "This is the hardest thing I have ever had to do."

"I would think, after this, the rest will be plain sailing in comparison." Michael replied, "Drink this. It will put you in a heavy sleep, but you must heal quickly and this is the only way to do it." Alice leaned forward and Michael helped her take sips of the drink through her broken lips, "Ah." Michael said calmly, staring into nothingness, "They have broken De Soulis, his magic has weakened all around us." he sounded relieved. "Alice." Michael said, raising the blanket above her shoulders as sleep began to take a hold of her, "To know you, is to love you."

Chapter Fifty-Six

(End of Time)
What Happened During the Battle

The Wizard Michael had said charms and spells to weaken the spells of protection that De Soulis had all around his castle, Michael was possibly strengthened by the magic of the Sea Rose working with him as much as it could. As the army walked forward towards the castle De Soulis' men had exploded out of the drawbridge in a dark rage of fury.

William Wallace yelled a war cry into the air, under which the very air itself seemed to tremble as his army took up the battle cry with him. They had come to fight, and this was their war. The men cast their branches to the ground and drew their swords and ran forward to meet their enemy. The first sounds of metal clashing upon metal resonated up the castle walls.

The battle was bloody, De Soulis' men fought without honour. Men on the top of the walkway fired burning arrows into the swirling mist, aiming at men at the back of the battle. What De Soulis' men hadn't reckoned for was their opposition to be a force the likes of which would never be seen again. The men took the hits of the burning arrows and still stood standing, refusing to go down on their knees they snapped the arrows off at their entry points, pushing on and striking ever onwards with their swords. The men were fighting to stop the end of time, they would not give in. Alice's army began to win.

De Soulis' man Brutus put up a good fight, taking down many men, but he was impaled in the shoulder by a blow from William O'Rule's sword, and his final death blow came from the blade in William Wallace's hands.

The two Williams looked at each other with blood splattered faces, their chests were heaving to catch their breath back, but in that moment they knew the battle had been won.

Chapter Fifty-Seven

(End of Time)
I am Vengeance

Arthur, Minn and Michael broke through and ran down to the dungeons while the three Williams headed up the main battle outside. Swords had been useless against De Soulis in the skirmish in the dungeon, though they did manage to disarm him by knocking his staff from his hand. Michael had then bound him with his magic silver rope and the men had managed to lock De Soulis in the chest in the dungeon, the same one that he had imprisoned Alice in, they locked the dungeon door as they took Alice to the safety of the wood, unaware of how badly injured she may have been. De Soulis was then guarded by William O Rule and six men until Arthur returned to them.

When the chest was opened, again, Arthur gazed upon the man beneath him, cocking his head to one side. "It's your day to die." Arthur said. De Soulis hissed at him. Arthur punched him in the face, slamming De Soulis's eye shut. "Cast a spell against that." he snarled, and punched him again, full force, breaking his nose.

"Who are you?" De Soulis asked through his bloody mouth.

"I am Vengeance." Arthur replied, "And you are living on borrowed time. Tick Tock, time's up." he slammed the lid shut.

Men lifted the chest and carried it up, out of the cellar, out of the castle and some distance away onto a neighbouring hillside. As advised by Michael, they found a set of standing stones at the top of the hill, in the centre was a cauldron hanging between two large stones, big enough to boil a man alive in.

"Light the fire." Arthur commanded.

At hearing that request from his wooden imprisonment, De Soulis started pounding on the chest. The men had brought the branches they had carried into battle with them, as well as some of the wooden platform of the ship from the castle, and they set about hastily constructing a bonfire. They had stripped the lead from the roof and fixtures of the castle, which were thrown into the cauldron to melt down into a molten liquid.

It took a while for the lead to break down, by which time the three Williams had joined Minn and Arthur to stand next to the chest, where De Soulis was still locked inside. They were joined by local people who had heard the battle and seen the movement of people going up to the standing stones.

Strips of lead were pulled from the heat of the cauldon, pliable and bendable. They opened the treasure chest and hauled De Soulis to his feet. His face was smashed up and covered in dried blood. They unwrapped the silver rope. He was too weak to protest, his limbs still sore from being locked in the chest. They wrapped the first strip of lead around his body, binding his arms to his chest. De Soulis screamed in agony.

"Beg for your life." Arthur said.

"Don't do this!" De Soulis said.

"Beg for forgiveness." Arthur said.

"Please, forgive me." Another strip of lead was pulled from the cauldron, and wrapped around De Soulis' legs. He sunk to his knees, crying out, "Stop this!"

"You have broken my Alice." Arthur stated, "And you were prepared to kill every person that has ever existed in your insane pursuit of power. Tell me, are you sorry for what you have done?"

"Yes, yes, I'm sorry, I didn't mean any of it!"

"You didn't mean to send a comet to earth to kill millions of people?"

De Soulis shook his head, whimpering, watching as a final piece of lead was carried towards him, and was pressed upon his ankles, binding them together. The smell of burning flesh was in the air.

"You are a liar!" Arthur snapped, smacking De Soulis across the face, knocking him to the ground.

The men tied ropes round his shoulders and hauled his body above the cauldron. The lead was allowed a few moments longer to liquify before they lowered the ropes and De Soulis feet touched the molten lead.

De Soulis' screams could be heard for ten miles around, taking on the supernatural volume of a man who destroyed and consumed a thousand souls. Arthur stood over the cauldron, the silver of the lead reflecting in his eyes. Minn, Wallace, O'Rule and Kinmont Willie stood next to him. The local people were cheering all around them.

"Burn in eternal hell." Arthur shouted, as De Soulis was lowered further into the burning lead cauldron. De Soulis' eyes met his one final time, "For all your crimes, for all that you have done. May the shadows of the darkness find you now and call you to pay for them all. Vengeance. For Milton Montrose if you even knew his name. For the crew of the Sea Rose. For all the souls you have stolen. And for Alice."

The villagers cheered and roared. De Soulis and his years of tyranny and debauchery were gone.

Chapter Fifty-Eight

(End of Time)
The War is Not Yet Over

Arthur ran back down the hill to where his Alice lay resting on a bed of blankets inside the main tent. Michael stood protectively in front of her, "She is sleeping, and she must sleep to heal." he said, "This is a magic sleep, it will speed her recovery, do not wake her."

"When will she wake?"

"With true love's first kiss." Michael replied, smiling.

Arthur frowned at him.

"Okay, sorry, she will actually wake up in a few hours."

"Did he ... did he?" Arthur asked.

Michael shook his head, "She was untouched. But she is severely traumatised."

Arthur gazed at Alice. Michael stared into the flames of the camp fire outside the tent, "I will go to the castle and remove the magic of the ship from its grip." Michael said, "You may be able to rebuild her yet. Or something like her. A phoenix from the ashes."

Arthur looked surprised at this.

"I can offer no promises, but I will see what I can do. It will not be the same as the one that sailed before it. I will not know what it is capable of doing until it is made and its voice can be heard. Fundamentally, though, I think I can do it. I will need some men to help me."

Arthur nodded, "Whatever you need."

"The ship will need to be bound to a Captain, just like the last one, as the new spells I cast will need to emulate the original ones as much as possible, so that the ship recognises them and answers."

Arthur looked at the Wizard Michael, then back at Alice, "It's me, isn't it, the Captain of this new ship?" Arthur asked.

Michael nodded, "But only if you agree, Arthur. Your brother being the Captain of the Sea Rose, this ship would answer to you like it would to no other man."

Arthur bit his lip, "I am what I am. I can be no other."

"Very well, it will be done. In the meantime, you will need to take the rest of your men and take Alice far away from here, back to your base to rest. We will meet you there when the work here is done. All going well, the ship will find you."

"It will be a relief to leave this godforsaken place." Arthur said.

Michael looked at him, noting the haunted shadows beneath Arthur's eyes, "There was no other way to deal with De Soulis." Michael said.

Arthur looked into Michael's eyes, nodding slightly. William Wallace walked into the tent at that time, taking in the figure of Alice sleeping on the bed, "Thank the Gods she is safe." Wallace said, "This is the first time I have ever seen her. Thee Alice. She is beautiful."

William O' Rule walked in as well, standing to the other side of Alice, "Beautiful doesn't cover it, man." he said, resting his hand lightly on Wallace's shoulder for a moment.

Had Alice been awake at this point, she would have looked around the room wondering who they were talking about, as they couldn't possibly have been talking about her, she had a big nose and a podgy tummy, but she wasn't awake so she couldn't argue with these men who said she was beautiful.

Kinmont Willie walked in and took his green beret off, holding it clenched in his hands. "This is the Lady Alice who we have fought for." he said in wonder, "Worth every drop of blood spilled today."

"I forget that you have never met her." Arthur said apologetically.

"Aye." Wallace said, "My father spoke of her beauty and the air she carried with her. Now I am in her presence, I can feel it in the air around us. Can't you?"

Arthur looked up at him, "I've never noticed it before."

"It's her aura." Michael said, frowning at Arthur, "Sometimes people can't see the nose on their faces in plain daylight. And sometimes that's how obvious it is to other people."

Arthur looked back on his sleeping Alice.

"Their work in this time is almost done." said Michael, indicating the three Williams and their men outside.

"Then we should leave?" Arthur asked the room.

"Let us be back at that friendly little Fatlips castle by nightfall." agreed Wallace.

"I can't thank you all enough." Arthur said, tears filling his eyes, "You have led an army when I could not, and still you stand by me now ready to soldier on until we drop on our feet."

William Wallace smiled, "She knew who to call."

The men were gathered, briefed and split into two groups, a larger portion made up of William O'Rule and Kinmont Willie's men to help with the clean up, and a smaller group of William Wallace's men to escort Alice back to the castle. Arthur secured himself onto the back of Alice's pony, which they had found amongst the herd of De Soulis' men's horses. William O'Rule lifted the still sleeping Alice, wrapped in a blanket like a newborn baby, in front of Arthur on the saddle. Arthur wrapped the blanket gently round her, and spurred the pony into motion.

"He really does love her." Michael said to Minn, "I only hope it is enough."

"Enough for what?" Minn asked, but already, Michael had turned and walked away towards Hermitage Castle.

Minn stared after him, sniffed, shrugged and jumped onto his newly acquired horse, "Damn magicians. Nothing but trouble." Minn muttered, spurring his horse into a canter, riding after Arthur.

On the long journey back to Fatlips Castle, Alice half opened her eyes only once, to gaze up at Arthur, "You are safe." he said to her, kissing the top of her head. She nuzzled into his chest, and that subtle movement of comfort and affection made Arthur feel as if his heart would burst.

The ride was hard, and the men and ponies were weary, the last climb up to the castle left them all exhausted. They did however, make it back by nightfall and set campfires ablaze to soothe their aching bones and muscles. Someone brought out meat and proceeded to begin cooking supper. The men suddenly found their appetites returned now that the battle was won. Tankards of ale were passed around and their journey-weary spirits began to lift a little into those of celebration and trumph. They stretched out, some kicking off their boots, others singing songs.

Arthur looked round at the army, a sight to behold even when less than half of them were there. Brave men, warriors, marched straight from the mists of time. Alice was lying by his side, still sleeping, wrapped in her blanket cocoon. William Wallace came over and sat next to him, "It will be time for me to leave soon lad."

Arthur nodded.

"I fear it will not be completely over for you yet." Wallace said, "That comet still sails in the sky above our heads."

Arthur looked over his goblet at him, across the fire flames, fear falling across his face.

Minn looked at them alarmedly, "Shouldn't it be gone? I thought it would be gone. How can it still be here if we destroyed De Soulis? Was it all for nothing?"

Alice opened her eyes at this point, feeling the heat of the fire on her face and hearing panic in her friend Minn's voice, breaking through the magic sleep she had been in. As she stirred, Arthur immediately reached over to her protectively. She flinched. The men quietened down around her and spoke no further of the threat in the sky when they saw she was awake. Alice stood gingerly to her feet, Arthur helping her. Alice nodded that she was okay and motioned for him to move away from her. She tried to smile reassuringly at him, but couldn't really move her swollen mouth to express a feigned emotion.

William Wallace stood up in the glow of the camp fire light, "It is time we were sent on our way home, Alice." he said, "It is time to light the beacon again."

"And I have more to do before this night is through." Alice smiled weakly, the side of her mouth eased only slightly, "Someone has to stop the comet."

Wallace strode over to her and embraced her, dwarfing her with his size, he was overcome with emotion, "It has been an honour, Alice." he said, "Once this is all done and dusted, you must come and see me again. Promise me you will not forget your friends." she nodded, "Send us home then, beautiful brave Alice."

Alice grabbed a long branch from the camp fire and walked along the narrow cragside to the beacon, which had been freshly set for lighting. Wallace's men stood up and gathered round. Alice placed the burning flame onto the beacon, and slowly it began to take alight. She raised her arms to the night sky. She didn't know what to say, so she made it up.

"William Wallace and all your men gathered before me. Your work here is done, the battle has been won. I bid you return to whence you came. Adieu, farewell, and may my eternal gratitude grant you a safe and speedy passage home."

Alice held her arms to the sky for a moment, then, when she lowered her arms, she could no longer see her friends faces on the other side of the flames of the burning beacon. An answering beacon fire lit up on the Bedrule hill nearby, and another lit up further away further up the Rulewater valley.

"Can you see them?" Alice said to Arthur, Minn, the Gypsy King and Eric, the last men standing with her, "They're on their way home."

Chapter Fifty-Nine

(Forever Fatlips)
Being Very Brave

Alice went back to the castle camp fire and sat down on her blankets. Minn and Arthur sat down near her.

"Alice, you must rest." Minn said.

Alice shook her head, "The magic must be done tonight or not at all."

"You're starting to sound like a damn magician." Minn said.

"Just what is it you think you have to do?" Arthur quietly asked her. He was sitting across from her. She looked at him sadly, poignantly.

"I'm going to do what they say can't be done." she answered, "I'm going to stop the comet in the sky."

Arthur frowned, "I won't let you go."

"But you must." she said, "I'm the only one who can do this."

"Says who?" Arthur replied angrily.

"Oh, pretty much everyone we've ever come across in the entire anals of history." Alice answered with more than a hint of resolute resignation in her voice.

"Well, they're all wrong! Someone else can take over from here. We're done with all this. We've done our part." Arthur said bitterly.

Alice shook her head, "There is no one else Arthur. Just me, and we have no time left. There is no going back after tonight. Our time is up." Alice stood up and went over to the castle, walking inside.

"Oh my god, Minn, we have to stop her. Lock her in the tower or something, where's the key, quick." Arthur said, desperately.

"She really won't thank you for that Arthur, seeing as she has just been freed from being locked in a chest, in a tower."

"Well we'll tie her up or something. We must do something Minn!"

"You know we can't." Minn replied, "And if you try to stop her, I will have to stop you. You have to let her go Arthur."

Alice came back out of the castle with a bow and quiver on her back. She had a rope over her shoulder that glimmered in the firelight, all were gifts from the Wizard Michael. She walked over to the campfire painfully, she was still so sore from being beaten at Hermitage.

"Stay here, please?" she asked them all, "If this doesn't work, I want your last evening to be spent together, drinking round the campfire, as champions and kings among men. That's how I want to remember the lost boys."

"Alice … " Arthur implored.

She turned to him, "Make a wish for me when I've gone, Arthur." she lightly brushed his face with her hand. He stared into her eyes.

Alice turned and walked away, down the pathway to where the ponies were tethered. She walked over to Casper, who was still saddled, and patted him. Arthur's neglect of removing the pony's tack while tending to Alice earlier had its benefit now.

"You carried me here before, thank you. Now I need you to run like the wind, one last time for me." she whispered into his ear, "Can you do that?" the pony snorted and stamped its hoof. "Thank you." Alice said, climbing painfully onto his back. "Onwards." she said, and off they trotted.

Alice's body ached, her muscles protested at the movement. She knew she had enough strength for this final journey, but no more than that inside her. She didn't think about what might happen after that. She concentrated on the winding steep downhill path in front of her, the moonlight getting brighter as they cleared the thick wooded hillside and entered the fields below. Then they reached the river crossing, the splashing water stung her aching body like biting snakes, each droplet burned her skin. Then it was a canter across the valley to reach Ruberslaw. Casper snorted, weary and tired.

"We are almost there my friend." Alice pleaded, breathlessly, "Please, keep going."

The little pony rallied and quickened his pace. The hill grew steeper and it was a long climb to reach the summit. Gradually he then slowed to a trot, a brisk walk and then to a complete stop. Alice jumped from his back and hugged his face, which was dripping with sweat.

"Thank you my little friend. You have taken me far enough. I can do the rest on my own."

Alice walked away from the pony, up the steep hillside. Pain and fear gripped her chest, ripping the air away from her lungs. She was terrified, and all alone. The comet appeared to be so close now. This was the last night before its destruction would not be able to be stopped, where it's pull on the moon and the earth, would begin to rip them all apart with irreversible consequences.

Alice's legs refused to walk further and she fought to catch her breath. She gazed across at her beloved Fatlips Castle, where her friends would be sitting round the camp fire. She could see the beacon fire light from where she stood, they had kept it burning brightly for her. It was as if the warmth from the flames warmed her, she summoned the very last of her strength to take the final steps to the very top of the hill. As she rounded the last corner of the pathway, the wind rose up around her, blowing in the right direction it helped hold her up as she couldn't hold her own weight any longer. But she was there, she was at the summit. Her hands were shaking and she was so cold that she struggled to lower the bow from her shoulder. She pulled the magic arrow out from the quiver, it shimmered once from point to tail. She tried and failed to tie the end of the magic rope to the end of the arrow. She tried again, and again she failed.

"I cannot come this far and fail now!" she cried, "Katniss never had this problem! Please just attach the rope to the flipping arrow!" she tried again, and the rope bound itself to the arrow, "Bloody magic spells." she sobbed.

Gingerly she tied the other end of the rope round her waist, grimacing where De Soulis had punched her, and finally looped the rope into her belt. She looked up at the comet in the sky and whispered to herself, "It's only a paper tiger."

She breathed in deeply, realising these were perhaps her final moments on this earth, and said, "I am coming for you Mister Comet."

Alice hooked the arrow to her bow, aimed it at the comet and let go. A shimmer shot through the arrow as it was released into the night sky, snaking down the rope line as the arrow shot up into the night and disappeared, the rope trailing after it. Alice watched it, then took a run and jumped off the top of the hill, arms outstretched. The rope grew taut as she leapt into the air, taking her last breath away from her as it careened her body upwards, into the night sky, and then, just like that, she was gone.

Chapter Sixty

(Lost in Time)
The Comet

The four friends were watching from the crags of Fatlips for any sign of Alice. They saw the white flash on top of Ruberslaw which looked like a bolt of lightning hitting the top of the hill. Minn grabbed Arthur as his friend sunk to his knees, a groan coming out from Arthur as if his very soul was trying to leave with her. "No. Don't you dare." Minn said to Arthur, "She knew what she was doing. Don't you dare leave us. You wait here. You wait right here with us."

Minn sunk down and wrapped Arthur tightly in his arms, as if trying to hold the very life within him. He kissed Arthur's head, "Stay right here." he whispered, tears falling down his face, "She knew what she was doing."

The Gypsy King walked over to Arthur, crouched down, and placed his hand on Arthur's sleeve. Eric walked over and crouched by Arthur's other side. Minn looked up at them, despair written all over his face. The Gypsy King sang a low murmouring haunting song, a gypsy prayer to keep them all safe.

"What was the last thing she said to us? Her last order?" Minn asked Arthur, "She asked us to make a wish Arthur. We have to make a wish, all of us."

The Gypsy King looked up with understanding, "We have to make a wish, together. Something that comes from our hearts. Up to the heavens. Alice is up there somewhere, and she needs to hear us."

"I wish my beautiful Alice would come back to me. Don't leave me behind." whispered Arthur, from beneath the support of their arms. Minn's heart gave a lurch of relief and he hugged his friend a little tighter. Arthur's last hope, his final wish, was for her to come back to him.

As they sat on the hillside, they each of them felt an energy gather amongst them, something stirred, something more powerful than all of them. They raised their heads as a sparkling energy rose up from the ground around them, it moved through their bodies, a spine-tingling sensation that rose up through their heads and as it burst out into the sky above them, it was a blinding light. It dimmed down as they raised their heads to watch what was happening. All around them was a rainbow beam. In the dark it shone bright, the brightest boldest rainbow they had ever seen, shining in the dark sky reaching upwards like a beacon searchlight. Caught at it's base, they were in amongst the colours, and all around them were tiny glittering stars. The sparkling stars passed through them, until all of them glittered and glowed from within. Their faces glowed bright with the sparkles. The rainbow beacon shone up into the darkness, and then it was gone.

The comet that had been conjured from the deepest darkest depths of space had almost completed its path toward complete obliteration of every time on earth. The astrophysicists of the modern day, Alice's original time, had tried and failed to deter the comet's path, sending up warheads and nuclear missiles. Nothing they did could alter or deter the comet's collision course. As you would expect for an end of the world scenario, just like all the movies, the media were in a frenzy. Everything that had stood to be important now seemed to be completely trivial by hundreds upon thousands upon millions of people all around the Earth. They were all powerless, and that was a humbling feeling. There were riots on the streets of town and cities where the people were out of control, overcome by a madness and despair that comes with regret and fear. Everyday work came to a standstill, the ftse stock market crashed completely, the value of money suddenly becoming completely irrelevant. But there were also the families and loved ones who were miles apart that travelled the impossible distances to be with each other, or made emotional long phone calls to say their final farewells. The ones who wanted their last words and actions to be of love. There is no need to spend page upon page describing the situation, the end of time is what it is. The end of the world as we know it.

But all was not lost. There was still a little wish upon a star that had been cast against the wicked wishes of Lord De Soulis, and it had reached its own collision course with a comet hell bent on human destruction.

Alice, as we knew her, was gone. She had become part of the bright and shining comet burning through the sky like an angel on fire. She had forgotten who she had ever been. The comet had consumed her body angrily in it's fire and rage when she rode the magical arrow to meet it in the sky. Time was so different up here, she had flown through the sky, sometimes she was the sky. Sometimes she was the light reflected in a tear in someone's eye. But she was on fire, always on fire, burning bright. She had travelled so far. So far. She was the ice, she was the fire, she was the glow. She didn't mind anymore, she didn't feel anymore. She was old, so old, and had an eternity to still fly across the sky, her only purpose was to sail, to sail across the sky.

Then there was a light, a blinding flash. The comet turned its attention, its entirety, it's rock, it's icy tail, it's dust, and its burning hell fire, it turned to briefly glance at the flash and in that moment, a rainbow pierced the fire and the rain began to fall upon the comet's fiery body. The rain held the wishes, from old friends who once knew a girl called Alice, wishes that the burning comet could not burn to ash. A shooting star must grant a wish, you see, and these were the greatest wishes of them all.

The wish remembered who Alice was. A tiny flicker of hope. A single beat of a heart not given up for dead by those who knew her and loved all she stood for. A heart beat came so faintly that the comet did not hear it.

Da-dum.

The rainbow still shone into the comet, refusing to be beaten by this failed remembrance. The heart was tired, and weak. But the wish insisted it knew a girl once, a young innocent girl, before the world turned her to fire. And the rainbow shone ever more, ever brighter. Who was she?

She was Alice. And she meant something to those pirates, down there, lost for dead on the dying planet, praying to a God they barely believed in, after all what sort of God would let a comet destroy them, praying for miracles to save them, just as every person on the planet was doing in every time that ever was. And who was she? She was a shining star in the sky. There was no Alice. Remember!

Da-dum.

There it was again. As the comet raced through the sky. Who dared disturb the comet's chosen path now. So faint, but irritatingly insistent, like the rain that was continuing to fall from the rainbow in the sky.

Da-dum.

What was that noise? The comet followed the rainbow to meet it's end upon it's burning inferno surface and delved it's gaze into it's own flames. There it was, resting at the end of the rainbow. A burned out little heart. The beat was so faint it was almost inaudible.

Da-dum.

The comet grimaced at the finding of the forgotten burned up wish. The comet was old and vast, filled with power, surging through the sky. How dare they make such a wish! No, it would not be fulfilled. Not on this day of days.

Da-Dum.

The comet turned its attention to the little noise of distraction, "Begone" he commanded.

Da-Dum.

But it could not be ignored. The comet knew the power of the magic held within the wishes of a rainbow of tears.

"What is this little beating heart that was beginning to sound so like my own?" the comet asked, "To whom does it belong?!"

The comet scoured the memories, so many that he held, hundreds of centuries of sailing through the sky, till he found the memories that beat in time with that insistent little heart beat, "Why, why are you still beating, Little Heart?" he asked the heart.

"For love." the comet heard a meek, soft and sad female voice speak through the fiery flames, "I beat for love."

"You speak of love?" the comet replied in a mocking, bitter tone.

"Yes." the little heart said.

"And what do you know of love, Little Heart?" the comet asked fierly.

"I know that it's worth fighting for." the little heart said sadly, "whether or not I survive, those I love will live on."

"They will not live!" the comet said defiantly, "You fight for them when all hope is lost. None shall live. No one shall survive. They do not deserve it Little Heart! They kill themselves and each other in the name of Gods.

They spread pain and suffering through the lands of my beloved Earth. It cannot continue. Gaia will rot to her very core with the poison your people play out on her surface. She herself will die. And you come to me and speak of love. I love her. I am here to save her. Who are you Little Heart, to come to me and talk to me of love. The Wizard sent me here, he awakened me, he told me you were all to die, and I know it is true. None of you deserve to live on my love, my Gaia."

"They deserve to live." the Little Heart said.

"Why, because they made a wish?" it mocked her, "And why should I answer their wish?"

"Because we love, and that is the most precious thing in the universe, and we will learn how to love each other better, and how to love Gaia better." the Little Heart said wearily, missing a beat.

The comet flinched as the sparkling raindrops began to fall and quench indiscernible flames on its surface layers. A hundred thousand wishes of a dying race had found their way through the rainbow and met with the wishes of the pirates in the raindrops that landed on the comet.

"You would lose yourself to try to save them all?"

"Yes, all of them." the heart said, "Please. Don't do this. They can change."

"A heart that has known sacrifice deserves a chance to beat, when so many others have stopped, it is a pity, I know, I have seen so much death and destruction in my wake, souls burned up through greed, I didn't know there was anyone like you left on Gaia. I was sent to destroy you all. Each and every one of your measly excuses for an existence. But you, Little Heart, you talk of love and you send their wishes to me, telling me to turn my course, and I must answer. Tell me who you love, little heart, down there."

The little heart found its last remaining light, and with that little light it called out a name up to the comet and then, the little heart beat no more.

Chapter Sixty-One

(Lost in Time)
Salvation

The comet glowed in the dusky evening sky, ever threatening in its presence. It had a white aura, a v-shaped glow emanating from the top. This aura had grown brighter in the last few hours. It was only a matter of time before the comet would shake the world apart.

"All hope is lost." Arthur said.

They sat watching the flames of the fire, not looking at the bright part of the sky that the comet shone in. It cast an eerie light on the night. They knew it was there. Death did not need to be watched constantly to know it was coming for them.

"Hope … " Minn muttered, "Where there is life, there is hope. Where there is a beating heart there is still hope. While blood flows in our veins, we still have hope!"

"Well I'd like to say we've been in worse situations than this, Minn, but we haven't. Thanks all the same for the rousing positivity, but I'd say we're all pretty much doomed." Arthur said. He glanced at the comet and did a double take, something had changed, the light was different. There was a rainbow about the aura, there was colour where there had only been white light before.

"What is it Captain?" Minn asked.

The Gypsy King saw it next, "Its her!!" he shouted, jumping to his feet, "Its Alice, the rainbow, she heard us!"

Journalists started broadcasting the change, documenting the comet's transformation of colours, not knowing what it meant, but asking everyone to remain calm. It unified them all. They were all in this together. It stopped the bickering, it stopped the wars. Everyone stopped to look at the comet changing in the sky.

The entire human race over every time and place stood in awe and watched the comet in the sky. A cloud like a twisting trail emerged from the front of the comet - no one was sure where or when it had come from, said the news reporters. No aeroplanes were flying so it wasn't a chem-trail. Two strands twisted like a DNA strand in the sky above their heads.

As the pirates watched, the cloud stretched, twisting and curving, stretching above their heads and it reached downwards. It went down and met the line of ancient alders along the river bank. And there was a brilliant white light, glowing in the river itself, at the very centre of the water. It hadn't been there before. "It's a portal." Arthur gasped, jumping to his feet and running down the from the castle, running as fast as his legs could take him down the steep hill and across the fields to reach the river bank before the light changed and the portal vanished.

Arthur leaped from the river bank into the air, and landed in the river, right in the glow of the light, and he vanished with only a ripple, deep into the waters' surface. Arthur was falling, falling, falling. It was so dark around him, after jumping through the blinding light. Then, he saw twinkles of light, and he realised they were stars. He stretched out his hands in front of him, he was floating through space, and then the gigantic comet soared into view.

"It is for you for whom her heart still beats." a voice roared in his head, Arthur winced with pain, it was a gigantium of a voice, it hurt to hear it.

"Yes." Arthur said out loud.

He stopped falling and hovered, suspended in space. He felt like he was being scrutinised. His mind filled with memories, all at once, images and emotions tearing through him, in milliseconds, or maybe it took hours. The comet stopped searching, it had found what it was searching for in Arthur's memories, it was looking at her, looking right into her eyes, looking back at him. Arthur's heart lurched in agony. The comet held her memory, spun her round and round, looking at her hair, her face, listening to her laugh, her smile. Arthur's heart tore, he missed her so much. The comet listened to their conversations and the way Arthur had fallen in love with her as soon as she had taken that first step onto the gangplank.

The comet watched as Alice came out of her house and sat in Arthur's little boat when he was a sorry wreck of himself. It watched them piece each other back together again. And it watched how she had taught him to smile again. Arthur cried in pain. No human was used to having their entire range of emotions played through and scrutinised by a being with a larger consciousness.

"There is still hope here." the comet said to him. Then there was a roar of fire, a roar of power, one statement, an order, a command, and an oath, "Love her."

Arthur then saw the memory of Alice's hand cast in front of him, as she reached for him that first day stepping across the threshold of the pirate ship, and had laughed her delicious sweet mischievous laugh at his tiny hands. Arthur found himself reaching out to touch the memory of her hand, as he had all those years ago, to help her across the threshold. And he touched something real, and entwined his fingers round a physical hand. He gasped, his heart was near exploding in his chest with the realisation that he was holding Alice's actual physical hand.

"Yes, there is still hope here."

Where there was the blackest of darkness in the starry night, the vast comet reached out and found the dark-matter that it knew would be able to re-create the body of Alice. Arthur held Alice's hand as tightly as he could. And the comet pulled Alice's body back into existence from Arthur's memories. She was completely lifeless, her eyes were closed and her body floated in the air, Arthur embraced her body in his arms.

"Thank you." he cried.

"I am done here. Begone Brave Little Heart." the comet said.

Arthur was swept upwards again, rushing upwards, the light of the starts becoming a blur, all the while he was holding Alice tightly to him. She was cold, so cold. He couldn't feel her breathing. Then it was light all around them. blinding light, and then Minn was hauling Arthur out of the water, as he was too weak to stand. Arthur was holding the body of his Alice in his arms.

The comet began to alter its path, but the pirates did not see it do this, and it shone, brighter than any given star had ever shone in history. It had changed the course of its direction away from the earth and the comet shone all of its love upon her instead of its hate.

Arthur sat at the river's edge, exhausted, next to Alice, refusing to let go of her hand, as if it would disappear again back into his memories if he dared let her go.

Minn checked her pulse, "She's alive." he said, "Just. I can hear her heartbeat. Its very faint, but it's there. I think she's in some sort of coma."

"She is real then? She is definitely here?" Arthur asked.

"Yes. She is as real as you or I." Minn replied.

Arthur lay back on the grass, "She has saved us." he smiled, "She's done it."

The pirates looked up at the comet then, and saw that the tail had moved, "It's changed direction?" the Gypsy King said, "Can you see that?"

"Impossible. But it's moved course? It has, hasn't it, the comet has moved!" Minn exclaimed.

The scientists of the modern day couldn't explain it. Television shows were going crazy with experts on every channel. Experts from every conceivable field, had all been wrong. When one scientist was being interviewed, he said, "There is no way to explain how a comet can avoid a course of a direct collision with a planet with no external influence."

"Are you now telling us that it was an Act of God?" asked the presenter, "Which religion are you?"

"None!" said the scientist, "I had proven to the world that there was no room for God in Science. But when I saw the comet, I began to pray. Even though I didn't believe in anything. Just like so many people in the world. I prayed to a God I don't believe in. Now I know, there has to be a higher force at work. Call it whatever you like. This cannot be explained by science as we know it. Its as if the comet itself just decided to alter its course to avoid our Earth. As if the comet is capable of *conscious thought*." the scientist stopped to wipe the tears of joy and relief from his eyes.

The journalist turned to face the camera, "People have wars in the name of Gods, they kill people in the name of God, commit atrocities on the planet, brainwash others into doing the same. That Comet *chose* to spare us. Does it believe in these Gods that we kill in the name of? What happened to make it change its mind? It makes everything questionable. The human race needs to change. There is a need for us all to unite, to work together as a human race, for the same goals. Let's find out what else is out there in space. What is actually out there? If a comet can *think* … " The journalist broke off, not comprehending what that meant.

The scientist continued, " ... If a comet is capable of conscious thought, then so is our planet Earth. And we need to learn how to communicate with her." he finished, "And I would think if we can do that, then we may be one step closer to the God that just answered all of our prayers."

Chapter Sixty-Two

(Forever Fatlips)
Remember the Sirens

Arthur slept by the campfire at Fatlips Castle, exhausted, with his arm wrapped round Alice's body. As he slept, one memory refused to settle back into the dusty depths of his conscious from where the comet had dredged them up. The memory of the sirens… Arthur opened his eyes just as the morning mist was beginning to clear around them, the natural mist of the morning dew. Minn was awake, tending to the fire they had kept burning all night to keep Alice warm, "We are to set sail." Arthur said.

Minn raised his eyebrows.

"We are to go to Honeydew Island, where the sirens are."

"Sirens?" Minn said, "But they'll kill us all? We've just narrowly escaped death here Arthur I think you need to rethink that bright idea."

"The sirens knew her as one of their own when they saw her. They'll know how to bring my Alice back." Arthur said, "I don't know how I know, but I just know."

"Well we would need a ship for that Arthur, and right now, we don't have one of those, which is probably a good thing as I don't particularly want to mess with the sirens anytime soon." Minn said.

"I think the ship might just be on its way." Arthur smiled.

The Wizard Michael had not failed them. The new ship appeared in the sky at right that very moment, sailing on the morning mist, glistening with a dazzling radiance of a newly born magical entity. It was beautiful, smaller than the original Sea Rose.

"It has come for us." Arthur said, "Avast ye!"

The lost boys boarded the new ship ready and waiting for her maiden voyage. Alice's body was laid out in the Captain's Cabin, Arthur placed her hands together over her stomach, he brushed tangles from her hair. He sat with her, trusting that the new ship would navigate this voyage safely without too much interaction. There had been no one on board the ship when it arrived for them, some sort of spell that Michael had cast allowing it to sail its first voyage unmanned.

The journey was, as Arthur anticipated, calm and uneventful. Minn knocked and entered the Captain's cabin, "We have arrived." Minn announced.

Arthur turned to look at Minn, "Thank you, my friend." I must go alone to them. I will take Alice with me. I will not risk your lives. If we do not return by dusk, take the ship to deeper, safer waters. Bring the ship back each morning until I return. If you have waited for seven days, leave without me."

Minn nodded, relief mixed with worry flitted across his face, "My captain."

"Help me?" Arthur asked, "Ready a row boat, it needs to be secure and comfortable for her."

"As you wish, Captain." Minn said.

Arthur's arms burned with the effort of rowing the length to the island from where the ship was anchored. Arthur was anxious, while he was driven by an instinct that the sirens would be able to help him, they could, on the other hand, just kill him on sight. Arthur looked over his shoulder towards the shore. There they were, the sirens, sitting on the rocks all around him, gazing down at him. Their long hair draping over their chests, their naked legs languishing on the surface of the rocks. He felt their gaze and their desires beginning to course over him, trying to get inside his mind. He fought through it, continuing to row. He reached the shoreline, jumping out and pulling the boat up to the shore so that it lodged onto the sand beneath it.

"We have been expecting you." A seductive female voice said near to him. Arthur looked up and there was a siren, close to him, standing on a large rock, enthrallingly beautiful, familiar to him. Luciosa, the Queen. Arthur turned to face her.

"Can you bring her back to me?" Arthur implored her, "She will not wake."

"We saw the omen in the sky and we knew our sister had melted the anger of the fire in his heart. But she has paid a heavy price. Her soul has been set on fire." Luciosa gazed affectionately down at Alice.

"My poor love. My poor beautiful sister. You have been so brave." she looked at Arthur, "Such a sacrifice indeed. She has saved each and every one of us. We are all in her debt now." Luciosa stepped down from the rock, "Bring her."

Luciosa turned and gestured to a path in the trees. Arthur lifted Alice's limp body into his arms. The sirens that had been on the rocks made their way down to walk behind them. The hairs stood up on the back of Arthur's neck, surrounded by so many sirens, he wasn't sure that while they may save Alice, they wouldn't let him leave unharmed. He concentrated on taking each step at a time, looking at the ground beneath him, and gazing at his Alice's sleeping face.

They reached a clearing in the dead centre of the island, Arthur saw a set of ancient standing stones which encircled a pool of water in the middle of the circle. Luciosa walked to the pool and motioned with her hand, "Lay her on the ground here."

Arthur gently set Alice down, and crouched protectively near her, brushing hair from her face. Luciosa turned to him, "To bring her back we must use the Old Magic, forgotten even by the fairy tales. But we sisters still carry some secrets." she smiled faintly at some amusement only she understood, "We guard them to the death. It is our burden and our blessing. Ourselves, existing in a world forgotten by the modern day world, are the ones who carry the ancient knowledge that can restore the Old Magic, but are bound to keep it secret." she looked down at Alice, "But perhaps things will change now. Perhaps the modern world will begin to believe again. Perhaps our worlds will merge again, and we won't be so … very lonely." her eyes flickered with hungry desire and died down again. "I feel it may be so. A change is in the very air. The mother earth has found a reason to live again, and so have we."

She turned to look at the pool of dark water in the centre of the standing stones. "Opening this doorway, this lost and forgotten portal, may lead to better things. Or it may not. De Soulis could not control the Old Magic, he twisted it with his greed and it consumed him. As was it's right, it claimed him. But open this door I must, for you have brought Alice to us, and we are indebted to her. There will be no going back to what once was, once this has been done." she said, "But it is to be done. It seems we are also to change the world with our actions … It is an honour …" she paused and looked towards the sky, at the comet soaring away from them, above their heads. "If you stay, you are bound to our secret. While you watch you must say nothing and do not intervene, under any circumstances. You must not tell anyone of what rituals we perform. The outside world, if it is to discover the old magic, will not find out from you. Is that clear?"

Arthur nodded, "My word, Luciosa, as a pirate, is binding. You have my word."

"Yes, or we will come for you. And we will have you." Luciosa added, looking hungrily at the man standing before her.

"Where do the standing stones go?" Arthur asked.

"To the land of the faeries." Luciosa replied, "They need to sprinkle their faerie dust on Alice to make her believe in herself again and restore her soul."

Arthur raised his eyebrows at Luciosa, "Faeries and fairie dust? Are you kidding me?"

Luciosa turned to look at him, her eyes flashed ever so slightly, but she was somewhat lighthearted in her response, "You're asking a Siren Queen if the Faerie realm exists, Time-Travelling Pirate? That is where she must be sent in order to come back again. They will find her lost soul and bring her back to you. Of course, I cannot guarantee that she will not be a little changed from her adventures that took her away from you, and additionally, no one comes back from the Faeries without being unchanged. But it is the only way you will get her back. The faeries hold the oldest magic. It is too dangerous for just any human to venture there alone, but they may just consider a request from the Queen of the Sirens for the soul of Thee Alice in the name of True Love."

Luciosa looked at Arthur with a deep yearning, "The taste of true love is the sweetest of all delicacies." she continued, "She would have to bring you back to us with that sort of love in your heart on a promise not to harm you." Luciosa sighed, then inhaled deeply.

A shiver went down Arthur's spine as if Luciosa had just breathed him in, scenting her lunch was standing next to her.

"A river can move mountains, just by flowing." Luciosa said loudly to her sister sirens, "Our sister must return by the water to soothe her burning soul. To the stones, siren sisters."

The sirens moved gracefully to take up standing positions between the archways of the stones. Some archways had gaps, which Arthur guessed were from the missing sirens that Alice had killed when she saved the pirate crew. Luciosa stepped down into the pool of water and looked at Arthur, "Give her to me." she asked, "Then, you will need to leave the circle."

Arthur lifted Alice's body and kissed her cold lips one last time, "Come back to me, my love." he whispered.

Luciosa took Alice's body into her arms, she dipped a ringed finger into the water and placed it onto Alice's forehead. A glow started to emanate from the gemstone of the ring, "Our magic has been woken. Begone from here pirate."

Arthur turned and walked away, as he walked out of the stone circle, he turned and saw the sirens in the archways raising their hands to the sky.

"Wait!" Luciosa called to him, "I was wrong. You need to stand over there. She needs to be able to see you." she pointed with the hand on which the ring glowed to one of the archways that were vacant. As he stood under the arch and raised his arms to the sky like the sirens were doing, as he wasn't sure what else to do, Arthur saw the sun beginning to set through the vacant archway of the standing stones directly opposite where he stood. And then, the Old Magic stirred.

Chapter Sixty-Three

(Mists of Time)
Dancing with the Faeries

Alice was in a room, which looked like a captain's cabin, she didn't know where she was, or how long she had been there for, or where she had been before, she just took in the surroundings in the room, sparkling light coloured their surroundings. Deep red drapes adorned the windows. There was a painting on the wall of a tower which she recognised as Fatlips Castle, it was homely and comforting. She sat down on a luxurious chair, feeling at rest after a long journey of some sort. There was a painting on the other wall of the ocean lapping upon the shore, the more she gazed at it, the more the waves began to roll back and forth onto the beach. To the left of the painting she noticed a pine door with a gold handle. The handle had a face on it, and the handle part was a long pointy nose. The gold glistened and beckoned her.

She didn't know what would lie beyond the door. She took hold of the handle and swung the door open. There was a wall of darkness, another room beyond, the same size as the room she was still standing in. Alice was hesitant. she didn't want to leave the nice warm room and step into the darkness, but it beckoned her. She could always leave the door open. Alice stepped into the room. She looked back, the doorway was still there leading back into the nice warm glowing room, she could always go back if she could see the way. She stepped further into the room, music was playing, haunting in a lilting lullaby.

There was a plinth in front of her, with two human figures lying side by side next to each other, draped in veiled robes covering their faces. She

275

couldn't make them out clearly in the dimness, the only light was from the doorway. There was a long ornate mirror on a stand at the back of the room, she walked over to it and held up her hand. Her hand appeared to be wearing a velvet glove in the reflection, and looked elegant and she was dressed in a fine evening gown. The mirror began to scare her, so she walked back to be closer to the doorway. As she turned she saw two small figures watching her, while they were lying on another plinth at the bottom of the larger one, between her and the doorway, she knew they were watching her with their little eyes. One was made of darkness, a silhouette of a miniature lady in a hooded cloak. The other was a skeleton. It was as the two little figures had waited for her, when her gaze fell on them, they jumped to life, standing and dancing a jig to the music of the lullaby.

"Dancing! Oh, I love dancing." Alice smiled and began to dance too.

She felt a presence near her, and raised her hands.

"Will you dance sir?" she held out her hands and raised them as if taking a partner's hand and shoulder, and began to waltz, a dance to the lullaby. She could feel the figure dancing with her, but they were completely invisible, not silhouetted like the little skeleton and lady dancing on the plinth near her. They were beckoning her towards the mirror, dancing closer and closer to the mirror. Alice gazed at the two human figures on the plinth, and knowing them to be resting, sleeping royalty, she did a curtsy, "Ma'am, M'Lord." she acknowledged.

On the wall, which she was now able to make out, were masks, strangely shaped masks that as she watched them, distorted and opened their fanged mouths at her, silently threatening her.

"Ah, but you stay on the wall and you will not dance with me." Alice said to them, unafraid.

The mirror beckoned her. Tentatively, she walked back towards it and gazed in the reflection. She could see a wooded glade, women standing round a circle of stones, and her Arthur, her beloved Arthur. She cried out and reached to touch the mirror, she placed her fingertips of both hands on the mirror, her left hand close to the frame, her right hand near the middle, she couldn't reach them.

A creature flew towards her from the room, and landed on her shoulder, it was shadowy, and dark, a thin humanlike figure with raggedy wings that looked like they had torn on something. She reached away from the mirror and towards the creature, which stepped into the palms of her hands. Alice giggled and started dancing again, she danced across the room with the little creature dancing in her hands, dancing across to the two figures lying on the plinth, where she stopped and curtseyed again. They did not stir, but she felt that the lady's face was smiling slightly.

The miniature lady and the little skeleton danced and waved at her as Alice danced about the room, dancing with the creature in the palm of her hand. It stopped dancing and pointed to the mirror.

"But, we must dance?" Alice asked.

The creature shook its head and gestured again at the mirror. It span around in her hand, fluttered its tattered wings, lifting into the air a little and as it gently landed back into her hand again it raised its hands and blew a kiss toward Alice, she felt the kiss land on her like a thousand snowflakes, melting into her skin as they landed. Her entire body tingled with an energy she had never felt before. Alice kissed the creatures little feathery forehead, placed it down upon the ground, and stepped towards the mirror. She saw her Arthur looking for her, and she stepped forward to meet him. She sighed with happiness.

She was there. His angel. Arthur could not believe his eyes. She stood before them, she had emerged out of the pool and she was there. He ran forward to her.

"We thought you were dead." he said to this glowing angel.

"Well, I was." she answered, simply.

"But you have come back to us."

"Yes, because you weren't dancing." she replied innocently.

But suddenly Alice remembered and she raised her hands in fear and pain, reaching out to Arthur, fearful that they all might disappear again, that somehow, they weren't real, and that she had dreamed them all, and she was still sailing through the dark universe, as part of a fiery comet.

Arthur stepped forward and swept her into his arms, he embraced her, breathing her in. His Alice had come back to him, she was real, she was there. Though she was not the same anymore, for she was tainted with a thousand sorrows, and an eternal flame burned in her heart next to a river of tears.

"I give you my heart, Alice, I will never let anything hurt you again." Arthur said.

"And I give you mine." she replied, smiling softly, "You found me."

"I will never lose you again."

"Forever is a long time."

"A lifetime isn't long enough with you, my sweet, sweet Alice. I'm yours. I have always loved you."

There was a silence between them in which Alice finally felt her heart melt completely. Alice looked into Arthur's pale blue eyes. "I love you Arthur." she replied, finally accepting it and admitting it to herself out loud.

Arthur took her in his arms and they kissed. The kiss of true love. The kiss of memories, of pain, of experiences, of high adventure, and of love. The greatest, the boldest, the bravest of loves there ever could be. The waves of the pale blue ocean quelling the fire in a burned out soul.

Alice pulled away and looked into his eyes, those beautiful blue eyes, sparkling back to life with their pirate magic, those eyes that she had once thought she would drown in, "I have always belonged to you, haven't ?"

"And you always will." he smiled, kissing her again.

There was a long pause.

"Well." Alice said, "I'm not doing that ever again."

"What, kiss me?" Arthur asked.

"No … ride a comet through infinite time and space. Wouldn't really recommend that to anyone." she replied.

"Oh." Arthur said.

"Kissing you is nice." Alice smiled again.

"Well." Arthur smiled back, "I'm happy to do that again."

"Just not round here if you don't mind." Luciosa muttered.

Epilogue

Somewhere, very far away, in the distant past, a newborn baby cried, screaming for its lost father, calling to all the evil in the land to hear its woes. A forgotten woman called Lady Marion soothed it bitterly to her breast.

The mother earth sighed a wistful knowing sigh of a planet that had seen this happen a hundred times before, those human children would never learn. She cast her gaze about to find some of her greatest heroes ever known, but instead she found herself distracted, just what were those mischievous lost boys on that time travelling pirate ship up to now?

"What if it's not him? It doesn't say anywhere in your history books that it is him." Arthur said.

"It is him." Alice stated with absolute certainty.

"But in the book, it says, 'skeletal remains of an unknown man who they thought was Sir Alexander Ramsay, De Soulis locked Ramsay away in the oubliette and he starved to death there."

"They got their names wrong." she replied, "They'll need to rewrite their history books."

"But it's a fixed point, you can't change a fixed point!"

"Watch me." Alice said defiantly, "There's rules for other people, and there's rules for pirates."

"You women and your bloody rules, there were never any rules before." Arthur moaned.

"Guys will you please stop arguing." Minn's voice piped up.

"He's right." Arthur said, "In fact, there's only one way I'm going to prove you completely wrong on this." Arthur grabbed the ship's wheel and turned it deftly, "Onward you scabbardly scumbags!" he shouted.

A man's eyes opened, struggling and weak, glistening in the dark, as if once, perhaps, they held a glittering ocean, which was now cast into eternal darkness. Alice shone her torchbeam down into the tiny cramped prison chamber and the beam caught upon the wreck of a man slumped in the shadowy light. "Hello Captain Milton Muldoon." she said, "Pirate Code Rule Number Five on the good ship the Misty Rose is this, sir: Never leave a man behind. Are you coming on board?"

He was unable to speak, but made a whimpering noise of incredulous disbelief and recognition. "I'll take that as a yes then." Alice said. She grabbed hold of his arm underneath his skeletal shoulder and heaved him up from a sodden ground covered in god knows what, and hauled him through the glowing magic portal with her.

So if you're out on a walk or a leisurely jaunt, and a somewhat magical mist falls down, know that there be pirates sailing in the sky, all around.

Keep your ears open for their cannons firing as the angels chase them across the clouds.

As the storm stirs, the thunder begins to rumble, and lightning begins to flicker across the sky, lookout!

When that lightning strikes the ground, Alice and the Pirates will be coming for you.

Get ready to change the world!

Avast Ye!

The End

The Author

G emma lives on a Scottish Borders farm with her husband James, her horse Murphy and her dog Marley. She loves to read, ride, and teach about the past and how it shapes our lives and futures.

If you enjoyed reading this book please leave a positive comment on the Amazon page:

http://www.amazon.com/dp/B01A1FRN4O

If you would like to learn more about some of the places that inspired this story, please visit Gemma's website: http://www.rulewater. co.uk

Thanks to Ailsa, Alison, Nicola, James, Wally & Betty for believing in me.

Gemma